RELICS OF CAMELOT

LH NICOLE

Book Three of the Legendary Saga

OMNIFIC PUBLISHING

LOS ANGELES

Omnific Publishing
1901 Avenue of the Stars, 2nd floor
Los Angeles, CA 90067
www.omnificpublishing.com

First Omnific eBook edition, January 2016
First Omnific trade paperback edition, January 2016

The characters and events in this book are fictitious.
Any similarity to real persons, living or dead,
is coincidental and not intended by the author.

Library of Congress Cataloguing-in-Publication Data

Nicole, LH.
    Relics of Camelot / LH Nicole – 1st ed.
    ISBN: 978-1-623422-30-1
    1. Fantasy — Fiction. 2. Fantasy — Arthurian.
    3. Young Adult — Fiction. 4. Romance — Fiction. I. Title

10 9 8 7 6 5 4 3 2 1

Cover Design by Micha Stone and Amy Brokaw
Interior Book Design by Coreen Montagna

Printed in the United States of America

To my family and friends
who have stood by me
and supported me through everything

PROLOGUE

The Underlord, master of death and the Underworld, stood and rolled his shoulders. His muscles stretched and his bones popped. That was a turn of events he hadn't seen coming.

"What have you seen, my lord?" asked his general, waiting at the bottom of the stairs.

The Underlord turned, his jade green and earthen brown robes rustling around him. He'd been gazing into the gold and onyx Well of Realms. Such a well existed in all seven realms and was accessible only to those strong and clever enough to control it.

He descended the worn, stone stairs. The area surrounding him was darker than a starless night sky.

"Is she all right?" A thread of frustration slipped into the general's usually calm voice. "Does Mordrid still hold her prisoner?"

"You haven't relaxed since Aliana first stepped foot in Avalon, General." It amused the Underlord to see his formidable warrior so tangled up.

The Destined One had a very special place in their world. Aliana's extraordinary powers and family line made her unique and valuable. Her heritage had gifted her the emerald eyes of the Fae queen's lineage. The only Fae to possess eyes any shade of green were those who shared Queen Titania's blood.

"She is free of him. For now." The tension didn't leave the general with the Underlord's assurance. "How did she escape the dark wizard?"

An almost amused sneer twitched the Underlord's sharp mouth. "After the Fae Queen got through the barriers protecting his pocket realm, she trapped Mordrid in another void and sent Aliana Fagan away. That is after Mordrid got his bargained kiss," the Underlord added.

The general's jaw clenched tight, hot anger flashing in his red-brown eyes like a Firebird's wing. "I will kill him for this!" That evil boy taking such blatant advantage of the Destined One was unacceptable to him.

The Underlord smirked at him. "I seem to recall you using a similar tactic to help draw your souls mate to your side, General."

The younger man, and one of the most deadly warriors in all the seven realms, narrowed his blazing eyes at the all-powerful ruler.

"You know you will never kill him. Hurt him, possibly, but never kill him." The Underlord's tone was dismissing the event like it was nothing more than a flickering light in the darkness. "She has her guardian, Lord Daggerhorne, with her again."

Vicious satisfaction rolled through the general as the Underlord told him of Lord Daggerhorne's purple fire burning Mordrid's face.

The Underlord closed his black eyes briefly, hiding his own approval of the guardian Dragon's actions.

"Where is she now?" the general demanded.

"She has been sent back into the past. There is much she must do in Camelot to ensure that her own present time, and her future, unfold as they already did and still must."

"You know how it annoys me when you speak in your time riddles."

A devilish grin broke out on the Underlord's harsh face, softening his hawk-like facial features just a fraction.

"Is she safe?" The general would have no peace until he knew that at least.

The Underlord sighed heavily. "As safe as she can be, considering the path she must travel to save the seven realms."

"What does Titania have planned for Aliana?" the general asked his king. A knife of fear and concern speared the general's heart. He must find a way to ensure the Destined One came to no harm, from whatever treachery the Fae was weaving.

The general clamped his jaw tight, his lips pressing into a thin line. He turned toward the magic Well only the Underlord used.

Before the general could speak, a cool loving presence rushed over him as his souls mate appeared by his side. She was the most beautiful woman he had ever had the pleasure of laying his eyes on. The moment he had seen her nineteen years ago, he had known what she was to him, and that he would have done anything to possess the lovely creature. She was far shorter than him, her glossy, rich brown hair curling at the ends around her shoulders, accenting her rounded face and vivid emerald eyes. Those eyes were the only thing one could use to tell that the two powerful women were related—an event the Fae Queen, ruler of the Isle of the Blessed, had taken many steps to ensure. Any descendant of one of the four rulers would be powerful indeed.

She bowed to the Underlord and then turned those big green eyes on her souls mate. "I'm sorry, my love, I could wait no longer for news about the Destined One." Her warm, caring voice soothed the edges of his frayed nerves.

"She is in Camelot," the general answered.

The Underlord nodded. "Merlin has been sent to her. She will be well cared for."

She gasped, her eyes widening and brows jumping up. "Did you know this was to happen? Did you know all along that traveling to the past was a part of her destiny?"

The Underlord said nothing as a current of power rippled around them. The trio vanished from the Well of Realm's hidden chamber. Seconds later they appeared in the courtyard of the dark, Gothic castle. The near black delicate blooms on the trees waved in the chilled breeze.

"My lord," she pleaded for an answer.

He gave it to her. "The war for the realms is fast approaching and there is still much to be done, both by the Destined One and by the new Knights of the Round Table." His voice lowered, the gravity of knowing the future evident in his perilous tone. "She is about to undertake her most dangerous challenge yet. And the foreign magics that war within her, for control of her emotions and heart, have not yet reached their cresting point."

"Can she not rid herself of those magics? How will she ever be able to decide her future for herself if other powers are trying to control her?"

The Underlord started to laugh, but it wasn't a kind laugh. "You two," he said, looking both of them in the eyes, "should know better than most what the greatest power in all existence is."

The two lovers shared a long, knowing look. Yes, they knew what the greatest power was, but it was not a simple power to survive. And the Destined One was so much younger than they were when they had faced it.

Nodding reassuringly to his mate, the general asked, "What is next?"

"Prepare yourself, my son. She will be here soon enough."

The general straightened, his shoulders squared as he gripped the long curved sword at his waist. He looked to his mate, and her own determination and excitement matched his. "Yes, Father."

I

Even the Fae queen, with all her accursed powers, doesn't understand how these pocket realms work as well as I do. That conniving woman thinks she's thwarted my plans to have Aliana, my Destined One, but she couldn't be more wrong. I know what none of them do, that blasted Fae has played right into my hands. Time is a tricky mistress, but she is a very good friend of mine, and MY Aliana will ensure that my past unfolds the way it did and that my destiny as King of Camelot and the seven realms is fulfilled. The Onyx Dragons will once again claim their rightful place of power and control. But I must wait for Morgana and our teacher to help release me from this temporary prison.

— Mordrid

It had been two weeks, six days and nineteen hours since the dark wizard Mordrid had taken Aliana Fagan, the Destined One, from her friends and the two men who loved her more than their own lives. Not that Flora was keeping track or anything. But really, who could blame the Pixie if she was?

Life had been hell in the weeks following Aliana's kidnapping. The Destined One had run away from the people who cared about her for a reason unknown to all of those still present except for the two men who loved her. After they had finally found her, thanks in large part to her best friend Wade Edrick, they discovered she had fallen into

Morgana LeFay's trap. The knights and their king, Arthur, had tried to save her but she had stepped in front of a magical attack that would've killed them all. They didn't even know for sure that she was still alive.

Then, nine days after her capture, Dawn's mother Michelle, and Aliana's godfather Joe, suddenly returned home, safe and sound, and with no memory of what had happened to them or where they had been. That was when they knew she was still alive. Mordrid and Morgana would've had no reason to return the pair without Aliana influencing the decision. The evil duo would've just killed them instead.

Then Merlin, the strongest Druid to ever live, and Daggerhorne, the Destined One's Dragon guardian, had the idea to try to create a link with Aliana through another kind of magic. Soul magic. And it worked! The little silver Dragon had managed to find her through an enchanted mirror Merlin had transported from his home in London. But the silver creature hadn't been seen since.

Now he *and* Aliana were missing, and every attempt to find them again had failed miserably. Their failure managed to drive a wedge of frustration and outrage deeper into the hearts of the new Round Table.

It had been three months since Aliana had first entered the realm of Avalon and discovered her destiny as the one person in all the realms who could awaken King Arthur. It was her duty to lead him on the path to find all of his Knights of the Round Table. Together, they would reclaim the lost relics that were the only hope of stopping the witch Morgana LeFay, and her power-hungry-cousin-of-a-wizard Mordrid, from unleashing a diabolical kind of Armageddon on the seven realms.

When she thought about it like that, it seemed so much bleaker. The Pixie wasn't one prone to such angst, but it was hard to keep your spirits up when every day she had to see the devastation that all in the house were suffering.

Flora flew through the narrow wood-planked hallway toward the office King Arthur had taken to hiding in when he needed to be alone.

The pale-haired Pixie knocked on the door. "Excuse me, your majesty." She peeked her head inside. She saw Arthur reclined in the brown leather chair staring at the cold, lifeless fireplace. "Your majesty?" she tried again.

He didn't even look at her. "What do you need, Flora?" His voice was somber and rough, not at all like the rich smoothness that normally came from his mouth.

"I wanted to see if you needed anything?" She didn't really know why she had sought out the golden king, but her instincts had told her to find him.

"She's out there, Flora," he insisted, his voice gaining a little strength. "I'd know if she wasn't." He rubbed his hand over his heart. "Safe, somewhere."

A small sigh escaped the Pixie. Despite their despair, no one had lost hope. "What can we do, sire?"

Arthur let out a heavy breath, roughly rubbing his stubbly chin. "Gather the others in the kitchen. It's time we stopped chasing our tails and moping and did something to get Aliana and Lord Daggerhorne back."

The confidence in his voice, and the way he sat up straighter, made the spark of hope in Flora's chest glow brighter. This was the king they needed right now.

She zoomed down the hall and out the open back door. The first place she needed to go was the beach. Owen and Leo had started going there when the house became too confining. She suspected even Gala-had would be found there, as it was the last place he had held Aliana.

Two figures came into view as she neared the white, sandy beach glowing with the hot, late August afternoon light. The two men were grappling with each other, their chests bare, their shoes dumped next to their T-shirts. Owen Nyhart and Leo Kell had become very close since Leo had found them in London when the Scot saved Aliana from Morgana, after they had walked right into one of the witch's traps. Owen was Aliana's cousin, a cousin she had never known about until after her parent's death, when she learned about her own adoption.

After discovering that painful truth, she had fled to London to try to find her real parents, only to learn that her mother was dead. But, fate being the ironic thing that it was, she found Owen the day she found her mother's grave, and the two hadn't been apart since. At least until Mordrid had kidnapped the Destined One.

Leo hooked his leg around Owen's knee and pulled it back, si-multaneously pushing himself forward. Caught off balance, Owen fell back and the two landed hard on the hot sand. Leo pulled back, his fist raised to deliver a blow that would knock the dark-haired British boy out cold.

"You left yourself wide open, mate," Leo chastised, dropping his fist and getting to his feet.

Owen glared up at his best friend, pushed himself into a sitting position and rubbed the back of his head. "And you're not pulling any punches today, mate."

Leo shrugged and held out his hand to help Owen up. The Brit grabbed the offered hand and got to his feet, grinning. Before Leo knew what had happened, Owen pivoted, his back hitting Leo's as he leaned forward and flipped the bigger Scot over his shoulder. He landed with a dull thud on the sand.

"Now who's not pulling any punches?" Leo asked, springing back to his feet after a moment.

Owen shrugged. "And you let your guard down. That can get you killed quickly. You taught me that, back in Camelot."

Flora smiled to herself. Owen was not the greatest fighter of their lot, even with the memories and skills Merlin had restored to all the reincarnated knights.

Just then the two guys turned to the Pixie watching them. "Is everything all right, Flora?" Leo asked. The Pixie never sought them out unless they were needed.

"King Arthur has requested everyone meet him in the kitchen immediately. He says it's time we found Aliana."

Owen's green eyes, so similar to their missing friend's, sparked with cautious hope. Every idea they had all come up with in the last few weeks had come to nothing.

Leo bent over, grabbing his shirt and tossing Owen his. "We'll go there now and fetch Merlin, Percy, Lancelot and Wade on the way."

Flora mourned the loss of the fantastic sight of the knight's muscular chests. Lacy, Dawn, and Aliana had a running joke about the guys secretly hoping to be *GQ* models. The gods know the women of the world would snatch the magazines up quicker than free money. They all may not be classically handsome, but they all had a charisma and confidence that seemed to draw the fairer sex to them.

Flora shook her head, snapping herself out of the hot-guy daze she had fallen into. "Is Sir Galahad out here as well?" She'd bet her hidden supply of Pixie dust he was, but it didn't hurt to ask.

Leo tilted his head to the left, past a high dune covered with tall grass. "He headed that way."

The Pixie shot off as the two boys took off toward the house. She made it to the knight's side in seconds, but he just stared out at the Atlantic Ocean, his mind so far away he may as well have been back in Camelot.

"Sir Galahad?" Flora asked, hesitant to disturb him. Since the last battle, there had been only two incidences when the knight had shown any real frenzied emotions: once after Mordrid had vanished with a limp Aliana in his arms; and then, after Lord Daggerhorne failed to return with his lost love.

Everyone knew now of the magic heightening his emotions, particularly when concerned for the safety of the people he cared for.

"What do you need, Flora?" Galahad asked. Much like Arthur, his voice was somber and gravelly, holding so much leashed pain and anguish Flora felt her throat tighten with unshed tears.

No one but Arthur, Galahad, and Aliana knew the details of what happened on the beach between them that night. All they knew was that the two best friends had gotten in a fight over the girl they loved and she had somehow rebuilt the shields that helped Galahad control his baser emotions.

"The king wants to see everyone in the kitchen. He wants to come up with a new plan to find Aliana."

Galahad sighed, still staring out at the ocean. His eyes turned to the Pixie who was the size of a small child, only three feet tall, with white blond hair and cerulean eyes that complemented the glow of her dragonfly-like wings. "I screwed up, Flora."

The Pixie's blue eyes widened at his admission.

"I never wanted to hurt her. I thought I had it under control. I knew what I was doing was wrong, that I was hurting and betraying her. I tried to stop myself, to free her, but my body betrayed me. My fear and need to protect her was like a demon controlling me."

Flora gulped down the scratchy lump in her throat. The brave knight's words were so heavy and tortured. How was he still able to think straight when he was clearly suffering so much?

"Then, when I saw Arthur kissing her, what little restraint I had left shattered to pieces."

"What?" Flora gasped. So that's what happened, why the two brother knights had fought.

"She foolishly got between us, stopping me when I couldn't stop myself, again. She grabbed on to me and I think that's when she realized what was wrong with me. I heard her in my head as she rebuilt my shields." Galahad's stormy blue eyes finally focused on the Pixie. "She was surprised that the magic Mordrid almost killed me with had damaged the protection she had created."

Flora remembered when they had returned from the Isle of the Blessed weeks ago and Galahad had thrown himself in front of a magic attack meant for Aliana. Aliana had nearly killed herself saving his life.

"I kissed her and then she pulled away screaming in pain. Everything happened so quickly after that, and before either Arthur or I could help her she just vanished."

Flora remembered Merlin mentioning that Aliana had managed to tap into shifting magic, something only extremely powerful magical beings could use. Even knowing what they did of Aliana's magic, the Druid had never suspected she had that kind of ability on her own.

"We will find her. I can feel it." And she could. Since she had awoken this morning, the Pixie had felt certain that today would be the day things changed.

Galahad took a deep breath, his body rigidly controlled. Since his last outburst, he had exercised an unyielding control over himself. He was even deadlier and more calculated when he sparred with the others, and Flora suspected he would be far more ruthless than any of them had ever seen when they found Mordrid and Morgana.

Galahad took a step closer to her. "We need to get to the house." He vanished in a blur and Flora shot off after him. Galahad had been trapped for centuries in a magic prison the Sidhe had used to confine him and that magic had enhanced the natural abilities the white knight had always possessed. He was faster and stronger than any normal human, and even most magical beings.

They made it to the house in seconds and saw Lacy Edrick and Dawn Anson, best friends and all but blood sisters of Aliana's, sitting huddled together at the island in their friends' kitchen. Dawn's voice filled the room:

"Before the darkest hour strikes, the Destined One shall come forth.
Avalon's lost daughter must thrice and alone prove her worth.
Then can she fully possess the power to awaken the king.
It shall become her destiny to reunite the Round Table.
Unearth and reclaim their lost relics.
Become the key to undoing the evil Mordrid has wrought.
Only with her can the Once and Future King prevail!"

Lacy groaned and dropped her head on her folded arms on the counter top.

Dawn sighed, just as exhausted and frustrated as her friend. "We have to figure out if there's anything in this prophecy that might help us find out where the heck Aliana is."

Lacy growled. "We've been over this stupid prophecy twenty-three times! Just like that stupid Fae queen, Titania, it's vague and of no real help to us finding Lia!"

"Stop this!" Flora yelled, her usually spunky bell-like voice taking on a more commanding tone. "Aliana wouldn't want you two fighting like gremlins over a leftover bone."

King Arthur entered the kitchen on the heels of the girl's statement. "Flora's right. We can't keep going for each other's throats at the slightest frustration."

Lacy scoffed. "Like you're one to talk, kingie. You and Galahad can't even be in the same room for longer than ten minutes without having a go at each other."

Flora knew it wasn't that Lacy disliked the legendary king, but Lacy firmly believed that Galahad and Aliana were meant to be together. The feelings that had grown between their missing sister and the golden king had only messed up the good relationship between Aliana and her white knight.

Arthur's golden brown eyes held hers for a second before flicking to his brother in arms, the man who had been Arthur's best friend since they were children. The others came into the kitchen. "You're right, Lacy. But that's going to change. We've had no luck trying to find Aliana with the means at our disposal. It's time we tried another approach."

"What do you mean?" Dawn asked, sitting up straighter. Unlike Lacy, the brunette firmly believed that Arthur was a better match for their friend. He was calm, rational, clearly devoted to Aliana, and unlike Galahad, not bogged down with an overprotective complex that had desolated their absentee friend's fragile heart.

Merlin Wylit took a seat at the kitchen table, the Druid spreading out several maps he had brought with him. Lancelot D'Arn helped his friend, adding several scrolls and papers of his own to the mix. One by one everyone took a seat around the kitchen table. The girls sat next to each other, Wade took the open seat next to Dawn, who'd given him the cold shoulder since the Aliana was taken. The dark-haired, lively knight had only managed to start thawing her frosty mood a few days ago.

Percy took the open seat on Lacy's other side. Unlike Aliana and Dawn, the blond girl had not shut out her gentle giant. She had been angry and hurt, sure, but she knew he had only wanted to protect her and their friend. He had sworn to her that he would never do such a foolish thing again.

Flora studied the immortal Druid and the cursed knight for another moment. Both men had been profoundly changed after breaking their vow to Queen Titania and leaving Avalon. Lancelot was tormented with the haunting memories of his Guinevere. Merlin's punishment had been strange, though. His banishment from Avalon, cutting off his link to his greatest source of magic, was bad, but Flora sometimes suspected there was more to it.

Arthur and Galahad took their seats, an open space between them where Aliana would've sat. Both men looked at the empty space, then each other. Their eyes clashed and held for what felt like an eternity, their bodies stiff and on guard. Then something palpable passed between the pair and they started to relax, finally turning their attention back to the others.

"I owe each of you an apology," Arthur said as two of the other Pixies, Sabine and Stella, joined Flora in the kitchen. "I have not been the leader you needed these last weeks, but that is going to change now. Aliana needs all of us."

"But we have no idea where she is!" Wade spoke up.

"Then we have to find out," Galahad said, his voice deep and rumbling.

Merlin agreed with his brother knight. "There are two possible sources that may help us find her location."

Lacy pulled out of Percy's embrace. "What's your *brilliant* plan this time?"

Dawn voiced her support. "The last *plan* you had involved shipping my mother and Lacy and Wade's parents on a two month cruise and banishing Joe to the west coast for a 'guest lecture sabbatical.'" Dawn made air quotes with her finders. "You still have no proof that he was betraying us to Mordrid and Morgana! You just wanted him out of the way."

"Enough," Arthur ordered, his I'm-the-king voice echoing around the kitchen. "You both know those decisions were for their safety more than anything else." He looked to Merlin, dismissing the girls. "Continue with what you were saying."

"We cannot dismiss the possibility that Queen Titania is somehow involved in her disappearance."

Everyone bristled at the mention of the devious Fae queen.

Merlin brought their attention back. "The other option is to find the Well of Realms. If we can locate it, we will have a way to find her, no matter where Aliana is in the seven realms."

"How? What is this Well, exactly?" Lacy asked, leaning back against her giant cowboy knight, Percy.

Arthur leaned forward, resting his elbows on the kitchen table. "I remember my mother telling me of the Well before, though I admit I don't recall all she told me of it."

"Because the Well is rooted in all the seven realms, it has a unique power to find anything." Merlin pushed up the sleeve on his right arm, revealing the barely visible tracking marks that circled his wrist. Every member of the new Round Table had an identical mark on their right wrist. "I used the same principle when I branded all of us with these marks. With their aid, locating Aliana through the Well's waters will be easier."

Arthur nodded. "We will split up. Myself, Lacy, Percy and Leo will go to the Isle and seek answers from Queen Titania." He turned to his friend. "Galahad, you, Dawn, Owen and Wade will go to Avalon and try to find this Well. You have the contacts in that realm, and Dawn—" his eyes went to the short girl "—you are a wood Nymph, and they live in Avalon. You will have another unique connection to the realm, and people that may help us find it."

Dawn gulped nervously, but bobbed her head up and down.

"What about Merlin and Lancelot?" Leo asked, his Scottish brogue rolling off his tongue.

"We are still banished from both realms," Lancelot murmured. "We will redouble our efforts to try to locate the Grail of Power." The knight's green eyes fell to Excalibur, hung over the back of Arthur's chair. "Now that we have Excalibur, the Grail is the last item we need before we can stop Morgana and Mordrid."

"Lancelot and I will go to Mt. Olympus. Rothik sent me a message that he may have a lead on the Atlantian who came to Olympus after fleeing his tribe in Atlantis." Merlin had introduced them to Rothik only a day before everything went to hell in a ripped-apart magical hand basket. The Chimera called Olympus home and helped teach the many who came to the famous realm to learn how to use and control their magic.

Lacy crossed her arms over her chest. "That's great and all, but how are we supposed to get into these realms? Aliana was the one who had the magic to get us in and out of them." It was impossible to miss the hurt and resentment in her voice. Since learning that Lacy was half Fae and that Dawn was half Wood Nymph, Merlin had been trying to help them both learn how to use their powers. But they hadn't had nearly the success Lacy had hoped for.

"I'll arrange for my jet to take Galahad and his team back to London. They can use the cave entrance Aliana first used to enter Avalon."

Galahad nodded at Merlin. He was prepared to do whatever he had to do to get Aliana back. He would prove to her that he had changed, that he could control himself, and that he trusted her and cared for her enough to let her make her own decisions. She had unimaginable magic and he knew it was wrong of him to think she couldn't take care of herself. She had proven she could many times.

And once she saw the changes in him, she *would* love him again, come back to him where she belonged. Assuming he hadn't damaged their sparking bond beyond repair.

"What about us getting into the Isle?" Lacy asked. "I still can't open the gate between the realms." Percy wrapped his arm around her shoulders and pulled the love of his life tighter against him.

"I will give you a talisman that you can use as a channel to summon the power needed to open the gate," Merlin said. "But you will need to be sure to push your own magic into the pendant so the Isle doesn't recognize it as mine. We don't know what would happen if to you all if it does."

Arthur stood up from the table. "Then it's settled. How long will you need to empower this talisman, Merlin?"

"I can have it ready by tomorrow."

Arthur looked at Galahad. The white knight inclined his head, his face set and eyes filled with life and purpose again. Much like Arthur's.

"Then we all depart tomorrow. Merlin, can you have your *plane* ready by then?"

"Yes."

Arthur straightened. "Good. Then we all need to turn in and get some rest. We are going to have very long and hard journeys ahead of us."

"If it gets us closer to getting Aliana back and finding the Grail then it's all worth it," Owen said, passion infused in his every word. Wade, Leo and Percy voiced their agreement.

Only the girls remained silent. They nodded to each other, a silent understanding between them. The guys, for all their cleverness, had no idea what the girls had secretly been planning to find their lost friend. There were still many mysteries surrounding this whole prophecy that Aliana had told them they needed to figure out. Answers that may hold the key to saving the realms and stopping their enemies. Answers that might give the Knights of the Round Table their lives and their freedom back.

2

Aliana tried desperately to wrap her mind around the place—scratch that—the *time*—she now found herself in. Even the beautiful dress Titania had put her in felt so foreign and out of place, just like her entire world right now.

Merlin's brows shot up. "And what answer did you expect to receive, my lady?" he asked in response to her shock of learning where she was.

Camelot. In the year five hundred freaking eighty-six!

Aliana opened her mouth then shut it again, not sure what to say. Dagg shifted on her shoulders.

She looked Merlin over again. Physically, he was the same. A few inches taller than her, his light brown hair was curlier than she was used to seeing it, but that's what happens when you don't have hair care products. His long silver cuff, branded with the Pendragon crest, a Dragon in flight, glinted in the sunlight. The wrist cuff was a sign that he was a member of the Round Table, and the king's inner circle of warriors.

He was so different, but still the same. It confused her to no end. His shoulders were more relaxed, even with a large shield strapped across them. He just seemed more *open*, almost happy, like he didn't have a care in the world. He even seemed to respect Titania, not hate her like he did in her time.

She really was back in time, back in Camelot, before all the horrible events that plagued her in her time had taken place. *"Does Titania want me to change history?"* she asked Dagg through their link, dumbfounded by the possibility. She could save all her friends the pain and suffering they had to endure for so long!

"Absolutely not!" Dagg's voice raged in her head. *"We must be very careful not to tamper with the events that are to come. One small deviation could have devastating consequences in our time."*

"I see you were not expecting that answer." Merlin's hushed voice drew her from her silent conversation. "You asked *when* you were. Not *where*." She could feel his bright orange magic testing and checking out her own bubble-sparkly pink powers. His eyes widened, his magic clearly telling him something she wasn't sure she wanted him to know. "Are you truly from the future?"

Aliana's jaw dropped. "How did you know that?" She gasped, slapping her hands over her mouth to keep any more secrets from falling out unintentionally. *Wait a second...So far as I know English wasn't a thing in the Dark Ages.*

"How do you understand me, and I you?" Aliana crossed her arms trying to get a grip on the crazy situation.

Merlin grinned. "I was told to cast a spell that would allow me to communicate with one not speaking my language."

Aliana's arms dropped along with her slack jaw.

Merlin laughed with amused disbelief. "Now, why are you here? How did you get here?"

Dagg jumped from her shoulders and hovered between the two of them. "The answers you want are complicated and dangerous to know."

Merlin's excitement dulled a bit, replaced with a seriousness that reminded her of the first time he'd tried to teach her magic. That memory felt like lifetimes ago.

"I understand, knowing the future is a very dangerous thing." He looked past Dagg to her. "Do you know what the purpose is to your being here?"

Aliana hesitated. "Kind of. We know of one reason, at least." The item they needed to find that would lead them to the Grail of Power. "But Titania always has many motives for doing the things she does." The queen *had* said that finding this artifact to lead them to the Grail of Power was not their true task here in Camelot, just linked to it. What would be more important than finding a way to locate the Grail, though?

Merlin stroked his chin. It was weird to see him accept her answers so easily, to not have him look at her like he's questioning her every move and thought, thinking it's wrong or stupid.

Oh god, if Merlin's this different, how different will the others be? Her stress level shot back through the roof. She had only just managed to get herself together after escaping Mordrid. Her thoughts shifted to Galahad. How different would he be? Or Arthur? Both guys had told her many stories about their lives in Camelot, though she suspected they might have edited a few details for propriety's sake. She remembered the last time she was alone with her brave warriors, on the beach by her house, and how disastrously the whole situation had ended. How was she going to be able to focus on anything if she had to worry about the magic bonds that existed between her and Galahad, and her and Arthur?

Dagg's claw gripped her shoulder, startling her from her panicked thoughts. Her green eyes went to the Druid knight, who seemed to be waiting on an answer from her. "I'm sorry, what was the question?"

"I asked if you know how you were sent here."

She shrugged. "Titania sent us. I have to complete some obscure task for her and there's something I need to find here. Something that I desperately need in the future…to save the realms." She didn't tell him from whom the realms needed to be saved. Dagg was right; they couldn't interfere with the time stream. She'd seen enough movies and TV shows, read enough books, to know that the consequences could be disastrous. She was going to have to be very careful from now on what she said and did. *Not like this wasn't hard enough already!*

"Then we will need to help you discover your purpose here."

At least Merlin seemed like he was going to be more of a help than a hindrance. Maybe telling him the truth had been the right thing. It made her wonder if there were others here she could confide in too.

"I'll need to find a place to stay." Aliana bit her lip trying to figure out how she was going to pull that one off without any money.

"You will stay at the castle, of course," Merlin answered like it was the most obvious thing in the world. "We will tell the king of your business here, that you are on a quest for the Fae Queen. He will welcome you as an honored guest. We already have one of her court staying at the castle."

"No!" Aliana and Dagg said together.

"He can't know why I'm here. No one can besides you. Clearly Titania wants you involved but we can't risk telling the others." She paused, Merlin's other statement breaking through her momentary panic. "What do you mean you already have a Fae staying at Camelot?"

"Delphina has been a resident of our court for several years now. You were sent by the queen, I am sure she will be of help to you as well."

Aliana looked at Dagg, her confusion and surprise surely all over her face. *"None of the guys ever mentioned a Fae girl in Camelot before!"*

Dagg's Dragon lips pulled tight. *"I am sure there is plenty they never told you about their lives in Camelot."*

Aliana felt her face turn three shades of green. She flashed back to Arthur's story in the Isle about kissing other girls.

"My lady, are you all right?"

Aliana mentally shook away those thoughts. "Fine, but I'm very clearly not from your world, and your Delphina is not going to know who I am."

Merlin unhooked his shield from his shoulders and turned from Aliana. "I can take care of that," he said, re-securing the shield to the side of his saddle. "We should cast a spell on you so you can understand the others, and they you. I can say I know your clan, that you are connected to my family. Arthur will accept that and I can make sure you have everything you need to get by in Camelot."

Aliana accepted the offer. Now she'd just have to be sure to figure out whatever it was Titania wanted her to do and what object would lead her to the Grail of Power. "I would like to draw as little attention to myself as possible, if I can. Not having to worry about communicating would help a lot. And we can't tell anyone why I'm really here or that I have magic."

He nodded. The Druid looked at Dagg then down to the ruby on her hand, set inside the soft cloth gauntlet Titania had given her. It was the Prophecy stone Titania had created to bind her prophecy of the Destined One and link all of Arthur's knights to this quest to save the realms from Mordrid and Morgana.

"There is no way for you to hide your magic completely. I could feel it well before I got to you. Any of the other magic users in Camelot will know you have magic." He looked at Dagg again. "And there is no way for you to hide your guardian here."

Panic rose in her chest. She didn't want anyone to know the extent of her powers, or anything else about her.

"Breathe, Aliana," Dagg commanded. *"We will find a way to make this all work. Remember Arthur has no objection to magic."*

Merlin spoke again before she could answer her Dragon. "That stone of yours has great power. If you want to keep that part of you hidden, I suggest you create a very strong magic cloak to hide it."

Aliana frowned at Merlin. "How do I do that and hide my magic?"

His brow knit together. "Do you not know how to use your magic?"

Aliana flushed. "Yes, I do. But I've had a bit of a crash course lately without a lot of real instruction."

Shrugging, Merlin came to stand in front of her and held out his hands. "Then I will help however I can. Having such great power without knowing how to use it or control it can be very dangerous to you and everyone around you."

Aliana crossed her arms. "Like I don't already know that."

He grinned. "Give me your hands, oh fiery one. We can also cast the language spell now."

Coughing a laugh, Aliana relaxed and placed her hands in his.

"Relax your mind and focus on your magic and that of your ruby."

She did what he asked as Dagg curled around her shoulders again and her magic soared.

"Good. Now imagine a veil surrounding both of them and seal it together, like tying off a sack."

Aliana even added a layer of shields around the thinly constructed veil.

"Very well done. Now focus on your voice and ears."

Her vocal cords tingled, a faint buzzing nagged her ears.

"Will your magic to make your ears understand all they hear."

The buzzing grew louder but Aliana kept her focus on her magic.

"Now command your voice to be clear and understood by all others."

The tingling in her vocal cords turned to an itch. The abuse of her senses ripped at her, but she kept focused on maintaining her magic. Her ears popped like she was surfacing from a deep dive. The itch in her throat soothed over like honey was coating her vocal cords. Her shoulders sagged, a big sigh of relief escaping her.

Letting go of her hands, Merlin stood back, a look of impressed awe on his face.

"Your power and your connection to Lord Daggerhorne is like nothing I've ever seen. I have never met another with magic like yours."

Aliana dropped her hands to her side, her insecurities and doubts flooding her as she bitterly stared at the ground. "Yeah, that's me, the freak magic user."

"You misunderstand me, my lady."

She looked up at the Druid, trying to put the lid back on her emotional hidey-hole.

"It is not a bad thing, to have magic like yours. It's amazing!" His jubilant mood dimmed for a second. "But there will be many who may want to try to use you. You will have to be very careful. The veil you created is doing a fine job of muting the extent of your magic, but I can still feel it."

She didn't need him to tell her that, but Aliana nodded anyway, slightly grateful that he didn't hold her magic against her. Curious, she opened her own magical senses and felt out Merlin's powers. She had never tested his strength before, because it always felt like an invasion, and she didn't want him doing it to her. But this Merlin was different, maybe he wouldn't mind.

His magic was there; right up front, no barrier hiding it. So vibrant and powerful, she had trouble breathing for a moment. She pulled back wondering why she had never noticed the strength of Merlin's magic before. No wonder he was said to be the most power-ful Druid who ever lived.

"Like what you saw?" A heaping dose of masculine pride colored his arrogant words.

"It's not bad." She made sure she sounded unimpressed. He certainly didn't need any ego stroking.

He laughed and gathered up the reins of his horse. His mount wasn't nearly as big as Belle had been, the Pegasus that had aided her in Avalon so long ago, but the animal before her now was no small thing either. "Is that sack there yours?" he asked, nodding his head to a spot behind her. Turning, Aliana's eyes fell on her colorful pack. Strange, she hadn't had it with her at Mordrid's…

"But how? Who?" She turned to Dagg, but the Dragon shrugged.

Trotting over, Aliana scooped it up and slung it over her shoulders. She knew it was hers; she'd have to go through it once she reached Camelot. Maybe Titania left her a clue as to what to do next? Only the Fae queen knew she was here, so no one else could have sent it.

Merlin deftly lifted himself up into the saddle and held his hand out to her. "We need to get back to Camelot before dark, and it is a long ride."

Aliana took his hand, lifted her foot into the stirrup and gripped the back of the hard leather saddle. He easily pulled her up behind him, her hands grabbing at his waist to help steady herself.

"What about your Dragon?" he asked.

She looked at her little silver guardian hovering next to them. "I will fly ahead and scout the area. When we get close to Camelot I will be sure I am hidden." Aliana knew he was referring to the bracelet form he took to keep others from seeing him.

Kicking the horse's sides, they took off in a fast trot. Aliana had to wrap her arms tight around Merlin to keep from sliding or bouncing from the back of the animal.

"You haven't ridden many horses have you?" Merlin's voice in her head surprised her, but she shook it off.

"I have, it's just been a long time since I've needed to."

They rode for several hours, stopping only to water the horse and eat a few pieces of fruit they found along the way. Merlin disappeared for a moment to "relieve himself" and Aliana had nearly fainted from embarrassment when she had to do the same.

One thing I definitely don't like about the past, she thought to herself, *having to use the forest as my toilet! So not sanitary.*

Thankfully Merlin didn't seem to notice her discomfort and they quickly set back out on the road. Late afternoon settled in on them as Merlin told her about Camelot and the people who lived there.

A pang of regret filled her heart. What wouldn't her father have given to get to see Camelot like she was about to? Well, her adopted father, but Aliana had learned there was more to family than just a blood relation.

"Your father would be proud of you, Aliana," Dagg assured her.

"Where are you?"

"I am a few miles ahead of you two. There is a strange power around here that I am not sure I trust."

Aliana looked around nervously, opening her own senses. All she found was the strong magic of the elements, just there waiting for her to take if she needed them. *"I don't feel anything."*

"I am going to look around, see if I can find the source of this power. I will meet you in Camelot. Please try to stay out of trouble until I return."

Aliana wished the smartass Dragon was near so she could glare at him. *"Watch it or I'll make you the pack mule again, or maybe I'll just clip your wings!"*

Dagg's laughter filled her mind before all traces of her guardian faded. Her last joke had her mood souring. The first time she had threatened to clip Dagg's wings was when she and Galahad were flying through Avalon on Belle, racing to find Arthur so she could awaken him. The aching sadness she had managed to hide away almost leaked out, but she corralled it back in.

Lost in her thoughts, Aliana didn't notice the riders approaching them until Merlin slowed their mount.

"Merlin!" a strong, smooth voice called. A voice she recognized.

3

Looking past the Druid, she spotted a giant on horseback with a long face, quirky large smile, whisky-colored eyes and broad shoulders. *Percy!* Next to him was another rider with longer, dark brown curly hair, late afternoon stubble and friendly hazel eyes. *Wade!* she thought happily, but kept the names to herself, reminding her over-taxed brain that they didn't go by those names here. Technically, she wasn't supposed to know who they were. They flanked both sides of her and Merlin, both men appraising her with open fascination.

"So, this fair maiden is why you took off from the castle so early this morning?" Wade joked with avid interest.

Aliana fought to not roll her eyes. *You'd think he's never seen a girl before!*

"Enough, Gawain," Merlin admonished, like a chastising father. "Lady Aliana is new to Camelot."

"Where are you from then?" Percival's too large smile calmed her with its familiarity.

"All over, I guess." What other answer could she really give without giving away where she really was from?

"And how does such a lovely creature know our killjoy Druid, Merlin?" Aliana giggled, turning toward Wade. His own silver Pendragon cuff was so well polished you almost missed the two long marks he had once gotten in battle. Percy's was still in pristine shape.

Gawain! She reminded herself. *He's Gawain here, and Percy is Percival!* She hid a sigh; this was going to be a lot harder than she thought.

"I have known Aliana and her family since I was a child," Merlin said when she remained silent. "She has spent many years traveling all over and has now decided to come see me in Camelot."

It was amazing how effortlessly he lied to his friends. It set her a little on edge, but she reminded herself that this little white lie was for the good of her quest.

"Will you be staying at the castle then?" Percy asked her.

She nodded. "Merlin was kind enough to offer me a place to stay for the duration of my visit." She cleared her throat. "And who are you two knights, if I may ask?"

"My lady, forgive our lack of manners. I am Sir Percival of Camelot and that loud mouthed oaf is Sir Gawain of Camelot."

"I'm not the oaf here, you tree shaking giant," Wade said with a fake heat to his voice.

"Pleasure to meet you both." She bowed her head to them and smiled. "I think we're all going to be good friends."

Merlin sighed loudly and looked at both his brother knights. "Now that that's settled, was there a purpose to you both finding us?"

"Arthur was looking for you. You didn't tell anyone where you were going and you've been gone for most the day." Gawain, the knight who in her time was all but her brother, flicked his eyes quickly to her then back to Merlin. "He said there is an urgent matter he needs to discuss with you."

Her interest piqued, Aliana tried to pretend she wasn't listening, hoping to find out what Wade, or rather Gawain, was talking about.

"How long do you plan on staying in Camelot?" Percival asked, drawing her attention when Merlin quietly answered Gawain. *Sneaky, sneaky Sir Percival!*

"I'm not sure." She shrugged, putting on a flirty playful smile. "I guess it will largely depend on when Merlin gets tired of having me around."

Percival laughed, the booming sound drawing the attention of Merlin and Gawain.

"If the king is waiting we need to hurry back." Merlin kicked his horse back into high gear. Aliana gasped and tightened her hold on his waist again, her legs and thighs clenched tightly to the horse.

The guys matched their pace and in no time they were clearing the forest road and entering a wide-open field filled with tall grass and a small patch of lavender flowers. The ground was wide open, and a lush, beautiful green was saturated by the sunlight. They made their way to a stark dirt road that led over a hill just in front of them. As they crested the top, as Merlin pulled on his horses' reins and brought their little party to a halt. His horse trotted sideways so she had a clear view.

Aliana's jaw fell open, her eyes widening in delight. Settled near the edge of a cliff was the tallest castle she had ever seen. Its five spires looked like they were nearly touching the sky, with bright red and gold flags flying in the strong ocean breeze. It had to be four stories high at its shortest points and close to double that in others. Walls stretched from the sides of the castle down the sloping ground separating a small city-like village. Shorter walls ran through the village like a maze. Large inns and smaller homes were built in the areas in front of the majestic structure with another shorter wall protecting it — a village at the gates of one of the greatest kingdoms in recorded history.

Aliana blinked and closed her mouth, but couldn't banish her huge grin. "It's *beautiful*, Merlin!"

"Welcome to Camelot, Lady Aliana," Percival said with a sweep of his hand.

"Home to King Arthur and his legendary Knights of the Round Table," Gawain added with a playful bow.

Merlin swatted at Gawain, hitting his muscled arm with a loud smack. "Enough, the king is waiting." He kicked his horse into a fast gallop, the other two knights racing beside them.

Guards called to each other to open the gates as Aliana and the knights made their way to the outer walls of Camelot. It was weird to see all the soldiers and citizens of Camelot bowing their heads to the guys as they made their way up the slight slopes of the city toward the castle.

The scent of roasting meat, herbs and livestock surrounding Aliana's senses threatened to steal her attention from the colors and sights of the vibrant, small village. The sound of soldiers marching, people rushing about, some pulling carts, and merchants talking loudly to draw customers, had her eyes darting everywhere so fast dizziness was starting to set in. It was almost overwhelming in its difference from what she had always imagined Camelot would be like. But that was the thing about the Dark Ages: no one had any real proof of what things were like back then.

Or is it now? This is going to give me a headache! Aliana shook her head as Merlin led his horse to the right and up a sloped alley into a wide open stable area. Servants scrambled to attention, rushing to the knights. A young boy — no older than maybe fourteen — rushed to Merlin.

"Welcome back m'lord." His smile was easy, excited and very friendly. And he couldn't stop staring at Aliana.

Fighting an uncomfortable blush and the desire to shy away, she offered the boy a smile. *Take a picture kid, it'll last longer.*

"Are you going to stare or help the Lady Aliana down, boy?" Gawain shot him an exasperated look. "You've seen beautiful ladies before."

The kid flushed, ducking his head, apologizing in a soft stuttering voice as he set down a stool another boy had brought over. The guys started laughing loudly and Aliana glowered at them.

"Leave him alone, boys."

The kid flashed her an embarrassed but grateful smile. Leaning into Merlin, Aliana lifted her leg over the horse. The boy's hand was at her waist steadying her as he took her hand and helped her down.

"Thank you," she said while Merlin and the guys dismounted. "I'm Aliana, what's your name?"

He never got to answer.

"Raven is one of our newest stable hands." Merlin looked like he was going to say more but another familiar voice drew his attention.

"You've finally returned." Lancelot's voice was the same as it was in Aliana's time, accented with just a touch of superiority. But the most surprising thing was the red-haired woman at his side, her arm tucked into Lancelot's. Her skin was pale with a light dusting of freckles and rich brown eyes.

"Lancelot, Guinevere!" Percival greeted the pair with a hard pat on Lancelot's arm and a kiss dropped on Guinevere's cheek.

"Look who we finally tracked down," Gawain teased, taking Lancelot's arm in a warrior's greeting, then kissing Guinevere's other cheek.

"And I see he didn't come alone." Lancelot regarded Aliana with an open and frank curiosity.

Clenching the loose pink fabric of her dress sleeve, Aliana took a breath trying to stow her building panic. As familiar as all these knights were, it was impossible to forget that these guys weren't *her* knights. They didn't know her from Eve, and it was going to take more than Merlin's vouching for her to get them to accept her.

But then maybe it would be better if they didn't really get to know her. It had been hard enough to not slip up with their names so far; what would happen if she slipped and gave herself away? She couldn't risk doing damage to the world's timeline.

Merlin introduced her to Lancelot and Guinevere, telling the same effortless lie that he had to Percival and Gawain. He told them about wanting to introduce her to Arthur and getting her settled into a room in the castle.

"Welcome to Camelot, Lady Aliana," Guinevere said, coming to her side. "It will be so nice to have another girl around here. These men can get a bit boring at times," she added in a fake whisper.

Aliana giggled. It seemed like she and Guinevere would get along very well. Her delight faltered at the thought, however, since Guinevere was supposed to die.

Before she could think on it too much, Merlin and the others led her out of the stables and up a staircase into a brightly lit hallway. The tall windows were exactly what she remembered from the ruined Camelot she had seen in the Isle of the Blessed, but they were much more beautiful now that the colored glass was whole and glowing in the late afternoon sun. Guinevere told her a little about the castle and the people who made their home there. All of the knights had their own rooms in the castle, as well as their own lands not far from the castle's city. She also warned her about some of the women that lived there. Aliana flashed back to Merlin's mirror room, at his house back in Aliana's world. She remembered Arthur telling her some of the horror stories of the women who had vied for his affection, including one about a girl ripping another's dress.

They walked down another hall way and up a curving flight of stairs she recognized. They were going to the throne room! Her anxiety ratcheted up, as her experiences in that room weren't exactly the best. Titania's bombshell reveal that Camelot could live again. Learning Titania was grandmother to her and Owen. Her finally opening up to Galahad about her past and her ex-boyfriend. Then of course there was Mordrid's attack that had nearly killed Galahad at the end.

She shook her head, trying to dispel that horrible, gut wrenching memory.

"Are you all right?" Guinevere questioned.

Aliana smiled quickly. "I've never met a king before, in his castle. I'm just nervous, I guess."

Guinevere laid a sympathetic hand on Aliana's shoulder. "Don't worry, I've known Arthur since we were children. He will welcome you to Camelot happily."

"Thanks." She took a breath and pushed aside her worry, for now.

Guinevere went to her husband's side as Merlin dropped back to join Aliana. "You ready for this?"

She nodded at the Druid. "I'm sorry you have to lie to your friends because of me."

He shrugged. "They would understand if they were in my position. Do not fret about it."

She still didn't like it, but it *was* a necessary evil right now. She would at least be protected in the castle and have Merlin's aid. She needed to quickly complete whatever task Titania wanted of her so she could get back home. To her family, to her friends and knights. They had to be going crazy by now.

The beach, where she had last been in Arthur and Galahad's arms, flashed in her mind, but the creaking wooden doors of the throne room opened, shattering the memory.

Golden sunlight spilled into the room, and the large pit in the center popped and hissed as a servant fed a few logs onto the building fire. More than a dozen warrior-looking men were gathered around a large round table just the other side of the pit, most of whom she didn't recognize as her knights. They all wore outfits similar to what her knights wore: dark-colored or white tunics, leather vests and jackets, dark pants and boots, and all the men were armed with their sheathed swords. Her eyes fell on one knight in particular, who had his sword strapped across his back. Leo. Owen stood on one side of his quiet friend.

All the heads turned to them as they walked through the doors. Aliana fought to keep her feet from freezing where she stood when she met Arthur's golden brown eyes across the fire. He was wearing a black shirt and leather jacket, his short dark hair swept across his forehead and tickling at his ears. He had the faint shadow of late day stubble and his features were just as strong and sharp as ever. But there was a presence about him, an utterly confident posture that was new.

Her Arthur, in her world, was plagued with worry and doubt, with so much at stake and everything to lose. She had seen glimpses of the King Arthur she now stood in front of, but never quite like this. *Then again, nearly dying, losing your kingdom and having to make a magic vow to Titania could definitely affect a guy's confidence.*

Merlin's hand rested on the small of her back and led her around the fire pit to where all the burly knights and advisors stood. Her eyes widened as she saw Excalibur secured across a tall chair beside the golden king.

Arthur watched them approach, as did all the others, but it was Arthur who had Aliana's hands trembling.

"Glad to see you're back, my friend." The king set his eyes on her again, openly appraising her, though not unkindly. She knew Arthur's looks, and she could tell by the tiny smile on one corner of his mouth that he was happy with what he saw. "Who is your companion? I don't believe I've ever seen her in Camelot."

Aliana bit her tongue. He didn't need to talk about her like she wasn't standing right in front of him.

Merlin grinned and nudged her forward. She curtsied slightly, feeling awkward with all the eyes in the room watching her. "Sire, this is Lady Aliana. Her clan has been well acquainted with mine for some time. She has finally decided to come and visit me here in Camelot."

"You traveled alone, my lady?" Arthur asked with a raised brow.

She hid her annoyance that he would be so chauvinistic, but this *was* the sixth century after all. "I often travel on my own, your majesty."

He smirked, then turned to the men gathered around them. "I think we are done for tonight." The men bowed and gathered their things before leaving hurriedly. Only Owen and Leo remained.

"Do you plan to stay in Camelot for long, Lady Aliana?" Arthur crossed his arms over his broad chest as he leaned his hip against the sturdy wooden table. Aliana's eyes roamed over his hot body quickly before meeting his eyes again.

"I guess that depends."

Merlin drew Arthur's attention from her. "I had hoped that you would allow Lady Aliana to stay here in the castle, during the duration of her visit."

Arthur's lips thinned as he thought over the request.

A door opened behind the group before he could answer. The only thing that kept her from gasping was the fact that all the air was stolen from her lungs. She watched Galahad stroll into the throne room, two girls flanking him on both sides. But she didn't really see the girls; her eyes were focused on her former white knight, and the world paused.

His wavy light brown hair was slightly shorter than it was in her world; it only just brushed the collar of his dark leather jacket and green tunic. His jaw was square and peppered with stubble around strong lips she had kissed too many times to count. The tall knight stopped as his clear blue eyes fell on her.

A thrill of excitement laced with worry arrowed down her spine. His eyes roamed over her, much like the others had. She saw the heat that started to blaze in those eyes, eyes that had the power to hypnotize her with their intensity. She had given her Galahad her heart, her love and her trust, and he had shattered the fragile bond between them with one deed.

"Ah, Galahad," Arthur said as the world seemed to move again. "Come meet our guest."

Aliana raised her eyes, deftly avoiding looking at Galahad, focusing instead on the two girls who still flanked him. The first girl, in a simple dark green dress with a thick silver belt around her waist, was short with long curling brown hair, blue eyes, and an air of innocence that made her seem no older than fifteen.

The other girl was a little taller, her gray dress highlighting her long apricot-flesh-colored hair and eyes of such pale green they were almost translucent. Her skin was a creamy pale with just a faint hint of blue.

She had to be the Fae Merlin had mentioned, but Aliana's overwhelmed brain couldn't recall her name. The exotic, curvy girl glided to Arthur's side, resting a hand on his muscular arm. Arthur turned and smiled at her, an air of such familiar comfort around them that a small spark of jealousy flared in Aliana's chest. They held each other's gaze for what seemed like forever, but really couldn't have been more than a heartbeat.

Clearly they had a very strong connection, one that Aliana thought she might actually be able to see if she wasn't hiding her magic. She felt the blood drain from her face as one mystery of her Arthur's past suddenly became clear.

Green eyes.

Green eyes that Arthur said were the only thing he could remember of the ghost girl that haunted his dreams. This Fae was his mystery girl! The girl he couldn't remember but knew that he had loved at some point in his past. The past she was now trapped in.

4

Merlin's hand touched hers inconspicuously, and she only then realized she had tensed up and clenched her fists. *"Are you well? What is wrong?"*

Merlin's questions in her mind were enough to snap her back to reality. With a ruthless determination she was sure would have met with Titania's approval, Aliana wrenched her emotions back in check and made her body relax. Her fingers pressed against his, twining together for a moment and she met the Druid's pale eyes.

"Sorry, I'm just feeling a bit overwhelmed. Remember this isn't my time. Is she the Fae you told me about earlier?"

"Yes." Merlin gave her a small smile of reassurance. Aliana discreetly pulled her fingers away hoping no one had noticed. From the questioning looks on everyone's faces, that was an epic fail.

"Lady Aliana," Arthur took a step closer to her, the Fae girl's hand falling from his arm as he did. "I would be happy for you to make Camelot your home for as long as you desire. You already know a few members of my inner circle, so please allow me to introduce you to the others."

Aliana smiled and looked to Owen and Leo. Of all the knights, they seemed the most similar to her knights, as they were in her time. Her soon-to-be cousin had his dark hair chopped short, his shoulders were wide, his long torso covered with a vest that seemed to be a leather version of chest armor. His slightly rounded face was open and honest, and his smile was just as easy as always.

The sandy blond Leo was slightly shorter than Percival, Galahad and Arthur, his vest similar to Owen's with the strap of his sword snug across his wide chest. His thoughtful dove gray eyes looked at her then to the side, in Galahad's direction.

Owen offered her a cool grin as he bowed his head to her. "I am Sir Owaine, it is a pleasure to meet you. It is rare we get to meet people from our Druid's past."

"I am Sir Leyon." His Scottish accent was present, just as it was in her time, but it was very surprising. What was a Scot doing in sixth century Britain?

"It is nice to meet both of you," she replied.

She looked away, meeting the green eyes of the Fae who held Arthur's heart. Aliana was stunned at the bold move the Fae pulled next. *"I am honored to greet one of the queen's lineage. May I greet you in the manner befitting one of your importance?"*

Panic resurfaced and Aliana replied hastily hoping to head off the girl. *"Please don't. Who my family is, is not something that is to be made known."* Aliana hoped the girl would assume that meant Titania didn't want her identity known. How else would she have convinced Delphina to not give her away? *"Thank you for the offer. I hope that we can have some time to get to know each other."*

That added thought felt a bit masochistic, but she couldn't stop herself from making the offer. Merlin had been right, she might be able to help figure out what she was to do.

The Fae dipped into a small curtsy. "I am Delphina, ambassador of Queen Titania, ruler of the Isle of the Blessed." Her voice was like that of a high pitched but soft musical note, pure and bright and genuinely warm.

Aliana mimicked her curtsy and smiled. "It's an honor to meet you." Out of the corner of her eye she saw Galahad step up to her side and she felt a small tremor of dread.

Knowing she couldn't avoid it, she turned to face him, her hands clenched so tightly she could feel her nails pressing into her skin. It didn't help that it felt like everyone in the room was watching her to see what she did, like she was the night's entertainment.

"I am Sir Galahad." He smiled boldly, his deep voice rolling off his tongue with his lovely accent that drew out his A's and E's. His blazing blue eyes drank her up like a man thirsty for water, just like they had when she first freed him from his stone prison, in the Sidhe's keep, so long ago. He had been out of control for those first few minutes, but then his sense returned to him and he became the man she had fallen in love with.

He held his hand out to her, just as he had then, but Aliana couldn't move her hand from her side. Thankfully the girl next to him cleared her throat loudly, drawing his attention, and he dropped his hand. Aliana knew she wasn't strong enough to handle feeling their intense silver sparking bond right now. Her heart was still too raw and bloodied from his betrayal.

"Forgive me," he said with a grin, not seeming to notice her discomfort or hesitation. He placed his hand on the girl's shoulder as she came closer. "This is my little sister, Lady Sophvira."

Aliana's eyes widened. This was his sister? Surprised, she smiled at the girl, saying hello as she took stock of the similarities between the two. Their hair color was the same, just like their paler skin tone and distinctly Roman features.

"Well, now that we are all acquainted I'm sure you'd like to get settled in to a room." Arthur's friendly words distracted her from Galahad. She looked at the man who, in her time, was one of her dearest friends.

"The rooms near to mine are empty, Arthur," Delphina offered quickly.

"Merlin," Arthur asked, "does that arrangement suit you?"

Merlin nodded. "Thank you, sire."

"I can show you to your rooms!" Sophvira said with delight.

"Why don't all the women show Lady Aliana the way? I'm sure you three can see she is settled in and comfortable." Arthur's golden gaze returned to Aliana and held hers for a long moment, nearly as mesmerizing as Galahad's.

Gawain broke up the moment. "Yes, we still have a few things that need to be discussed."

Arthur gestured to Leyon and Owaine who started to redistribute the papers and maps that were on the round table.

Guinevere came to Aliana's side while Delphina led the way, Sophvira giddily following them. As they reached the door, Arthur called out to them.

"Lady Aliana, I hope you will join us for dinner tonight. You must be desperate for a good meal after traveling all day."

Her stomach twisted at the thought of food. She hadn't really eaten since before the whole beach thing with Arthur and Galahad. With the way time flowed between the realms and now her traveling to the past, who knew how long it had been since that last meal?

"I would be honored," she said, more than grateful that Merlin had helped her create the language spell.

He turned back to his knights who all were hunched over the legendary Round Table. All except Galahad.

His eyes met and held hers before she could tear them away. Her heart raced like a dragonfly's wings and her mind screamed at her to look away. Another arrow of distress shot up her spine and she quickly broke away and motioned for the girls to show her the way to her room.

She could feel the emotions she had been working so hard to deny. The proverbial dam was close to breaking. The sooner she got to a room, and the girls left, the sooner she could have her impending breakdown.

Later when the heavy door to her room closed behind the three girls, Aliana was barely able to make it to the small wooden chair beside the tiny fireplace before her legs collapsed and the tears started to flow.

In a matter of twelve hours she had gone from seeing Mordrid torture Morgana to the point beyond endurance; making a bargain with the devil—a devil she ended up kissing—to watching him be sucked into a black void; Titania sending her to Camelot, almost fifteen hundred years in the past without any clear indication of what she was to do; finding out Merlin knew she was from the future; meeting all her friends and while they were similar, they weren't *her knights*; meeting two girls, who both seemed friendly, loving and wonderful, who were supposed to die; *and* she'd met the girl who haunted the dreams of the man she was falling in love with.

She didn't even want to think about Arthur and Galahad. But she couldn't stop recalling the way they both had looked at her with open interest.

And she was lying to all of them. How was she going to survive all this?

"Aliana?" Dagg's voice floated into her mind.

"Dagg?" She lifted her head, her tear-filled eyes landing on the small snake-like Dragon flying through the open window next to her bed. She rushed to him, almost knocking the chair over as she got up. The Dragon met her halfway, a look of panic on his long angled face. She snatched her guardian up in a tight hug, his front claws wrapping around her neck as his wings curled around her hunched shoulders.

She started sobbing harder, sinking to the cold stone floor.

"Aliana, please tell me what's wrong!"

His worry broke through the fog, but Aliana couldn't get her throat to unlock to answer her friend. She did something she swore she wouldn't do again. She dropped her shields, exposing most of her memories and feelings and thoughts to him.

A thin streak of purple smoke started to flow through her, soothing her ragged emotions and injured heart enough that she was able to take a full breath instead of coughing sobs.

It was several minutes later when Dagg had seen almost everything and she was able to rebuild her shields and speak with her raw voice. "What am I going to do, Dagg?"

The Dragon pulled back, his claws gently cupping her cheeks. "We will tackle one problem at a time, together, as a team. You are not alone in this."

"But what about..." She couldn't say their names, afraid that she would break down again.

"We cannot change what has happened." Aliana thought that the Dragon was talking about more than just her heart's issues with Galahad and Arthur.

"You mean Guinevere and Sophvira?"

He nodded sadly. "Their fate is out of our hands. We can only do what we were sent here to do and hope we get home in time." His marble-scaled face tightened. "But I think there is something you need to tell me now."

Aliana felt her face go pale.

"Something you and Merlin have been hiding."

Aliana's heart kicked. She knew exactly what he meant. "The scroll."

Dagg jumped from her arms to the floor. "Why did you keep this from me?"

Hands twisted together, she answered, "I was scared what you and everyone would do. You know how the guys would have reacted!"

Dagg actually growled at her. "And you didn't tell *me*, why?"

Aliana threw up her hands in frustration, her emotions zinging around inside her. "What was I supposed to say? According to a stupid piece of paper, from that ridiculous iron-box-of-death, the only way the *Destined One* can defeat Mordrid for good is to sacrifice herself?" She shook her head, sucking in air. "You know you would have told the guys and they would have gone bat shit crazy."

The Dragon didn't deny the accusation. He just stood there on the pale stone floor, disappointment pouring from him.

Aliana fought the return of her tears. "It feels so hopeless, Dagg! Like I have no control over anything anymore!"

"I am your guardian! More than that I am your friend. If you can't trust me or our friends—no, our *family*—then we have already lost this war."

Aliana shoved both hands in her hair trying to quell her guilt. "I know, but it's not that easy! I hate the thought of lying and keeping this from everyone, but it seemed like the best decision at the time."

Dagg growled again. "How did you convince Merlin to stay quiet?"

Pulling her hands from her messed up braid she looked at her right palm. "I convinced him to make a magical promise to not say anything."

"And you promised—" Dagg paused like he was remembering what he saw "—that you would not intentionally place your life in harm's way."

Aliana's shoulders slumped, her braid slipping over her shoulder.

"And that's the real reason you couldn't leave the house before Merlin sealed it when the knights went to confront Mordrid."

Aliana shrugged. "Now you know." As hard as it was for Dagg to know, not having to hide it from him felt like a burden being lifted from her stressed and ravaged soul.

Dagg's stiff posture relaxed. "There's nothing to be done about it now. But you know you'll have to tell the others *when* we get home."

Aliana ran a finger over the nearly invisible brand around her wrist. Everything was so out of control.

"It only feels that way because you're letting your emotions take over. You must bring them back under control, just like when you are using your magic."

She let out a loud heavy breath. He was right, as always. "You're a little know-it-all, you know that right?"

Dagg grinned. "Don't think I won't remind you of it when you try to argue with me."

She giggled and got to her feet. Her pack was on the bed, covered with heavy blankets and two pillows that looked like they were stuffed with feathers or maybe something a little firmer. The room she was in was nice, with a tall dresser for clothes and even a small table with a bench and a mirror made of a brightly polished oval of metal. On a smaller table by her bed was a bowl filed with clean water and a cloth lying next to it.

"You must have made quite the impression to have Arthur giving you such an extravagant room."

She flicked the teasing Dragon and tilted her bag upside down, its contents spilling out onto the bed. Considering that Titania had sent her the bag — after doing who knows what to it — it was hardly surprising when three beautiful dresses, several smaller pouches that rattled and clanged, and a pair of boots hit the bed.

She had secretly hoped her camera would be one of the items tucked into her bag, but much to her dismay, it was absent. *It's for the better I suppose. That would definitely give me away.*

She grabbed one of the two leather pouches and pulled the flap up. It was filled with gold and silver coins and even a few precious stones. "How *nice* of her to be sure I had money to survive with."

Dagg fixed her with an exasperated look and opened the other pouch. It had a small round tin and three very small chopstick-like pieces of wood and iron. He grabbed the tin and removed the cap, sniffing the contents. "It's a magic-based ink." He sounded almost awed by that fact.

"Spell it out for me, Dragon boy."

He didn't even glare at her this time. "It can be used to reveal hidden messages."

"Spying and passing covert messages old school style, fantastic. Who am I supposed to get secret instructions from?"

"Aliana," he admonished sharply.

Her lips pulled to the side, pouting. "Sorry, but why couldn't she put something useful in here — like a blasted clue as to what the heck I need to find that will lead me to the Grail in our time! Or how about some slight hint as to this crazy *mystery* task!"

"Calm down. Being hysterical won't help us." He jumped up and wrapped himself around her shoulders. "For now I think it's logical to try to find out whatever we can about the Grail. Maybe then we can figure out what this Grail item is. We also need to remember, the eclipse Mordrid needs to take over our world happens every fifteen hundred years."

"That means there should be one happening here soon, if it hasn't already happened." Aliana leaned against the footboard of the bed. She stroked one hand down Dagg's leathery wing. "Who would be the best person to ask? Merlin?"

Dagg's chest rumbled. "Yes. But we should take care with how we phrase it. Just to be safe and not give away any knowledge of our future."

Aliana rubbed at her swollen eyes with her palm. "If I'm going to attend dinner, I need to clean myself up."

Dagg jumped into the air, hovering. The water in the bowl was cool and refreshing as she splashed it on her heated and splotchy face. She rubbed her wet hands over her neck and shoulders, wishing she could have a nice long soak in her tub at home. "How do people take baths in this time?" she asked, patting her face and neck with the surprisingly soft cloth.

"I believe they used the bath houses like the Romans used to. I'd suggest you ask Delphina. She will be the least likely to think it an odd question."

Aliana sat on the bed, surprised again when she sank a little into a softness she hadn't expected. Dagg started putting everything but her dresses back into the pack. "What do you think about her?"

Dagg opened his mouth to reply, but froze, his head twisting suddenly toward the doors. *"She is coming."*

Aliana shot off the bed as Dagg instantly shrank and hardened into his bracelet form. As she secured him around her wrist a light knock sounded at her door.

"Lady Aliana?" Delphina's soft voice floated in as she pushed the door open a fraction.

"Delphina? What are you doing here?"

"I was hoping to speak with you for a moment before we join the others for dinner."

Aliana motioned her in, not sure what to say. "What did you want to speak to me about?"

Delphina stepped in closing the door. "I wanted to know if Titania sent you to see the progress of my quest here in Camelot."

Aliana frowned, her brows pulling together. *What did* that *mean?*

As if she heard her silent question, she answered. "My quest to build a lasting and beneficial union with King Arthur and Camelot."

That makes sense. But something didn't quite feel right. "In what way?"

"In any way possible."

The simple answer worried Aliana. She had put enough together from her interactions with Titania, as well as the things Mordrid and Morgana had hinted at, and all the things the guys had shared with her about the queen's deeds. Had she sent Delphina to enchant Arthur and marry him?

The thought of Arthur being deceived by a girl she knew he cared about deeply infuriated her. Even if the King Arthur here wasn't *her* Arthur, she still refused to let him be hurt in such a way.

"*Don't jump to conclusions,*" Dagg counseled.

Clearing her throat, Aliana shook her head. "No, that's not why I am here. Titania wishes me to find something here, and an object that will help me and my friends on another quest."

The Fae nodded, her curly apricot hair bouncing. "I will gladly assist you in any way I can." The sincerity in the offer caught her off guard. Maybe her rash assumption *was* wrong. "We should go. They will be waiting for us by now."

Aliana followed her out the doors, noticing the guards that were stationed at the top of the stairs and the few servants that made their way through the long hall. "How many others are in this part of the castle?"

"Both Galahad and Sophvira have rooms in this side of the castle, and Arthur's royal chambers are just down that hall." She pointed to their left as they stopped at the first step. "There are a few others, members of Arthur's council, but you will not notice them."

They started down the stairs. "Okay." Great, she was between Arthur and Galahad again! Why did the universe keep playing this cruel joke on her?

They entered the throne room again and saw everyone gathered around either the table or the fire pit.

"I'm glad you joined us, my lady," Arthur said, coming to the girls' side. "Is your room to your liking?"

"It's wonderful, thank you. Much more than I could've ever expected."

Arthur grinned and held out his hand. With a quick glance to Delphina—whose face was carefully neutral—she took it and let him lead her to the table.

The table was set with plain looking plates and metal goblets, jugs of wine, platters of roasted meats, vegetables, nuts and fruits. The others all gathered around, a smiling Guinevere between Lancelot and Leyon, then Owaine. Sophvira was seated on Lancelot's other side with Galahad between her and Delphina—who was seated on Arthur's left side. Aliana was on the golden king's right, Merlin on her other side next to an empty seat. Gawain and Percival took the last two places.

They all waited to take their seats until Arthur sat. When he did they all followed, Aliana wondering whom the empty seat was for. She couldn't think about whom else would have a place at this table.

Maybe Merlin's lover? Aliana gasped at the recognition.

The doors creaked open. In walked Morgana, her long curled hair laced with thin braids and a few small flowers. She wore a blue dress similar in fashion to what Aliana and the other girls wore with accents of gray. Her hazel eyes went to Merlin's immediately and she smiled so brilliantly it was like being struck with lightning. Aliana couldn't believe what she was seeing. The blond girl who had murdered her parents, tried to kill her and her friends and even sided against her cousin, the king, looked as fresh and joyful as a summer day at the beach.

Morgana approached the table, stopping long enough to curtsy to Arthur and moved to her seat next to her Druid lover.

"We were worried you wouldn't return from the market in time, Morgana," Arthur said in way of a greeting.

"My apologies, sire. I got tied up helping a woman home."

Really? There was no way this was the same power-hungry-vixen-witch that had made her life, and that of her knights and family, so miserable and dangerous.

"We do not know when she turned to the side of evil, Aliana. She may well be sincere at this time." Dagg's words rubbed her the wrong way, but he was right. None of the guys knew when or why she had started to betray them.

5

The memory hit like a hundred arrows. But it was a pain I'd happily endure again. I thought I was going crazy at first, remembering Aliana in Camelot, Merlin introducing her. Even then she had captivated me, in the first glance. It was not her understated beauty, but the spirit in her emerald eyes and a feel about her that called to the deepest part of my soul. It felt like, for the first time in ages, I was whole again. That something I had never realized was missing was within arm's reach. Then Wade and Owen said they had the same memories return. Something very dangerous is at play here. But I must maintain absolute control. For her.

— Galahad

Aliana swallowed down her disbelief, deciding that she would have to keep an eye on Morgana and try to solve this mystery. She felt Morgana's eyes on her.

"And who are you?" she asked, a friendly curiosity in her voice.

"This is Lady Aliana," Merlin told her. "She is visiting with me for a while."

Aliana swore she could see a small spark of jealousy flash in those eyes she was used to seeing filled with hate and cunning. "My family knew Merlin's when we were children."

Morgana seemed satisfied with her answer and sat back, taking a sip from her goblet.

Aliana looked around the table. All the knights and Arthur were wearing their Pendragon cuffs, unintentionally shown off as they started grabbing meat and vegetables and chatting among themselves. Aliana filled her own plate, her stomach grumbling at the scent of the roasted duck and pork. A servant ladled some thick soup into a small bowl for her. It was strange to eat with her fingers and the small, but sharp knife that was set out, but the fork wouldn't be invented for another thousand years or so.

She mostly ate in silence, enjoying the sight of the knights and the women interacting together. Percival, Leyon, Owaine and Gawain were engaged in a loud discussion of which weapons were better suited for close combat, each guy telling what had to be exaggerated stories of glorious fights, with Lancelot playing the referee. Guinevere was carrying on a conversation with Sophvira. It was almost like she cared for the girl as a mother would her child. It was easy to imagine that Sophvira was the most cared for among them. Poor girl, Galahad was probably the most overbearing, protective brother in the history of the world.

Her eyes landed on the knight which her thoughts couldn't seem to escape. He was leaning into Delphina, seemingly involved in the conversation she was having with Arthur, but she caught his eye when he glanced across to her. He was intense and inviting; Aliana looked away, spooning a little of the soup into her mouth to distract herself. She caught Sophvira staring at her from the corner of her eye and felt heat rush to her cheeks.

"Why don't you tell us more about yourself, Lady Aliana?" Morgana's pleasant invitation caught her off guard.

"There's not much to tell really." She didn't want to have to tell any more lies than she already had.

"Nonsense," the Sorceress said with laughing denial. "Merlin said you traveled here, but you came alone?"

Already asked and answered, she wanted to say, but held it back. "I did, yes. I've actually spent most of my life traveling from place to place with my parents." Okay, so that wasn't a lie. Maybe this wouldn't be so hard after all.

"But they didn't accompany you here?" Guinevere asked, confused. It wasn't normal for women to travel alone in this time.

Aliana shrugged, swallowing the emotions that threatened to surface at the mention of her parents. "I've pretty much traveled on my own for the last few years. Every now and then some friends will join me, but mostly I am on my own. My father and one of my dearest friends taught me how to defend myself."

"Really?" Sophvira asked excitedly. "I want to learn how to shoot but my brother simply refuses to let me handle a weapon."

"You don't need to know because you'll never be without protection, little sister." All the guys voiced their agreement while Guinevere and Delphina hid wide smiles. Aliana imagined this was a running joke with all them.

"I happen to be very good with archery," Aliana said, allowing a little pride to color her words.

The guys all burst out laughing, with even Morgana joining in the clear disbelief of her statement. "Where all have you been, Lady Aliana?"

She bit her cheek trying to think of the easiest answers. "I've been to Rome and many of the surrounding territories. I've also traveled through many of the kingdoms here in Brittan."

"You certainly have had you adventures, my lady." Arthur seemed almost impressed.

Boy, did he have no idea how spot on that statement was.

Delphina turned the conversation away from Aliana by talking about the upcoming celebrations and games that Camelot would be hosting in honor of Camelot's creation. The knights went back to talking about the contests they would be entering, each boasting about how they would win.

A touch of cold air brushed the back of her neck and Aliana immediately recognized the feel of Morgana's magic. She seemed to be discreetly feeling out the strength of her magic. Acting on instinct, she tightened the veil hiding her true strength.

As if the blonde sensed she'd been discovered snooping, the cold magic instantly disappeared. Aliana turned, meeting the confused witch's eyes. Morgana looked away quickly.

Aliana looked at Guinevere, who was openly frowning at the blonde. *What had Guinevere noticed?* The redhead looked to her and her expression lightened. Aliana got the distinct impression she wasn't the biggest fan of Morgana.

Dinner finished soon after. Morgana excused herself, kissing Merlin's cheek and saying she would see him in their rooms. Aliana watched her retreating figure, worried about what she was up to. Was she already working in the shadows to hurt Arthur and his kingdom?

Guinevere called her attention back. "Would you like to join Sophvira and myself for our nightly walk, Lady Aliana?"

Glad for the chance to see more of the castle she nodded. "Yes I would, and please call me Aliana. I'm not much for formal titles." She looked to Arthur and added, "With exception of you, of course, your majesty."

Arthur chuckled, leaning closer to her. "In all honesty, I'm not really fond of them either."

Did Arthur just give me permission to call him by his name?

Guinevere and Sophvira rose from their seats and Aliana followed suit. They left out the door they came through but headed toward a different set of stairs. Torches now lit the halls, the windows adding an eerie glow with the light from the moon.

"Can you really shoot a bow, Lady Aliana?" Sophvira asked, distracting her from the beautiful castle.

"I can shoot and fight with a bow staff and my hands. And please, both of you call me Aliana."

The girl's light blue eyes widened with excitement. "Can you teach me?"

"Sophvira!" Guinevere admonished.

"What?" she whined. "Even you know how to handle a sword, Guin."

"You do?" Aliana asked before she could stop herself. That wasn't something she had seen coming.

Guinevere grinned at both of them. "When we were kids, Arthur and Lancelot used to teach me in secret. My parents and King Uther would never have approved."

"That is fantastic!" Aliana already felt more at ease with both girls. But pain twinged in her heart. It hurt to know what was to happen to them.

"Where are we going, Lady Guinevere?" Aliana asked, turning away from her sad thoughts. Guinevere stopped outside another door, grabbing the iron bar that served as a door handle and opening it.

"It is a surprisingly warm night. I thought you might enjoy seeing the castle from one of the ramparts. And if I may return your kindness, Aliana, please call me Guin. All my friends do."

"And I prefer to be called Vira!" Sophvira's lively face scrunched up in annoyance. "Though I can only seem to convince Guin to call me that."

"When I'm not trying to get a point across to you," Guin added.

They ascended the stairs quickly and went through another door. The briny ocean air hit Aliana first, reminding her of home. "Oh my stars!"

It was no wonder the window had glowed so brightly. The moon over the ocean was full and so large it looked like she could reach out and touch it. Leaning against the edge of the wall she watched the crashing waves, white tips glowing so familiarly.

Guin's hand touched her shoulder. "If you think that a sight, come see the city."

Obediently, Aliana followed her and Vira.

Her jaw dropped. The city was lit with blazes of firelight, some from the torches that lined the walls running through and around the city. Larger cauldron-like blazes spread through the streets to help the patrolling soldiers see the areas around them. The entire city seemed to have its own living heartbeat, strong and sure. "This kingdom is so amazing. I've never seen another that seemed so…alive."

"Even with all the places you've been?" Vira asked.

"I have certainly seen my share of breathtaking places, but truly, none of it can compare to Camelot." A different kind of sadness settled over her. She was living another dream she had always shared with her archaeologist father. They had both always wished to see this ancient city, to learn what it was really like, how the people lived, and what kind of king Arthur really was.

Vira's small hand touched hers. "Why do you look so sad?"

She exhaled, trying to decide if she should answer. "I was just thinking about my papa."

Vira scooted closer and Guin curled her arm around the girls' small shoulders, cocooning the young girl between them.

"He and I always wanted to come here. To see this city so many people tell amazing tales about. I never thought it could actually happen. I wish he was here to share this with me. He would be as excited as a child getting new toys."

The three of them laughed and the heaviness on Aliana's heart lightened a little. It felt good to talk about her father. To remember all the good times they had shared.

"I still can't believe he lets you travel alone! Galahad is always so worried. He doesn't let me to go anywhere on my own."

Aliana took Vira's smaller hand in hers. "I don't blame him. It *is* dangerous out there."

The girl pouted, her bottom lip jutting out. Aliana had to bite back a smile.

They stood silently for a few minutes before Guin took a step back. "We should be going in now. My husband will be wondering where I am. And so will your brother, Vira."

Sighing dramatically, Vira followed, still holding Aliana's hand. She expected her to let go, but the girl kept her hold and led them down the stairs.

Guin parted from them when they reached the stairs that led to Aliana and Vira's wing of the castle. As they came to the top of the stairs, Aliana saw a small alcove off to the right and smelled the night air.

"You go on to bed, Vira," she said. "I'd like to have a few more minutes before I go to my room."

Looking slightly dejected, Vira disappeared down the hall. It was only a few steps to reach the alcove, and Aliana was thrilled to see the little spot hidden by stone walls, like a secret hiding place.

Resting her arms against the open window ledge, she gazed out at the sea and glowing waves. The sound was so familiar; if she closed her eyes, she could imagine herself back on the beach behind her house, her parents by her side as her papa told her one of his many stories.

"My lady?"

A large warm hand brushed her elbow and Aliana was snapped from her memory. She wheeled around, heart thumping in her ears, but she stopped suddenly when her eyes tangled with Galahad's brilliant blue ones.

He smiled charmingly, like she had seen him do so many times before, and her heart fluttered in response. "Forgive me, I didn't mean to frighten you."

Aliana let out the breath that had frozen in her chest, her hand lying over her heart. "It's not very polite to sneak up on a girl, Sir Galahad."

"Galahad, please." His smile was still in place. "May I call you Aliana?"

She nodded automatically.

Galahad stood in front of her, either intentionally or unintentionally blocking her only escape. His shoulders and chest were broad and so large she could hardly even see past him into the hall. "I thought you would be resting by now. Merlin says you've had a very long journey to get to us."

She remembered being on the half-ruined dock where she had watched her parents die in the horrible explosion Morgana had created. "It certainly feels like that."

He looked down briefly and took a small step forward. "You seem to have made quite the impression on my sister. It's been a long time since she's been so excited about anything or anyone."

Aliana's head tilted to the side, her curiosity clear. "She's been nothing but outgoing around me."

"I'm grateful that she is. I worry that she's too closed off at times." His arms crossed over his wide chest, the worn, soft leather not making a sound. "Even among our friends, she's only really close with Guin and Morgana; Delphina at times."

Aliana bit her lip, holding back something she would have had no problem saying to her Galahad, but not so much with this one.

"You seem like you want to say something."

How can he read me so clearly already? "It's not my place."

He stepped closer again, and Aliana shifted back a fraction before realizing she had done it. He immediately stepped back, the corner of his luscious mouth turning down. "You made my sister happy. That entitles you to speak your mind with me."

She pondered her words carefully. "Maybe…if you gave her just a little freedom to spread her wings, she could find some confidence to be herself."

His face darkened a fraction, and he ran a hand over his evening stubble. Aliana held her breath, wondering if she had over stepped.

He finally nodded once. "Perhaps. I will consider it."

Delight filled her and she felt a crack splinter through the walls she had built after her Galahad's betrayal.

"You are a good brother, Galahad." She took a step to the side hoping that he would let her pass. Her savaged heart couldn't take exposing herself again.

But he didn't move aside. If anything he shifted closer. "You intrigue me, Aliana." His voice was so soft and sexy, and it was trying to worm its way past her defenses.

His eyes were hypnotizing her again with the familiar confidence he always seemed to have. She was reminded of their moment in Avalon when they had been alone after escaping the Sidhe.

Marching boots and the thunk of a staff hitting the ground just behind them startled her from Galahad's spell. It wasn't until his very warm hand moved on her bare shoulder that she saw she had instinctively moved closer to him.

"It was just one of the guards," he murmured, but he wasn't looking at her. He was instead focused on his hand, the hand that was touching her bare skin.

What was more terrifying was the fact Aliana felt none of the accustomed silver sparks that had always been so present between them.

Where had their bond gone?

6

Aliana spent the night dreaming about the encounter on the beach, her last moments alone with her Arthur and Galahad. There were so many unresolved emotions zinging around her head and heart it felt like she was missing some unseen meaning of the dream.

She was woken the next morning by a soft knock on her door. A servant girl brought in small plate of bread, fruit and oatmeal-like soup. Waving away the girl's offer to help her dress, Aliana poured a glass of water, swishing it around before nibbling on a piece of mint next to her plate. It was the closest to toothpaste she was going to get here.

"I want to explore the city a bit today," she told the Dragon from behind the changing screen next to her bed. "It may be a long shot, but maybe I'll get some idea of what it is Titania wants us to find here."

"You should invite Delphina to accompany you."

Aliana bristled at his suggestion. "I know I should…"

"You cannot allow what you fear Arthur feels for her to discount her aid. Right now she's our strongest ally."

Tightening the last string on the back of a very soft purple dress, Aliana held back a sigh. He was right again, but that was only because she knew of her connection to Titania. She slipped her feet into the thick soled boots Titania had clothed her in when she sent her here and pulled on the cream belt that had been wrapped with her new dress.

Stepping out from behind the screen, Aliana stared out of the thin window that overlooked the ocean. She saw herself on the beach with Arthur, their passionate dance in the moonlight and the moment he had almost kissed her. It was only when he did kiss her, a week after that encounter, that she had realized that she had fallen hard for her golden king. She could still remember her distress when Galahad had seen them and attacked Arthur.

Aliana massaged her temples, the shadow of those sharp connections with the guys trying to cut at her, making her ache all over again.

"Are you all right?" Dagg's cautious question made her think he knew what she was remembering.

"How much did you see last night, exactly?"

The little guardian silently regarded her. "You know what I saw. Your secret from the others, and all that happened while you were trapped with Mordrid."

Aliana's heart kicked into a panic. Had he seen the kiss the dark wizard had laid on her? Or her memories of her parents' deaths?

"I didn't have to see your memories to know that you are connected to both Galahad and Arthur. But I now understand why you disappeared from the beach."

She sagged a little, her knees almost giving out with relief. Maybe he hadn't seen her personal nightmare. Heck, maybe he could even help her understand her feelings.

"Those kinds of bonds, the way they live inside me can't be normal, right?"

He sighed. "There is not much about you that *is* normal, Aliana."

She flinched back. She had managed to get past a lot of her issues and doubts, since she first found out that she was the Destined One, but that one ache had never gone away. Knowing that her magic was so different that even the most powerful Druid who ever lived couldn't explain it had also corroded away at her self-confidence.

Dagg jumped from the bed, his leathery wings spreading wide as he soared to her side and wound himself around her shoulders like a stole. "You know I didn't mean it like that, Aliana." He rubbed his warm scaly cheek against hers, like a cat.

She set the ache aside for now and scratched him behind his ears.

"Okay, let's get out of here and do some exploring." She held out her hands for him. He dropped from her shoulders, his body shrinking and hardening to his bracelet form. Holding him in one hand, Aliana ran her finger over his bent wings which formed the cuff before securing him.

Her fingers drifted from him to the prophecy stone that looked almost like it was fused to the top of her hand. The intricate pattern of winding silk-like strands formed a strange patterned glove that hooked around her middle finger and wrist. Opening her magical senses she felt the now familiar swirling burgundy-pink-colored magic that had fused itself with her own pink core of magic.

"Time to go." She grabbed the small pouch of money and hooked it to a small loop she had discovered in her sleeve. She didn't think that was a normal place for people to keep their money, but clearly Titania had wanted her to use it.

The heavy doors of her room swung open with a tiny creak, the heavy metal clicking behind her as she closed it. She made her way toward the stairs she had used last night, hoping that she would find Merlin in the great hall. He should know where she was going; he might even know someone she could talk to. She came to the hall on her left, the hall that led to Arthur's rooms. Not knowing why, she glanced down the bright hall.

Her eyes widened when she saw Delphina step out of a room, followed closely by Arthur.

The king's hand was wound together with the Fae's and they talked in voices so low Aliana couldn't hear more than a few murmurs. Then the girl laughed, stretched up and placed a lingering kiss on

Arthur's cheek. The very space surrounding them seemed charged with some kind of magic that wound itself around the pair, almost like it was connecting them.

Something in her heart cracked and she turned away, dashing as quietly as possible toward the stairs. She blinked back unexpected tears. She knew what Arthur's touches felt like, how they made her feel. She knew what he tasted like and how his lips felt against hers. Witnessing his affections for the woman who had haunted Arthur for so long was like a hot poker being stabbed into her stomach.

The only reason Arthur could have fallen in love with *her* was because he truly didn't know if his ghost girl was real. That had to be the reason her Arthur had let himself fall for the "Destined One."

"Aliana," Dagg's voice did little to soothe her as she all but ran down the steps and past the door to the great hall, deciding that she just needed to get out of the castle as quickly as she could. How could she have thought she would be able to handle seeing those two together?

She was going to have to avoid them both now, if she could.

A few passing servants gave her strange looks as she dashed past them. Only then did she realize what she must look like. Forcing her feet to slow down, she took a few deep breaths, calming her emotions and focusing instead on what was going on around her. She followed the path Merlin and the others had led her on last night, bypassing the throne room completely.

She considered reaching out to Merlin mentally, to tell him her plans, but she had never tried to do it before when he was more than a few feet away.

A pair of large hands gripped her shoulders, abruptly halting her movement. "Lady Aliana?"

A large chest covered in a loose gray shirt and brown buckled vest was right in front of her. She looked up to meet Leyon's questioning gaze.

"I…I am so sorry," she stammered, stepping back when his hands fell from her arms. "I was lost in my thoughts."

"So it would seem. Are you searching for Merlin?"

She nodded.

"He is in the front courtyard with several of the others." He pointed to her right. "It's this way. I can take you if you so wish it."

Since directions weren't her strong point, she told him to lead the way. They walked in silence, Leyon glancing at her covertly every now and again.

"Is there something you'd like to ask me, Sir Leyon?" He was whip smart, in her time. No doubt he'd be just as clever here in Camelot. One thing she'd learned about her knights and the ones here, they were all *very* alike. Not totally, but still.

"Nay." He opened a door in front of them. "But there is much more to you, lass, than you'd like for people to notice."

She moved to go through the door but he blocked her. He wasn't aggressive or threatening, and despite his words he appeared more curious than fearful she might be evil.

"Merlin wouldn't speak for someone if he had any worry they meant harm to Camelot or King Arthur." It was like he had read her mind. But he was wrong, and so was Merlin, who had after all spoken for Morgana. "You are a fascinating puzzle, lass."

She grimaced. She really needed to keep a low profile from all of the knights. None of the guys remembered her in her time, so she couldn't do anything that might make them remember her and inadvertently mess with the timeline.

"I believe you were taking me to see Merlin, Sir Leyon." What else could she say or do?

He smirked. Her hands started to shake, but she raised her chin, stepped around him and headed down the stairs. She heard the click of his boot heels and the rustle of his leather clothes as he followed her down the narrow stairs and through a small arched door.

Raising her hand against the bright sunlight, she saw Owaine, Merlin, Gawain and Percival all circled around Galahad, swords drawn, shields on their arms. Her adrenaline spiked as she watched the scene in front of her, Leyon hovering at her back.

The guys were attacking him in turns, but Galahad was fierce in his defense and he fought all them back with powerful strokes and reverberating clangs of sword against sword and shield.

Gawain attacked him from behind, as Galahad deflected a blow from Percival. Before Aliana could cry out a warning, Galahad swung around quickly and kicked Gawain's shield so hard the shorter knight lost his balance and stumbled back. Her fierce knight whirled again and in a few moves had Merlin disarmed, Owaine on his butt and Percival trapped with a sword pressed to his neck.

Her heart galloped in her throat, her eyes glued to the sharp sword set so dangerously against her best friend's boyfriend's neck.

Galahad smirked and his whole demeanor changed. He pulled his sword back, sheathing it and tossing his shield to the ground. Percival laughed, his head bobbing up and down in amusement before he turned and helped Owaine to his feet.

Merlin and Gawain were back on their feet by the time Sophvira slipped through the fence and handed her brother a piece of cloth, a proud grin on her Pixie-like face. "That was faster than last time, big brother."

He smiled and ran his hand affectionately down her hair. He said something to Gawain that had all of them laughing.

Leyon cleared his throat and Aliana started. She instantly felt stupid for getting caught up in the guys' training. She had seem them go at each other dozens of times, but seeing it now was a totally different experience.

Leyon led her toward the others, his grin widened to a satisfied smile.

"Good morning, Aliana." Sophvira beat her smoldering brother to her side.

"Morning," she said, finally peeling her eyes from the knight who was somehow still intoxicating even while wiping sweat from his face.

The guys all gathered around, and she felt like a circus show again as even nosy servants openly watched them. Morgana, who Aliana hadn't even noticed, came to join them.

Shaken from her discomfort, Aliana asked, "Merlin, can I talk to you for a second?"

He set down his shield and vaulted the fence. Aliana had to admit that the handsome Druid was an impressive sight, even with such a simple display of strength.

They walked a few feet away, the guys turning back to their training. The tension between her shoulders lessened a little.

"Is everything all right?"

She smiled tightly. "I was thinking of going into the town for a while. I need to see if I can figure out what Titania sent me here for." She glanced past the Druid and saw Morgana standing with Sophvira and Gawain. The blond witch was watching them from the corner of her eyes.

"There is a woman in the lower town," Merlin said. "I have had some dealings with her in the past. She seems to have an uncanny knowledge of the Fae and the Isle of the Blessed. She may be someone who can help you. And her shop has some…*unique* items, if you can get the crone to show them to you."

"And how am I supposed to do that?"

"I'm sure you'll find a way." He chuckled before telling her how to find this person as they rejoined the others.

"What are your plans today, Aliana?" Sophvira asked when they came to her side.

"I am going to go explore the city for a while." *And get some much needed space from the craziness of the day.*

"That sounds like a wonderful way to spend the day," Morgana said. "Perhaps you wouldn't mind my accompanying you? I need to buy some new dress material as it is."

Aliana's voice failed her in her surprise. Morgana seemed sincere, her face open and friendly.

"Can I go too?" Sophvira questioned, looking as excited as a kid about to go on a ride. "I can show you some of my favorite places in the town."

Both girls looked at Galahad. Aliana was worried he would say yes, but insist she be protected. That was the last thing she needed today. She racked her brain trying to figure out how she could tell Sophvira no without hurting her feelings. More voices came from behind them and Aliana glanced over her shoulder to see Arthur and Lancelot making their way toward them.

Galahad spoke first. "If Aliana would not mind your company I see no reason you can't go."

Sophvira smiled brightly. Aliana bit her lip. Now she was going to have to deal with an armed chaperone.

"Whom will you send with us?" the girl asked.

Galahad met Aliana's eyes again. "If you promise to stay with Aliana and Morgana, I see no reason for you to have an escort."

Aliana's eyes widened. Everyone in the training yard stopped talking to look at him in varying expressions of shock and disbelief.

"Really?" Sophvira's voice was hesitant.

Galahad ran his hand down her hair again and nodded.

"Deal!" The girl was nearly bouncing up and down.

"Galahad?" Arthur questioned. "Are you sure?"

Galahad inclined his head to Arthur. "I think she will be safe enough with a Sorceress and an accomplished traveler."

Aliana couldn't hide her proud smile anymore. Galahad had listened to her, and actually taken her advice. Another crack formed in the walls she had constructed around her savaged heart.

Looking away from Galahad she saw Morgana's open disbelief, which she quickly covered with a smile when she noticed she was bring watched.

"Let's go then," Sophvira said, grabbing Aliana's wrist and all but pulling her toward an arching stone pass. "Before he changes his mind," she whispered with a wave to her brother.

She followed, Morgana giving Merlin a quick kiss before she joined them. Aliana didn't miss the way Arthur looked between them. His handsome golden face was tight but carefully blank, a look she recognized as the kingly mask he wore when he was hiding his true feelings.

The knights disappeared from her sight as Vira turned a corner of the castle and they entered the market. They passed a man selling straw from the back of his ox-pulled cart. The three of them were soon passing many of the merchants she had noticed when she arrived yesterday. The sounds were so foreign, all the loud voices jockeying for attention as the people milled about. Men and women came and went, barely noticing Aliana and her two companions. There was just so much vitality and life happening all around her it was almost overwhelming.

Morgana stopped at the third fabric vendor they passed. Vira looked over the fabrics, holding up a green one that complemented her pale skin.

"What do you think?" she asked.

"I like it. That color suits you wonderfully."

"It will look beautiful on you, Sophvira," Morgana added, holding tails of white and yellow fabric in her hands. "Maybe you could even have a dress made in time for the Feast." She held up both of her selections to the girls. "Which do you think is better?"

"Yellow," Vira said quickly. Aliana smiled and agreed. The color should have washed out the blond girl, but instead she imagined Morgana would practically glow with brightness.

"How about you, Aliana, do you see anything you like?" Vira asked.

She glanced down, her hands touching a piece of reddish pink material. "I don't think I need anything."

The girl seemed shocked. "But you'll have to have a dress to wear to Camelot's anniversary celebration!"

Aliana shook her head. "I doubt I'll be going, Vira."

"Nonsense," Morgana said. "Arthur won't hear of you not attending."

Aliana took a calming breath. She needed to focus on finding what it was Titania wanted her to find, not open herself up to getting closer to the two men who could both shatter her completely. Or let herself get closer to any of the others, even Vira, knowing what she did about their futures.

Morgana turned back to the elderly man who had been watching them with assessing eyes. "It is a lovely color for you, m'lady," he wheezed, no doubt anxious to take their money. "And my daughter could make such a dress for you with it."

Aliana wavered. She would love to see such an extravagant party; maybe she could just slip in and slip out again? How could she pass this chance up? "Okay." She caved and Sophvira laughed.

After Morgana bartered the price and all three girls had been measured by the man's two daughters, they continued through the city. It was a fun and relaxing trip, set at a lazy pace. The tension in Aliana's shoulders eased as she, Morgana and Vira fell into a rhythm of friendliness. She found that Morgana was actually pleasant company to be around. The Sorceress even talked about how she had grown up in a castle outside the village she was born in, and how she was trained to use her magic alongside several other girls. She was smart, and very enthusiastic when she told Aliana more about the celebrations and tournaments that would be held in less than a week. And it was impossible to miss the affection in her voice when she talked about her cousin, King Arthur, and Merlin.

They bought some fruit and pieces of cooked meat on sticks for lunch and finally made it to the lower town.

7

A prickling of magic hung in the air and Aliana followed it to a small barn-like stall that was packed with two large carts of wares and rough looking jewelry. She glanced back at Morgana and Vira, who were caught up watching a man on a short platform who appeared to be telling a grand story.

Satisfied they were okay, she walked over to the first cart, the magic getting stronger with every step she took. The wooden displays were in surprisingly good condition, pieces of glass and colored ribbon dangling from the long planks of wood that held the thatched roof in place. Scrolls and books littered some of the cart shelves along with wooden and stone-carved artifacts. There were pieces of fractured geodes and bundles of dried herbs and small bottles of various colored liquids.

She walked to the cart opposite and saw more of the same. Leaning in to get a closer look at a round piece of dull bronze, a book just a little ways down from it fell to the dirt ground with a thunk.

"Really?" she muttered as she bent down to pick it up, hoping it hadn't been damaged.

"It would seem the fates desire ya ta' see that."

Aliana straightened, gripping the hardbound book tightly in her hands. An older woman was watching her from the doorway to the house the stall was attached to. She regarded her shrewdly, but then she smiled and ambled over.

Her magic senses flared as a familiar feeling overcame her. This woman had Fae blood in her. Just like Lacy. "What do you mean?" Aliana asked.

"Books don't just jump out at any person gettin' too close. Destiny is tellin' ya there be somethin' ya need to see in that tome."

"I don't think—"

The woman waved her hand. "Mark my words m'lady," the woman warned like an old crone from some witches story. "You be needin' the wisdom in those pages sooner than ya think."

Aliana looked down at the bound pages in her hand. The hard brown cover was plain, just like the spine. Running her fingers down the rough paper edges, a flash of brightness flared.

"I think this woman may be right," Dagg whispered.

Convinced, Aliana took out the small pouch of money Titania had sent her. "How much for the book then?"

The woman's eyes danced with satisfaction. "One silver piece."

Not even bothering to barter, Aliana paid the woman and left the stall. She glanced around to see if anyone was watching her, but no one seemed to notice her presence. Taking the chance, she plucked a bit of the ruby's power, and just like with her magical bow, she envisioned the book disappearing into her prophecy stone. Suddenly, the book became a streak of pink and shot into the heart of the gem.

Aliana made her way back to Morgana and Vira. As she joined them, the man on stage finished his storytelling and the people clapped, a few even dropping some coins onto the base of his platform.

"What did you think of the story?" Vira asked.

"Um…" Hadn't they noticed she was missing?

Morgana frowned, her eyes flicking over Aliana quickly before turning away.

"It was nice," Aliana said, not sounding very convincing even to her own ears. But if Vira noticed, she didn't let on. Instead they started to make their way back toward the castle, "window shopping" as they passed more stalls. They were halfway back to the castle when the trio heard laughter and music filling the large square just ahead of them.

They stopped just outside a tavern over flowing with burly, loud and drunk men and women in very low cut dresses floundering about them. Serving wenches, apparently, never really changed from culture to culture.

Two giggling girls, maybe eight or nine years old, ran to Morgana. The blond witch knelt down and opened her arms as the duo wrapped their small arms around her.

Aliana laughed along with the girls, her guard lowering even more as she again realized there was a lot more to Morgana than she had known. She was openly affectionate with the little girls and Vira, and it was impossible to miss the love that showed on her face every time she looked at Merlin.

A heavy drumbeat kicked up and two men playing lutes joined in at a fast pace. A small troupe of musicians had set up since they had passed through this part of town earlier. Children started to dance as a gypsy-looking woman sang in a language she didn't recognize.

The two girls leapt from Morgana's arms and dragged the blonde behind them into the foray. A few onlookers laughed, swayed to the beat and started clapping. Vira, who had been talking with two girls she seemed to know, ran over to Aliana giggling, her friends hot on her tail. "Come on!"

They all grabbed Aliana, her mood soaring even more. Following Vira's lead, Aliana raised her hands in the air and spun alongside the others. They kicked out their feet in little jumps and danced in a loose circle. Several of the smaller girls linked hands and started to dance-weave through the older girls, laughing and skipping as the beat kept growing and picking up pace.

Happiness spilled from all of them, and Aliana felt like her worries and fears were temporarily banished. Vira looked so happy, and there was a confidence to her moves that Aliana hadn't seen from the sweet girl before. Out of the corner of her eye she saw several of the guys standing there laughing and clapping along. Arthur's grin nearly took over his face. Galahad was looking at his sister, a deep-set happiness on his brotherly face. Aliana lost herself in the music again.

Men cheered and women laughed. Morgana twirled her way next to Aliana as Vira danced off with her two friends. She took Aliana's hands and they started to swing around in a wide arc, spinning under each other's arms and clapping to the rhythm.

A small girl was trying to copy them. Aliana snickered, her head thrown back, feeling, for a small second, like she was at home again with her best friends.

The little brunette stumbled back and knocked into a drunken man, causing him to drop his mug of ale.

Aliana froze.

"Why you little tramp," the drunken man roared, swinging his catcher's glove-like hand at the girl who had fallen to the ground.

Aliana rushed forward, anger rising up like a soaring Firebird, and blocked the man's hand, slapping it away in a practiced block she had memorized many years ago. The little girl sniffled and scrambled behind Aliana.

"You filthy wench!" The man's hand pulled back, even as he swayed a little off balance. She saw the punch coming. The clumsy oaf swung and she bent herself back in an arch and then pulled back up, her feet shifting at the same time. She sidestepped the man as he stumbled forward onto his hands and knees.

Out of the corner of her eye she saw Vira and Morgana placing themselves in front of the children. The sound of heavy feet and weapons surrounded them as guards and the knights closed in, blocking any routes of escape.

Red-faced, the angry man pushed himself back onto his feet and bellowed as he came at Aliana again. She ducked his meaty fists as her anger and adrenaline kicked her fighting instincts into high gear. She blocked and deflected his blows easily enough, but she could see the rage building in this man. She knew she needed to end this.

He managed to grab her arm in a tight grip, but he only had one hand on her. Blocking his free, raised hand, Aliana flung herself forward, slapping her hand onto the hard, sweaty chest and jabbed it up, with all the strength she had, into his throat. He coughed, spit and blood flying from his open mouth as he choked. Using her momentum she spun, her hands grabbing his arm as her back hit his chest and she bent forward. The heavy man went sailing over her shoulder and hit the ground in a heap of sweat.

The whole scene hadn't taken more than a minute but it felt like much longer. Breathing heavily, her anger starting to ebb, she looked up and saw Galahad, Arthur, Percival, Lancelot and Gawain watching with surprise and amusement. Their swords were partially drawn, but they pushed them back into the sheaths.

Holding her head high, she walked past the groaning man and went to Vira's side.

Vira's eyes looked at her with an awe that made Aliana extremely uncomfortable. But the awe morphed into fear as the girl looked behind her. Reacting on instinct Aliana slid into an attack stance; half-turned and snapped out her leg. Her boot slammed into the man's jaw, the sound of breaking bones mixing with the cries of outrage from the knights. Her foot came back down, her hands balled, her arms in the guard pose, tucked tight to her sides, and she glowered down at him. A stained dagger lay just inches from the man's hands on the dirt street.

He was curled up in a ball, his hands clutching his face and neck as the tips of four swords were suddenly pressed against the moaning, pathetic drunkard.

Aliana stared at the dagger until Vira's small hand on her arm distracted her. For a second she thought the dagger looked familiar, but she couldn't place from where. It seemed like something she'd seen in a dream, or maybe a nightmare, long ago.

"Take him to the dungeon!" Arthur's clipped order startled her. Clearly his easy-going demeanor from moments ago was gone. "A few days in the stocks should teach him."

Gawain and Percival got the choking man to his feet and dragged him away. The drunkard had blood and spit leaking down the already purple and blue flesh of his jaw. She had likely broken his jaw and probably done some serious damage to the guy's esophagus. Her hands trembled with the remains of her adrenaline.

Vira's big awed eyes were focused on her again. "How did you do that?"

Huffing out a breath, Aliana said, "I told y'all, I have been trained to defend myself."

Arthur came to her other side. "I guess that is a lesson to all of us." He seemed calmer now.

"Waste of a good weapon," the white knight remarked, handing the dagger to Merlin. "Do you think you can use your magic to make this a decent piece again?"

Morgana came to Merlin's side, studying the deadly instrument as she wrapped her arm through Merlin's and pressed close to him. "What do you think, my love?"

Morgana's head tilted slightly, her hair slipping over her shoulder. "It is worth trying, but I wouldn't hold out much hope."

Aliana's stared at the pair. What were they talking about? Then she remembered Merlin's brief lesson on enchanted weapons. She remembered how magic could be used to restore or even make certain weapons undefeatable. Just like the one she had made for *her* Galahad before their trip to the Isle.

Galahad wrapped his arm around his sister's shoulders, but Aliana could feel his blue eyes on her. "We should get back to the castle."

Aliana refused to look at the knight for fear of what her heart might do.

Arthur placed his hand on her back, leading them up the path back to the castle. "Dinner will be waiting for us," he said as they entered the training yard again.

"If it is all right with you, your majesty, I'd rather skip dinner tonight." And she needed to start reading through that book!

The king frowned, pulling her slightly to the side as the others passed them.

"Are you feeling unwell? Did that brute hurt you?" His rage returned like hot lava.

Aliana placed her hand over his. "I'm perfectly fine, Arthur." She paled, then felt her face flush. "Er…your majesty."

His anger cooled as the king smiled. "I'm glad you are comfortable enough to call me Arthur." He stepped closer. "I truly wish for us to get to know each other well enough to be so friendly, Aliana."

Her mind was empty for a long second. Was Arthur hitting on her? "Um…Arthur…I don't think Delphina would appreciate that." It was hard but Aliana forced herself to take a step back.

His brow pulled together, the corner of his mouth turning down. "What does she have to do with any of this?"

Aliana shook her head to clear away the image of Delphina and him in the hall earlier. Clearly they had just "been together," how could he turn his emotions around so quickly?

"I'm fine, really. I just want to relax a little and go to bed early." She wasn't going to dignify his question with an answer. Delphina was the girl he loved, and she needed to accept that fact.

With a frustrated sigh, he relented. "I'll have a servant bring you a plate of food and some wine."

Grateful for his acceptance, Aliana turned, familiar enough with this hall's layout to make it back to her room on her own. She pushed the door open, slid through and closed it, and leaned against the hard wood.

A feminine voice cleared her throat. Aliana's eyes shot up to meet the pale sunlight eyes of a tall woman with very dark honey-colored hair. She was standing beside the small table and chair by the lit fireplace.

Aliana looked around the room quickly to be sure it was hers. "Forgive me, but I am in my room, right?"

The woman smiled, a throaty laugh escaping her. Her face was slightly familiar, but she couldn't figure out why.

"Yes," she said, amusement in her tone. "I am Queen Igraine. My son and Merlin were telling me about you after my return earlier today."

The blood drained from Aliana's face. This was *Arthur's mother!* She curtsied quickly not wanting to offend such a powerful woman.

Jeeze this day just keeps getting better and better!

"I see I have startled you. Please sit down."

Aliana steeled herself, pushed away from the door and went to the woman's side, but didn't sit. "I am fine, thank you. You just surprised me."

"I was on my way to see to dinner when Sir Gawain and Sir Percival brought in a man who looked in dire need of healer and a remedy for drunkenness. They told me what happened and I simply had to meet such a brave young woman."

"Um…" For the second time today, Aliana couldn't think of what to say.

The queen's long face softened even more. "Please do not feel uncomfortable by my presence. My son has told me you will be staying with us for a while. You seem to have made quite the impression on many people since your arrival."

"Everyone's been very kind." Why did she feel like the queen was trying to tell her something her misfired brain wasn't seeing?

"Yes, dinner will no doubt be ready, are you joining us?"

Aliana shook her head. "Thank you but no. It was a…long day today. I haven't really gotten to rest since we entered the city yesterday."

The queen headed toward the door. "Then I will not keep you any longer. I hope we will have some time to talk tomorrow."

Aliana nodded and the queen left looking satisfied. Though why she was, Aliana had no clue.

"What was that all about?" she asked Dagg as soon as he became his normal self.

"I think we just met a piece of the puzzle we have been missing."

Aliana wheeled around to the Dragon who was perched on the top of the chair. "Say what?"

His lips pulled back, amused. "You didn't feel it did you?"

"Feel what?"

"The air humming around the queen."

Aliana straightened trying to recall it, but failed. "No. What does that have to do with anything?"

Dagg jumped from his perch, hovering before her. "She's a Dragon. A Golden Dragon to be precise."

8

After Dagg's monster bomb drop, Aliana barely remembered crawling into bed, the magic book totally forgotten for the night. How could Arthur's mother be a Golden Dragon? Arthur sure as heck wasn't one, at least not one hundred percent Golden Dragon. Dagg had reassured her of that. But he also explained that the more diluted the blood magic, the less likely a descendant was to be a true Dragon, able to take beast form. The fact remained he did have *some* Dragon DNA in him.

Aliana wondered, before fading for the night, if Arthur's talent for getting people to not only listen to him, but do exactly as he ordered wasn't because of his Dragon heritage. What if all of his years spent trapped in Avalon's magic enhanced his Dragon blood and brought out more of its powers in the king?

Since the queen was a Dragon, it was likely she realized the presence of another Dragon, so they both agreed that they would talk to the queen and find out her story. Maybe she would turn out to be another ally.

Lying in bed, the morning light illuminating the stone room, Aliana tried to remember what Arthur had told her about his mother. But she couldn't remember much. She knew that his father was deeply devoted and in love with her, that she worshiped the old gods and not the Catholic beliefs of Rome. Only his mother had been able to cool his father's raging temper, and Arthur loved her very much.

She was starting to realize, despite how well she knew her Arthur, there were still many things about him that were a mystery to her. She wanted to know more about him. Her heart squeezed. Maybe she could, if she got back to her time.

"When," Dagg corrected her, probably feeling her doubt. *"We will get home safely!"*

Shelving it for now, Aliana rolled out of the bed and padded across the bearskin rug to her changing screen. This time she put on the dark blue dress Titania had sent her with a white belt. A few minutes later she was lacing up her heavy boots and Dagg changed to his bracelet form again.

She headed toward the stairs, hoping that the throne room would be a good place to find the queen. But then she remembered her first trip to Camelot, weeks ago, in the Isle. They had passed a beautiful room Arthur said his mother used to pray to her gods. Hoping she remembered the way, she passed behind the throne room and turned down another hall. Several more servants and scholarly people passed, a few giving her a curious glance before moving on.

It took her only a few minutes to find it. The wooden door was closed, the fragrant scent of burning herbs filling the hall.

"Aliana?" She turned at the sound of Arthur's rich voice coming up beside her. "What are you doing outside my mother's prayer rooms?"

She flushed, realizing they were totally alone in the long hallway, and she had no way to explain how she'd known to come here without lying. "The queen said she wanted to talk to me." She fumbled with her belt's hem to hide her trembling fingers. "I was shown the way here."

"Just not by anyone here." Dagg laughed in her mind.

Arthur looked relaxed in a white tunic and red vest. "Yes, she said she had spoken to you briefly last night." He took a few steps closer, crossed his arms across his broad chest and leaned his shoulder against the wall. "Yet another person you seem to have won over in your brief stay with us so far."

Everyone seemed to love telling her that. She felt her cheeks flush, not sure if it was because of his praise or the fact she was enjoying the sight of his broad chest and flexed arms. "I think you're giving me too much credit. Give it a few days and everyone will get bored and forget all about me." She could only hope it would be that easy!

"I very much doubt that." His soft words cut straight to her rapidly beating heart. "I cannot imagine you ever being boring, much less forgettable. There is just something about you that makes it hard to think about much else." He straightened, reached out and pushed her hair back from her shoulder. His long fingers slowly threaded through the thick, dark mass. "I wonder what it is?" he murmured, so quietly she thought he might not have realized he said that out loud.

Aliana held totally still, her eyes trapped on his. He seemed fascinated. Something so simple shouldn't feel so intimate, but she couldn't help feeling like he was somehow trying to weave a kind of claim over her.

The door opened behind them. Arthur didn't show any kind of startled reaction, but his fingers slid from her hair. Aliana sucked in a breath, not realizing she had stopped breathing.

"Arthur, Lady Aliana." His mother's voice was bright and musical.

Arthur turned to the golden-haired woman. "Good morning, Mother."

The sunlight eyes of the queen shimmered with happiness as she looked between both of them, noticing just how close Arthur was hovering next to her.

Snapping from her thoughts, Aliana curtsied quickly. "Good morning, your highness."

She laughed, her voice light and airy. "I do not believe such formality is needed, do you?" She looked at her son and winked at him. "Please just call me Igraine. I am glad you came, my dear."

"I suppose I will leave you two to your plans." Arthur kissed his mother's cheek and gave Aliana a smoldering smile. "I hope we can finish our conversation later, Aliana."

She watched him walk down the hall.

"Come, my dear." Aliana turned back to Igraine. "We should speak privately, I think."

Aliana followed the woman, admiring the cream-colored dress and golden belt that she wore so elegantly. She couldn't help comparing the Dragon Queen with the Fae Queen. Both women were mysterious and had airs of ultimate power, but where Titania was cold and calculating, Igraine was open and friendly. Two very powerful women who were very different, but still similar in many ways.

They turned another corner and Igraine led her into a large room with a wide table, richly decorated walls and a large, lit hearth. The same servant girl that always attended Aliana was there, straightening the queen's bed.

The girl turned as soon as they stepped in the room and curtsied low. "Could you please excuse us, Clara?" She rose, grabbing a basket filled with several dresses and pieces of cloth.

As soon as the door closed Igraine took a seat at the table and waved her hand for Aliana to take another chair. She did, her hands folded together and resting on the tabletop. "You said last night that you wanted to speak to me."

"But first I think you should introduce me to your companion." Igraine waved a tapered finger toward Dagg's metal form peeking out from beneath her sleeve.

The Dragon didn't hesitate to take his true form. "My lady." He bowed his head, one claw covering his chest. "It is an honor to meet you. I am Daggerhorne, guardian to Aliana."

She smiled. "You are quite the charmer, DragonLord." She looked between the two, her sunlight eyes flashing a dark gold quickly, a swell of hot magic filling the room and Aliana's magic senses.

"Wow," Aliana said when the power faded in the next instant. She studied the queen with a new respect. Her magic could easily rival Titania's!

"I echo your sentiments. It is rare for a half Fae and Dragon to have such a strong bond."

Aliana jerked up. "You know I'm half Fae?"

"Of course. You hide it well, but I have walked this earth for many long ages. It takes much more than a veil to hide your true powers and heritage from me. I imagine Queen Titania is quite pleased with you."

Aliana sank back against the chair's back.

"I see you did not expect anyone to know your secret."

"You could say that." Aliana flushed, realizing how informal she was being. "I'm sorry, I shouldn't have said that, your highness."

"Igraine," she reminded Aliana, "and I do not think the two of us need to stand on such formality."

Aliana smiled. "It'll be nice to have someone else to talk to about this."

"I am glad you feel that way. I have the feeling your path has not been an easy one, and may only get worse for you."

Aliana dropped her eyes to her folded hands. "What did you want to talk about?"

"What do you know of Camelot's history?" Igraine asked.

"Not much." Aliana shrugged. "I've heard so many stories *of* Camelot, but nothing about how it was created."

"Legend says that Camelot was built by two Dragons. A Gold Dragon and an Onyx Dragon. Only Gold and Onyx Dragons have the ability to take on human form, and these two had long wished to bridge the distance between their home realm, Tir Na Nog, and the mortal realm. So they built a great city, hoping to create a kingdom where humans, Dragons and other creatures could co-exist. But the Onyx Dragon didn't want to live with the humans, he wanted to rule them.

"Realizing his folly too late, the Golden Dragon fought the Onyx Dragon and banished him from Camelot. But many of the magical creatures were too scared, after the battle, to venture to the Golden Dragon's new kingdom. So Camelot became a kingdom made up of mostly humans. The Golden Dragon ruled for many long years, watching over his people as the city thrived and grew. But near the end of his long life the king realized that because of the magic he and the Onyx Dragon had weaved to create the kingdom, only one who was of their kind could ensure Camelot's eternal rule and life.

"He understood that if he did not have an heir, the Onyx Dragon could once again stake a claim on his kingdom. His whole vision for his city was to be one of welcome for all races, so he decided he needed a half mortal son. He found a human woman who captivated him like no other and took her to his bed. Shortly after their union, she bore him two children, a son and a daughter. He raised them to follow in his footsteps, taught them all he knew before he passed on to the stars, his human wife following soon after.

"The king had ruled for so long as a human, many forgot his true lineage, until it became nothing more than a bard's tale. But ever since his death there has always been a Golden Dragon ruling Camelot, even if no one really knew."

"Are you his daughter?" Aliana asked in awe.

Igraine smiled, her eyes crinkling. "My brother ruled Camelot in many different guises for centuries. I had wanted to see the world, and the different realms. But then he came under siege and eventually lost his life. Camelot started to fall into ruins as a human warlord conquered the city. I returned too late to save my brother, but I knew I had to carry on my father's wishes and restore Camelot to what it once was. So I married the warlord's son and Camelot thrived again."

Dagg spoke this time, "Was that Uther?"

"No, Uther came many years later. Like my brother and father I hid my long life line creating many different lives for myself."

"Did you have any other children besides Arthur?" He had never said anything to Aliana about having a sibling.

She shook her head. "My brother had two children, but they both wanted to have their own lives in Tir Na Nog. Arthur is the only child I have let myself conceive. I know my long years are soon coming to an end and I want to be sure that Camelot will not fall into darkness again. The descendants of the Onyx Dragon have never forgotten their own claim to this kingdom."

"How did these two Dragons have enough magic to build a whole city?" She remembered the eclipse, the unimaginable power it was said to unleash.

"I suspect you may already know," the queen said shrewdly.

"The eclipse and alignment that happens every fifteen hundred years." It was a statement, not a question. "I know of it, but I don't understand or see how it works." *Or how the Grail plays into all of this.*

The queen leaned back in her chair. "They are not one event, but rather two that happen within one day."

Aliana let the information sink in. "Can you tell me more?"

The queen was thoughtful for a moment before answering. "First the stars and other celestial bodies align with our world. When that happens, one magical location, somewhere in our realm, will be immersed in the strongest magic ever known."

"The one random point of earth's magical grid," Aliana said to Dagg.

"Yes, we cannot forget that."

Igraine continued like she hadn't noticed their silent exchange. "Then, half a day later, the sun and other planets in the sky will align with the moon, eclipsing all the light of the sun. It's then that all the gates of each realm will be vulnerable. If one was able to harness the power of the first alignment, they could use that magic to open all the gates during the eclipse. They will all only seal again after all the forces of the universe have left the alignment and the light fully returns to the realms."

Aliana fought a shudder. The thought of Mordrid having all that power…she couldn't let herself go there. "How do you know all this? Planets and alignments, workings of the universe?"

The queen smirked. "You know what I am, and I know many others of my kind, far wiser than me, who have shared their knowledge."

"Is the eclipse how your father and the other Dragon built Camelot?"

"Yes," she confirmed. "Over three thousand years ago."

Aliana's jaw dropped. The queen's laughter echoed around the room. Aliana had to clear her throat before asking, "When is the next time this is supposed to happen again?"

"Not for another fifteen hundred years, give or take."

At least that's one less think to worry about while we're here.

"My Lady, what happened during the last alignment?" Dagg's ageless voice was soft and a little worried.

"Nothing, thank the Golden Dragon." Her hand touched her stomach absently. "Since my father and the Onyx Dragon used the power, none have ever been able to successfully harness it again."

"That's a heck of a back story." Aliana frowned. "Why don't Arthur or the knights know anything about this?" Arthur and the others would not have kept all this from her! Especially Merlin!

Her eyes widened in surprise. "How do you know they don't?"

Blood drained from Aliana's face. *Darn it!* "Um…well I don't, um…"

Igraine studied her with a new curious suspicion. "You are not from this time, are you?"

Aliana's panicked eyes shot to Dagg. He just shrugged, not looking put off in the slightest.

"I understand." Igraine's assurance didn't make her feel better. That was two people she'd failed to hide her secrets from. She *had* to be more careful.

Her resolve crumbled. She needed to talk to someone other than Dagg about this. *In for a penny in for a pound.*

"I'm so confused, and so worried. I have no idea what I'm doing!"

Igraine's warm, soft hand covered her clenched ones. "You are not alone. I do not believe one as powerful, spirited and smart as you will not be able to handle the tasks you've been sent to complete."

Aliana studied Igraine. Her reassurance reminded her of her mother. Her heart fluttered. It had been so long since she'd had any kind of motherly influence in her life. "Why are you so understanding? How do you know I don't mean harm to Camelot or Arthur?" No one had treated her with any kind of dangerous suspicion since she arrived.

"Because." She patted Aliana's hands and stood. The queen came to stand behind Aliana, her hands covering her smaller shoulders. "Besides seeing your true power I can feel the goodness radiating from you. I think that even those who don't have magical abilities can sense it in certain ways."

"So Arthur and the knights do know who you are?"

Igraine nodded and brushed a wrinkle out of her skirt. "Only Arthur, his inner circle, and our family know the truth." Aliana bit the inside of her cheek. "What do you wish to ask, child?"

"I heard that King Uther had hunted many magical creatures, killed many magic users, but he married you. Did he know?"

The queen sighed. "He did. He was hunting me." The nostalgic smirk on her lips surprised Aliana. "He fell into one of his own traps, foolish man. I saved his life, turned from my Dragon form to my human form. My magic saved his life and he fell in love with me. I knew the type of man he was and refused his advances, but over the next few seasons, he changed. He became more tolerant of magic and magical creatures. He passed a law that, so long as they do no harm to others, no one would do harm to them. He still didn't trust magic, or those who used it, but as long as they followed the law..."

"Son of a biscuit, he must have really loved you."

She sighed wistfully. "I came to him after that, agreed to marry him. At first it was only because I needed to be in power once again, to help Camelot thrive. But I too fell in love with him. And then Arthur was born...and he is a gift I thank all the powers in the world for."

"And his father's way of seeing magic clearly didn't transfer to him."

Igraine laughed. "Uther tried, to a degree, but I taught Arthur that, much like a weapon, magic is not good or evil, only those who wield it are. For many years I feared Arthur would become like his father was, then Delphina came to our court and everything changed. Arthur finally understood what I had been teaching him."

Envy twisted in her gut. Aliana held back the questions she wanted so badly to ask. But what if she did ask, but wasn't supposed to? Frustration and stress tightened her muscles.

Soothing waves of warm sunlight flooded her and the anxiety melted away. She turned and looked up at Igraine, confused as to why she didn't feel like the queen's calming magic was an intrusion like she had once felt Dagg's to be.

The answer came to her immediately. She trusted this woman. The desire to tell the queen about Morgana's coming betrayal took root in Aliana's throat.

"There is one thing you must do: Promise me you will tell no one here of what the future holds. No one, not Arthur, any of the knights, not one single, living soul."

"But, you need to know—"

"No!" Igraine's voice thundered around the room and Aliana's mouth instantly snapped shut. "Say nothing of the future, or you risk destroying everything you know, and the lives of the people you love."

Aliana nodded, her throat tight and eyes downcast.

"I would hear your promise, Aliana."

She raised her green gaze. "I promise." Aliana wouldn't do anything to jeopardize her friends or home.

The queen's gentle hand touched her shoulders. "Thank you. I know it will be hard, but I believe you can do this."

9

Leaving the queen's chambers, with Dagg back in his hidden form around her wrist, Aliana now felt calmer than she had since before they found Excalibur in the Isle of the Blessed. She had a strong ally now, one who was so much like her mother it almost hurt. For a second she had felt disloyal to the woman who had loved and raised her, but she knew her mama would be happy she had someone to rely on.

She wandered the halls, heading back toward the throne room, hoping she could retrace the path she and Lacy had taken back in the Isle's Camelot. It was easier than she had thought, and in minutes she was standing outside the room filled with wall-to-wall books and scrolls.

A servant had said that the court historian used this room as a storage room for all the tomes that had been amassed in Camelot's long history. Aliana glanced down the gray stone halls, wondering how she could have gotten lucky enough to have them deserted. She pulled, but the door was locked. Glancing around again, she raised her gauntlet hand and pushed her magic into the iron lock. It slid open and Aliana quickly ducked in, being sure to close the door behind her.

The room was pitch dark, and old panic rose like a vicious demon. Her throat closed up and it was hard to breathe. Dagg's magic flowed into her, calming her enough to grab at her magic and create several balls of pink magic light. The breath whooshed into her lungs as the fear lost its grip and her heart started to beat again.

"I really thought I was over that stupid fear!" she murmured, resting against the door.

Dagg sprang from her wrist. "Some fears take a long time to be soothed away."

Aliana spread out the balls of light, the room now brightly lit. The sheer number of books amazed her. The room was three times fuller than it had been when she and Lacy had seen it. It reminded her of the book hidden in her ruby that she really needed to read. *Later, after I talk to Merlin. I need to tell him about it.* She went straight for the bookcase that hid the secret hall and room.

She ran her hands along the sides of the stone and under the shelves looking for some kind of catch or lever but found nothing. Sighing, Aliana remembered that it had only opened once Lacy had kicked it.

Dagg laughed when she told him about it. "I don't think we need to be that dramatic. Try using your magic."

Aliana opened her sense and gathered a small amount of the air element's abundant power. The door opened a second later, her balls of light flowing into the dark hall filled with cobwebs and stone dust.

"It certainly looks unused." But that didn't mean that no one was here. Holding her hand over her ruby, Aliana called her magic bow to her hand. A few more steps and she was at the knotted door. Using the element's magic she opened the door, her bow at the ready, and drew a pink sparking arrow.

The hidden chamber was cold and dark, not a sign of life or magic anywhere to be seen or felt. Stepping in, her magic light illuminating the tight space. Aliana was shocked by its emptiness. Where were the scientific vials and workstation, the books and magical items?

"Maybe she hasn't betrayed them yet." Aliana's heart lightened at the hope. "If Morgana hasn't turned against them yet, maybe there is a way we can keep her from ever turning evil!"

She glanced at her Dragon, surprised he hadn't objected to her thought. But he remained silent flying around the room.

"Okay, clearly, we're good for now. We should probably head back."

Dagg's long angular head bobbed up and down as they left the room and hall. Aliana sealed both doors with the element's magic and quietly cracked open the wooden door of the small library. Dagg reattached himself to her wrist and she poked her head out into the hall.

It was empty!

Grateful for her luck, she slipped out and locked the door. The last of her pink sparks had disappeared when she felt the prickle of warning that she wasn't alone any more.

"What are you doing, Aliana?"

Aliana's spine went stiff at the sound of Sir Owaine's curious voice. She turned, forcing herself so smile, hoping it didn't look too forced.

Galahad stood beside Owaine and Gawain, all three dressed in heavy leather and their swords.

"Don't they go anywhere without those?"

"Not usually," Dagg answered.

"That was a rhetorical question, Dragon boy."

"Aliana?" Gawain drew her attention back.

"Sorry, I'm a bit distracted this morning." Time to see if she could be a good actress. She let out a nervous giggle and shrugged her shoulders. "I'm also more than a little lost."

"Then why were you trying to get into that book storeroom?"

Aliana widened her eyes. "I didn't know that's what this was." She hoped she was convincing them. "I thought there might be someone in there that could help me figure out where I am."

Gawain grinned. "For someone who travels often, you seem to get easily lost."

She scowled, and then saw his teasing devil-may-care grin. An ache of longing for her best friend, Wade, throbbed, but she set it aside for now. "Very funny. Can one of you tell me where Morgana or Merlin is?"

Owaine and the guys stepped to her side, her soon-to-be cousin answering, "Merlin is with Percival and Arthur in the training yard. I would suspect Morgana's with them too."

"We can show you the way, Aliana." The way Galahad said her name, the ever present burning in his blue eyes, and the way he gently touched her back made her heart race like a cheetah. The pressure from his hand had her keeping pace next to the tall knight.

"Where did you learn those moves you used in the market yesterday?" Gawain asked. "I know you said you could protect yourself, but I hadn't quite imagined you had those kinds of skills."

She grinned, recovering slightly from Galahad's warm touch. It wasn't fair that his touch still felt so intimate and strong, even through the heavy fabric of her dress. "My papa had me trained. And one of my dearest friends is a great fighter. Most of what I know I learned from him."

"Him?" Galahad's question held a slight edge to it. "Who is this friend?"

Aliana gulped, not looking at the knight who had broken her heart. Or rather, would break her heart. Instead she focused on Gawain. "His name is Wade. You remind me a lot of him."

Galahad's fingers flinched on her back so quickly Aliana wasn't sure if she imagined the reaction.

They turned down another hall. "Where is your friend now?" Owaine asked.

"I'm not sure, really." And that was the truth. She had no idea what all her friends were doing; she just prayed they were safe. "We separated a while ago. I'm hoping I will hear from him or some of our other friends soon."

They turned another corner and Aliana relaxed a fraction, recognizing the hall Leyon had taken her down yesterday. "I can find my way from here." She took a hurried step toward the door, more to get away from Galahad's tempting touch than anything else.

Galahad smiled. "We were on our way to join them when we found you."

"Are you guys doing more training?"

"Of a sort," Gawain said, leading the group down the winding stairs.

Owaine explained, "In honor of Camelot's anniversary, we are hosting one of the biggest tournaments the kingdom has ever seen. We all plan on taking part in the games."

"Oh, sounds like fun." And it really did. Maybe she could bond with Morgana a little more, if the girl was really with the others in the training yard.

Aliana stepped out into the training arena. The sky was overcast, a few darker clouds and the heavy scent of water in the air hinting that it might start raining later. Merlin, Arthur, and Percival were all in the fenced off arena.

Arthur was carrying on an intense conversation with Merlin while the giant knight oversaw the servants setting up several targets, all at different distances. Aliana worried about what had Arthur so tense. Morgana and Delphina caught her eye before she could think on it any more.

The two girls came to her side as the guys went to Arthur's.

Aliana didn't miss the hot way Galahad's eyes traveled over her before he went to his king. She repressed a shiver. She didn't have time for his attention.

"I'm glad to see you, Aliana. We were worried when you didn't join us for dinner last night." Morgana linked her arm through Aliana's.

Delphina walked beside the two girls as they made their way to the fence. "Are you going to join us and watch the knights practice, my lady?"

"It's Aliana, Delphina. And I'd like that. It should be entertaining." Aliana saw the servant, Raven, enter with his arms loaded down with quivers of arrows and a few bows. Two more bows were strung over one shoulder, another two gripped in his smaller fingers. There was also a long strip of leather hanging off his other shoulder with more than a dozen sheathed daggers. "What are the guys practicing today?"

"A little of everything," Delphina said, resting her arms on the long wood. "Knife throwing, sword play, hand to hand combat and archery." Her sea green eyes went to Arthur. "At least that's what Arthur told me this morning."

Aliana tried to not let that last comment sting too much. Morgana released her arm and mimicked Delphina. "This will be a most entertaining afternoon, Aliana."

Aliana nodded but watched the boy approach Percival.

Several of the bows shifted in his arms and the boy stumbled awkwardly, trying not to drop anything. Percival saw the boy and chuckled, but helped him by taking the bows from the boy's hands. Raven set his load of weapons down on the table next to them for Percival to inspect. Several of the guys joined them, but Merlin, Arthur and Galahad all came over to the girls.

Merlin placed a long kiss on Morgana's cheek and the blond girl flushed, her hand going to Merlin's shoulder. Winking at his love, the Druid turned to Aliana. "Good morning. I hope you are feeling better today."

"I am thanks."

"Did you meet with the woman in the market yesterday?"

"Yeah. I think I may have found what I need to get one step closer to figuring out why I'm here."

The Druid nodded, pleased.

"Sophvira was hoping to spend some time with you later today, Aliana," Galahad informed her. "She and Guinevere went into the market to pick up some things, but should be back soon."

Aliana couldn't help but tease the knight. "Under armed escort, I'm sure."

"Quite the contrary, none at all."

Aliana's brows shot up, and then a smile bloomed. "I'm glad." She noticed Arthur watching them warily. "So what are you guys practicing first?"

"We are starting with Archery," the king explained. "I, Leyon, and Galahad are the best marksmen in Camelot."

Aliana bit her cheek to keep from agreeing. She did know how good they were. He and Galahad had helped trained her after all, back in London, before their first battle with Mordrid and Morgana.

She stayed beside the others and watched in fascination as the guys all started to train in earnest. Arthur, Merlin, Leyon, and Owaine all took up bows and arrows while Galahad, Percival, and Gawain sparred in hand to hand combat.

The longer the three went on, the fiercer they became. Despite the gray sky, it was getting more and more humid. One by one they all started to shed layers of clothing, the heavy vests going first, then their tunics later.

Aliana's eyes adored Galahad's toned chest, the way his muscles flexed as he fought. Even now she still found it hard to believe a warrior could move with such grace and precision while wielding a heavy sword. Arthur and Merlin soon joined the fray, both also casting their tunics aside.

How she longed for her camera to capture the show of male hotness she was witnessing. She imagined how Dawn and Lacy would be drooling by now, a thought which only made her miss her best friends more.

Aliana looked down at her hand where her ruby gauntlet was still hidden by her magical veil. She still hadn't looked at the book. She needed to stop letting herself get distracted and focus on her reasons for being here: Titania's mystery task and finding a way to the Grail.

Aliana's mind made up, she excused herself from the other girls. "I should head back in. There's something I need to do."

"My lady?" Delphina sounded worried.

"Delphina, I need to focus on my quest for the Fae Queen. Please try to keep the others from distracting me for a while."

The apricot-headed Fae nodded once.

Vira pouted. "Do you have to?"

"Yes. But I *will* see you at dinner."

The girl looked satisfied. "After dinner we have a surprise for you."

Aliana quirked a brow, looking from her to Guinevere. The redhead shrugged, but her amused look told her she knew what the secret was.

"Then dinner better get here and done soon!" They all laughed as Aliana turned to leave.

Lancelot came barreling out of the castle, the red cape he wore flapping behind him. "Arthur!"

Everyone stopped to focus on the harried knight. "What's happened, Lancelot?" Arthur's demand was harsh.

"Villagers just came to the castle saying that their village had been attacked by some magical beast." He stopped to suck in a fresh breath. "They said it's the second one to be attacked in as many days."

Fury arched on Arthurs face. "Why didn't we hear about his before now?"

"They all only just arrived. The first village was on the borders of our lands and the Fisher King's."

Aliana's gut twisted. A whisper in the back of her mind said this was somehow tied to her quest here in Camelot.

"Send out a scouting party, immediately. Raven," Arthur called the boy to their side.

The boy scrambled over in a flash. "Yes, sire?"

"Have our horses saddled and a small battalion ready by first light. Pack enough provisions for three days." Arthur looked back at his men. "We will not allow this creature to destroy our people."

The guys all nodded, serious and heavy determination hardening their faces.

"Merlin, I need to go with you."

The Druid's pale eyes snapped to hers. *"No, it's too dangerous, and if we get into a fight you might accidently expose yourself."*

"I won't! This might be somehow tied to my quest. How do I convince Arthur to let me come?"

His mouth thinned, and Aliana feared he was going to tell her no. Not that it would matter if he did. She'd just sneak out and go on her own. The more she thought about the creature, the more she was sure she needed to find it.

"You can't convince the king. But maybe I can get him to agree. Give me until dinner."

Grateful, Aliana accepted the concession, her fingers brushing over her hidden power gem. That gave her until dinner to search the mystery book for more clues. Maybe she would even get lucky and find something to help them against the beast attacking Camelot.

Aliana's head dropped against the blanket of her bed, where she was stretched out on her stomach, as she groaned. Her eyes were aching from reading the magical book for the last three hours. And the book was definitely magic. She had confirmed that as soon as she had tried to open it. Because it wouldn't open at all.

Dagg had been the one to figure out that she needed to use the energy element's magic to open it. Her momentary excitement had quelled when she realized the book was a history of the seven realms.

Merlin and Dagg had already told her so much about the different places, and if she had any questions, surely her guardian or even the queen or Merlin here, could tell her what she needed.

"This book came to you for a reason!" Dagg had chided. "There must be something here you need to find out on your own."

So far she had skimmed through the parts about the Mortal realm, Avalon and the Isle of the Blessed. There *had* been plenty of information there she didn't know, but none of it stood out to her as important.

Aliana massaged her eyelids with cramped fingers. "My eyes feel like they're bleeding, Dagg!"

"We still have time until dinner, Aliana. We need to keep reading until then."

She moaned reluctantly. "Fine." She flipped the page and saw a drawing of what she could only compare to a haunted-looking Gothic church. There were two towering, square parapets, and a large window in the center that appeared to be made of spiraling glass and metal. A wickedly dark labyrinth seemed to spider out from the eerie castle. Below it was a description written in a language she didn't know. It was made up of clipped wavy lines and curves that *maybe* could be compared to Mandarin.

She looked to her Dragon. "Do you know what this says?"

Her small friend studied the writing from his perch on her shoulder. He had spent the last few hours curled up on her back, like a cat.

"It's the language of the Underworld."

The grimness in his voice piqued her interest. Of all the realms, she knew the least about this one. "But what does it say?"

"Galkamish."

"Bless you. Wait…what?"

Io

I felt horrible for Lacy when we first approached the tree to enter the Isle of the Blessed. The lass had gone paler than the Banshees that had nearly killed her brother. I had been about to say something to her when she pulled herself together and opened the gate. We ended up much close to Notien than we had last time. I allowed myself a brief moment to think of Freya, the sweet Fae we had met last time. It was more than fortunate that Aliana's Pegasus, Belle, and several others, came upon us when they did. Flying with them will get us to the Fae Queen in no time, and maybe some answers too.

— Leo

"Galkamish. It's the castle of the Underlord. It's surrounded by the endless labyrinth." Dagg's amethyst eyes started to glow as the page turned on its own. The words on that page were also written in the creepy scrawl but when Dagg's eyes shimmered again they wavered and were suddenly in English. He'd had to do the same trick for the pages on Avalon, which had been written in the king's language.

Aliana started to skim the pages when a heavy knock had her scrambling to her knees and Dagg falling from his perch. The Dragon zoomed behind the changing screen as she opened the door.

"Arthur?" Aliana stepped back, opening the door for him to enter.

"Good evening, Aliana." His normal calm and friendly voice was gone. In its place was a heavy and slightly upset tone.

Her heart sputtered as she closed the door. "What's happened? Another attack?"

He shook his head, his golden brown eyes looking around her room and landing on her bed. Or rather the book on her bed.

"A little light reading before dinner." Her attempt at lightening his mood didn't work.

"I've just come from a very long *discussion* with Merlin."

Aliana gulped. This wasn't going very well. She wasn't used to Arthur being so angry with her.

"He seems to be under the impression that you need to accompany us tomorrow when we set out to fight the creature attacking my people."

Aliana twisted her fingers together behind her back. He wasn't going to allow her to go. And worse, she could only imagine how angry he would be when she would follow them.

"When I asked him to justify this *suggestion* he couldn't give me a more suitable answer other than 'she has to go.'" He took a step closer and she pressed against the wooden door. "Why is my Druid, my friend, telling me that I have to bring a woman, no matter how well she can defend herself, into a battle party?"

Aliana opened her dry mouth but nothing came out. His hot gaze was stealing her voice as he crowded closer. She cleared her throat. "Arthur..."

"I'm listening."

"Arthur, I can't give you a better answer than I *have* to go." She took a calming breath. "One way or another."

His mouth pulled down in a frown, his eyes narrowing with anger. This was such a different Arthur than the flirting one who had run his fingers through her hair, just this morning. It almost seemed like he had another personality coming through. Could this be the influence of his Dragon blood?

"I am the King of Camelot. You are here because you are a friend to Merlin. Now I have you and him telling me what I must do."

"We're not—"

He silenced her with a finger to her lip. "You have shown us you are a very capable woman, but I don't allow the females I care for go into dangerous situations."

Aliana's eyes widened at his impassioned admission.

"The fact I care for you surprises you?" The leashed frustration from moments ago eased a little as he dropped his finger.

"No. Yes. Um…" Aliana mentally smacked herself. This was Arthur; he cared about everyone in his life. And he was in love with Delphina. Her lungs squeezed. He hadn't meant that the way she wished it did.

"I'll ask again, why do you believe you must go with us tomorrow?"

Aliana pressed back into the door. "I have encountered several different kinds of magical creatures over the years. I may know what the one attacking your people is and how to stop it."

She felt Dagg's approval through their shared link. Arthur eased back a little.

"You continually surprise me, Lady Aliana. You are the only woman I have ever known who can do all the things you do. Part of me says you are too good to be true, or that you are hiding a very big secret that makes you so special and unique."

Aliana silently held her breath.

"My instincts about people are rarely wrong."

"All you need to know is that I can be of help to you and your kingdom." She hoped he'd see her sincerity. "If you'll let me."

He eased back a little more. "I will think on it. I shall give you my decision soon."

Realizing there was nothing else she could do, Aliana suggested they head down to the great hall for dinner.

"You'll have to stay up here for dinner. I'll be fine. I am going to read more of the book."

They couldn't risk Dagg revealing himself when Arthur was around. Clearly he was suspicious enough already.

They left her room and were outside the great hall in minutes. Everyone was already there when they entered. More than a few curious pairs of eyes seemed to wonder why they were coming down together, Delphina's chief among them.

Everyone took the seats they had two nights ago, except this time Igraine's seat was between Arthur and her.

Worry and anxiety twisted Aliana's insides together so much she could barely enjoy the roasted vegetables and fried meats that were placed in front of her. The guys were talking strategy, surmising what they would do depending on the kind of beast they would be facing.

Lancelot revealed more of the villagers' details about the creature. "It was a monster with a red body, like a lion's, but it had a barbed tail, the wings of an eagle and a face that, according to the people, was almost human."

"It sounds like a Manticore," Aliana said when no one else spoke. "But they don't normally have wings. Griffins do." She thought about Belle. "Or Pegasuses." Everyone's eyes were on her and her discomfort ratcheted up.

Galahad's eyes darkened. "How do you know this?"

Aliana glanced to Arthur quickly. He just studied her, his hands pressed together as his elbows rested on the round table.

"I've heard stories about them all my life. The legend originates from the Persians. Manticore means 'man eater.'"

"They are also creatures that are rumored to be inhabitants of the Underworld." Merlin's words had her attention shifting back to her book. Maybe there was something about Manticores in there!

"Lord Merlin is right." Igraine's quiet voice carried around the room. "Manticores are also creatures born from magic. No ordinary weapon will be able to slay it."

Aliana stayed silent for the rest of dinner. She had no more to offer right now, but she was determined to read every word about the Underworld in her book. She had to prove to Arthur that he should bring her.

They all got up to leave when Vira came to Aliana's side. "I still have that surprise for you."

Aliana hesitated. "I really don't have time tonight, Vira."

"It will only take a moment!" she pleaded.

"It might be a nice mood lifter," the redhead said.

She sighed and gave in.

They made their way to Vira's room. It was slightly bigger than Aliana's and decorated with pale-colored fabrics. Candles were in every corner, all lit, incense giving the room a very calm herbal scent.

A wrapped bundle sat in the middle of her small table. "Open it!" Vira said when Aliana looked at it.

Aliana picked up the cloth-covered thing. "It's heavy."

Vira watched excited as Aliana pulled apart the bow, the covering falling away.

Her breath left her and Aliana's hands gripped the gift and held it up. It was the most gorgeous dress she could have imagined! The dusty pink was even more beautiful than she remembered it being in that marketplace. The square cut neckline was trimmed with thick pieces of cream and pale purple. The cloth belt was cinched and pinned at the waist following the same pattern, with gold stitching along the edges.

"It's beautiful!"

"It will be perfect for the anniversary celebration." Guin stroked her delicate hand down the fabric. "You will catch the eye of most of the men there."

The praise had Aliana hesitating. She didn't want to draw their attention like that. She needed to stay as invisible as possible, but it seemed like she was already failing miserably at that task.

"You have to go!" Vira insisted.

"She's right." Guin laid a hand on her shoulder. "I have a feeling we will all need some good entertainment after this ordeal with this *Manticore* is done."

Aliana gave in. She didn't want to argue with the two girls. Thanking Vira for getting her dress, Aliana went back to her room, laying the dress carefully over the changing screen.

"That's quite stunning."

Aliana ignored the Dragon's words and sat back down on the bed, where he was perched over the magical book.

"Were you eavesdropping on us during dinner?"

Dagg frowned. "No. I was reading more about the Underworld."

She leaned over him, her hair falling to the side like a curtain as she looked down at the book. "Is there anything about Manticores?"

Dagg jumped to his feet, his long neck curving around as he looked at her with glowing eyes. "Why are you asking about Manticores?"

"Because that is what we believe has been attacking the villages in Camelot. Is there anything in there about them?"

Dagg turned back several pages. "They are one of the three guardians of the Underworld." He pointed a claw to the passage he had quoted.

"Sphinxes, Hell Hounds, and Manticores guard the gates to the realm of the Underlord. They are fierce and cunning and only those who prove superior can enter without having to first face their own death."

"It goes on to say that there is only one way to kill a Manticore. Only a weapon touched by the strongest magic can pierce the one weak spot in the monster's impervious hide."

Aliana ran her finger along the passage, but saw no mention of *where* the weak spot was. "How will we know where to strike? And what weapon is made from the strongest magic?"

Dagg gave her a droll stare. "A clue: we watched Arthur reclaim it."

Aliana shuddered. Of course! Excalibur was the answer.

For the second time, there was a heavy knock on her door. Dagg disappeared behind the screen again.

She opened it, not surprised to see Arthur.

She spoke before he was even fully in the room. "A Manticore has only one weak spot on its body! We'll have to find it before you can kill it with Excalibur!"

He frowned and closed the door. "I've made my decision."

Aliana braced herself for the rejection, already planning how she'd sneak out of the castle.

"You can come with us."

"But, Arthur, you'll need me! There's more I can te—" She stopped, his words sinking in. "You mean you're not going to try to stop me from going?"

"I will allow you to go, with the understanding that you are never to be out of mine, Merlin's or Galahad's sight. And you will stay back, protected, when we find and slay this beast."

"Okay," Aliana agreed readily. She wasn't stupid. Arthur had the only weapon that could kill the Manticore. She could still help Merlin find its weak spot while staying out of direct combat.

"We leave at first light."

To say everyone was startled to see Aliana being allowed to go would be an understatement. Even Galahad had protested her being with them. But Arthur silenced them all. Guin handed her a brown hooded cloak made of thick, dense fabric to help keep her warm on the journey.

Aliana had imagined there would some big send off or fanfare this morning, as they all set out to track down the Manticore. But only Vira, Guin and Morgana had been there to see them all off. Vira hugged her brother tightly, her face buried in his chest as he stroked her hair and assured her he would return. Aliana had looked away, only to see Lancelot and Guinevere in a passionate kiss, his hands stroking her cheeks, the strength of their love as bright as a lighthouse on a dark night.

It struck her again how different Lancelot was with Guin by his side. Her heart ached, knowing what was to come for both of them. She *had* to figure out a way to help them both.

Even Morgana and Merlin were saying a quiet good bye. Of everything in Camelot, the complete difference in Morgana resonated the strongest. The Sorceress brushed kisses on his cheeks as the Druid held her tightly to him. A fluttering sensation danced in the air around them. Curious, Aliana opened her magic senses, just enough to figure out what she was feeling. But what she saw was something else entirely.

Rays of shining sun and cool blue magic flowed around them, blending together seamlessly. It was intimate and pure and so beautiful it almost hurt.

"What is that?" she asked Dagg.

Her Dragon's answer made her heart clench. *"They are souls mates. The magic you see is the proof of their bond."*

Souls mates. A tremor ran through her, her fingers convulsively tightening on the reins of her horse. Could it really be true? If so, it was no wonder Merlin had become so cold, distant, and bitter in her time. The person he loved beyond compare, the other half of his soul had betrayed them!

She closed off her magic senses and pulled on her gloves. She couldn't think about such things now. Especially when she hoped...

Aliana shook her head and smoothed an imaginary wrinkle on her heavy sleeve.

Igraine had come to her in the very early hours and given her a pair of warm pants, a long sleeved yellow tunic and a heavy wraparound vest lined with dark animal fur. She left as quickly as she had come, saying, "You can't very well ride across the kingdom in a dress."

It was strange to have her own horse. So far, on this grand adventure, she had always ridden with one of the guys. It wasn't hard to control the beautiful white mare Arthur had told her was hers, but the ride was also a workout for her muscles. Moving with the horse, knowing which muscles to use to help her keep her balance was a challenge she was starting to enjoy.

They rode at a steady pace for hours, most of the time not speaking. Everyone was focused on the upcoming battle. Her thoughts turned back to the Manticore and the information she hadn't told Merlin yet.

Aliana reached out to Merlin mentally. *"Merlin, I need to talk to you."*

"Are you all right?"

"Fine. But there's something I need to tell you about the Manticore." She told him all she and Dagg had discovered in the book last night.

During the catch up, Merlin moved back to ride beside her. *"Arthur mentioned the weak spot last night."*

"He did?"

Merlin nodded. *"He came to see me after he talked with you. You seem to have sway over the king."*

Aliana felt her face heat up. *"It's nothing like that Merlin. I just think he realized I was either going to go with you guys or sneak out and follow anyway."*

The Druid frowned. *"Hear me in this, if Arthur wanted you to remain in the castle he would have seen to it. And don't believe for one moment that he won't send you back the instant you try to go against his orders. You going off on your own could be dangerous. To all of us."*

She sent him a hard look. *"Geesh, relax. I know that. I won't do anything stupid. How are we going to find the Manticore's weak spot? Arthur has to be the one to kill it with Excalibur, but he won't know where to strike if we can't figure this out."*

Merlin scratched his chin, deep in thought. A prickling of awareness trickled down her spine. She cast a curious glance over her shoulder and caught Galahad's hot stare. He had been very somber all day, the only words she'd heard from him today were his protests about her coming with them and his good bye to Vira. There seemed to be more eating at him than just her going with them.

She turned away quickly, taking a steadying breath. Mixed in with the smell of the horses was the mineral scent of the rich earth and the dew on the leaves of the trees. It was slightly balmy, but there was a chill in the air when the wind picked up every now and then. Best she could tell, it was early autumn or late summer here in Camelot.

She wondered what that meant for the timeline of her own time. How long had it been since she was captured by Mordrid? What if she was here so long that she didn't get back in time to stop Mordrid before the eclipse in April? And despite her search of her secret book, she'd yet to find any mention of the Grail or a way to find it.

"Can you and your Guardian connect in a way that lets you see through his eyes?"

Merlin's sudden question almost knocked her out of her saddle. *"What?"*

"Can you connect with the DragonLord to use his sight as yours? If so, he can circle the creature, when we find it, and you can look for its weak spot. Dragons see things differently than humans. His eyes should be able to find what we need."

She hesitated but opened her and Merlin's mental channel to include Dagg. *"Can we?"*

The Dragon was silent for a moment. *"Our bond grows with each day. It may take practice, but I think we can do it."*

"I will need to be beside Arthur and the knights fighting the creature; most of my powers will be focused on that."

Aliana shivered at the image Merlin painted.

"My connecting with Dagg won't do us any good if he has to remain hidden on my wrist. He can't be seen by anyone!"

"I can cloak myself from sight."

Aliana got the feeling there was more. *"But?"*

"But keeping myself invisible from so many will take great magic. I won't be able to maintain the enchantment for long."

"Can you draw from me? I have plenty of power."

Merlin shook his head beside her. *"I do not think that wise. He could end up leaving you vulnerable."*

"How? I've always been able to pull strength from him without hurting him. Why is the opposite so different?"

"Because your magic core is not like most," Dagg answered first. *"Your greatest magic comes from the prophecy stone; even with it bonded to you, I cannot ever seem to draw on it."*

Aliana huffed, not liking the thought. She had to help Dagg do this. He was always helping her. *"We can figure that detail out when we get there. For now, at least, we have a plan."*

She would find a way to help her Dragon.

<h1 style="text-align:center">II</h1>

Arthur and the riders started to slow ahead of them. Aliana tugged lightly on the reins of her horse, the animal slowing at her command.

Arthur turned his horse to the side, pointing to a place just past the trees on their left. "There is a clearing large enough for us to make camp for the night. We'll set out again at first light."

Twenty minutes later several fire pits had been built. The few servants who had accompanied them were gathering wood and preparing food that they had brought. It wouldn't exactly be comfortable, but at least the ground was even, not covered in branches and tree roots like the forest was.

She watched the Druid and Arthur talk as she helped Raven build a tower of kindling to start the fire, only partially listening to the boy's prattling. The king seemed to take the new information in stride. As soon as Merlin turned away, Galahad pulled Arthur quietly to the side. He looked even bleaker than he had earlier. It frustrated her that she still worried for him even after he'd betrayed the bond between them. *But it wasn't* this *Galahad that hurt me,* she reminded herself. It was still so hard to believe he was a different man than the Galahad she knew.

Arthur clapped Galahad on the arm. The knight said something else, then turned and headed back to his horse that was leashed at one of the more deserted areas of the clearing.

"Excuse me, Raven." She brushed off the grass from her pants as she went to Galahad. "Are you leaving?"

He turned, blinking a few times like he was coming out of a trance. "I am doing some scouting."

The lie was obvious to her as he pulled his sword from the side of his horses' saddle and belted it at his waist. He had two more daggers around his belt, and one more she knew he kept tucked in his boot.

"You're lying." The words slipped out before she could stop them. "Something's been bothering you all day."

He opened his mouth, but she cut him off. "And it's not just my being here." Like it or not, she knew all the ways he liked to deflect conversations.

He frowned, adjusting the wool covering he wore to combat the chill in the air. "This is something I have to do alone, Aliana." He softened a little and touched her shoulder reassuringly. His hand seared her even through the layers of her clothes. "I will be back soon."

He turned and headed off into the woods. Glancing around, she saw no one paying any attention to her. She made the decision to follow him. Aliana had been wondering all day what had him so upset, and there was nothing for her to really do at the camp.

If Galahad knew she was following him, he didn't let on. She had caught up quickly, but stayed back a bit, hoping to avoid being noticed. She wasn't technically breaking Arthur's decree.

"If you wanted to keep me from knowing you were following me, you should learn how to move unheard through the forest."

Galahad's words froze her on the spot. He turned swiftly and motioned for her to join him. She went to him, falling in step with him as he led the way to wherever they were going.

"You know I could have Arthur send you back to Camelot for this. You are disobeying his orders."

"No I'm not. He said to stay in sight of him, Merlin, or you."

He snorted. "Arthur won't see it like that when we return." He glanced down at her. "But at least you are safe with me."

"Where are we going?" she dared ask.

He sighed heavily. "Do you know how I came to Camelot?"

She did, but she shook her head anyway.

"My parents were murdered when I was a child. We used to live around here. Our home was tucked in the woods because my mother was a healer and she loved being around all the healing plants that grow here."

"That sounds kind of lonely, being so far from a village."

He shrugged. "It is not really that far, only half a day's ride. Sophvira and I never knew any different. We were playing when they came." His face darkened as he stared ahead. "Raiders attacked us. My father hid me and Sophvira in a secret room in the house. They were slaughtered. If Sir Belvoir and his men hadn't heard the attack and slain the murderers, they would have found us too."

Sadness washed over her. Galahad had told her about his parents before, but he had never given her any real detail. "I'm so sorry."

"Sir Belvoir was my father's cousin; he took us in, raised us as his own. He was also Lancelot's father, so he, I and Arthur all grew up and trained together to be knights."

He quickened his step. "It's been a long time since I was here last. When I realized we would be coming this way I told Arthur I wanted to come."

The sun momentarily blinded her as they stepped out from the covering of the trees. The small cottage was like a ghost hidden behind plants growing all around the yard and walls outside. The fence around what used to be a garden was covered with moss, looking like it would break under any extra weight. Galahad had really lived here?

The knight stood still for a long moment. He finally stepped forward. He went to the front of the cottage, running his hand down the side of the weathered doorway. His eyes swept the area, lingering on the garden, then on a spot to the left just behind the house.

Swallowing the emotions that threatened to choke her, Aliana went to him. "How old were you when you lost them?" Her voice broke the cold silence of the glen.

He looked at her again, his eyes regaining a little of their brilliant Carolina blue color. "I was seven. Sophvira was only two." He stepped into the house, pushing aside the hanging plants.

She followed him into the darkened, earthy interior. It was bigger than she had first thought. Crumbled remains of a bed and table littered the floor like they had been left after a fight. There was a small little alcove off to the side with two small beds.

That must have been where he and Vira slept. She looked at him again. He was just standing there looking lonely, lost and heartbroken. Another crack formed in the already weakened walls protecting her heart.

He finally moved. He kicked aside a small pile of debris and slammed his foot down on the wooden floor. It crumbled away, revealing a small hidden hole.

Aliana went to his side and laid her hand on his tense arm.

"I could hear them die." His low, choked whispers seemed to echo through the house. "I heard them run my father through and heard my mother's screams before they slit her throat."

She gasped, tears burning her eyes, but she blinked them back. She couldn't stand to see him hurting so much. Grasping a small wisp of her pink magic she sent a wave of comfort to his heart, hoping to help ease his aching suffering and give him some small measure of relief.

His eyes found hers, boring down on her like he knew exactly what she was doing. They stood there for what felt like ages, some small part of Aliana's heart healing in the process. His hand cautiously wrapped around hers. When she didn't pull away, he tugged her outside and around to the back of the house.

She saw two long piles of stone overgrown with delicate little wildflowers.

"We buried them here. My mother would have never wanted to be far from her plants."

Her tears returned, thinking of her own adoptive parents' graves and that of her birth mother. She hadn't been to see her mama and papa since the funeral. Now that she knew their truth, she vowed to go see them again. And she would see her birth mom's again too, just as soon as she got home.

She gripped his hand tighter. "I know this won't make it any better, but I know what you're feeling."

He looked at her with surprise.

"I only recently found out that my parents had adopted me. My real mother died giving birth to me." She looked back to the graves. "Just before I discovered the truth, my parents were killed." She saw the boat explosion again behind her closed eyes. "They were murdered too."

Her hate for Morgana resurfaced, and it warred with the friendship she had started to form with the Morgana of this time. How could she have changed so drastically?

His fingers threaded with hers. "How?"

"They were on a boat when it was intentionally set on fire." She remembered that fire trying to stretch toward her, to claim her too. She now knew that Morgana *had* tried to kill her as well. In a way she had succeeded. The girl she had been before their deaths was long dead. She wasn't as carefree or open as she had once been. Trust was now a luxury for her.

"We are two of a kind it would seem."

She dashed away the tears that had returned, and the few that escaped. "I'm sorry, Galahad. I should never have followed you and intruded on your time with your family."

He tugged her closer, a gentle arm wrapping around her waist. "I find that I am glad you came. I think your presence has made this a little easier for me. I don't feel as burdened as I did earlier."

Funny how she felt the same. Going against her better judgment, she wrapped her arms around him, ignoring the press of his weapons against her sides as she hugged him tightly. His arms tightened around her, one of his hands burying itself in her own wind-tangled hair as she laid her cheek against his heart.

She could hear its thundering beat and felt her own rush to meet it. After a moment she pulled back, but he wouldn't let her escape. His blazing blue eyes claimed hers and held them like a thief would a treasure.

His head dipped lower, pausing as their lips hovered inches apart. His hot breath tangled with hers. She remembered their first kiss, when he had stolen a heated, branding kiss to free her from the trap of the Sidhe's magic.

Her eyes closed as a tear squeezed out. His lips barely brushed hers when she pulled out of his arms. "I'm sorry, I can't."

She wrapped her cloak around her like an extra shield against the new kind of pull that she felt for him. Their sparkling bond may be nonexistent here, but she was discovering a whole new kind of attraction to him. Something that went beyond the more physical attraction she had felt, ever since first awakening the white knight.

"What's wrong?"

How could she explain this to him? "We're just caught up in our losses." She shook her head, looking anywhere but at him. "My heart has already been broken too many times. I won't survive if it happens again."

His fingers gripped her chin and gently pulled her eyes to his. His thumb swiped away the stray tear track. "And what if I don't break your heart, but help heal it?"

She shook her head and stepped back again. It was too late for that.

"We should get back." She looked at the graves again. "If you're ready to go."

He sighed, but nodded. She had expected him to look solemn and upset again, but as she watched him say one last silent good bye to his parents she saw a new determination on his face.

Arthur, Lancelot, Merlin and Leyon were immediately on them as soon as they returned to the camp.

"Where have you been?" Arthur demanded. His angry eyes softened, however, when he seemed to notice her downturned mood.

"Are you both all right?"

Aliana opened her mouth to answer, when a screaming roar pierced the twilight-colored sky.

Aliana's eyes went toward the sound as the guys turned and drew their weapons.

Diving straight at them was a giant beast with matted, devil red fur, wings bigger than a Pegasus's and a barbed tail that swung through the air. It was the fiercest monster she had ever seen.

And its fathomless, glowing night eyes seemed fixed on Aliana.

"Take cover!" Arthur ordered her over the chaos that had exploded at the Manticore's roar. He drew Excalibur, holding it high in the air. "Knights, to me!"

"Get to the trees!" Galahad drew his own sword and grabbed his shield, the same shield she had seen at the Sidhe's keep. Round with crescents on both sides with a single sword identifying it as his.

Aliana stumbled back, wide eyes meeting Merlin's over the top of his own shield with a bronze sun. The Druid nodded once, telling her silently to do what she could.

The Manticore dove, heading right toward them.

"Go, Aliana!" Arthur roared, hefting his shield.

She took several steps back, her eyes focused on the beast. The Manticore screeched again and rushed for them. Soldiers and knights formed a battle line as she spun on her heel and dashed toward the shelter of the trees.

She ducked behind the biggest oak, watching the Manticore's claws batter at the warrior's shields. Arthur and the knights held fast. Owaine, Lancelot, Percival and Gawain threw their spears, but they bounced off the creature's impervious hide. It made another pass, its barbed tail and claws tearing through several of the soldiers' armor and scattering the battle line.

Aliana's throat constricted, her energy and fear jumping in her stomach. "Now would be a good time to get your scaly butt in the air, Dagg!"

Her guardian sprang from her wrist, his presence hidden by the wide tree trunks, as he landed in her outstretched hands. "You must open your mind to me if you are to see through my eyes."

Her eyes widened. He wasn't asking her to do what she thought he was, was he? "You mean all my shields have to come down?" She didn't know if she could make herself do it. There were so many things she didn't want Dagg or anyone else seeing or feeling from her mind.

His eyes glowed bright purple. "Now is not the time to be worrying about what you wish to hide!"

She took a breath and forced her mind to calm. She could do this, if it meant destroying this creature and helping Arthur and his men. One by one she let the layers pull back, like a rose in bloom.

"That's good enough." Dagg surprised her. She had only pulled back about half of the shield she'd constructed. His purple-silver magic

rolled into her like a gentle fog. It sang through her muscles, rising higher until her vision turned to gray clouds. Her panic resurfaced.

"Stay calm!" She blinked furiously. A burst of purple took over, her vision returning seconds later. It was like she was seeing the world through a rich, high-definition photo filter. Everyone and everything was crisp and clear. Faint shades of shimmering colors came from the knights and soldiers, almost like she was seeing the strength of their souls.

"Oh my stars!"

"Unfortunately, now is not the time to admire how I see things." Dagg's serious tone brought her back to the situation.

"Now it's my turn." Before Dagg could react, she pulled back the veil that hid the true strength of her powers and shoved a small bubble of her pink magic into him, just enough to make him stronger without sacrificing any real power of her own. He vanished from her hands, even her new Dragon sight unable to see any trace of her guardian.

"You shouldn't have done that!" Dagg was furious, likely worried she was going to leave herself vulnerable.

"Too late!"

The Manticore dove again, its hooked talons catching two more soldiers, ripping through their flesh, blood spurting and staining the ground where the dead warriors landed.

Merlin's powers clotted the area, streaks of orange lightning zinging down from the sky, crashing into the Manticore. It roared, soaring back into the sky as more bolts came toward it.

"Get in the air. Now!" Aliana felt Dagg shoot off from her hands. He climbed high into the air, all the while keeping focused on the monster. The beast's red fur oozed a brown kind of aura that made Aliana's stomach clench. The power and menace surrounding the creature was almost unbelievable. The Manticore's wings flared, it arched in a flip, avoiding the balls of magic fire and spears coming toward it.

Dagg rose higher until he was above the Manticore. They both scanned the length of the creature's body, from its barbed tail to the human-lion-like face. Its brownish aura was like sludge. Her heart raced, sweat trickled down her neck and forehead as the knights continued to battle the creature with weapons and magic. Nothing seemed to stop it, and Merlin's power, as great as it was, only managed to slow it down for a few seconds.

Dagg kept pace with the creature, all the while dodging the deflected spears, arrows and volleyed swords. Dagg's eyes caught sight of the carnage littering the ground. The green grass was bathed in the blood of the fallen soldiers. Her knights were battling side by side with the other two dozen men who were left. They couldn't last much longer!

Worse, the Manticore was staying out of reach of Arthur and Excalibur.

"Its weak spot has to be here somewhere!" She blocked out everything else, focusing on the creature alone. It banked to the side, the current shift causing Dagg to curve as the Manticore almost smacked into him. A pale flash caught her attention. *"There! Between its wings!"*

Dagg went in closer, their eyes landing on the small strip of flesh between the wing joints. The area, no bigger than a rolled scroll, was a pale patch of furless skin.

"Merlin, we found it! Tell Arthur he needs to strike it between the wings, just below the beast's neck!"

"We need to find a way to get this thing on the ground for him to have that chance."

The Druid was right. So far the Manticore had only come within striking distance a handful of times. And each time it did, more men died. What if one of her knights was its next victim?

Icy fear clogged her blood, but she fought past it. *"I can help you bring it down!"*

Merlin and the knights all dove to the side and the Manticore's tail and claws rained down on them again. *"You'll expose yourself."*

He was right, but he also didn't seem too worried about that.

"Maybe, but I can't let anyone else die. I can work my magic from here."

12

Aliana broke her connection with Dagg. Her vision returned to normal between blinks as her shields folded back into place.

"Dagg, get back here before you become visible!"

Aliana looked out at the knights. They were shooting useless arrows as Merlin called down more cracks of power. The knights were slowly being pushed back toward the trees at the creature's relentless attacks.

A movement on her left caught her attention. Raven was inching out of the cover of the forest, his dark eyes fixed on the creature's every move. The Manticore's glowing white eyes landed on the boy.

Its roar-screech was ear piercing as it dove straight for him, several yards behind the guys.

"Raven!" Aliana reacted, rushing toward the stunned boy who just stood there like he was waiting to be attacked. Aliana ran faster than she could ever remember pushing herself, pulse pounding in her ears as she and the Manticore drew closer.

She slammed into the servant, both of them hitting the ground in a tangle of limbs and fallen twigs and leaves. The guys hollered as the Manticore suddenly pulled back. The knights were on it immediately. Aliana's magic pulled and wavered, sending shudders through her body. Gusts of wind rushed through the trees, hitting the creature between the wings and forcing him lower to the ground.

Aliana looked down at the boy in her arms. He was still and pale, his eyes closed, his dark hair matted with dirt and leaves. "Raven?" She laid him on his back, her fingers going to his neck in search of a pulse when he didn't stir. It was an excruciating half a second before she felt his steady heartbeat. He was just knocked out.

She sagged for a moment then scrambled to her feet. Dagg's small silver form shimmered back into visibility as he came straight at her. She opened her arms, the Dragon flying right into them and she hugged him fiercely. *Did you create that wind tunnel?*

"Yes!" He immediately shrank back to his bracelet form. *"That was too close. I was barely able to hold the concealment spell I cast with your magic once we separated."*

A loud crack drew her attention back to the raging battle before she could answer. Merlin pounded the creature with blast after blast of fire and orange lightning. It screeched and tried to rise back to the safety of the sky. Galahad and Gawain grabbed long rolls of ropes and chains from one of the wagons and started to throw them around the thrashing body. The others joined in as well, but the Manticore broke the chains and slashed through the ropes.

They dodged the tail that swept toward them. The monster reared up on its back legs, its wings flapping. They couldn't let it get back in the air! Aliana knelt on one knee and dug her fingers into the ground. The earth element's magic jumped at her command, bending and shaping itself to her will. Whip-like vines shot out of the ground, lashing around the swinging tail and thrashing claws.

It roar-screeched again, but Aliana leashed it tighter with more vines. New sprouts circled the Manticore's wings. Her pink magic sparked and bubbled up as she added more power to the vines. The Manticore struggled to break free, but Aliana held fast. Its wings were pulled out, exposing the only weak spot on the monster.

It struggled harder and Aliana felt her magic starting to falter, more sweat beading on her face. Another magic fought back, a crackling darkness that seemed to come from the creature.

The knights all yelled to each other, throwing more chains and ropes as leashes. Arthur charged toward the restrained creature, Excalibur gripped tight. Merlin turned from the Manticore, his hands flung out as two long spears of orange magic formed in the air beside the creature. As if on cue, Arthur jumped, landing on one of the magic bolts, then jumped to the next. He leapt up, his momentum sending him sailing through the air as he twisted Excalibur around and landed on the Manticore's back. He drove Excalibur down into the soft, vulnerable flesh between the wings.

The Manticore bucked harder, its glowing night eyes dimming as it roared and screeched like a banshee. Golden light burst from its body like fireworks. Between one breath and the next, it disintegrated into brownish black ash.

Arthur dropped to the ground, landing on his feet, Excalibur's tip sinking into the ground.

Relief flooded Aliana as she released the elemental magic and rehid her own behind the veil before anyone noticed her still glowing ruby finger glove.

"Lady Aliana?" Raven's groggy, soft voice called to her.

She helped the boy sit up. "Raven, are you okay?"

He held his hand to his head wincing. "You saved me."

She frowned at him, her brows pulling together. "What were you thinking walking out onto the field like that?"

He opened his mouth to answer, but snapped it shut as Merlin, Gawain, Galahad, and Arthur rushed to them.

"Are you both all right?" Gawain asked, stooping down next to Raven.

Aliana nodded, still trying to calm her pulsating heart, heaving lungs and shaking hands. She looked up at Arthur. "You did it."

He smiled and offered her his hand. She took it and he pulled her to her feet. She wobbled, her legs weak from the use of magic and fading adrenaline. Arthur and Galahad both grabbed her arms, steadying her.

"Are you sure?"

Aliana smiled. "Right as rain."

Gawain got Raven to his feet as Lancelot came over to them. "We need to check for survivors."

Arthur let her go. All the knights went back onto the bloodied field to see if any more soldiers had survived besides the eight that were still standing. Aliana turned away from the gruesome sight and focused on Raven.

She gently turned his face to inspect any damage. Mostly he seemed to be fine, just covered in dirt, leaves and sweat. "Are you hurt? I'm afraid I may have tackled you pretty hard."

He shook his head. She hugged him, realizing then just how tall he really was, taller than her by a few inches actually. There was something so familiar about his dark eyes, but she couldn't decide what.

The young man's hands gingerly touched her shoulder. Aliana winced. "M'lady, you are bleeding."

Aliana released him and turned her head, looking down at her right shoulder. Smears of blood stained the torn fabric of her vest. Aliana sucked in a painful breath through her teeth as she moved her arm.

Raven's eyes clouded with worry. "You need Merlin to heal you."

She didn't need Merlin to heal her, but this boy didn't know that. "I'm fine, really." She gingerly touched the wound. It stung but the bleeding seemed to have already stopped. "I've had much worse before."

Raven protested but she silenced him with a shake of her head. "Merlin can take care of me last." She looked out at the field where Percival, Galahad, Leyon, and Lancelot were carrying the bodies of the dead men to the wagons. Gawain was supporting another man, the injured man's arm thrown over his shoulders as they went over to Merlin.

The Druid had already set up a small area next to one of the few tents that remained standing. Two men were already at his feet, Merlin's orange magic pulsing as he worked to heal them.

She looked back at Raven. "Are you feeling strong enough to go help the others?"

"I am, m'lady."

"Then go see what they need of you. I'm going to help Merlin."

Raven headed toward the two other servants that had accompanied them. Aliana was glad they had remained safe during the fight. She jogged to Gawain and helped him sit the injured man down before the knight went back out into the field to search for more survivors.

"What can I do to help?" she asked the Druid.

He looked up from the groaning man on his left. "I'm using my magic to heal those who are the most desperate."

"I can help heal with my magic. I'm good with that."

His mouth twitched. *"I have no doubt of that. The magic you used was incredible, but I can feel your exhaustion. I can heal those most needy."*

"Sir Owaine is seeing to the men who are not in need of magic healing. Help him with those men, cut up fresh bandages, whatever he needs," he said aloud.

Aliana got up, heading toward her soon-to-be reincarnated cousin. She hadn't really gotten to be around him since she arrived. It would be nice to get to know him better. He was only a yard away from Merlin, four men leaning against another wagon as Owaine tied off a bandage around a fifth man's head.

"What can I do to help, Sir Owaine?"

"Do you know how to clean and bind wounds?"

She swallowed down a small pool of bile that rose in her throat. Injuries she could handle, but blood and ravaged flesh? That was a whole other story. But she could do it for the brave men who had survived.

Owaine motioned to the left as Leyon and Lancelot brought over two more men. "See to them." He handed her a bowl of water, cloth and bandages.

Aliana gritted her teeth and set to work. The hours passed as she saw to the injured. A few times the hanging flesh had looked so bad she used a small dose of her magic to help along the healing. Dagg had scolded her, Merlin too after the fourth time he had felt her flare of power. She was feeling the drain that came with using too much magic so she reluctantly pulled it back.

Working beside Owaine had been great. He was diligent and thorough with his work, his calm manner helping to relax the men when they would get a little anxious. Leyon, Percival, and Arthur had come over a few times to help and check on their progress and the men. Percival had been the first to spot the tear in her clothes, but thankfully Dagg had been working his own magic and had already healed her wound. The bloodstain had seemed to worry him and Owaine, but when they looked her over, and saw no evidence of a wound, they accepted that it was nothing.

The knights had been the luckiest; besides torn leather, bruises and some minor damage to their hands from the ropes and chains, they had come out of the battle unscathed. The injuries to Galahad's hands had been the worst. The chains had pinched and torn his gloves leaving welts and small scrapes all over them. Owaine had handed her a salve to soothe the pain and help with the swelling.

Not daring to look at him, she focused on his hands, trying to be as gentle as possible. Her heart raced, because she could feel him just watching her. Diligently, she wrapped his hands in clean bandages and wiped away the blood and dirt that had covered his arms, all while trying to keep her breathing steady and even.

He didn't try to draw her into conversation. She attempted to control the tremble of her hands as she rinsed out the dirtied rag when her work was finished. "All done." She gathered up the other bandages, still not meeting his eyes, and dumped out the soiled water.

His large, calloused hand covered hers. Despite her resolve, her eyes shot up to his.

"Thank you for your care." His eyes blazed dark blue and her heart stuttered like it always did when he looked at her like that.

"You're welcome." Her voice was breathless and soft. He raised his hand to touch her face, but Lancelot interrupted them before he could.

Night was already in full swing by the time all the injured were seen to. The field had been cleared, dinner cooked and tents reset up. Aliana sat between Galahad and Arthur, her brown cloak helping to battle against the chill night breeze. Aliana ate the rabbit stew that Raven handed her. The boy was very attentive, and only left after Arthur ordered him to go eat his own supper.

"I think the boy is infatuated with you," Galahad whispered, leaning into her slightly. "He cannot seem to stop fawning over you."

She pursed her lips. "Galahad, I think you're exaggerating just a bit." She thought she had noticed him staring at her throughout most of the evening. Her discomfort ratcheted up a little.

"Merlin," Arthur's voice drew her attention. "I have not said it yet, but without your magic today, we may not have killed the Manticore. Thank you."

Merlin's gray blue eyes cut to her quickly. "*I am not comfortable with taking all the praise. Your magic is what trapped the beast.*"

She frowned. "*They can't know. You deserve to take the credit. Your magic was just as effective as mine.*"

He smiled at Arthur, but it was a little strained. "Thank you, sire. We were fortunate."

Leyon spoke up, setting down his empty bowl. "What we need to worry about is how the Manticore came to Camelot."

Owaine nodded. "Yes, Merlin said himself that the Manticore is a creature of the Underworld."

"One of its three guardians," Aliana added almost absently, remembering the passage from her book.

The guys regarded her for a moment, but none said anything.

Arthur spoke up, his hand rubbing his jaw in thought. "If it is a guardian, then it was most certainly sent by someone."

"Not the Underlord," Merlin said quickly. "Of all the rulers of the magic realms, he has never shown any desire to claim more kingdoms for himself."

Merlin's words felt true to her. The book had said that the Underlord was one of the four strongest powers in existence; his realm was far larger than any of the others. During the war eons ago that had resulted in all the realms sealing up their gates, he had never actually attacked any of the realms, only defended his own with his army of death.

Aliana shivered and pulled her cloak tighter. It made no sense that the Underlord would attack Camelot.

"Then who is powerful enough to release such a deadly creature on Camelot?" Percival's question fell on heavy silence.

Aliana thought of Mordrid and Morgana. It had to be one of them; it was the only thing that made sense. But did it make sense? By all appearances, Morgana hadn't yet turned against Arthur, why would she send this monster? She wasn't even here to control it!

"We should all get some rest," Arthur said, standing up and taking Excalibur in hand. "I want us back on the road to Camelot at first light."

Everyone stood and went their separate ways. Aliana's head was still spinning from the events of the day. She needed some space from the camp, but knew she couldn't go far.

Aliana edged her way toward the trees lining the clearing, right where she'd saved Raven earlier. Her stomach was a tangled mess, so worried about them being attacked again, and wondering who had sent that Manticore after them in the first place.

"Why have you wandered alone from the camp, Aliana?"

Aliana whirled around, frightened by Arthur's silent appearance, stumbling off balance.

Arthur's hot hands gripped her waist, helping to steady her.

Her own hands came up to rest on his hard chest. "You scared me."

"Good. You should not be off on your own. I told you I would only allow you here if you stayed by me or Merlin or Galahad."

Aliana's cheeks heated. "I'm sorry, I just needed some space to shake off...everything."

His temper cooling, one of his hands came up to twist strands of her hair around his fingers. "Since I am here, is there any way I can help you?"

Her pounding heart tightened in her throat. Her breath came a little faster as desire for the king raced through her. Being wrapped in his arms was making the stress of the day fade away. "You holding me seems to be helping." The words slipped out before she could stop them.

Tiny tingling sensations brushed her skin. She hadn't been this close to Arthur since *her* Arthur had kissed her on the beach. She couldn't help her eyes dropping to his mouth quickly, remembering the way he'd kissed her, with such pent up passion. His summertime scent, slightly sweet and fresh like morning dew, surrounded her. A part of her healing heart ached for Arthur to kiss her again.

"You can't look at me like that. I'm not strong enough to resist," he moaned gruffly. Arthur leaned in slowly, his intense eyes searching hers for any sign of rejection. But she didn't have the resistance to deny him. She closed her eyes as his lips brushed hers. He was gentle and sweet at first; he bit her lip softly. He pulled back a fraction, his half hooded gaze finding hers. His mouth came down on hers again, more passionate and slowly, deliciously taking over.

She circled his neck with her arms. His hands cupped her cheeks then burrowed into her hair as they kissed over and over again. His taste was sweet and warm and addictive. It stole through her, drawing her in that much more.

It felt like his kiss was claiming a part of her very soul, binding them even closer. She felt the tickle of strings glide over her skin. He shuddered against her, like he felt the same sensations. Aliana pulled back a fraction, sucking in air. She could almost see the golden threads weaving together, between and around them.

She gasped as her clouded brain realized what she was seeing. Before she could fully process it, Arthur took her mouth again. His warm tongue danced with hers before he slowly pulled back.

Aliana looked up at him, feeling dazed and blissfully content for the first time since arriving in Camelot. They both stayed in each other's arms for a long moment before it finally dawned on Aliana what had just happened.

Her pulse spiked again. She stepped back, feeling the reluctance in Arthur's hold before he let her slip away. She'd just kissed Arthur! Again.

"I'm sorry," she stammered, "I shouldn't have…" She felt the desire to both run from him and go back into his arms. But the latter wasn't an option. Arthur had Delphina, his green-eyed ghost girl, waiting for him back in Camelot. "I should go back to the camp."

The king looked confused and frustrated but she forced herself to ignore it. She scurried through the camp, ducking into her tent, trying to understand what had just happened but failing. She couldn't let it happen again. Arthur had Delphina, and like it or not, this wasn't her Arthur. She needed to remember that. And that she was here to fulfill her quest for Titania and find a way to locate the Grail of Power. That had to be the only thing that mattered.

Aliana woke from her restless slumber when a heavy hand shook her awake. Not even opening her eyes she pulled her cloak over her head. "It's too early! Five more minutes."

Merlin's amused chuckle filed the tent. The guys had all insisted that she have one of the five that had survived the attack. "You need to get up. We are getting ready to depart for Camelot."

Aliana peeked out from under her cloak that had served as her blanket. Merlin set down a metal cup of fresh water next to her bedroll. He knelt there, staring at her with a raised brow.

She sighed heavily and sat up. "I'm up. Happy now?"

"Immensely," he said dryly.

Aliana drank down the chilled water, grateful to get rid of the cottony feel in her mouth. "Why did he have to wake me up?" she muttered quietly.

Merlin snorted. "Were you hoping for someone else? Galahad or Arthur maybe?"

Aliana felt her face turn hot as a cooked crab. Flashes of Arthur's kiss from last night returned. "N-No that's…that's not what I meant."

Merlin's chuckle did nothing to ease her flustered mood. "I did not get the chance to ask last night, but do you think this Manticore attack may be tied to your purpose for being here in Camelot, Aliana?"

The thought had crossed her mind last night, while she was trying to nod off. "Possibly. But I don't see how. What reason would I have to get involved, to any degree, with the Underworld?"

"I do not know. But the Underlord is not the only powerful being in the Underworld. His son is his top general. He is rumored to be fierce, deadly, and even more cunning than the Underlord himself."

Great! Aliana sighed. "Have any other magical creatures ever attacked Camelot?"

Merlin sat back on his heels. "A few, but none that have ever been so closely tied to one of the four rulers."

Aliana looked down at Dagg, still in his bracelet form on her wrist. When they got back to Camelot she needed to go to Morgana's bad-magic-potion-lab-secret-hidey-hole, as Lacy had called it. She hoped with all her heart that she was wrong and Morgana hadn't sent the Manticore.

Merlin stepped out of the short tent as Aliana retied her cloak around her shoulders and straightened her clothes. She had no idea how Arthur was going to react this morning, but right now she was determined to pretend like nothing had happened.

Merlin offered his hand to her as she came out, helping her to her feet. Galahad was already looking in their direction as he tightened the saddle on his horse.

Raven and another servant boy came up and started to pack up the tent and bedroll. She and Merlin went to Galahad, her own horse next to his and Arthur's. *I'm so over this cruel joke of yours, Universe.*

"Did you sleep well, Aliana?" Galahad asked as Merlin went to his own mount.

"I did. How about you? How are your hands?"

Galahad stepped to her side, holding them out for inspection. Trying to control the trembles in her fingers she untied the bandages. She released a soft breath when she saw they were almost healed. Only a few patches of red skin remained. She retied the bandages as Arthur came up to them.

"Good morning." His golden eyes were weary but there was also a glint of hope.

She smiled, trying to pretend like her heart wasn't pounding. "Morning."

That little spark of hope seemed to fade. "We are going to ride ahead of the rest of the men," he informed her, his tone all business. "Merlin, Percival, Leyon and Owaine are going to see the wagons with the dead and injured make it safely back to Camelot."

Aliana frowned. "Why won't we stay with them?"

Galahad answered her. "The wagons will be slower because of the extra weight."

Arthur nodded, his face set in his I'm-appearing-calm king mask. "I want to get back to Camelot as quickly as possible and see if we can't find out who sent this creature to attack my kingdom."

"I hope you are ready for a fast paced ride, Aliana." She nodded at Galahad and mounted her horse with Arthur's strong hands on her waist helping her up.

Lancelot and Gawain directed their mounts next to Galahad's, along with two other soldiers. "Are we ready, sire?" Lancelot asked.

"Yes." He looked back at Merlin who was securing his shield to his saddle. "Be sure you return to Camelot by tomorrow. My cousin will be furious that I am returning without you, Merlin."

He grinned broadly. "Tell Morgana I'll be back with her soon."

Aliana remembered the beautiful bond she had seen between Merlin and Morgana as they left Camelot. Their souls mate bond. She couldn't help but wonder if either the golden, net-like bond between her and Arthur, or the sparkling silver one she shared with *her* Galahad wasn't something similar. But how could she share such a pure connection with two men? There were a few rare moments since she had felt the connections to both her warriors, where she felt their feelings were almost forced on them. But that was foolish. No one could be powerful enough to do that.

Dagg spoke up in her mind. *"I am afraid I may have a theory about that. We will discuss it once we've returned to Camelot."*

Aliana's heart lurched, her hands tightened on her horse's reins. *"I'm not going to like this, am I?"*

13

Wind rushed past her, blowing Lacy's hair out in a wild tangle. She knew she was going to hate it later, but right now she didn't care. She was flying on a Pegasus! This was just too much fun!

Hopefully she, Arthur, Leo and Percy would finally be able to track down Queen Titania and get some answers about Aliana. Could she really be in Camelot's past? It'd scared the holy daylights out of her when the guys had doubled over in pain from the memories. *Things can't get much stranger at this point.*

Lacy and her pack of knights were searching across the Isle and Aliana was suddenly a time traveler! *If I wasn't living it, I wouldn't believe it!*

Surprisingly, the whipping wind didn't sting her eyes as she looked at the jewel-colored ground and forest below them. They hadn't been flying long when she felt the tingling and bursting power she felt last time they were in Notien.

Titania's towering, living tree palace came into view. It was beautiful and Lacy wished Aliana could see it. No doubt her missing friend would die to see the castle from this angle. She frowned and pressed her chest and cheek against Percy's back. One of his large, strong hands covered hers, the slightly callused skin of his fingers soothing her.

They got closer to the Fae city, but the Pegasuses didn't slow, or start to descend. They tucked into a tight formation with Arthur on one side of her and Percy and Leo on her other side.

"What's going on?" she heard Arthur ask from her right.

Lacy tried brushing her moonbeam-like magic against Belle's. She felt an instant snapping connection to the creature. There weren't exactly words, but Lacy understood that the Pegasus was taking them where they needed to be.

"I don't think Titania's in the city!" she yelled to the guys, her voice carrying on the wind. "I think they are taking us to where she actually is."

At this point they really had no choice but to go where the Pegasuses took them.

Belle whinnied and started to descend, leveling off minutes later, as a tall mountain of gold, purple, orange and white loomed closer. A clearing of blue-green earth appeared and the Pegasuses dived. Lacy's stomach jumped and spun with excitement, before they pulled back at the last second and set down on the open valley ground.

"That was *so* much better than a rollercoaster ride!" she said when she could catch her breath. Lacy loosened her grip on her boyfriend, ready to jump down, but Belle and the other two Pegasuses started trotting into the woods.

"Where are they taking us now?" Leo asked for all of them.

One hand still gripping the white mane of his mount, Arthur reached back into the pack on his back and pulled out one of the maps. Lacy was impressed when he bravely let go of the animal to open the map, only his strong legs holding him in place on the moving Pegasus.

His golden eyes scanned it quickly. He found what he was looking for and folded it into a more manageable size. "I'm pretty sure we're here." He pointed to the top corner, his finger brushing over a single mountain peak.

If she remembered correctly, they were pretty close to Camelot's ruins.

Leo took the map from Arthur and held it close to his face. "There's something written here," he murmured. "But it's more like an impression, rather than writing." He angled the map another way. "Got ya, you sod!"

Startled by his outburst, everyone pulled their mounts to a stop and gathered around the Scot.

"What'd you find?" Percy drawled, stretching to look over the map.

"I can just make out a symbol. I recognize it from one of Merlin's other maps, sire. I believe it's the symbol for the Well of Realms, but only Avalon is supposed to have one. That's what Merlin said, right?"

"Well, it seems someone's been doing his homework, even if it is wrong!" The almost snide, high-pitched voice surprised them all.

They looked to the side and saw Puck floating a few feet from them.

"Where's the queen?" Arthur demanded.

Puck tsked and waved one orange-skinned finger like a chiding teacher. "Now why would you want to see the queen when I can offer you all the help you want?"

"We have no reason to trust you, trickster. And I have business to discuss with the queen," Arthur said forcefully. Something had changed in Arthur since they had come to Charleston. A weird energy sparked around him at times. It had only become more evident since Aliana's kidnapping.

Puck came a little closer. "That *business* wouldn't happen to have anything to do with the Destined One, would it?"

Arthur actually growled, anger seeping into his face. His Pegasus shot forward so fast that not even Puck had time to react before his white tunic was being gripped in the king's hand, Excalibur suddenly at his throat. "If you know what is happening with her, why we suddenly have memories of her in Camelot, tell me now. Or I might decide you'll look better without your head."

"Arthur!" the three of them called out, startled and worried. Lacy couldn't let him hurt Puck! She needed answers.

Puck gulped, but didn't seem *too* worried. He raised his hands in surrender and held Arthur's furious gaze. "Relax, I'm here to help. I actually like your Aliana."

"He speaks the truth," a softer voice said from the forest.

A Fae girl, no taller than Lacy, emerged from the purple hued bushes. She had lavender hair that faded into pink, and pale blue eyes, and she ducked her head before looking to Arthur.

"We are both here to help. But the queen does not know it."

Ever so slowly, Arthur lowered Excalibur and released his death grip on the trickster's shirt.

He zoomed several feet away, his hands flicking down the material like he was trying to brush away the wrinkles. "Geesh, talk about tightly wound!"

Arthur dismounted his Pegasus, his eyes locked on the trickster.

"Sire, he's trying to get a rise out of you," Percy said, swinging a leg over Belle's bent head and sliding to the ground. He turned and helped Lacy down, tucking her close to his side as they went to their king.

Leo went to Freya and they stared into each other's eyes for a long moment before gathering with the others.

"Now," Arthur said, taking a calming breath. "Explain what you two mean."

The trickster grinned as another came out of the tall brush.

The king and the knights were wide-eyed.

Arthur took a step toward the pale, apricot-haired Fae with beautiful green eyes. "Delphina?"

Dawn snuck another glance at the dark-haired elf leading them through the forest. J'alel was exactly like Lia described him. *Though she failed to mention how hot he is, being a dark-haired version of Legolas and all.*

Their little party of four, plus an Elf, was hoping the Elven Elders of his people would be able to help them find the Well of Realms. Just after leaving Deidre, the Lady of the freaking Lake, the guys all lost it and suddenly had memories of their lost friend in Camelot.

Camelot! As in the Dark Ages. *I wonder if she's freaking or floating on cloud nine?*

"We need to cross the Garnet River before we can reach the village." J'alel's regal voice carried through the thick forest vegetation. They had been walking on a thin path through the thick, winding trees of the Red Wind forest.

They trekked up a sloping hill covered with green, gold, red and other autumn-colored leaves until they final reached a long, wide river with rushing water.

Dawn took a leery step back. "We have to cross this to get to your village? Anyone else but me think that's a little dangerous with rushing water and all?"

J'alel shared a smirk with Galahad. The Elf whistled a long sharp note. For a second nothing happened, then the water started to tremble as large flat stones rose from beneath the waters forming a path to the other side of the wide river.

"Shut the front door!" It was just like the one scene from her favorite movie!

J'alel's smile broadened. "You sound like your friend, the Destined One." He leapt gracefully to the first stone. "We must hurry. These stones will not remain above water for long."

Galahad followed him, both guys easily stepping from stone to stone with a little hop until they reached the other side. Owen was close behind, only Dawn and Wade remained.

"Ladies first, sunshine."

Dawn narrowed her eyes at him. He knew how she hated that nickname. She also knew he only used it to get a reaction. "Then by all means go ahead, maybe there'll be some hungry crabs waiting for you as you cross over." She couldn't resist the taunt. Verbally sparring with Wade had always been like her own form of catnip. One whiff and she was a goner.

He crossed his arms over his muscled chest. "I already apologized for hurting you, but you must know that we did what we thought best at the time. We only wanted to protect you and Aliana and Lacy!"

Dawn remained stone faced, but her hands trembled. She could see Wade's own guilt. Honestly, she had already forgiven him, but she didn't know if she could place herself in the position to have him disappoint her again.

"You can't stay pissed off forever."

She clenched her hands and lifted her chin. "And you've done nothing to show me that I can trust you again. I'm not some mindless bimbo who needs a guy to make all her decisions for her." Not letting him respond, she stepped on to the first stone then the next until she reached the other side.

Wade followed, and she swore she could hear him mumble, "I'll show you that you can believe in me still."

J'alel's silver eyes were asking Dawn what had happened, but she ignored the Elf as he led the way. It wasn't until the Elf used his longbow to pull aside a heavy curtain of green and orange ivy that she stopped caring about ignoring her knight.

Trees and stone towers had grown together, blending so seamlessly that the intricate detail of the carved stone and the rich green leaves of the trees were almost one. The towers stretched as far back as the eye could see, stone stairs leading up to wondrous homes. Even more breathtaking were the translucent, bubble-like blooms that glowed with colored orbs. Each flower was lit with the different colors of the magic living inside them, lighting up the village like small lanterns.

"Wow!" was all Dawn could say, slowly taking in everything, not wanting to miss a single detail. Her heart started to race, her blood rushing through her veins, and the tingling Merlin had taught her was associated with her Wood Nymph magic blazed to life. The magic was almost calling to her.

"Welcome to my home," J'alel said, stepping back to allow them to enter. "This is the forest village of the Elves of Red Wind forest and the Wood Nymphs."

Dawn snapped to attention. "Wood Nymphs?"

"Dawn is part Wood Nymph," Galahad told J'alel. "It cannot be a coincidence that her people are here with the elders who can lead us to the Well of Realms."

J'alel studied Dawn with heavy eyes. "I can see it now, your magic," he said softly. "The magic of this glen must be bringing forth the true strength."

The Elf led the way through the living city until they reached a wide set of connected towers held up higher in the trees than the other homes they had passed. Gold, orange and green leaves blanketed the forest floor, standing out in stark contrast to the pale gray stone stairs.

"Fantastic, we get to climb a mountain of stairs," Dawn mumbled.

The guys chuckled as they all started their journey up. The trip up was beautiful, giving Dawn a better view of the village from the high vantage. *Aliana would kill to photograph this place!* The thought sobered her a little.

"Are we sure this Well of Realms can transcend even time itself?" She'd managed to get a private moment earlier to contact Lacy using the talisman they'd created to communicate across the realms. She wanted to see how their mission was going, as well as to ask if they also gained memories of Aliana in Camelot too. If Aliana was really in Camelot, their time mirrors were even more important!

"Nothing is impossible for the Well of Realms. But it will be no simple task. I know of few who can truly harness the Well's great magic."

Galahad's jaw tightened. Even though Dawn totally thought King Arthur was a better match for her missing sister, she couldn't deny that the knight was hopelessly in love with Aliana. And he had one heck of a strong will. Merlin had taught her that magic was only as strong as the will of the person who wielded it. The white knight was most likely their best hope for controlling the Well. It was *almost* scary how in control and focused he had become.

Finally they reached the top of the curving staircase. It opened up into a beautiful rounded courtyard filled with stone statues of serene looking warriors and elegant women playing instruments. Small pools of glowing water were placed in an even pattern around the edge, each pond filled with more of the glowing bubble flowers under the crystal waters.

A soft, feminine voice broke their awestruck silence. "You have returned, J'alel."

The Elf knelt on one knee, his right hand covering his heart. "My Lady."

Galahad and the guys bowed to the short woman. Dawn followed suit, feeling all kinds of silly. But she wasn't from this realm, and they couldn't risk offending the people who could help them.

"Please rise," she commanded. "I am Lady Varaness."

Dawn took a second to look over the raven-haired, pointy-eared Elf. She was dressed like a Roman empress in draped silk of pale blue, purple and white. The stola dress had a darker colored limbus layer of silk and intricate pleated folds. It was all held in place by a white cord belt under her small bust and around her waist. The dress hung to her delicate shoulders by strands of colored jewels and a long pale blue cape draping behind her.

She was radiant. The men surrounding her were dressed much like J'alel, in long dark tunics with gold accents and belts that held long curved sabers. All of them were unimaginably beautiful, and deeply terrifying to Dawn. The power flowing from them was almost palpable.

The two women on the right had pale, freckled skin and earth brown eyes. One's hair was golden blond and the other's a light chestnut similar to Dawn's. They wore dresses similar to Varaness's but in tones of gold, brown, red and green. Tiaras of flowers were weaved into the piles of curls their hair had been styled in. They truly looked like Roman goddesses. Roman goddesses with rounded ears, not pointy ones like the Elves.

They must be Nymphs, she realized.

"It has been long since we last shared your pleasurable company, Lord Knight." The Elf woman held out her hand to him, a way too familiar glint in her stunning eyes.

Galahad took it and placed a formal kiss to the delicate flesh. "You have grown in grace and beauty, my lady."

She drew her hand back. "I was a young woman, new to adulthood, the last you saw me. I am now regent of the Red Wind forest, thanks to the grace of my elder brother, Lord Oberon."

Oberon? Oh boy, we are in real trouble now! Dawn remembered every terrifying detail Lacy and Aliana had told her about the crazy Elf king.

"And whom have you brought, Lord Galahad?"

Galahad motioned for Dawn and the others to step forward. "My lady, may I present my fellow Knights of the Round Table, Sir Owaine and Sir Gawain, and our dear friend and companion Dawn Anson?"

She walked up to Owen and Wade, looking each knight up and down several times. "I was led to believe your fellow knights had perished at the hands of the vile Mordrid and Morgana LeFay."

"We did, my lady," Owen said. "But thanks to Queen Titania's help we were reborn to finish the fight we began in Camelot."

"Yes, I have heard much about the queen's doings." She favored J'alel with a knowing look. "And I have heard much about the Destined One. Does she not travel with you?"

"That is why we are here. Aliana, the Destined One, has been taken. We now have reason to believe she may be trapped in the past, in Camelot. We wish to find the Well of Realms so we may find her."

The Elf princess stepped close to Galahad, her silver eyes searching his. Her delicate hand came up to touch his whiskered cheek. Galahad's flinch was barely noticeable, but Varaness immediately dropped her hand.

"You care very deeply for the Destined One, love her beyond measure."

He nodded slowly. "And it was because of me she was taken from us." Galahad's deep voice was even, but his hands were clenched so tightly his knuckles were white.

"I understand." Varaness stepped back. "J'alel told me all about what happened when the Destined One was last here in Avalon. Where is King Arthur? I would have thought the Golden King would be as vested in finding the Destined One."

Wade spoke up this time. "He is in the Isle of the Blessed with the rest of our friends, seeking an audience with Queen Titania. We believe she may have had a hand in Aliana's appearance in Camelot."

Varaness's purple painted lips tightened. Dawn got the feeling she wasn't the biggest fan of the Fae Queen. *Join the club, sister.*

The Elf woman's eyes jumped to Dawn like she had heard her thought. "And how is it that you have come to join these valiant warriors, fair lady?"

Dawn squared her shoulders, not liking the skeptical look she was giving her. She was already suspicious of the almost *intimate* connection between this princess and the white knight. "Aliana is my best friend. My sister in every way but blood."

"Indeed. How strange that a half blood wood Nymph is so closely linked with the Destined One."

Dawn's hazel eyes widened. "You know what I am?"

"Of course. I have lived among the wood Nymphs all my life. I will always recognize one who bears their heritage." She indicated to the two Nymphs standing behind her. "Lady Iris and Lady Isis are two of the Wood Nymph elders."

"Lady Varaness." Galahad drew the Elf's attention. "We do not have much time to spare. We need to find the Well of Realms."

The princess turned to the tallest man behind her with dark brown hair. "Summon the guardian at once." The Elf and two others bowed and left quickly. "J'alel, see to Sir Galahad and the knights, I wish a moment with Lady Dawn."

Wade took a step toward Dawn but Galahad stopped him with a hand on the shoulder. He shook his head and steered Wade toward J'alel, who led them toward the other side of the courtyard.

"I am correct to believe you have been feeling the power of these enchanted woods since your arrival, yes?" Varaness asked in a low voice when everyone around them was far enough away.

Dawn nodded.

"How long have you known the truth of your heritage?"

"Not very long. I was hoping I might learn more about the Nymph side of me while I'm in Avalon."

"There are many wood Nymphs here who would be happy to tell you all you wish to know. I fear you may be in my demesne for some time."

Dawn's anxiety dimmed the excitement of learning more about herself. "Like Galahad said, we don't have a lot of time to spare. I do have a question, Lady Varaness."

The Elf inclined her head.

"Do you know of something called 'time mirrors?'"

The woman raised her brow. "I think you should already know. You did just say you were here to gain access to the Well of Realms."

"No freaking way!" Dawn's jaw dropped. She shook her shock away. "Then that means I need to tell the knights what Lacy and I have been planning," she said more to herself than the Elf princess.

She looked to where the knights stood with J'alel, all watching the two of them. "Then you must hurry, the guardian will be along soon."

Nodding, Dawn went to the guys. "We need to talk."

Galahad frowned. "About what?"

"Look, I don't want you all to get your sword belts into a twisted mess, but before we left home, Lacy and I had been working on our own plan to find Lia." She ignored the reproachful glares the guys all fixed on her. "We found out about these things called time mirrors. They can let anyone see into the past or future. In some cases, you can even talk to people through them."

Owen stepped closer. "That would be a powerful tool to possess."

Wade crossed his toned arms. "Why are you only telling us now? What were you and Lacy planning to do once you found these time mirrors?"

Dawn gave Wade a *duh* stare. "Lady Varaness just told me that the water from the Well of Realms *is* the time mirrors. From what Lacy and I read, we may be able to at least figure out how to use them to contact Aliana, if not bring her home!"

The guys reeled back.

"Lacy and I were going to try to use them at the same time. Maybe together we will be strong enough."

A door on the opposite side of the courtyard opened before the guys could get a word out. Lady Varaness and the two Nymphs, flanked by a giant Elf dressed in all black with a wicked looking sword made their way to Dawn and the knights.

Varaness strode forward with all the grace and authority one would expect of a ruler.

"Why do you wish to gain access to the Well of Realms?" the Elf man, with jet black hair asked, his voice aged and wise.

"We are on a quest to save the seven realms from the dark wizard, Mordrid," Galahad stated. "We must find the Destined One, Aliana, and find a way to bring her back to us."

"Are you implying you have lost the Destined One?" the giant Elf boomed.

"She was kidnapped by Mordrid," Dawn said, boldly stepping forward. "And now we think she may have been sent back to Camelot, in the past, by Queen Titania."

None of the council openly showed any astonishment at the news, but Dawn could almost feel the shock of the two Nymphs.

"And what purpose would the Fae Queen, consort of our Lord Oberon, have for doing such a thing?" another Elf asked.

"In exchange for a way to find Excalibur, in the Isle of the Blessed, Aliana, the Destined One, made a bargain with the queen. It is the only reason we can think for her doing such a thing." Owen explained what happened in the Isle and the deals that had been struck.

"And the Fae Queen now possesses the sword of the fire Elves?" another of the Elves asked.

"Yes," Galahad answered.

Iris stepped to Varaness's side and asked, "Even should you gain access, there is no guarantee you will be able to harness its great powers."

"We understand," Wade replied.

"I may know of a way to use it," she said to Varaness, hoping she appeared confident and not the tangle of nervous mess she felt like she was. "I know about the Well and the time mirrors."

Some kind of silent communication passed between the Elf princess and the others with her. Suddenly, Varaness nodded. "Knights of the Round Table, we have long allied our forces with that of the Golden King's. Elves and Nymphs are creatures of the light. The darkness Mordrid would spread could spell our doom."

Varaness's eyes fell on Dawn. "To prove worthy of using the Well, here in Avalon, the one who would wield its powers must first defeat its guardian."

Dawn's brows pinched together. "I don't understand."

Isis spoke, nodding to the Elf in all black. "Trial by combat. You or your champion must best the guardian."

Well isn't that a kick in the knees? Fantastic, how the heck am I supposed to beat an Elf? Dawn's hands started to tremble, but she clenched them tight.

"Do you accept?" the dark-haired Elf asked.

"Choose your champion!" Wade hissed in her ear.

Damn, why didn't I put that together? "I accept, and I choose Sir Galahad as my champion."

Galahad stepped forward. "I am ready to face this challenge."

Varaness's eyes seemed to light with satisfaction. "Very well."

The Elf in black stepped forward, standing in front of Galahad. "I am Marius, Guardian of the Well of Realms." Both men locked in an epic stare down. "I have heard much of your skill as a warrior, legendary knight. Be warned, I am no easy opponent."

The white knight's gaze never wavered. "And I have no other purpose right now, other than finding the Destined One. I will not fail her."

Dawn could almost hear the silent "again" he didn't say.

Lady Varaness clapped her hands once, the sound vibrating around them. "Then it is settled. We will have the battle arena prepared."

Dawn looked back at Galahad. He was talking quietly with J'alel and the knights. She made a wish then, that the white knight would be as strong as he appeared. Like it or not, he was their only chance to find Aliana right now.

14

Guin, Vira, Delphina and Morgana came running into the stable yard as the horses slowed and everyone dismounted.

"Thank the gods, you're back!" Guin threw herself into Lancelot's arms and kissed him fiercely.

Vira ran into Galahad's arms. "I'm so glad you are safe, big brother." Galahad kissed her head and stroked her hair before Vira pulled away and came over to Aliana.

The girl hugged Aliana, and tears suddenly formed in her eyes. How was she going to just let Vira die? She could still remember the hurt she'd felt from Galahad when he had told her about losing his family and then his little sister, before things had blown up between them.

Delphina talked quietly with Arthur, her fingers lightly tracing down his arm. He smiled at her with such fondness Aliana's lungs tightened with pain.

Vira pulled out of her arms and stepped back as Morgana came to Aliana. "I am relieved you are all well."

Aliana smiled, searching her eyes. She saw none of the darkness, evil or hate that she had spent months trying to fight against. Her gut told her Morgana hadn't turned against them.

Not yet.

Aliana reached out and hugged the Sorceress. Morgana hesitated then returned it. "I'm sure Merlin wishes he could have ridden back with us."

Morgana pulled back, her lips wavering. "I know. He sent me a message earlier this morning. He is making sure that our dead return home safely so they can be buried properly, with the honor they deserve."

Aliana looked around the small-enclosed area, noticing more guards than usual hovering on the tall walls and by the entrances. Come to think of it, there had been a lot of men than usual patrolling the streets of Camelot. "What's with all the added guards?"

Morgana's face fell. "A few servants have claimed to have seen two strangers roaming the castle." She shook her head. "We have found no sign of them, but the queen has doubled the guards to be sure."

Aliana nodded as Delphina approached. Morgana didn't seem too worried, and neither did Vira or Delphina, so Aliana let it go for now. The Fae bowed her head to Aliana as Morgana stepped back and went to her cousin and Gawain.

"Welcome back, my lady. I thank the Fae Queen you have returned, uninjured."

Aliana knew it was just a figure of speech, but Delphina's mention of Titania still made her uncomfortable. That and the guilt that was ripping at her for kissing Arthur.

Delphina motioned for Aliana to head toward the castle. "The queen and I have had a bath prepared for you. I am sure you wish to wash away the angst of your battle."

Aliana followed the Fae girl up to her room. She was surprised to see Igraine waiting by the fireplace with a large copper tub filled with steaming water.

The two girls curtsied to the queen. "I thought you would appreciate the comfort of being clean and a new dress." She pointed to the pale purple dress hanging over the changing screen.

"Thank you." Aliana turned to Delphina. "Both of you."

Delphina smiled brightly. "I can stay and attend to you, my lady, if that is your wish."

Aliana shook her head. "I will be fine on my own."

They left, telling Aliana that a late dinner was being prepared.

As soon as the door shut, Dagg sprang from her wrist. "You don't even need to say it."

Aliana smirked. "I'm glad you haven't forgotten my rules."

The silver Dragon smiled broadly. "Yes. Though I hardly think it's fair that you threaten to kick me out for snoring, when it is you that snores!"

"I do not!" Aliana cried in mock outrage. She playfully threw a small towel at the Dragon as he zoomed behind the changing screen. Aliana quickly undressed and blissfully sank into the warm water. She sank all the way under, letting the feel of the water soak into her pores and through her dirty hair.

Breaking the surface, Aliana ran her hands through the tangles of her long dark chocolate hair wishing desperately for a good conditioner. She opened her magical senses to see if anyone with magic was close by. Sure she was alone, she used a pulse of bubbly pink magic to smooth out her hair and another to clean it and her whole body.

"Aliana," Dagg growled from behind the screen.

"What?" She shrugged and lay back, relaxing. "Why shouldn't I use my magic to get clean?"

Her guardian sighed heavily. "Your magic is meant for more than beauty regimes!"

Aliana rolled her eyes. Her magic was hers to use as she saw fit, but a small part of her conscience said he was right. "I won't do it again," she lamented.

"Thank you."

Dagg stayed silent as Aliana relaxed. Her magic sense still opened, she felt cool droplets of magic like rain against her magical core. She gasped at the tickling sensation. She was feeling the magic of the water element, she just knew it!

"How?" she asked her Dragon a second later. "Back in London, when Merlin was first training me to connect with the elements, I couldn't touch the water element!"

"Your powers are growing and with that your ability to tap into the elements you couldn't before." Dagg's answer seemed too simple, until he continued. "And connecting to the earth element is not like what you do with the air or with the energy elements. Remember you only connected to the fire element's magic after you got very angry with Merlin and me."

Aliana remembered. Merlin had insisted that she had the ability to connect with all five magic elements, but she had refused to have anything to do with the fire's power.

Back then, none of the guys knew about the explosion that had killed her parents, and now she understood why that hellish fire had scared her so much, why she had had nightmares for two long years about it.

She felt Dagg's silent question in her mind. "Even knowing what I do now, I still don't think I can connect with the fire element's magic."

"You cannot keep denying your connection to it. Remember what happened just after we got to your home in Charleston."

Dagg didn't need to remind her about the magical sparring session with Merlin that had gone horribly wrong. The Druid had used his fire attacks against her and she had lost control of her magic, hurting herself as it surrounded her and raged out of control.

"Speaking of magic, what did you mean earlier, when we broke camp? The theory you're not keen on telling me." His reluctance flooded her. "Just say it, Dragon boy."

"You were thinking about Merlin and Morgana's souls mate bond, and the ones you share with Arthur and Galahad."

Aliana nodded, even knowing he couldn't see her through the screen.

"I have no proof, and no explanation, but I believe there to be more to the bonds you share with them. I don't believe it's anything evil, but I have never known one person to share such strong bonds with two people."

Aliana hugged her knees to her naked chest. "You mean they're not real? Just another side effect of my freak magic?" She hated the bitterness she could taste on her words.

"No, that's not it. I felt the strength of the bonds. When you opened your shields to me days ago, I saw them. There is no faking what you share."

He sounded so sure, and he certainly knew more about those kinds of things than she did, but…Aliana splashed the warm water on her face, scrubbing away the one tear that leaked from her eye.

"I'm sorry to upset you further."

Aliana shot a hard look at the screen. "Just because you can feel my emotions doesn't mean you always have to."

Dagg sighed heavily. "I think we need to tell the knights a little more of why we are here. We have the book, but we have found nothing about the Grail or a way to find it. We need their help. Camelot's achieves and libraries are famed for all the knowledge they contain."

Aliana took the subject change as an olive branch. "You heard the queen. She said we can't reveal anything to the knights."

"She said we can't reveal the future, or the fact we are from the future. But telling them of our quest here…"

Dagg's words hung in the air. He was right. "But I don't want to reveal anything about my magic. As much as I wish it won't happen, if or when Morgana betrays everyone, her knowing my true strength could give her and Mordrid an advantage."

"I agree."

Aliana swirled her hand around the water.

"I don't want to worry about that now." Aliana focused again on the water element, relaxing again as the magic came back to her. Aliana cupped her hands with the water and blew gently. Spheres of water rose up and hovered in front of her like glass ornaments. Giggling, she twirled around a finger and they started to dance for her. "This is so cool!"

A knock on her door startled her, breaking her concentration. The spheres burst and the water fell back into her tub.

"Who is it?" Aliana asked, pulling her knees up and wrapping her arms around her chest.

"It's me, Aliana," Vira called back. "May I come in?"

"One second." Aliana got out of the tub, grabbed the heavy cloth the queen had left and wrapped it around her body. "Come in."

The door opened and Vira slipped in, closing it behind her. "Would you like me to help you dress for dinner?"

Aliana shifted, uncomfortable with Vira seeing her naked. Not even Lacy or Dawn had seen her totally naked! "I'll be fine, thank you."

Vira's eyes dropped to the ground, her hands folded in front of her.

"But I wouldn't mind the company while I get dressed."

Vira brightened and sat down in the chair by the fireplace as Aliana stepped toward her changing area.

"Dagg, I hope you've found a different hiding place!"

He chuckled in her mind. *"I have. I am under the bed."*

Aliana dried off and pulled on a pair of modern panties she had magically created days ago. She noticed Dagg hadn't said anything about her using her magic for that purpose. She answered Vira's questions of what had happened during the fight.

"I heard you even saved Raven from getting hurt."

Aliana stepped out from behind the screen. She was trying to tighten the strings on the back of her dress, but they were proving difficult.

"Let me help." Vira didn't wait for her response. She came up and efficiently laced the dress, pulling it just enough to fit without being too tight.

"Thank you. And I wouldn't say I saved him. I'm sure the knights wouldn't have let it get him. I just got there first." Aliana picked up the matching belt for the dress and secured it around her waist. "Who told you anyway?"

Vira turned pale. "Um…"

Aliana tilted her head, searching the girl's young face for the truth.

"I…pried it out of my brother."

Aliana heard the lie, but felt like there was more to it. "Are you sure?"

Vira nodded vigorously. "We should really go down to dinner now!"

Aliana frowned but allowed the girl her secret. She had her own after all.

Dinner was quicker than usual, though it was still filled with the knights all talking about the battle and how they had all fought to defeat it. It was the same bragging and teasing that was common of the dinners she had with her knights, back in her time. Loneliness set in, but then Igraine's hand touched her arm and she felt a little better.

Aliana returned to her room as soon as dinner was done. "I just realized, Dagg, how have you been eating since we got here?"

The Dragon smirked from his perch above one of her pillows. "I've been hunting a few times."

"Hunting?"

"I am a Dragon, Aliana. We do hunt for our meals on occasion. Though I admit some hunting may have been in the castle kitchens."

Aliana snorted a laugh and sat down on her bed. She held up her hand, willing her ruby glove to appear. Concentrating, she imagined the book lying on the bed. A soft weight hit the bed as the book appeared in a flash of dark pink. With the fire still burning in her fireplace, Aliana flipped open the book, got comfortable on the bed and continued to read through the pages until her eyes could no longer stay open.

Rays of sunlight hit her eyes, and Aliana moaned, stretching her legs before pulling the blanket up over her head.

"You need to get up, Aliana." Dagg's own, ageless voice sounded like even he was still trying to wake up.

"Why?" she asked, still buried under her blanket.

"Because we're about to have a visitor."

Aliana flipped the covers back and looked at the Dragon through squinted eyes still trying to adjust to the light.

A soft knock came before her door opened. "Pardon, my lady, are you awake?"

Aliana recognized the voice of Clara, the servant girl who came to check on her every morning. "I am."

Aliana sat up and stretched, then ran her fingers through her hair. Her magic from last night seemed to be doing its job, because her hair was still tangle free.

"You slept in your clothes, my lady?"

Aliana looked down at herself. "I guess I did." She looked at the book still open by her pillow and quickly snapped it closed. Her eyes fell on her visible ruby. Aliana pulled her sleeve forward to cover it. "I must have fallen asleep reading last night."

Clara seemed not to notice her sudden behavior. That's when she noticed the burnt-orange-colored dress in the girls' hands.

"What's that, Clara?"

Clara laid the dress out on the bed. "The queen sent it for you."

Aliana stared at the dress. She was grateful, but she couldn't understand why the queen was being so generous. "Please thank the queen for me, but really, she's already done so much for me. I can't accept this."

Clara shook her head. "Her Highness was quite insistent." Clara leaned in closer to Aliana. "Besides, these are her old gowns. I think she is only pleased to see them worn again."

Aliana sighed. "Has there been any other news of Merlin or the knights?"

Clara nodded. "The king received word that they will be here before midday. He also asked that you meet him in the throne room at your earliest convenience."

Clara left the room and Aliana quickly hid her ruby behind her veil again and returned the book to its magical depths. She changed quickly, but instead of going to see Arthur she made her way through the halls to the record room that led to Morgana's secret room. She would see Arthur after she satisfied the need to know if anyone had gone into the room after she had. The hall was empty again, and so was the hidden magic lab.

It reinforced her belief that Morgana *hadn't* been the one to send the Manticore after the people in Camelot. But then who? Mordrid? *"Dagg, can you go find the queen? I need to speak to her. I want to see if I can get her thoughts on who could have attacked Camelot. And I want to let her know that we're going to tell the guys more about why I'm here."*

"I can, but I do not like the thought of leaving you alone."

"Dagg, I've been wandering around alone several times. I'll be fine. I promise, I'm going straight to Arthur." His reluctance was heavy in her mind, but he changed to his true form and disappeared through the door.

She exited the room, this time without Galahad and the others catching her. She stopped to gaze out one of the windows. It overlooked the sea and its crashing waves. Aliana opened the window and breathed in the briny breeze. Her mind wandered, so many different questions rolling around that needed answers. Not the least of which was how her friends were doing. She missed her magic sisters, Lacy and Dawn.

A burly, sweaty hand appeared out of nowhere and clamped over her mouth. Cold, sharp steel pressed against her neck. "Scream, an' I slit y'ur throat."

Aliana fought back out of reflex. Her hands gripped the one on her mouth and the one holding the weapon against her. The knife bit into her skin and the hand around her mouth clamped down with a force so hard she knew she'd have bruises.

"Donna test me, gurl." His hot breath was like foul smelling acid against her ear. His voice was heavily accented, like a strange form of Leyon's Scottish brogue, but vile as opposed to the smart and smooth voice of the knight.

"Y'ur gonna come with me, nice an' quiet."

Her chest heaved as she struggled to calm her racing adrenaline. She jerked her shoulders again, but she couldn't get free.

"If y'u donna stop strugglin my friend will kill the li'ttl pretty one y'u all seem so fond of." Aliana immediately stilled. Vira!

She forced herself to relax enough to call out to her guardian. *"Dagg, help! One of those intruders has a knife to my throat."*

She felt his anger and the swell of magic through their bond. *"I am coming!"*

"No! There's another one that has Vira! You need to tell the queen and go save Vira!"

"You are my charge, not her!"

"And she can't protect herself like I can! Tell the queen, save Vira and send Arthur and the knights! He wants me to go with him, that means he doesn't want to kill me! Please, Dagg!"

His loud growl filled her head. *"Stay calm, do what you must to protect yourself, even if it means exposing your magic!"*

"Les' go." The brute pulled her back from the window. "If my friend donna get my signal, he *will* kill her."

The knife eased on her throat and Aliana's training took over. She pulled at the blade-wielding hand, pushed her body back and jabbed her elbow into his soft gut at the same time. He cursed as she slipped from his arms and turned to get out of his reach. Her foot caught the edge of a loose stone on the floor and she stumbled. The brute's hand smacked her into the wall, her head cracking against the pale surface as she cried out in aching pain.

15

Stars burst behind her eyes, her vision swam and spun as something wet trickled down her temple. The man jerked her back into his arms, his hand clamping down on her mouth again and the other wrapping around her stomach. The long knife pressed harshly against her ribs, just under her heaving chest. She tried to clear her mind, to grasp her magic, but she couldn't focus enough to even touch the bubbling sparks.

She heard the sound of tearing fabric and felt the cold of the blade cut into her skin. She moaned behind his hand, the sound barely registering as she felt him force her through the deserted hall and down a set of stairs she couldn't remember seeing before. She felt Dagg's foggy presence roll through her, her head clearing along with her vision. Light pounded her eyes as her captor pulled them out into a small courtyard. She saw an open gate, one that she remembered led to the stables.

With a clearer head, Aliana grabbed his thick sweaty wrists again and tried to break free. But he had her off balance and stumbling side to side so she couldn't get a strong enough stance to shake him off.

"Let her go!" The roar of Arthur's fury was almost as loud as the sounds of pounding feet, jingling chainmail and the hiss of drawn swords.

The brute gripped her tighter, the knife sawing into her skin as he turned them both in circles, his panicked breath puffing against her. Arthur, Lancelot, Gawain and dozens of soldiers surrounded them. Their weapons were drawn, all in fighting stances, watching for their moment to strike. But she was still his human shield. None of them would be able to attack him as long as he had her.

She felt the man's hand slip and Aliana bit down hard on his fingers. He cried out, but his grip didn't loosen. Instead his fingers gripped her throat like a vice. She choked and struggled, trying to draw breath. The little calm she had managed to gain shattered.

He repeated his threat from earlier, his voice barking loud. "Y'ur gonna let us walk out'a here or the li'ttl one y'u all so keen on is gonna die."

Arthur's anger was a living entity in the open yard. The king snarled at the man. "You mean by this fool's hand?"

Two more men appeared, dragging a bleeding, limp man between them.

She relaxed for a half second. Vira was safe. Her eyes flickered up. She caught sight of Galahad atop one of the walls that surrounded them, his bow trained on them.

The man jerked her side to side again. He looked at the warriors who clearly wanted to kill him, then to his partner's dead body. "Dosnna matter. Y'u still canna harm me without hurtin this pretty one."

He pushed the knife harder into her ribs. She couldn't hold back her cry as blood started to flow around the blade.

Arthur took a threatening step forward, Excalibur trained on them. "This is your last warning. Let her go or you will beg for death before I send you to hell with your pathetic friend."

Aliana had seen Arthur angry before, but this was a level she had never thought him capable of. Her eyes flicked back to Galahad. He pointed to his left bicep.

What was he doing? She had a psycho trying to kidnap her! Now really wasn't the time for Galahad to show off his muscles!

The brute's left arm tightened around her waist again, the blade slicing even deeper into her skin. The white knight touched his arm again as she hissed in pain and he drew his bow. Her eyes widened as she realized his intent.

Arthur ordered him to release her again, distracting the brute as Galahad took aim. Her blood sang, her nerves tingled and shook as everything slowed. She never took her eyes from Galahad, trying to force stillness through her screaming tight muscles.

Galahad released the arrow. Her heart jackknifed, afraid for a second that he would miss and hit her instead. Time sped up again and the arrow sliced into the man's arm. The knife fell from his hand as he jerked, his grip loosening. Aliana grabbed the hand around her throat with both hands and pushed her hips back, flipping her would-be kidnapper over her shoulder. He landed in a heap, like the last man she'd done that to.

Arthur and the knights rushed them, Aliana stumbling into the king's outstretched arms. She buried her face in his neck and inhaled his scent, calming a little as it surrounded her. Her throat ached, her lungs felt like they were going to burst. She gripped the bleeding wound under her breasts, whimpering in pain.

His arms tightened. She could feel the pommel of Excalibur pressing into her, but it didn't hurt her. "Seize him!"

Aliana peeked back at the brute, yelling in pain as he struggled against the soldiers that held him. Lancelot and Gawain glared down at him, their swords still held ready to skewer the guy. With a hard jerk the man broke free, grabbing one of the soldier's swords.

Aliana tensed and gasped as he rushed forward like a deranged man. The knights moved forward, and then Arthur's hand was suddenly cupping the back of her head blocking her vision, his own head pressing down on hers as he cradled her close. "Don't look," he ordered.

She heard the man's gurgled cries and the sound of lots of steel pushing through flesh. She tried to look again but Arthur's grip was gentle, yet unyielding. "Some things, you do not need to see."

She heard the body drop to the ground and looked over Arthur's shoulders to see Galahad rushing through archway, barreling toward her.

Arthur's grip relaxed as he turned and gently placed her in Galahad's arms. "Take her to the healers' chambers. Mother will be there waiting!" Galahad nodded sharply and herded her inside the castle. She turned to look back at the knights, to see the dead body of the man who had harmed her, but all she saw was the guys gathered around him, and Arthur's last heavy, molten look before she was taken completely from the courtyard.

"How badly are you hurt?" Galahad sounded strained.

"I…I'm not sure," she croaked. It hurt to talk; her esophagus felt like it was swelling and throbbing. She started to tremble and her legs shook as Galahad took her through another unfamiliar door and up a few stairs. Her hand pressed harder against the still bleeding cut, trying to call her magic to stop the flow.

She moaned again, the pain in her head and body too much to focus enough. "*Dagg!*"

"I'm waiting for you in the healers' room!"

Galahad stopped and turned to face her with eyes wild with worry. Aliana sagged back against the stone wall, Galahad following her movements. His hand gripped her waist steadying her as his eyes roamed over her. His fingers stroked her cheek, just below the blood trail from where her head had hit the wall. His fingers carefully tilted her head to the side and looked at the angry marks she felt on her throat. Then brushed over the ones around her mouth.

"When I find the person who ordered this, I will kill them with my own hands!" he raged.

Aliana trembled again and tears burned her eyes. She opened her mouth to tell him to calm down but his silenced her first.

His warm lips claimed hers, gently at first then his tongue slipping into her open mouth with a desperate passion. He kissed and kissed her like he was trying to assure himself that she was still there, in his arms and safe. A dam of emotions burst inside her and Aliana gripped his leather vest and flexed arm as she kissed him back with all the aching loneliness and rekindled feelings that had been stirring in her since she arrived. She forgot about everything and let the rolling emotions anchor her to this world and not the one of fear and pain she had felt since that guy first grabbed her.

Galahad pressed into her, caging her against the wall. She cried out in shocked pain as he pressed into her bleeding wound.

He pulled back with wide eyes and looked down at the pulsing cut. "Damn! Forgive me, I…"

She tried to tell him it was okay, but he swept her up in his arms before she could speak. They were up the winding stairs in minutes then rushing down a hall toward the waiting queen, a tear-stained Vira, and an anxious Delphina and Guin.

Igraine took command as soon as they reached her. "Set her down on the bench, quickly, Sir Galahad."

Galahad entered the room and did as told, setting her down on the long table with exquisite care.

The queen followed, grabbing a rag from a bowl of water and wrung it out. "Vira, Delphina, go to my rooms and get her a fresh dress." Both girls disappeared.

Galahad moved to her other side, gently pressing her back onto the table as she tried to sit up. "Stay down, Aliana."

Igraine dabbed the cloth on the long cut on her ribs. Aliana hissed in pain, her eyes squeezing shut as a few tears escaped.

"Aliana!" Galahad's hand gripped hers and she squeezed back, hard.

"Sir Galahad, I need you to leave."

The knight glowered at the queen silently.

Igraine's sunlight eyes narrowed. "Now, Sir Galahad."

"Why?" he asked, his voice rough.

"Because I need to remove her dress to treat the wound, and I cannot do that with you hovering."

Aliana felt her face heat. She squeezed Galahad's hand drawing his eyes back to hers. She nodded once and let go of his hand. Guin came to his side and pulled the hulking knight until he finally relented and let himself be led from the room.

Guin shut the heavy wooden door. "I swear, he can be so pig-headed sometimes!"

Igraine took Aliana's hand and gave her a wadded piece of cloth. "I need you to hold this against your ribs, to stop the bleeding." Aliana did as ordered, moaning again.

"Guinevere, you and Delphina *have* to keep the men calm and outside until I've finished!" The redhead slipped from the room.

As soon as the door closed, Dagg shot down from the rafters, landing at her side in an instant. His silver scaled hot claws touched her face and she felt the immediate rush of his healing magic enter her body.

"That's enough, DragonLord." The queen's voice held an edge of authority that even Dagg couldn't deny. His powers drew back.

Her head stopped spinning, her vision was clearer and the headache that had formed disappeared.

Igraine gently wiped away the dried blood from her temple. "We cannot heal her too much with magic. The salves and potions I have will do enough." She set the rag back in the water bowl and helped Aliana sit up. Her entire body still ached and she felt cold and shaky. Shock, she realized with a numb thought.

The queen's eyes flared with magic. "The three of us need to have a long talk."

She met her guardian's glowing purple eyes. She felt his worry and gnawing guilt for leaving her side.

"It's not your fault, Dagg." Her throat felt marginally better. The swelling and pulsing pain had receded, but the external bruises still stung. At least it didn't hurt to talk anymore.

The queen chimed in. "Of course not," she said kindly. "I'm sorry to say but your dress will need to be cut off." She pulled out a strange looking pair of scissors.

Aliana looked back at her Dragon, trying to smile at him. She wanted to ease her friend's despair as much as she could.

He turned his back as the queen cut away the top of the dress and sleeves. Aliana flushed with embarrassment as Igraine helped her out of the tattered cloth. She pressed another towel into Aliana's hand, which she used to cover her exposed chest. Aliana hissed as the queen cleaned the cut on her head.

"How did you save Vira?" she asked, trying to distract herself from the stinging.

"I was already with the queen when you called to me," Dagg said, his wings covering his eyes as well. "We were close to her chambers, and we got there just as the man made an attempt to grab Lady Sophvira."

"Galahad was furious," the queen added. "He killed the man on the spot. Not that he didn't deserve to die. He would have died anyway, by Camelot's laws. Even Delphina looked ready to murder him."

Aliana's eyes went wide. "He did?"

"The man had drawn a weapon, Galahad acted in self-defense." Dagg's assurance calmed her a bit, but she still worried.

"Wait, if you and the queen were there with Delphina and Galahad, were the others there? Do they…does he…did they see you?" Her guardian's hesitation told her all she needed to know. "They did!" Her blood raced, her adrenaline spiking again as panic made it hard to breathe. Everything felt like it was spinning faster and faster out of her control.

Dagg wheeled around, his eyes glowing. "There was no other choice. We had no other way of getting the knights to you in time. I had to reveal myself and tell him where you were."

"You were the one who was so gung-ho about *not* telling anyone in the first place!" Aliana clutched the sheet tighter to her chest. At least dealing with this news was making it easier to forget about Galahad's amazing kiss a moment ago. "Turn back around!" she snapped.

He did so with a low growl. "It was the only way to get to you in time."

"Your DragonLord is correct. I do not have the connection to you that he does. It was the only way to know where you were. If Merlin had been here, maybe it could have been done differently."

Aliana's shoulders slumped. "But, what if all of them knowing about Dagg has changed the course of history?"

The queen looked at her sharply, her hands pausing as she cleaned the long cut on her abdomen. "Time is one of the greatest mysteries of the realms. Many have fallen, even gone mad trying to outwit it."

Aliana said nothing. The fact was, not one of the guys remembered knowing her here in Camelot. What other explanation was there?

As if reading her mind, Igraine spoke up. "I have walked the realms and this earth for centuries. There are many thoughts among magic kind about tampering with time. Most believe and accept time is largely unchangeable."

"If that's the case, then why don't I just tell the guys everything?"

The queen's pale gold eyes snapped up to hers. "Because even I do not know the answer to time, or know what danger such information may bring. You worry so about affecting the timeline, here in Camelot; telling them could do just that." The corners of her mouth tightened, tiny wrinkles making the queen appear older than Aliana had ever seen her look. "Trust me when I say the consequences of meddling in the toils of time is not one you want to bear. Even if the future is set, knowing what is to come, knowing your own fate and that of your loved ones is a terrible burden to bear. Who wouldn't be tempted to change fate if they thought it would be for the betterment of someone they loved?"

Aliana closed her eyes as the queen rubbed a thick salve over her cut and wrapped it tightly with bandages. Soothing warmth flared around the cut and the pain lessened immediately. She relaxed just a little more, her heart rate returning to normal.

Igraine opened another jar of floral smelling salve. She gently rubbed it on the bruises on her neck and around her mouth. "There are many ways to tamper with events, and people's memories, without changing history."

Aliana pondered that wisdom until a sharp knock came from the door.

"Dagg, hide!" Her guardian frowned but moved up to the rafters.

Igraine shook her head. "I think it's too late for that." Dagg mumbled his agreement as the queen said, "Come in."

Vira opened the door at the queen's permission. Aliana spread the cloth covering her naked chest a little more as she caught a glimpse of Arthur and Galahad. Guin and Delphina were next to them, both apparently doing as they were told and keeping them calm and outside. Igraine took the dress from Vira.

The small girl smiled a wet, wobbly, relieved smile before closing the door.

Dagg returned to her side. "Aliana, the queen is right. We…I have only been assuming that the king and his men do not need to know all about us."

The dark-haired girl sighed heavily. "Can we take that chance?"

"I believe," Igraine started, "that you would be wise to see how things proceed from now. They now know of your guardian. I would recommend revealing more of yourself to them. Your purpose here, at least." The queen stepped back, offering her hand to Aliana so she could stand. Aliana looked pointedly at Dagg who turned his back and moved his wings to hide his eyes again.

"We were already thinking about that. It's why we were going to find you before…well, you know." Aliana slid off the table, her legs wobbling, the long cut on her chest throbbing again.

Aliana steadied herself, clutching what remained of her dress and the cloth that covered her chest. Igraine held up the mauve dress she had worn when she first arrived in Camelot. Blushing madly, Aliana let Igraine help her into it, only wincing a few times.

"I still don't get why the guys have no memory of me. If the queen's right, they should have remembered me when Merlin restored their memories in London. I know Galahad would have remembered me, at least."

Dagg turned back as the queen tightened the strings to her dress. *"I do think the queen may have given us a clue to that answer; we just need to figure it out."*

Aliana ran her fingers through her hair as loud knocks sounded against the door.

"Mother, what is happening in there?" Arthur's worry tangled with his loud demanding question.

The queen sighed, shaking her head. "I suppose we have tried their patience too long."

Aliana's mouth turned up in a slow smile as Igraine slid back the bolt on the door.

16

Everyone swarmed the room at once, Arthur and Galahad making it to her side first. Both knights seemed focused on the bruises on her throat. Arthur's large hand came up, tracing the edges of the tender skin around her mouth.

Aliana looked between the two brooding men battling for her attention.

"You can both see she is well." Igraine's hands appeared on both guys' shoulders, prying them back from Aliana. "Let the girl have some room to breathe."

Gawain came to her side when Galahad and Arthur stepped back. Aliana smiled at him, his concerned eyes so much like her best friend's. She reached out and hugged him. He hesitantly hugged her back, his arm careful not to hold her too tight. "Not many women are able to keep themselves calm enough to do what you did. You were very brave."

"Lucky Galahad is such a good shot."

"Lucky you have a small Dragon to warn us of danger."

"About that…him…um."

Lancelot crossed his arms, "Yes, what about him?"

Gawain snorted. "We all knew you were hiding something. Who would have guessed it was a DragonLord?"

Arthur cleared his throat. "I'd like to know why you have a Dragon companion, as well as his name."

Dagg jumped from the table hovering beside his aching charge. "I am Daggerhorne, Aliana's guardian."

"Why would you need a Dragon guardian, Aliana?" Guin asked, her brown eyes lit with curiosity.

"That's a very long story and one I think best left for when it doesn't hurt to breathe." There was no hiding her reason for being here now, but she wanted to talk to Merlin about it first.

Gawain raised a mocking brow. "Well, this was certainly one way to start Camelot's anniversary celebrations."

Everyone laughed a little and the tension eased back. Aliana hugged the girls and Morgana, who had apparently come just after Guin had left the room. She didn't miss the blond-haired Sorceress's long pensive gaze at Dagg and her.

Aliana again wished Lacy was here to get her opinion. Her half Fae sister was always so good with judging people. Thoughts of Lacy segued into thoughts of Dawn. God how Aliana missed her best friends and magical sisters!

A knock on the open door drew their attention.

A short soldier stood just outside the room. "Sire, forgive the interruption." He bowed deeply.

Arthur nodded. "What is it?"

The soldier lowered his eyes, shifting from foot to foot with anxiousness. "Lord Merlin and the other knights have returned. They said they have urgent news."

Arthur dismissed the man with a nod of his head. He and the guys left the room, Morgana following.

Guin spoke first. "I wonder what is wrong."

Aliana wanted to know too.

"You need to rest," Igraine implored.

Aliana's hand covered the cut below her chest. The aching wasn't too bad now, but she was still having difficulty talking deep breaths. Vira and Delphina led her back to her room. She'd have to find out later what was happening.

Aliana winced as she took a too-deep breath. Her wounds were healing remarkably fast, but the cut on her ribs still hurt. Aliana suspected the rapid healing was because of the queen's salves. She needed to find Merlin and see what his urgent news was. She hadn't gotten the chance last night. Instead she had been stuck in bed trying *not* to think about Galahad's kiss and what she was going to say to all of them about herself and her quest.

"Merlin," she called out, knocking on the door to his room.

The door creaked open. Merlin looked confused for a second then motioned for her to come in. The room was small, filled with wooden benches, colored jars and so many different kinds of hanging herbs and flowers it was like stepping into a potpourri factory.

"What is this place?" She caught sight of several maps hanging on a far wall.

"This is my workshop. Morgana and I do much of our research and magic in here."

Aliana turned back to him. "I don't understand? Magic, your magic and mine, comes from inside us. We don't need potions to use our powers."

Merlin shook his head. "True, but there are times that it is far wiser to have magical concoctions at your fingertips. Magic may be accepted in the kingdom, but there are still many who fear and hate it. Openly using magic in front of the populace is not wise. And a great wielder of magic knows that it takes more than just our own pure magic to defeat our enemies or heal people."

"Oh." Aliana hadn't even thought of that, but then, short of the day she was in the market, she hadn't really interacted with too many people outside the knights and the girls. But why had Merlin never spoken to her of any of this? It was almost the opposite of what he had first taught her about magic.

The Druid smiled ruefully. "I am sure you are grateful for the salves that have been using to treat your wounds."

"Yeah, I am, but Dagg could have healed me just as well. I've even healed myself in the past too."

"I have never met one who is able to heal themselves." He shook his head, huffing a laugh. "I should not be surprised. How are you feeling? Everyone is talking about what happened."

Aliana's hand went to the cut on her ribs that she had rebandaged this morning. "Better. I still can't figure out what they wanted with me or how they even knew to find me here in Camelot."

Merlin leaned back against a table. "Could it be tied to your quest?"

Aliana shrugged. "No one here knows about my quest but you. Delphina knows I was sent here, but I didn't give her any specific details." And the Fae girl didn't seem the traitor kind. She clearly cared too much about the people here.

But then again, so did Morgana.

"Perhaps it is just a coincidence." Merlin didn't sound like he believed that any more than she did.

Aliana shook her head. "There is a new problem. Dagg had to reveal himself to the others yesterday."

Merlin didn't look surprised. "Yes. The topic has also been quite the source of debate."

Aliana twisted her fingers together. "Do they hate me for not telling them?"

Merlin laughed. "No. They would never hate you. But you certainly surprised them. Galahad, however, spoke with me at length about it. He was very irritable when I wouldn't give him all the information he wanted." The Druid was grinning like he enjoyed annoying the white knight.

"How do I handle this? What do I tell him?"

Merlin stroked his chin again. "The queen told me of your conversation. I share her thoughts about the working of the timeline.

But, I think you should listen to your instincts. One thing I have learned with magic is to trust what they tell you."

Aliana chewed her cheek. She needed to think about what her gut was telling her. "What was the news you brought yesterday?"

Merlin straightened. "As we were returning to Camelot, we came upon a village that said they were being haunted by a dark spirit. We found no evidence of it, and I felt no trace of magic. But this is not the first report of a malevolent spirit in that area. Three other villages had reported the same sighting, and dozens of mysterious deaths. I fear if we do not figure this out soon, people will start to panic."

"Do you think it could all be connected to the Manticore being drawn from the Underworld?" Aliana remembered Galahad telling her once about the many strange and dangerous occurrences that had happened just before Mordrid and Morgana's treachery was revealed.

"I do not know. But we've sent patrols to scout the areas."

Aliana trampled down the desire to once again tell Merlin of Morgana's coming betrayal, remembering her promise to the queen.

"I've read through that book I got from the old woman." She had, in fact, finished it last night, making use of the queen's enforced bed rest. "The only thing that sticks out to me is the passages about the Underworld, but that might just be because of the Manticore."

"I know you fear telling me too much, but is there something in your time that you were searching for?"

Aliana sighed. *"What do you think, Dagg? I think it's time I tell him about the Grail of Power?"*

She felt the Dragon's approval. *"I think it worth the risk. He did possess it, after all, when the queen's prophecy was created."*

Aliana looked back up at Merlin, her nerves spinning. "What do you know about the Grail of Power?"

Merlin's eyes nearly bugged out, his mouth dropping open for a brief second. "You search for the Grail of Power?"

Aliana shrugged. "In a way. You know I'm from the future, and in my time, my friends and I need to find the Grail so we can stop this really bad evil from trying to take over the realms. But the Grail of Power has been lost for ages, and we have no way of finding it."

Merlin nodded slowly, still reeling from shock, his shoulders hunching forward just a little. "So you want to take the Grail from this time?"

"No. That would mess up your timeline." Aliana started pacing the room. "Titania was very clear when she said I need find an object that will *lead* me to the Grail." Unfortunately, finding this artifact was only *tied* to what Titania wanted her to do here.

"This is very disturbing." Merlin's eyes watched her as she wandered the room, her fingers skimming over table surfaces and colored bottles.

"You don't need to tell me that. All this mystery crap is really starting to annoy me!"

Merlin's mouth turned up in a sardonic smile.

"So do you know of anything that would lead the way to the Grail?"

Merlin scratched his stubbled chin. Apparently the Druid hadn't bothered to shave today. "Give me a few days. I may be able to find some answers in the ancient scrolls and books that fill Camelot's archives."

"Is there anything I can do to help?"

Merlin shook his head and came to Aliana's side. "I will look for your answers; but it will take time. I suggest you take the next few days to recover and enjoy the celebrations. Or try to discover what your other purpose here is."

Aliana didn't feel as sure as Merlin, but agreed. She opened the door to leave, but hesitated. She wondered again about the choice, even wisdom, of not telling the Druid of Morgana's coming betrayal. He clearly loved her so much. It's no wonder he was so closed off, angry, and mysterious in the future. Maybe she could just give him a hint. It wouldn't hurt anything as long as she didn't outright say anything, right?

"Was there something else, Aliana?"

Aliana swallowed the warning words on her tongue. "Just…thanks for the salves. They have really helped."

Merlin's head tilted. "It is not I who makes them. My souls mate, Morgana, is the one gifted with such a connection the earth and the magic its herbs and flowers supply. She is the most talented I have ever known when it comes to such things. It is only because of her that I started to use them myself."

Aliana held back her shocked gasp. *Morgana* had been the one to create that healing magic? Could the differences in the Morgana of Camelot and the Morgana of her time get any crazier?

Aliana found her way back to the rampart Guin and Vira had taken her to the first night she had arrived. Fortunately, she had avoided the others. She still needed to wrap her head around what she and Dagg had agreed to reveal to the guys. She looked out at the crashing ocean waves breaking against the cliff face below. It wasn't her beach back home, but it felt very close. The sound of pounding, yelling men and moving wagons drew her attention to another side of the castle. She watched workers and servants scurry about, just outside the Castle walls, and through parts of the walled city, setting up an arena and dozens of tents.

This must be the preparation for the games tomorrow. The games that all the knights were planning on taking part in. Even Arthur had said he was going to be entering the tournament. Aliana wondered what would happen. He was king; would people not fight as ruthlessly for fear of harming him?

"Are you excited for the games tomorrow, Aliana?"

Aliana turned, her face almost colliding with Galahad's wide chest, her heart beating in her ears. "You really must stop sneaking up on me, Galahad."

He smiled broadly. "It would seem I have a talent for finding you when you are lost in your thoughts."

Aliana's stomach started to fill with butterflies. Before the very perceptive knight could read her she turned back around, leaning her elbows on the cold stone of the rampart. "Are *you* excited for the games?"

He took a spot next to her, his arm brushing against hers as he mimicked her pose. "There are many things about these coming festivities that excite me."

"You mean you're excited to prove you are the best of the knights of Camelot?"

"Perhaps." His body pressed a little closer against hers. "There are few things that I enjoy more than facing a worthy opponent. And these games bring out the best in Camelot and the other kingdoms."

Aliana giggled lightly. *He is such a guy!*

"You laugh at me?"

"No." She glanced at him. "Well, maybe. Part of me is afraid to ask what you enjoy more than beating on other warriors."

His grin widened. He turned his body so he was facing her, one arm leaning on the stone wall. "I enjoy being with those I hold most dear." He tucked a strand of hair behind her ear.

Heat raced through her, but not the silver sparks that she had had always felt from his touch. In movies and TV, this is the part where the girl would look at the guy and they would share a passionate kiss. But Aliana's resolve had already weakened once. She took a step back. She wasn't sure she was ready to let it happen again.

She heard his quiet huff of breath. Aliana had agonized over the frenzied kiss he had laid on her after she was freed from her would be kidnapper. All the raging emotions she had worked so hard to run from had come rushing back, and hadn't given her a real moment of peace since.

"I have not had the opportunity to talk to you since yesterday. There is much we need to discuss." His hand pulled up her sleeve, revealing Dagg's bracelet form. "So this is how you have kept him hidden."

Aliana pulled her hand away, being sure her sleeve covered her guardian again. "Why haven't you gotten upset about him?"

He scoffed. "I was none too pleased last night, thinking about it. I hope now that you'll tell us the rest of your secrets."

"You're asking a lot of me."

He shook his head, his wavy dark hair moving in the soft breeze. "I'm asking you to trust us."

"Trust isn't an easy thing for me to give," she said through clenched teeth. "But there's more to it than that."

"It can't be so bad. And even if it is, you will have us, the Knights of the Round Table, the armies of Camelot to aid you."

Aliana stiffened again. Maybe it would be a good thing to tell everyone. If they knew, then they would think that was the only thing she was hiding. But doubts still lingered. "You guys barely know me. How could you be willing to risk so much?" She turned back to him, letting him see the seriousness of her question.

He regarded her silently. "Merlin speaks for you. Moreover, you have shown us your heart, who you are. I can imagine you as many things, but never a danger to Camelot or our family."

No she wouldn't be, but Morgana would. She turned back to the field not really seeing the commotion below. "Merlin…"

Galahad stepped closer. "Merlin enjoys playing the mysterious Druid with everyone. He is not always right to do so." He shook his head. "How Morgana puts up with him, I will never understand."

He wasn't going to give up on this, that much was clear. "I will tell you, all of you. Just give me time."

"Then perhaps you would rather discuss that kiss we shared."

Tension radiated in her shoulders and down her arms. "Galahad, we can't."

His frustration was palpable. "You keep saying that." His fingers cupped her chin and pulled her eyes to his blazing blue ones. "But you kissed me back."

She couldn't deny it. She wrapped her hand around his, pulling his grip from her chin. His fingers closed around hers as she straightened and moved to step back.

He pulled her hand to his lips, his eyes locked on her as he kissed her knuckles sweetly. He kept her from escaping.

"Galahad, please," she begged quietly. A part of her wasn't sure if she wanted him to let her go or kiss her again. She had been seeing a side to Galahad that she only saw on rare occasions, back in her time. He was more emotional, more open and relaxed. Maybe it was because he still had Vira here. Or maybe it was all the years he spent in Avalon, protecting Arthur before his capture by the Sidhe, that had really changed him. Whatever the reason, there was more to her feelings for Galahad than the overwhelming physical attraction that had first kick-started their relationship.

"Is your reluctance because of the king?" His voice was rough, his face intense.

Her eyes widened. Did he somehow know about the kiss the king and her had shared? "Why would you ask me that?"

He drew closer to her, as she felt rooted to the spot where she stood. He was only a few inches from her now. "I have seen the way you two sometimes look at each other. And Arthur is one of my oldest friends."

She couldn't deny it. Arthur *had* made his feeling for her fairly obvious, even before he'd kissed her. But there could never be anything between them. Delphina was the one he loved so much he couldn't completely forget her, even in an enchanted sleep.

"There isn't anything between Arthur and me. He has Delphina. I am not the type of girl who would get between two people who care for each other like they do." Not intentionally, at least.

Galahad's brow pulled together, confusion replacing his frustration. "Delphina and Arthur are not—"

The door to the stairs opened. "Aliana?" Arthur called.

17

Galahad's grip tightened when she tried to pull her hand away. Arthur came around the corner, coming to a dead stop when he saw the two of them.

The silence stretched for a tortured moment.

Arthur broke the silence. "I did not realize you were up here with another, Aliana."

"I'm not…I wasn't…" Aliana's breath sped up, like the beat of her heart.

Arthur studied Galahad and their still entwined hands.

"I sought Aliana out." Galahad leveled her with a blazing look. "We had some things to discuss."

Aliana tugged, finally freeing her hand. "And I have said all I need to on the subjects."

Frustration returned to his handsome face, almost mirroring Arthur's, aggression spilling into the air around them. She twisted the fabric of her dress around her fingers. It seemed, no matter what she had told herself, she couldn't escape being caught between two such brave, loyal and fierce knights.

A chilled breeze blew past them sending shivers down Aliana's spine. "I should be heading back in."

"Wait." Galahad took a step to block her escape. So did Arthur. Both guys stared each other down for a heated moment.

It seemed that even in a different time period she was destined to come between them.

Galahad broke their stare first, those determined eyes returning to her. "There is still more to say about your reasons for being in Camelot."

"And I told you I needed time."

"You will have it, Aliana," Arthur declared, stepping forward. "But I can't imagine you have much to spare."

Her mouth opened and closed, totally lost for words. They both were right, but there was also the problem of Morgana. Aliana didn't know when the witch would show her true side. What if she revealed all to them and that gave Morgana and Mordrid a dangerous advantage? That thought alone reaffirmed her determination to keep her secrets. She'd tell them about her quest, that she was here seeking a very powerful tool. But her magic, her parentage and definitely her future would stay her secrets.

"You're right, but even I don't have all the knowledge you think I do."

He looked resigned but a determined spark flickered in his golden brown eyes. For a second she almost thought she could feel the crackle of fire around her. It was similar to the natural presence that always seemed to surround Igraine. Maybe this was another look into Arthur's Dragon side.

"Thank you for understanding. I think we should head back in. There is a party tonight after all." She smiled to both of them, putting on a show. "I'm sure Delphina would like to see you before the banquet."

"What do you mean, Aliana?" Arthur asked.

Aliana scoffed, what the heck was wrong with him? "I mean, don't you want to see Delphina?" The Fae he loved so much. And she couldn't stop the flare of jealousy that tried to surface.

Arthur and Galahad both spoke up.

"Galahad and Delphina are not intimate any longer."

"I tried to tell you, Arthur and Delphina have not been together in several years."

Aliana's eyes went big as saucers. "What?" she whispered, beyond confused. "You've…both…*been*…with her? As in the biblical sense?"

Neither guy said anything.

Aliana rocked back on her heels, blinking rapidly, trying to expunge the images her imagination was creating. "So." She pointed to Galahad. "You and Delphina have *been together*." Then pointed to Arthur. "But she's the girl you are crazy in love with."

Arthur took a step closer. "Who told you this, that I am 'crazy in love' with her?" He cast a dark glance at Galahad.

Galahad crossed his arms, meeting Arthur's accusation. "It was not me. I tried to tell her otherwise before you interrupted us."

"It doesn't matter how I know. I know that you are in love with Delphina."

The king shook his head. "I care for her yes, but it has been years since there was anything between us. At least not like you seem to think. She is a trusted friend and confidant. Nothing more."

Aliana wrapped her arms around her middle, wincing when her cut ached from the pressure. Arthur was one thing, but Galahad…She looked at him briefly. That was not something she had seen coming.

"Aliana." Galahad's accent made her name sound like an intimate caress.

She didn't have time for this. Aliana never thought she would *really* ever regret kissing Galahad, but now she did. If she had kept her emotions in check after that attack…*And I'm done. My brain has reached its limits for processing today.*

"I really need to get back inside. I was supposed to meet Merlin about…something." She moved to walk past them. Both held their arms out to try to stop her. She looked at them with wide, hurt eyes. A hurt she told herself she didn't have a right to be feeling. "Please, don't try to stop me."

They both stood aside. She walked past them, trying to appear calm, but her legs wanted to dash away. She refused to give into the desire. She made it down the stairs, not hearing any sign that the guys had followed her. Arms still wrapped around her middle, she walked in a daze toward her room.

"Aliana?" Morgana's warm voice snapped her out of her mental fog. "Are you all right? You look upset."

Aliana blinked, her eyes meeting Raven's dark ones. *What was he doing with Morgana?*

"I'm fine," she assured the blond girl.

Morgana didn't appear convinced.

"M'lady?" Raven's worry for her made her smile. He was a sweet boy. Though, she probably shouldn't call him a boy. He appeared to be almost as old as her.

"Really, I am fine. I'm just…" Aliana trailed off as the door she had just exited opened again. Both Arthur and Galahad stepped into the hall.

Aliana looked away from them and took a steadying breath. "I'm actually looking for Merlin. He was helping me with some research." She had let herself get distracted for too long. It was time to do what she came here to do, find a way to the Grail and complete Titania's mystery quest.

"I believe he is in the archives," Morgana replied.

"I can show you the way, m'lady," Raven offered. She smiled at him, noticing again just how much of a boy he *wasn't*. He motioned for Aliana to follow him. Thankfully they were going in the opposite direction of the two knights that still stood there watching her.

She felt their gazes until they turned a corner. Theirs and Morgana's.

Jaw dropping was not an adequate description for the enormous library she now stood in. Yes, it was only one level, but it looked like four large rooms had been built together and stuffed with more shelves than you could count.

"M'lady?" Raven's hand touched her. An electric chill brushed over her body. Both actions snapped her out of her amazed state.

"Sorry," she said, stepping away from his touch. "So where is Merlin in all this?"

"I'll show you the way."

She followed him through the dust covered isles of book cases overflowing with bound volumes and three times as many scrolls. "This is unbelievable!" she said when Merlin came into view.

The Druid looked up from the two tomes lying open in front of him. "It is indeed." He looked to Raven, who was hovering quietly. "You can return to your duties."

The boy bowed his head and disappeared back the way they had come. Merlin waited another moment before saying, "If you've come to see if I've found anything, you'll be disappointed."

Aliana sighed, Dagg leaping from her wrist. His glowing eyes scanned the shelves before he dug himself into one of the many piles of scrolls on a far shelf.

"I wanted to see if I could help. This is my quest, and I need to do more than I have been." She leaned over his shoulder, reading the pages he was staring at. Her bandages tightened over her still healing wound. She hissed out a heavy breath.

Merlin scowled. "You should be resting." He snapped the book closed. "I have yet to find anything, but I still have many places to search."

Aliana wasn't going to give up that quickly. "Would it help if we got the others involved?"

Merlin's surprised face was a picture. "You're ready to bring them in on your secrets?" He pointedly looked at her right hand, where her magic ruby glove was still concealed behind her magic veil.

Aliana laid a protective hand over the invisible glove. "Not that, no. But they know I'm here for a reason beyond seeing you. I've been meaning to talk to you about that since you got back."

Merlin studied her. "What do you plan to tell them?"

"That I need to find a way to locate the Grail of Power. Nothing else for now." She wondered again about finding a discreet way to warn him about Morgana but stopped the thought. The queen's warning was a heavy weight.

"I'm glad you are telling them. And I know Owaine, Leyon and Percival are anxious to see Lord Daggerhorne."

Aliana nodded. "We can…" Clicking footsteps silenced her.

Merlin stood, both looking to see Guinevere coming around the corner.

The redhead smiled. "Raven told me I'd find you both here."

"Is Lancelot with you?" Aliana looked past her, half expecting the fierce knight to appear.

"No. He's with Arthur and the other knights welcoming the warriors arriving for the tournament tomorrow." She looked at the books on the table. "I wanted to see how you were feeling."

Aliana smirked at the murmured words. The girl's eyes were looking at the books and not her.

"I'm getting better. Thanks."

Several scrolls fell to the ground with cascading thuds. Aliana flinched back. Dagg crawled out, his amethyst eyes back to normal, his tail wrapped around one scroll, another clenched in one claw.

"Are you trying to give me a heart attack?" Aliana snapped.

Guin giggled and Merlin rolled his eyes.

The Druid gathered up the scrolls on the floor and shoved them back into the cubby shelf. "What do you have, Lord Daggerhorne?"

"I wasn't sure at first, but these scrolls have the feel of Dragon magic." He jumped from the shelf to the table, his leathery, silver veined wings flaring. Aliana hid her smile at Guinevere's awed gasp. Her little guardian was pretty impressive. Not that she'd ever tell him that.

Dagg looked to Aliana, his Dragon smirk showing.

"Vain much?"

His amusement filled her.

"Why are these scrolls so special?" Aliana asked. "*The queen is a Dragon, and Arthur is part Dragon. Not to mention Igraine's father, the original Gold Dragon and his son. Any of them could have touched those scrolls.*"

He shook his head once. "*These have the feel of my clan, the Silver Dragons. I am curious to know why.*"

"*Curiosity killed the cat, you know.*"

"*Good thing I'm a Dragon then. A pretty impressive one.*"

Aliana pursed her lips.

"Are you two communicating magically?" Guin's eyes ping ponged between them.

Aliana flushed with embarrassment. "Yeah, it comes in handy."

Merlin snorted. "Time to get down to work." Merlin opened one of the scrolls.

"If you tell me what you're looking for I may be able to help. I know this library very well, even the hidden rooms." Guin smiled proudly, and not bothering to hide her frank curiosity.

"Did you say secret rooms?" Her mind automatically went to Morgana's evil hidden compartment.

The redhead nodded. "There are two in this library and one in a smaller archive room. But there's nothing left in that one."

Aliana bit her tongue so hard she tasted blood. It wasn't going to stay empty.

Merlin cleared his throat. "Are you going to tell her?"

She swallowed the mild copper taste before answering. "I'm here in Camelot because I was told there was an artifact I could find that would lead me to the Grail of Power."

Guin blinked. "The Grail of Power?" Her eyes jumped to Merlin. "You told us about it, when we were kids, but I didn't think it really existed."

"Oh, it's real!" Aliana ran a hand over her still cloaked ruby. "I need to find — whatever it is — that can lead me to it, so I can return home." She didn't mention the battle that would follow her return.

Guin looked around the library. "Merlin, have you checked in the hidden room in the back?" she whispered.

The Druid shook his head. "That is the only one I haven't checked."

Guin wrapped her arm through Aliana's. "Then you and I will go take a look."

Aliana hesitated. "What about the scroll Dagg found?"

The Dragon swished his tail. "I don't know what is in them. You should still go search that room."

Guin led Aliana through the row of book shelves, past a few statues and an old man who was hunched over a smaller desk in one corner.

"That is Sir Magnus. He is the court record keeper," Guinevere whispered as they cut him a wide berth.

"Does he know about the rooms?"

"Not as far as I know. Arthur, Galahad, Lancelot, Merlin and I found these rooms by accident as kids. Magnus would always get angry or suspicious when we would all come, but he never found us in the rooms. Even now he still gets temperamental about us roaming around. These archives are his life's work."

They stopped in front of a tall shelf with a beautiful, long flag bearing the Pendragon crest hung next to it. Guin let go of Aliana's arm and ran her fingers down the stones on the edge of the shelf. Her fingers stopped halfway.

"Ah!" The faint sound of stone scraping startled Aliana. She half expected the bookcase to spring forward, like it did for the other room. Instead the redhead pulled the flag aside, revealing a door crack. She pushed the hidden door open, motioning for Aliana to follow.

But Aliana stood frozen. The room was totally dark. Darker than a true midnight sky without stars.

"Come, Aliana." Guin motioned her forward.

"You are safe, Aliana. Do you need me?" Dagg's calming effect helped to release the tension in her stiff body.

"I'm okay." And she would be, darn it! She wasn't going to let her fear of what may be hiding in the dark stop her. She was already facing down one hideous monster that hid in the darkness.

Aliana moved her feet forward before she could chicken out. She stepped through the thin door and past Guin who was watching her with worried eyes. The door shut and Aliana's heart seized the instant before she could stave off the small burst of panic.

Lights flared and burst on her right then her left. The torch fire glowed with an almost orange light.

"Merlin enchanted all the torches here to light with magic fire whenever we come in here." The redhead smiled as Aliana let out her breath.

"You could have told me that sooner," Aliana said with an embarrassed flush. Now Guin knew her stupid fear.

"I apologize. Come, we should spread out." She took down one of the torches and handed it to Aliana before taking another one for herself. "I vaguely remember finding an old tome once that was filled with drawings and stories of magical artifacts. If we are going to find you an answer it may be here."

The two girls started at different ends, opening book after book and scroll after scroll. Thoughts of her papa invaded Aliana as she worked her way through the shelves. What he would have given to see all these books and scrolls?

With every discarded book, Aliana felt her frustration grow. She wished again for her camera. Maybe it would have somehow helped her find what they were looking for.

"Where is this stupid book!" she hissed, shoving another thick, old and smelly book on a dust-coated shelf.

"Here!" Guin said, grabbing a book on the shelf she had been searching.

Aliana smacked the dust off her hands and went to Guin. They flipped it open as Aliana eyes grew. On the page was a drawing of Excalibur and words written in a scratchy language, like the writing in the Fae book she had read. It was the language of Tir Na Nog!

Guinevere handed Aliana the book. "Take it. We should get back to Merlin and your DragonLord. See what they make of it."

Aliana followed Guin like a puppet, her eyes roaming over the dusty, spider web infested room of secret treasures. Aliana hoped she'd get the chance to explore this room more before she had to leave.

Merlin and Dagg looked up as they returned. "Did you find anything?" The Druid closed the book in front of him.

"I think so, yes." Aliana handed him the book. They all gathered around the table as Merlin started searching the pages. There were drawings of Excalibur, a strange looking spear, a magic flower and dozens of other cool, mystifying artifacts, but by the halfway point there was still nothing about the Grail.

Aliana felt the desire to yank out her hair. "This is getting us nowhere." She pushed up from the table.

Before Merlin could respond Dagg leapt up in the air scrambling to the top of a shelf and out of sight. The serving girl, Clara appeared.

"Pardon, m'lord, m'ladies, but the queen has asked to see Lady Aliana before the banquet starts."

Guin gasped, shooting up from the table. "We forgot all about the feast!"

Aliana bit back her reply. She wanted to keep searching for any ideas of the Grail. But then again, how many chances would she get to ever attend a party at Camelot?

"The queen awaits you, m'lady." Clara curtsied and left quickly.

"Take the book," Merlin said, pressing it into her hands. "You can keep going through it after the feast."

Guin left quickly on Clara's heels. Dagg drifted down to her side as Merlin left to.

"I feel guilty, Dagg." She turned the book over in her hand. "I should be focusing on this task, but I want to see what the feast is like."

Dagg's hesitation touched her.

"You don't approve of my going?" Aliana ran her hand over the book. If she went to the feast, she'd have to face Arthur and Galahad again. She wasn't sure she could handle that after earlier. Delphina was like the perfect person, or Fae, rather. It was no wonder both guys had been taken with her.

Aliana's jaw tightened, like her grip on the book. "You're right. I shouldn't go."

She fled the library as the words left her mouth, heading straight for her room.

Dagg flew through the small open window of her room as she closed the door. "You know you cannot avoid them forever."

Aliana glowered at the Dragon. "Shut it."

"I agree you need to focus on our quest, but running away from your feelings won't help us either."

Aliana flopped down on her bed and opened the new book, ignoring the ache in her ribs and forgetting the queen's summons. Holding out her right hand, she retrieved the Fae woman's book from her ruby. Lying both side by side, she started to flip through both sets of pages.

I⁸

I still find it difficult to believe Merlin was wrong about there only being one Well of Realms. It makes me wonder about the Druid. He never made such a mistake in Camelot. Even more astonishing was Lacy's revelation about her time mirror theory and her and Dawn's plan to use them. It frustrated me knowing the lasses kept such a large secret from us. I know Percy and the king share my anger. Freya and Delphina had been the ones to calm us all. Now we just have to wait for Puck to reappear. Lacy seems to believe that the trickster can help her understand how to use the Well's waters. Fortunately Freya and Delphina have agreed to stay with us until we return home.

Leo

It wasn't easy to ignore the immense disapproval from her guardian, but Aliana did so by burying herself in the mysterious book she hoped would help her complete her quest. She reread the segments on the Underworld, and the information terrified her all over again. The Underlord was thought to be one of the more even tempered of the four great rulers of the realms, but his general worried her the most. If the Underlord was anything like Titania, she could handle that. But this General Alaki was known to be ruthless, treacherous and in the mortal realm he was known as Death himself. The Egyptians had called him Anubis. The Hindi called him Yama. The Japanese knew him as Izanami, and the Greeks called him Thanatos. A man, no, a magic being like that was not one to be taken lightly.

If her task here did involve the Underworld in some way, it was a good bet that she'd have to deal with this guy.

"A task you may need the help of the knights and Arthur for."

"Dagg, enough! I get it, you don't like that I'm hiding up here while there's a party going on."

A knock on her door stopped their argument. Dagg's eyes flared purple, sensing who was there. "It's the queen." No sooner did he speak the words then her door opened and the queen entered.

She was dressed in a pearl and gold gown, a thick band of gold and jewels circled her head, crowning her pale blond waterfall of curly hair. The matching belt at her waist was clipped together by a thick circle of bronze engraved with the Pendragon crest.

"Should you not be getting ready?"

Aliana looked down at herself, still in her blue dress from earlier. She shrugged, feeling like a child waiting for her mother's approval. "I guess I got caught up researching."

"Ah." The queen didn't sound convinced.

"I have so much to do, so much about my journey here that I don't understand. I can't…let myself keep getting distracted by guys… by things that can't…"

Igraine sat down on the edge of the bed. "I've seen the way you look at my son, and at Sir Galahad. You care deeply for both of them."

"That doesn't matter. I'm not even from this time period!" Aliana closed her eyes against the memory of Arthur and Galahad fighting over her on the beach by her house. "And I don't want to be the cause of problems between Galahad and Arthur," she lamented.

"Is that the truth, or are you really only afraid to acknowledge what your heart feels?"

Aliana looked to Dagg. His amethyst eyes and smug expression telling her he silently agreed. She felt torn. She really did want to see what parties were like in this time, and maybe she would discover something new tonight. Didn't she owe it to her father to learn as much about Camelot and its people as she could?

Aliana relented and gave Igraine a wobbly smile.

The queen smiled warmly. "It's settled then. Get into your dress and I will help you with your hair."

Less than an hour later Aliana nervously followed the queen down the stairs toward the side door of the Great Hall. Her pink dress fit her like a glove through the bodice, the long sleeves flared at the end, trimmed with the same cream and lavender twined ribbons and gold detailing that made up her heavy belt. The queen had left her hair down, a few segments pulled away from her face and held back by metal pins and ribbons.

Aliana had to beg the queen to let her go in through one of the unobtrusive side entrances. She didn't want anyone to notice her until she was ready. Delphina was waiting when the side door opened.

"My lady, I am happy you joined us." She greeted Aliana with a curtsy. If anyone saw her, they would hopefully think the gesture was for the queen and not her.

Aliana ignored the wave of jealousy trying to form. "Thank you. You look lovely, Delphina." And she did. Her apricot hair was practically shining and her eyes were accented with dark liner and a touch of pink that made her pale green eyes stand out against her darker green dress and china white-blue skin.

Aliana cleared her throat then whispered, "And thank you for keeping my secret for so long. I know it couldn't have been easy."

"I think we should join the assembly, ladies." Igraine smiled warmly and moved toward the crowd. Many parted and bowed to her as she passed, drawing the guys' attention. She felt Arthur and Galahad's eyes first, but before she could start to panic, Merlin and Owaine appeared. The two were dressed in their colors, Merlin's heavy shirt dyed a dark orange, his silver Pendragon knight cuff standing out in contrast. Owaine's was a lighter blue, almost the color of the sky.

"You look beautiful, Aliana," Owaine said with a crooked smile as he looked over her and her dress. "You and Delphina outshine all others here."

Delphina sent him a sideways grin.

"Flattery and charm will get you nowhere with us, Sir Owaine," Aliana teased and winked at the knight.

They all laughed. "He is not wrong though," Merlin said bowing his head to her. "You do look very lovely." Merlin offered Aliana his arm.

Looping her hand through his arm, Delphina taking Owaine's offered arm, they made their way through the throng of partiers dancing along to the drums and lively music. The hall was lit with hundreds of torches, streamers of colored fabrics and fresh flower garlands hung from the upper railings and along the walls. People talked and roared with laughter, all dressed in clothes much finer than she would have thought possible for this age. Aliana caught sight of the other knights, all spread out through the room. All were dressed like Merlin and Owaine, only in their family's colors. There were two banquet tables filled with roasted and fried meats and seafood, ripe fruits, nuts and cheeses and breads.

Aliana's stomach rumbled at the scent. "The hall looks amazing! And the food smells great, Merlin."

The Druid laughed and led her to the table, handing her a plate that a servant rushed over. Aliana nibbled while Merlin, Owaine and Delphina told her more about the party and the visiting people that had come, even dignitaries from other kingdoms. Gawain and Leyon joined them, each with a woman pressed closely to their sides sipping wine.

"Glad you decided to join us, Aliana," Gawain said.

Aliana sent him a cheeky grin, feeling much more relaxed than expected. "Well, I was told this was supposed to be a grand celebration. How could I pass that up?"

Aliana remembered the gallery party where she had last danced with her best friend. Before the homesickness could set in Lancelot, Guin and Morgana joined their growing party. Morgana's dress was the beautiful yellow fabric they had looked at the merchant's stand, and Aliana had been right then; Morgana practically glowed with warmth and magic and beauty. Both girls had their hair piled up in curls in a very Roman fashion, each wearing delicate gold or silver necklaces.

Merlin went to Morgana's side, his arm wrapping around the Sorceress's waist as she happily leaned into her Druid. Guin stayed at Lancelot's side, their hands entwined the whole time. They laughed and joked and Aliana took in all the splendor she could not have imagined being possible in this time. Vira danced in the center of the room with two girls she recognized from the market. Several younger boys were watching the trio with avid interest, taking turns trying to push each other forward toward the three dancing girls.

The song changed and the boys made their approach. Aliana smiled as Vira blushed when one with blond hair kissed her hand.

"Someone better head Galahad off," Morgana teased.

Aliana looked past Vira and saw the knight, dressed in dark green, black and silvery white accents, heading toward his sister with a frown. Sir Percival got to him before he got within a few feet of the flirting teens. The giant knight laughingly shoved Galahad's shoulder, saying something that had Galahad's mouth breaking into a grin.

"Arthur!" Merlin and Owaine greeted, drawing Aliana's attention from the dance floor.

Gawain wrapped his arm around her shoulder. "Look who decided to grace us with her presence."

The king was dressed in a fancy red tunic and dark pants, Excalibur strapped to his waist, the gold of the hilt matching the gold, peaked crown adorned with half a dozen blood red rubies that rested on his dark head. Even his brown eyes seemed to glow like gold in all the candle light.

Aliana tried to calm the nervous churning of her stomach and keep her face impassive instead of letting on just how apprehensive she felt around him. What was she supposed to say to him after earlier? Galahad too, for that matter. She didn't want to spoil the good time everyone else seemed to be having. The best thing for all of them would be for her to forget it; act like it never happened and didn't matter. Maybe she'd convince herself of that too.

"Sire," she greeted, bowing her head. "This feast is wonderful."

"Thank you." Arthur took Gawain's place as the knight stepped back and stole Guin from Lancelot for a dance. "I am glad you came down," he said in a low voice, leaning into her. "I am sorry I upset you earlier. Especially when you still have not recovered from the attack yesterday."

She gave him a smile. "You don't need to apologize. I overreacted. Who you care for, or are with, is none of my business."

Galahad and Percival joined them before Arthur could reply.

"Where is your Dragon guardian, lass?" Leyon asked, drawing her attention from the two men.

Aliana held out her wrist, Dagg's silver form gleaming. "He rarely leaves me."

The Scot's eyes were bright with excitement. "Aye, we all knew there was more to you than meets the eye." He smiled. "There is still more to learn of you though, I suspect."

"You're right, but it can wait until after the games tomorrow." That way she'd have a little more time to learn what she can, to best explain her need to find the Grail without breaking her promise to Igraine.

Aliana caught the queen watching them all from the other side of the room, sitting in the smaller throne she recognized from when they were in the Isle. The arching, carved wooden one next to it was Arthur's. Igraine smiled, looking very pleased with herself.

"Aliana!"

She looked away from the queen to see Vira making her way through the crowd. The girl was beautiful in the green dress she had gotten from the market and her cheeks were flushed with a rosy blush. The teen was practically shining, her blue eyes that were so much like her brother's aglow.

"Looks like you were having fun!" Aliana hugged the girl when she came to her.

Vira squeezed her tightly before stepping back. "I was looking for you earlier."

Aliana flushed. "Sorry, I couldn't decide how to do my hair."

Guin and Gawain returned. Lancelot leaned over and kissed his wife's cheek, whispering something in her ear that made the redhead blush wildly.

"Now that we are all here, I say we really enjoy ourselves!" Merlin said, raising his glass, his other arm securely around Morgana.

"And may the best knight win the tournaments and the spoils!" Gawain added loudly.

Everyone cheered and raised their glasses, Aliana following suit with her cup of water. Out of the corner of her eye she caught sight of a dark-haired woman, but before she could figure out why she looked so familiar, the woman disappeared into the crowd.

Aliana brushed her fingers over Dagg's bracelet form before grabbing her pouch of money and hooking it to the little loop in the sleeve of her mauve dress. She was supposed to meet Vira and the other women in a few minutes before Queen Igraine officially opened the games, and the first contests got underway.

"Good morning," Guin said, looking up when Aliana found her and the girls in the training yard. Everyone looked a little tired, all having stayed late at the party. Aliana had left with Vira, when the girl couldn't stop yawning. She had only had two cups of wine, but it seemed that the alcohol put the teen to sleep. Galahad had tried to follow, but Delphina had pulled him away for a dance.

Aliana's heart had hurt a lot when she watched the Fae dance so closely with Galahad. She hadn't even looked in Arthur's direction at the point. Yes, he said he didn't care for Delphina like that, but she knew differently. Maybe she was supposed to help him see that? Maybe that was the reason Titania wanted her here? After all it was plain enough to realize the Fae queen wanted to have her own power here in Camelot. Why else would she have saved Arthur, created this prophecy and magically transported the ruined kingdom of Camelot to her Isle of the Blessed?

"Are you all right, Aliana?" Morgana's question brought her back to the present.

"Sorry, my mind tends to wander on occasion."

"Well, I hope it was wandering toward the arenas," Guin said playfully. "The opening ceremony is about to start and I want to go to the tents and wish them all luck."

"I cannot wait to see Galahad win!" Vira gushed, leading them toward the tents where the fighters were suiting up.

Men were having their armor readjusted, or getting in some last minute practice with their weapons as they made their way through the small area. Many of them followed the girls' progression with leering glances; some even made a few cat calls. Aliana had to mentally restrain herself from telling a few of them off. Fortunately, the Knights of the Round Table and King Arthur's tents were clustered together. The girls separated. Aliana went to where Leyon, Percival, Owaine and Gawain were talking and adjusting their capes or securing their pieces of armor.

They all grinned broadly when she came over to them. "I wanted to wish all of you good fortune with your matches today!" She kissed each of their cheeks.

"Is that all we get for luck?" Gawain teased, playfully winking at her. She laughed and hugged him too. "There!"

Merlin and Morgana stepped out of another tent. The Sorceress's cheeks were flushed and her lips looked a little redder than they had been. Guess Merlin got a make out session for his good luck. Guin and Lancelot looked just the same.

While everyone was distracted with their well wishes, Aliana slipped into Arthur's tent.

The king had his back to her, adjusting the Pendragon cuff on his forearm.

"I hope you don't mind I came by to wish you luck."

Arthur turned, his strong square face lighting up with his smile. "I am glad you did." He stepped closer. His leather armor was tight over a heavy layer of chainmail, like the others had been wearing. His red cape draped and dragged on the ground behind him, Excalibur proudly displayed at his waist. "I wanted to wish you the best of luck." She quickly gripped his shoulders, rose up on her toes and kissed his cheek.

He looked surprised, then pleased. He caught her hand as she was pulling away. He brought it to his mouth and placed a butterfly soft kiss on her knuckles. "Thank you," he said, releasing her.

Aliana started to turn.

"Wait."

She looked back at him. He pulled out a thin string of leather she realized was a necklace. At the end of the cord hung a round pendant, the edges lined with bronze, and small dots of gold circling a silver center that was engraved with the Pendragon crest.

"What is that, Arthur?" she asked as he pulled it over his head.

He held it out to her. "My mother gave me this when I was younger and first learning how to fight." He took her hand again, laying the warmed piece of metal in her palm. "I hope you'll wear it during the games."

Aliana looked at it, then Arthur. "I can't."

He cut off her protests. "You can." He closed her fingers around it. "It would make me happy to know you wear something of mine while I compete."

Aliana still hesitated, looking at their hands. "You should give this to Del—"

"I want *you* to have it." His free hand cuffed her chin, bringing her eyes back to his. She felt herself falling into the warm sincerity and intense emotions behind his gaze. "Please, wear it for me."

Aliana gulped, tried to find her voice but couldn't. Instead she took the necklace and put it on, tucking the warm pendant under her corset.

"Thank you." She gave him a last smile and left the tent.

Vira came up to her immediately. "My brother did not say it, but I think he wants to talk to you before we take our seats." With that she went into Arthur's tent.

Aliana noticed Gawain, Owaine, Merlin and Leyon all watching her. She flushed a little and ducked into the tent she guessed was Galahad's.

The dark-haired knight looked up from the piece of paper he was reading. "Aliana." The way he said it was like a caress on her skin. "I wasn't sure you'd come."

She shrugged. "I'm wishing everyone luck."

He came closer to her. "I did not get the chance last night to apologize for upsetting you. But I had to talk with you." He took her hand and pushed back her sleeve to reveal Dagg. "I still can't believe it. I never knew Dragons had this kind of magic."

Aliana pulled her hand back. "Dagg is a special case, I think. He's my guardian."

"You do seem to have a way of drawing trouble to you." His fingers came up and touched her cheek. His warm fingers traced over where the red marks had been on her cheek then trailed down her neck to where those bruises had been.

"I'm all healed, Galahad." She took his hand in hers. "You saved me. You and the others."

"I have something for you," he said when she pulled away. He turned and grabbed something from the small table. "Here." He held up a purple iris bloom. "I do not remember as much about my parents as I'd like, but I do know that when my mother would get mad at my father, he would always give her a flower. Irises were her favorite."

Aliana touched the soft dark petals. This was something she had never thought to expect from her big bad knight.

He reached out and tucked it into a twisted part of her hair she had pulled back. "I am sorry for upsetting you. But I couldn't let what happened go undiscussed."

Aliana was well and truly speechless for a long moment. Her heart was racing; her finger trembled for a second as she touched the delicate flower in her hair. "Thank you." She stared up at him, watching as he hesitantly leaned forward.

Her pulse beat louder. Could she do it? Could she kiss him and risk losing her heart to him again?

"Galahad!" Owaine's laughing call broke the moment. "We need to enter the lists."

Aliana drew back. "Good luck, Galahad."

She left his tent, not daring to look back for fear she'd go and kiss him like her heart was telling her to do.

19

Raven waved to Aliana as she walked past the guys. "M'lady, I am to show you to your seat. The others have already taken their places."

They stepped onto a raised platform that surrounded the largest of the constructed arenas. Guin, Morgana, Vira and Delphina all sat on a long bench to the left of a tall covered area with the thrones. Vira saw her first and waved, the girls' eyes seemed to be fixed on the purple iris in her hair. A bright, knowing smile formed on the teen's mouth.

Aliana thanked Raven before shuffling past the other well-dressed spectators. The girls made room for Aliana between her and Delphina.

The crowd rose to their feet, cheering as the warriors paraded into the center of the dirt arena. The roaring of the crowd died down as the last man entered and Igraine stepped up onto the covered platform looking every bit the powerful, beautiful and commanding queen she was in an elegant ruby red and gold dress.

She raised her hands, silencing the cheers that had erupted at her entrance. "Citizens of Camelot, it is my pleasure to welcome you as we celebrate the anniversary of our beloved kingdom and our noble king!" Arthur stepped forward and bowed his head to his mother. "Today these brave warriors will put their skills and courage to the test in the tournament of these celebrations. Only the best among you will advance to the final rounds of competition, and only one will claim victory. May the supreme among you win the glory and honor of being known as the greatest fighter in the lands. Let the games begin!" The crowds cheered again. The queen took her seat as the knights filed out of the arena.

The course was a long, wide oval, much like the Circus Maximus, where all of the chariot races took place in Rome. Racing was dangerous, and it would be even worse with the whole knocking people off their horses thing. She repressed a shiver; humans were so violent sometimes.

"This is so exciting!" Morgana gushed.

Aliana just looked at her with an are-you-crazy expression. *I sure hope she's stocked up on her healing potions and salves. I've got a feeling there's gonna be a lot of knights needing it.*

"Yes, it is certainly popular, but also one of the most dangerous." Guin wrapped the thin stole tighter around her shoulders.

The excitement between them all was palpable. Aliana's stomach was twisting and turning more than it had since the Manticore attack. "Yes, because nothing says fun like boys knocking each other off horses with a stick."

Horns sounded. Riders lined up next to each other, six all together, Arthur on the inner corner with Leyon right next to him. Every knight was wearing thick mail with chest and shoulder armor as well as helmets with flapping cheek guards for better visibility. Their spears were wide and long with rounded wooden ends. They reminded her of very old school *bokken* swords Wade and Lacy used for their martial arts training, just about five times bigger.

"How does the elimination work here? What if none of the knights fall off?" Aliana asked.

"No more than two riders can advance. If there are more remaining on their horses at the finish line, then the first two to cross will be the winners," Delphina explained.

The horses pranced and shuffled next to each other, ready for the signal to go. Igraine stood and walked to the edge of her platform, a red square of cloth hanging from her fingers. The queen held it out, looked at her son, then dropped the fabric.

The riders took off like a shot. Arthur and another two unknown knights got out in front right away, their wooden weapons swinging toward each other. The golden king leaned forward, ducking a strike that would have taken his head off. The knight on the outer side took advantage and clobbered the middle rider hard on the side.

He flinched and tilted to the side of his saddle, but avoided falling all the way out.

She gripped Delphina's hand tight, chewing on her thumb nail as Arthur and Leyon continued to work together as they raced closer to the finish line. Two more riders were trying to advance and separate the pair, but at the last second both Arthur and Leyon veered slightly and their aggressors ran chest first into their extended spears. Both men fell backward, one flipping right out of his saddle.

The race was happening so quickly, but so slowly at the same time. The remaining four were entering the next turn; they only needed to make one more circuit around the course to win. Arthur and Leyon had a good lead on the other two so they focused on the race rather than fighting.

Arthur looked back just as the other man raced to catch up. Leyon cut another swipe at the man attacking him, the wooden spear smacking right into the other knight's helmet. Man and horse immediately veered to the side, almost doing a one-eighty as he was left in the dust.

The king crossed the finish line to a deafening roar of approval from the crowd. Aliana jumped to her feet with the others clapping, but looked right back at their friend. The Celt leaned forward even more, his horse seeming to find one last burst of speed as he sprang forward, beating the last rider by almost half a horse length.

Arthur and Leyon threw off their helmets, their hair matted and faces covered with dirt and sweat, both smiling bright and proud.

Igraine got to her feet clapping as her son and Leyon pulled their horses in front of her and bowed their heads to her. Both men left the lists, waving to the girls as they passed.

Everyone sat again as servants cleared the ground of broken wood and helped the injured knights.

"I'm not sure I can take much more of this," Aliana said, her hand resting over her racing heart. "What if someone had died?"

Vira reached over Morgana and patted her thigh. "It's rare that that happens."

Somehow that didn't make Aliana feel any better.

"Owaine, Percival and Lancelot are in the next round!" Guin said, clapping her hand in excitement.

"I suspect the outcomes will be much the same as the king's race." Morgana flashed a happy smile. "I would wager most of our men will work together to advance."

"If they are indeed riding in the same elimination races," Delphina added.

"Are any of them in races on their own?" Aliana wondered aloud.

"I believe Galahad, Merlin and Gawain ride alone." Guin shook her head. "Those will be the races to watch; fortunately all three men are expert horsemen."

Aliana still didn't feel any comfort from that. "*I definitely don't think I can take much more of these races.*"

Dagg's amusement spilled into her mind. "*I am sure the knights are more than prepared to handle this challenge.*"

Aliana fought down a *humph*.

Vira left as the track was cleared and set for the next race. Aliana reached up and touched the flower in her hair. The leather chain of Arthur's necklace shifted on the soft skin of her neck.

Delphina spoke up, distracting her. "My lady, I was hoping to get the chance to speak with you alone."

"What about?"

"Perhaps we should go for a walk."

Aliana stood when Delphina did and followed the Fae. They started up a side path, toward one of the other arenas, at a slow pace.

Delphina cleared her throat. "I hope you don't think me too forward, but would that flower happen to be from Galahad?"

I didn't expect that question! "Ah…yes. He wanted to apologize for a fight we had."

Delphina's pale flesh blushed slightly purple. "I hope I was not the cause of your disagreement."

Aliana's gut clenched, guilt creeping into her. "You may have come up," she admitted very reluctantly. "But no, our fight wasn't about you." Aliana shook her head. "It doesn't matter." She started walking again, Delphina keeping pace. She was Arthur's green eyed ghost girl, and she was going to have to live with that.

"I'm sorry to hear you two were at odds. I am glad it's been set right." The Fae looked around. "But this was not the reason I wished to speak with you."

Aliana's brows pulled together. "Then what was?"

Delphina tugged Aliana past a few more tents, toward an area with stacked crates and barrels. "Your quest," she whispered. "You told me that you were here searching for something. Merlin came to me asking if I knew of a way to locate the Grail of Power."

Aliana felt herself go pale. Why had Merlin gone to her? "Did he tell you that?"

She shook her head, her apricot curls bouncing. "He merely asked if I knew of any object that could locate the Grail. It is, after all, an item created of Avalon and the Isle of the blessed as well as man."

"It is?"

The Fae nodded. "I told him we did not need anything to help us locate it. Everyone knows the Grail is locked away in the Fire Caverns of Avalon."

"That doesn't sound good."

Delphina shrugged. "Merlin insisted he needed something to guide him to it. I made the inference that he was asking for you. I imagine that is what you plan to tell the others after the games."

Excitement rushed through her blood. Finally something was going right! "Do you know of anything that can lead me to the Grail?"

"There is something, but it is far more dangerous seeking that out as opposed to retrieving the Grail from the Fire Caverns."

Aliana looked around this time to be sure no one was over hearing their hushed conversation. "I don't need the Grail, just a way to get to it. What is this object and why is it so dangerous to get?"

The Fae's pink lips pursed together in disapproval, but she finally relented. "The Grail of Power was created by a small group of powerful humans, Fae, Elves and a Sapphire Dragon using the magic of all the realms."

"Wait, I thought a Dragon alone created the Grail."

Delphina tilted her head slightly. "Did a Dragon tell you that?" There was a playful tone in the Fae's musical voice.

Aliana bit her cheek. "Maybe."

"With no offense intended to your DragonLord, very few know the true origins of its creation. But it was more powerful than any of them had ever expected. They fought over how to use it, and one of the creators, the Dragon, decided to steal it and hide it away where the others could not use its great magic."

Aliana's jaw dropped. "Talk about a double cross!"

"Indeed. But the others were not willing to let the creation go, so they used the leftover magic to create a way to find it, a map. No matter where the Grail is, the map will lead the way to it. It worked, they found the Grail, but a terrible battle ensued. The one who stole the artifact managed to get the map and made a bargain with the only being powerful enough to protect it, while she once again hid the Grail."

Aliana leaned forward and whispered, "Who?"

"The Underlord."

Aliana reeled back, her head almost hitting the crate she was standing behind. "Son of a biscuit!" If she wanted a way to forget her boy troubles, she certainly got it.

Delphina's yellow brows shot up. "I am not sure what that means."

Aliana fought back a giggle. "Does your story tell you how to get the map from the Underlord?"

The Fae shook her head. "All I have heard is that it is guarded by the fiercest of guardian of the Underworld."

Aliana breathed deep. "Then I need to find a way to the Underworld."

Terror leaked onto Delphina's face. "You cannot! It is too dangerous."

"I don't have a choice. My friends and I need that map! I can't go home without it."

Fear mixed in with her confusion. She stared at Aliana as if assessing if she was serious. "I will, of course, help you in any way I can."

The horns announcing the beginning of one of the games startled both girls.

Aliana took Delphina's hand and pulled her toward the sound. "We should hurry or we're going to miss the next race. And thank you for telling me what you know."

Delphina lead the way back to their seats.

After this she was going to have to sneak away and do more reading on the Underworld. "*We finally have a lead to follow, Dagg!*"

She felt his amusement. "*We do, and I can already see the distraction it is proving for you.*"

Aliana sent a wave of annoyance at her Guardian. "*Shut it, I will not talk about this right now!*" Now that she knew what she had to do to get home, she was determined to see it through, no matter how much it might hurt her heart. Arthur deserved to be happy with the girl he loved.

They made their way back through the crowd. The second race was to start soon. Vira and Galahad met them halfway, the teen all smiles and excitement.

"I was wondering where you two went!" Sophvira grabbed Delphina's arm and looked at Aliana. "We need to hurry and get back before the race starts."

"I believe Owaine and Percival and Lancelot should be competing next."

"Yes," Galahad confirmed, leading their small group toward the tented area. "I am in the third race, so I must get ready."

Vira hugged her brother again and pulled Delphina away. Aliana made to follow, but Galahad grabbed her hand before she could. "Are you well? You appear distracted."

"I'm all right. Just…" She tried to think of what to say. "Just thinking over something Delphina just told me."

"If I can help in any way…"

"I know." She squeezed his hand comfortingly. "Thank you and good luck in the race." Maybe she would stay long enough to be sure he made it safely through that competition.

Galahad released her and Aliana went off the way Vira had gone. A woman in a pale cloak bumped her shoulder. "Pardon, my lady."

Aliana opened her mouth to reply, but the woman was already moving on. She glanced back and Aliana caught sight of the same familiar black blue hair she had seen at the feast. Most of the woman's face was obscured, but something about the sharp, caramel toned cheekbones, lavender gray eyes and the powerful but soft lilt of her voice pulled again on the strings of a memory she couldn't quite grasp.

She was still trying to place the woman's face when she met all the other girls in the stands. They were again sitting next to the covered platform where Queen Igraine awaited the start of the match.

Owaine, Percival and Lancelot entered the lists with four more knights, all seven men looking more than ready and eager to compete.

Men! Aliana thought, rolling her eyes.

Their three knights were scattered among the starting line with six other burly men. The queen gave the signal to start. As soon as the cloth left her fingers, Lancelot and Owaine took the lead, getting off the line first, Percival very close behind them.

Two more riders immediately shot up to the front line as they went into the curve; only one of them managed to avoid Lancelot and Percival's powerful strikes. Owaine and Lancelot remained in the lead, Percival advancing from behind to a close fourth. They looked at each other then struck at the rider between them. The sound of wood reverberating off the metal was almost as loud as the crowds' cries of excitement. The middle rider seemed stunned and veered to the side, almost into Owaine's horse. The crowd roared again as a different knight, further behind, was kicked from his saddle and went crashing to the ground, dirt and dust puffing up in clouds. The man lay absolutely still for a long moment and Aliana feared he may be dead from such a fall. Then the man moved and she was able to breathe.

She looked back to her knights as pages and servants scrambled to pull the man from the horses' path.

It was down to their knights and one other stranger. The interloper attacked Percival like there was bad blood between them. The big knight fell out of the lead, fending off his attacker.

Lancelot raced toward Owaine, who was still in the lead.

With a move that was all kinds of dangerous, Percival brought down his wooden weapon on the last racer then kicked the teetering rider from his saddle. Lancelot and Owaine were a good deal ahead of him, but he didn't seem to be giving up.

The three raced neck and neck, through the final lap until Lancelot's horse lagged just a moment allowing Owaine and Percival to cross the finish line and advance.

20

I feel bad for upsetting the guys so much I knew they'd be pissed, but the disappointment I felt, especially from my sweet giant cowboy, had hurt me the most! It makes me feel even worse for sneaking off to see Puck. He's reluctant to face Arthur. I don't think it has anything to do with kingie threatening him, despite what he says. Dawn's told me about her adventure in Avalon, and Galahad's battle. She has people there helping her learn to use the Well's waters so I need to as well if the plan is going to work. If I didn't think Puck would disappear completely, I'd bring my Percy with me. But if the guys knew of the danger in our plan...Nope, I'm not saying a thing. Yet.

— Lacy

The rest of the races were fierce to watch and nerve-racking. After each race there was a long break between rounds. Aliana used the time to sneak away and do more research on the Underworld and trying to locate a portal with the holographic-magic map Merlin had taught her to use so long ago.

As it turned out, there was a portal several miles outside of Camelot.

The hard part would be getting out of the castle to go to the Underworld without drawing suspicion from the knights. Maybe Merlin would be able to help her. He seemed to be much more willing to be helpful than he did in her time.

With that thought in mind, Aliana made her way toward Merlin's tent, set up next to Galahad's. The Druid had battled through his round advancing into the final race. It had been very impressive, even more so because he hadn't used magic the entire time. There was so much more to her Druid than she had ever realized, or that he had ever let on in the months they had spent together.

"Merlin?" Aliana called out. "Are you in there?"

She heard the faint sound of footsteps crunching on the ground. Seconds after, a half dressed Merlin pulled the cover back. Aliana's eyes widened looking him up and down; he was ripped!

"Do you enjoy the view?" he asked, leaning one muscular arm on the wooden support, a supremely smug grin on his thin lips.

Aliana hid a smile. "It's all right." She stepped in the tent and closed the flap when he moved back. "I need to talk to you about my quest here."

Merlin grabbed a loose burnt orange shirt hanging off the end of a table. It was a shame to have his amazing figure covered up, but she was here for a purpose. Dagg leapt to life from her wrist, taking his proper form. Fortunately, her guardian agreed that this task was something she needed to do without the aid of the others; the only problem now would be convincing Merlin of that.

"What do you require of me?"

"Aliana and I need to go to the Underworld."

Merlin couldn't have looked more shocked than if Dagg had told him Morgana was going to die by his sword. "Delphina told you about the map then?"

Aliana nodded.

"That is a dangerous journey to make. Arthur will not let you undertake it alone. Moreover, the Underworld's portals are different than the other realms. Getting you, me and the other knights in will not be an easy task."

She cut him off. "I think I need to do this alone, Merlin."

His pale blue eyes hardened, his shoulders tensing as he took an aggressive step toward her. "You cannot enter the Underworld alone. It would mean certain death for you."

"You don't know that." She made sure to keep her voice calm while not showing him his intimidation tactic was affecting her. "*I* was sent here to do this."

His gaze didn't waver as he stared her down. "You now have the most powerful group of warriors in all the five kingdoms who care for you like you are our own. It would be folly to think we would allow you to walk into such a dangerous realm without our help and protection."

Aliana flashed back to her father's office when she and Merlin had argued over the paper they found in the iron-box-of-death. Just like then she refused to back down, but this time she was going to go about things differently.

"Merlin, to have the others come with us would risk revealing I'm from the future. We can't do that. You and I can make an excuse to be gone for a day or so. I found a portal to the Underworld a few miles from here, maybe half a day's ride at most."

Merlin's face pinched, his arms crossing over his broad chest.

Aliana ran her fingers through her hair. "It's close to where the Manticore attacked us. Honestly, I can't believe I didn't think to check for a portal when we were there."

"Your plan will not work. You must know that time flows differently in each realm. We could be gone for far longer than a few days. The king and the others would get 'involved' when we did not return." He looked to Dagg for support, but the Dragon kept his face neutral.

She placed her hands on her hips. "And what if we are gone for only a few hours? That could be just as likely as us being gone for a long period of time."

"I cannot allow you to do this. It is too dangerous." He leaned back on the short table behind him. "And you have still not told the others of your quest here yet."

Aliana rolled her eyes. "I told you, I plan on telling them after the games are over! And I know it's dangerous. That's why I am here, talking to you." She dropped her hands. "I *have* to find this map, but I am not so ignorant as to realize I don't need help." She laid her hand on his still crossed arm. "Your help. That has to be why Titania sent you to find me the day Dagg and I arrived here."

He held his unwavering gaze on hers for another moment before letting out a breath. His arms dropped, one hand rubbing over his freshly shaved face. "You may be right," he mumbled. "But we will need to be extremely careful about when and how we bring this to the king. He will not be happy with it."

Aliana twisted her fingers together. "But it should be privately, and probably after he's had a few drinks."

Merlin glared at her.

"Or not."

"I have a suggestion," Dagg butted in, flying between them to break the tension. "It should be a satisfactory solution for everyone."

Merlin studied the silver creature. "And what is that?"

"We tell the king the truth…" When Aliana opened her mouth, he held up a claw to silence her. "We say that Merlin and Aliana need to go to the Underworld, and we can be sure to have several of the knights accompany us. You and they can stand guard at the portal while we do what we must to find this map."

Aliana saw Merlin's conviction start to waver against Dagg's plan and jumped on the opportunity. "It's a simple and effective solution, Merlin."

"They'll never allow you to go into Death's domain without them." His knowing look caused her stomach to churn. She knew exactly what he meant, or rather who. Galahad and Arthur.

"They won't have a choice. It's far more dangerous for them to enter as opposed to me." She didn't know how she was so sure of that fact, but every instinct in her was screaming she was right.

Reluctantly, the Druid agreed. "We will broach the subject after the tournament finals and *after* you have told them why you are really here." Merlin grabbed the leather vest he usually wore and slipped it on quickly and efficiently.

"You have a small tear on the shoulder," she pointed out. "I can fix it for you real quick if you want."

Merlin glanced over his shoulder at her as he secured his large Knight of the Round Table cuff. Aliana stepped close to the clean scented Druid and traced the tear with her finger. Closing her eyes she summoned a small bubble of her sparkling pink magic, commanding it to seal the tear like it had never been.

When she opened her eyes the tear was gone, and the door to Merlin's tent flap opened.

Morgana stood frozen, her eyes wide and confused until she noticed how close Aliana was to Merlin, who had stopped in the middle of tying the cords on his leather vest. Her fine face frosted over as Aliana took a step back from Merlin.

He smiled warmly at the sorceress. "Hello, my love."

How was the Druid blind to the jealousy so evident in Morgana's gaze? "Merlin and I were just discussing a problem we need to talk to Arthur about," Aliana offered, hoping to cool the blonde's chilly demeanor.

"Indeed." She went to Merlin and wrapped her arms around him possessively. "My lover and I need some time in private."

The order was clear in the forced, polite statement. Aliana nodded and turned to leave the tent, Dagg returning to her wrist. *"I will be happy when we return home and I do not have to spend so much time in bracket form."*

"You can always stay in my room." She stifled a giggle at his immediate, heated burst of annoyance. *"I was joking, Dagg."*

"Your safety is not something that will be left to chance again!"

Aliana sighed and took her time navigating her way back to the arenas.

A head of bluc-black hair caught her wandering eye.

She scanned the area, catching sight of the dark-haired, lavender gray-eyed woman who had bumped into her. But she was so far back in the crowd, with so many people shifting in front of her, Aliana couldn't get a clear look at her. Maybe she would see the woman again at the feast tonight?

The final race was about to start in the oval arena when she finally returned. From the sound of the people in the stadium, it was the biggest turnout yet. Arthur, Galahad, Gawain, Merlin and Leyon were part of the final eight in the race. Percival, Owaine and Lancelot had been eliminated during the last match.

She pushed her way through the crowd, toward the seats she and the others had been using, next to the queen's throne. The knights who weren't competing in this final race were all seated next to the girls, their face bright with energy.

Vira waved her over when the shorter teen caught sight of her. All the girls were there, even Morgana, her blond hair a little disheveled and wearing a new dress.

Aliana's brows rose than fell. *"Guess I know what she was doing with Merlin. I'll bet she used magic for that quick change!"*

"We feared you would not make it in time!" Delphina said as the Fae patted the open seat between her and Vira.

Aliana tried to catch Morgana's eyes as she passed, but the Sorceress pointedly ignored her by carrying on a very loud conversation with Guin about the feast that would be held in honor of the winner.

She sighed and took her seat. Seconds later, the knights entered the arena on their mounts, decked out in their armor with the long wooden lance-type swords in their hands. They lined up in front of the empty throne where the queen would be sitting.

Her eyes skipped to Arthur's. His full lips pulled into a very assured grin before his gaze fell to the pendant that was hanging around her neck, safely hidden underneath her bodice.

Aliana felt the heat creep up her neck as she looked away.

"Who do you favor in this contest, Aliana?" Vira's excitement matched the crowds and she continued before Aliana could even open her mouth to respond. "I believe my brother will win. He is the best with horses!"

There seems to be an endless list of the things he's the best with. On the heels of that thought, Aliana looked at the white knight.

He was already facing her, his eyes fixed on the purple iris tucked in her hair.

Her nerves were starting to flare to life again; she was about to watch what amounted to a blood sport. One life had already been claimed in the second race of the day; and several others had been seriously wounded.

Aliana blinked, returning her focus to Galahad rather than the gruesome knowledge. He inclined his head to her. She said a silent prayer that all their knights would come out of this race unscathed.

Queen Igraine stepped up onto her covered platform and raised her hands to quiet the cheering masses and draw all attention to her. "Welcome to the final contest to determine our champion!"

The crowd's cheering returned, and then stopped again when the queen motioned for quiet.

"The knight who wins this final race will be known throughout the lands as the greatest champion of Camelot!" She looked at all the men, her smile a little brighter as her son bowed his head to her.

The pride on her face was as bright as her sunlight-colored eyes. But Aliana knew that pride was for more than just Arthur, it was for all the knights. Igraine had mentioned at dinner, the night before, that she considered all the knights, and all the girls, to be her children.

"Knights of the realm, take your starting position and may the grace of the gods smile upon you!"

The crowd clapped as the racers lined up a few feet away at the marked starting line. Igraine held up another red piece of cloth and the excitement in the air thickened and pulsed like a drum beat against Aliana's skin. No one dared to breathe as the horses danced behind the starting line, awaiting the sign to go.

The cloth fell from the queen's long tapered fingers and the racers were already barreling past her, and the girls, before the scrap touched the dirt. The thundering hoof beats was close to drowning out the crowds' screams and cheers as the knights wasted no time attacking each other and jockeying for position. The three other racers targeted the knights closest: Leyon, Galahad and Merlin.

Leyon bent forward, ducking a volley from his attacker while simultaneously cutting his weapon upward. It landed in the crook of the other guy's arm, from the cry of pain, and the way the man dropped his weapon. The mangled racer cradled his arm against his chest and fell to the back of the pack.

Merlin was the aggressor in his battle, swinging and stabbing his lance into the side of his opponent. The other man's weapon scored a hit to Merlin's back causing the Druid to push forward and veer his horse a little to the side, but Merlin quickly regained control and struck the guy's side hard enough that he tipped in his saddle then fell to the ground. Some of the crown moaned in sympathy pain, but most cheered as the man rolled out of the way of the racing horse hooves.

Galahad struck his challenger with a heavy hit to the upper part of his chest; the man nearly came clean out of his saddle. His body bent backward, his horse veering to the side as man and beast lost control. The white knight wasted no time maneuvering his horse to catch up to Arthur and Gawain who were exchanging blows at the front of the pack.

The king and Gawain were holding nothing back, attacking each other like it was their life on the line. It looked for a second like the golden king was about to get the better of Gawain, until Leyon and Galahad came up on either side of the two men. Arthur shifted his attention to Galahad, Gawain's going to the Celt and Merlin who had joined the fray. The attacks were relentless. Whatever camaraderie had been between the Knights of the Round Table in past races was gone now.

Merlin swung his weapon at Gawain's head, the devil-may-care knight meeting it in a thudding clash that splintered and broke both men's sticks. Leyon capitalized and hit Gawain in the stomach. His body flinched forward, his grip on his horse's reins slipping causing his mount to zigzag, unintentionally colliding with both Merlin and Leyon. The three of them fell back a few paces behind Galahad and Arthur.

If either the white knight or golden king realized, they made no show of it. Both men were completely focused on each other; both their weapons clashing as they angled their horses to try to get the other to swerve aside.

Aliana's heart was in her throat, one white knuckled hand gripping the bench she was on, the other holding Vira's tightly. But the teen didn't notice, her blue eyes fixed on the two brothers in arms.

"I've never seen Arthur or big brother go at each other like this!"

The shock of Vira's word drew Aliana's eyes from the race for a split second. "What do you mean?" she asked.

"All our knights have always been competitive, but Sophvira is right, this is a new level of intensity." The Fae's eyes met Aliana's quickly before looking back where Arthur was currently striking at Galahad.

Trepidation mixed with fear and sank her stomach like the Titanic. Were they being so aggressive because of her?

The two thundered past the girls in the final leg of the race. Merlin, Leyon and Gawain were not far behind, all three racing to catch up and maybe pass the two fighting knights. Blood dotted all their clothes and faces; they all were going to need Igraine's and Morgana's salves.

The crowd's cheers got louder as both Arthur and Galahad knocked the others' weapons from their hands. Both men turned forward and spurned their mounts to go faster. Now it would all come down to who crossed the finish line first. And the other three were gaining quickly. Not wanting to miss the lightning fast ending that was coming up, Aliana grabbed a small bit of her ruby magic to speed up her vision so it was like watching a scene in slow motion.

Galahad looked at Arthur quickly, as the finish line drew closer—Aliana chewed off one of the last nails she had left—and said something which got lost in the roars of the crowd. But Arthur ignored it. The king kicked his heels into his horse just feet from the finish line. Everyone got to their feet; it looked like Arthur was going to win.

At the very last second Galahad shot forward, his horse barely getting a third of the way across the finish line before Arthur's.

The crowds ignited with cheers and elation as Aliana felt her heart damn near explode in her chest. She released the magic quickly, her hand clutching her top, over her heaving chest, as she struggled to suck oxygen into her starved lungs. When had she stopped breathing?

Vira's screams of delight were close to ear-piercing but Aliana managed to tune it, and all the other noise, out as the guys pulled their horses to a stop. Galahad's blazing blue eyes found hers first as he hefted his helmet up in victory.

2I

Aliana breezed through the tents that were being disassembled by servants, stalking toward Galahad's. "Dagg, I need you to give me some privacy," she whispered. No one was around them as the Dragon returned to his natural form.

"Aliana…"

She cut him off. "No. I will be with Galahad. I need you to get the others here so I can talk to all of them." She turned her pleading kitty eyes on him full force. "Please, Dagg."

He frowned but nodded. "I will return shortly." He flew up into the air, heading toward the castle, his small body looking like a bird from that height. The last of the sunlight lit the sky in shades of red, purple and pink, a beautiful sight, but Aliana couldn't appreciate it. She was too worried how the knights were going to react. Finally she came to his tent, heard voices inside but didn't bother to announce herself as she flung back one flap and entered.

Galahad was sitting on a stool, his shirt set aside as Raven finished gathering up his chainmail and other pieces of armor. The knight's intense eyes met hers, his posture straightening a little. Galahad motioned for the servant to leave.

He bowed to them and left, only the healer who was applying an herbal-smelling salve to the knight's back remained.

Aliana steeled her nerves and went to the old woman healer. "I'll do that."

The lady set aside the jar in her hand, bowed to Galahad and left.

Aliana moved to where the old woman had been, picked up the clay jar and scooped up a small bit of tacky salve. She bit back a gasp at the dark, green and brown bruises, old and new, all over his body. "My god, how were you able to stand?"

"I have had far worse injuries." His muscles tensed as her fingers touched his hot skin, gently rubbing the healing balm on the bruises.

Galahad's shoulders slumped, his head falling forward as her fingers moved higher on his back, over a puckered scar and on to a new ache on one broad shoulder.

When she finished, the knight stood, stretching his thick arms. Flushing from the hot sight of his toned body, Aliana handed him his shirt and tunic. He was just finishing dressing when the tent flap opened. One by one the knights, still dirty from the race, entered. The girls, Guin, Delphina and Vira followed. Aliana frowned, not seeing Morgana among the group. Maybe her absence was for the better.

"Thanks for coming," she said after clearing her throat. "There's something I need to tell y'all about."

Leyon raised a brow. "Are you finally ready, lass?"

Aliana nodded as Dagg settled around her shoulders. "Some of you already know, I was sent here to find something, a relic that will help me locate the Grail of Power."

Several of the guys sucked in surprised breaths. Galahad and Arthur fixed her with heated glares.

"Sent by whom?" the king asked.

Now came the tricky part. "Queen Titania." She glanced at Delphina hoping the Fae would back her story. "She meant for Merlin and Delphina to help me on this quest."

Everyone remained silent. Aliana chewed the inside of her cheek trying not to combust in the silence. "Someone please say something." Her stomach twisted tighter. Would they throw her out now?

"Why Merlin and Delphina?" Gawain finally asked, sending a dark look at the Druid.

It was Delphina who answered. "Because I know a little of the Grail's history."

Merlin jumped in. "And I owe the queen a favor. My helping Aliana is payment."

Aliana stared at him. *I didn't know that. Damn mysterious Druid!*

The guys all exchanged heavy looks, the jubilation from the games all but gone.

"Do you know what it is you seek?" Sophvira asked, speaking for the first time.

"A map. A magical one."

Before anyone could ask any more, the tent opened.

Clara blushed furiously before bowing low. "Forgive me, sire."

"What is it, Clara?" Arthur asked as the tension eased back a little.

"The queen sent me. She wonders where all her knights are and why they are not preparing for the feast."

"We will be there shortly," Lancelot said, dismissing the girl who took off like a scared cat.

"We still need to finish this conversation." Galahad's voice was as tight as his narrowed eyes.

"Tomorrow. I'm still not even sure on all the details myself right now."

She could see their reluctance, but Guin spoke up for her. "She's right. We will get nothing accomplished tonight."

Arthur agreed. "We finish this first thing in the morning."

Aliana ended up being late for the dinner feast. By the time she came through the side door almost everyone was seated. Entertainers flounced around in the middle space left by the long tables that had been set out for the entire court. Arthur was the first to notice her; he raised his golden goblet to her, looking almost relieved. She smiled back and took the open seat between Guinevere and Delphina.

"Sorry I am late," she said, trying to pretend like everything was all right.

"That's quite all right. You have come just in time." Delphina took a sip of her wine. "Our evening entertainment is about to start."

Aliana filled her plate, glancing at the head table where Galahad and the other knights had gathered and were laughing and drinking together in celebration. Galahad sat on Arthur's right side, a place of honor, wearing a thick cloak of animal fur. Curious, Aliana asked Vira about the cape, and she said that it was to honor the champion.

Different entertainers, all dressed in masks and colorful outfits, took turns entrancing the audience. One spit flames of fire with the help of the wine sack in his hand. Two others had knives and daggers of different lengths, all very sharp, as they demonstrated with flamboyant flare, and juggled them between each other. The last one was an archer who performed feats with his long bow and arrows. He would throw things in the air and pierce them with his arrow, or he would have each of the previous performers stand with fruit on their heads and shoot them off one by one. In a way he reminded Aliana of J'alel. They looked nothing alike, but their presence was similar.

It was an evening full of loud celebration. The knights all relaxed, the unattached ones flirting outrageously with the available women at the feast. At one point Aliana was sure she saw Gawain sitting with two ladies in his lap. Even Owaine and Leyon were swarmed with female company. Galahad had a throng of admirers swarming him and Arthur. Both men politely kept sending them away. At one point Sophvira even came up and helped get rid of the more stubborn women before she went off with some friends.

Aliana moved to join the teen, to try to talk to her. She wanted to know how she was holding up with the revelation she had just learned. Aliana's brows pinched together as she looked around the room. It was a few minutes before she saw Vira, in her pale blue dress and long braided hair, duck out another side door with a guy just taller than her with white blond hair and a familiar presence.

Puck!

Aliana pushed her way through the crowd, following the white blond hair. She lost sight of them when they slipped out of one of the side doors. She kept following, recognizing the hall that led to the queen's rooms. It deadened. There was no sign of Vira or Puck.

"You saw him too, right?" She looked around.

"Yes, I felt his presence. Just as I did after we first arrived here in Camelot."

"You never told me that!"

She felt his frustration. *"I never actually saw him, just felt his magic. Though I feel no trace of it now. Or Sophvira."*

Aliana ran a hand through her curled hair. She may not totally understand or like the half Imp, but she felt certain he wasn't a danger to Vira. One thing for sure, she was going to have one heck of a conversation with Vira tomorrow about it.

A warm hand fell on her shoulder. Aliana looked over her shoulder into Arthur's liquid gold eyes. "Why are you out here? Is everything all right?"

She tuned. "Yeah, I just wanted to talk to Sophvira, but I must have taken a wrong turn or something and lost her after she left the party."

Arthur grinned. "She normally leaves these parties early. I'm sure she's up in her room."

Aliana wanted to go check to be sure, but if Arthur wasn't worried…

"Is your Dragon guardian with you right now?"

Aliana nodded pushing up her sleeve as Dagg took his true form.

"I would like a private moment with Lady Aliana, DragonLord."

"I'll be in our room. I will go through the books some more."

"Thanks. I'll be there after this."

He shook his head. *"You deserve a night of fun. Enjoy the rest of the party."*

Surprise filled her as Dagg flew out a window.

"You two can communicate with your minds?" Arthur's question was more of a statement.

She shrugged. "It comes in handy."

"So we have discovered." His eyes darkened, remembering her attempted kidnapping. He quickly shook off the thought. "Are you returning to the feast?"

"I shouldn't. I still need to try to learn more about finding the Grail's map."

"You don't have to do this alone."

"I know," she said with a small smile. "I've got Dagg and Merlin and Delphina."

Arthur shook his head. "That's not what I meant, and you know it."

She knew what he had meant but she still feared him and the others getting involved too much. The more they knew the more she'd have to hide. The fact they had yet to turn her away or get upset with her for keeping all these secrets proved that they trusted and even cared for her. Sadly it only made her miss her knights, friends and home even more.

Arthur's finger gently traced down her cheek. "Why do you suddenly look so sad? Is it because you regret me kissing you?"

"No…I don't know." She blinked away the beginning of a tear. "I just remembered how much I miss my home." And she missed having her Arthur to confide in. Her homesickness made her curious if this was what Arthur had felt since she had awoken him in Avalon.

The king tensed, his golden eyes filling with cautious alertness. "Are you unhappy here?"

"It's not that," she assured him. "As great as Camelot is, as wonderful as you and the others are, this just isn't my home. I miss my family and my friends. And I'm worried about them." It felt good to say it, to talk to Arthur like she was used to. It helped ease a little of the homesickness. "They're in just as much danger as I am if I can't find this map to the Grail."

Arthur had his king mask on but she saw right through it. He was worried for her. Her heart fluttered but she squashed the feeling before it could sweep through her. Arthur wasn't concerned for her like that. Despite everything, he had Delphina. His ghost girl. His true love.

The war that had started to rage in Arthur seemed to settle as he nodded once. "We, I, will do everything I can to help you complete your quest. Do not doubt that."

She did trust Arthur, this version and hers. "I know, and I'm truly grateful."

"I also know there is more to your story."

Aliana looked down twisting her fingers together. "I have my reasons for keeping my silence."

The king took a step closer. "I will learn all your secrets, one day, Aliana."

"I'm not really that interesting." She had to find a way to deter him from his inquiries. "I'm sorry I've upset you, but I can't give you the answers you want."

"We should return." Arthur took a step back. He offered her his arm. "May I escort you back to the party?"

She looped her arm through his. They walked back through the door, several pairs of eyes moving to them, Galahad's and Delphina's among them. The beautiful Fae was standing very close to Galahad before she came over to them.

Aliana hid her flinch remembering again that not only had Delphina *been with* Arthur, but Galahad too.

The white knight looked like he was going to follow the Fae until another knight, one of the visiting men, distracted him.

"Sire, Aliana," Delphina greeted them with a curtsy. "Arthur, I was hoping I could speak to you for a moment."

Arthur seemed reluctant to leave Aliana.

She smiled at him. "Go, I'll be here." He deserved to have time with his ghost girl.

He left the hall with Delphina and Aliana distracted herself by looking out at the people still partying. She wasn't sure if she was hoping to see sign of Puck or Vira or even the dark-haired, violet eyed woman, but she kept scanning the crowd.

"Who are you looking for?" Guin asked, approaching Aliana, Lancelot's hand tangled with hers. The glow she remembered seeing surround them, when they left to battle the Manticore, pulsed faintly.

"I was looking for Vira, actually. I haven't gotten to speak with her recently." It was a pleasant, but painful surprise, realizing how much she like being around the teen that was fated to die.

"She went to her rooms a little while ago," Lancelot answered.

Gawain and Percival stumbled up to the trio, both men clearly drunk by the faint smell of ale and the way their normally graceful movements were slower and unsteadied.

"Sir Lancelot!" Gawain called loudly, his muscular arm flinging around the shorter knight, causing both men to sway unsteadily. "You're not leaving the party yet are you? Arthur's already abandoned us for Delphina's fine company…"

"And that ponce Merlin spirited Morgana away an hour ago!" Percy drawled, cutting his sloshed friend off. "The night is still young, my friend! It's our duty—" *hiccup* "—to see this night through to the dawn!"

The two friends cracked up, the giant Percival nearly falling over. Aliana rushed forward to steady the big knight. His arm curled loosely around her shoulder. Aliana wondered how pissed Lacy would be at her and Percy if she had seen this.

Galahad appeared from nowhere. "I believe the night is over for the two of you." He lifted Percival's other arm around his shoulder. "Lancelot, you and Guinevere can see Gawain to bed, yes?"

The souls mates nodded.

"Then Aliana and I will see Percival makes it safely to his."

The six of them parted company, heading toward opposite doors of the great hall.

"I can support him, Aliana," Galahad said a moment later, seeing her struggle to keep her own balance with the humming, swaying and heavy knight between them. "You get the doors."

She sent him a grateful smile and ducked under the leaden arm of their giant friend. Galahad readjusted his brother knight as she opened the door. Aliana trotted alongside them as they made their way through a part of the castle following Galahad's directions.

Galahad came to a stop in front of an unfamiliar door. "It should be unlocked."

Aliana squeezed in front of them and pushed opened the door. Galahad maneuvered his friend into the room none too gently, laying his now-snoring friend face down on the large bed. He hefted Percival's long legs onto the mattress while Aliana grabbed the thick fur blanket form the foot of the bed and covered him with it.

"Is he going to be okay like this?"

Galahad chuckled. "He's slept off much worse than this before. I'll see that Merlin gets him a tonic for the morning to help with the headache he's sure to have."

Aliana giggled behind her hand. Galahad motioned for them to leave, and she followed him out. They stood outside his door for an awkward second.

"Shall I walk you to your room?" the knight asked. "We are going in the same direction after all."

With no real excuse to refuse she agreed, the two of them walking silently for a few minutes.

"Um…do you know if Sophvira had plans tomorrow?"

Galahad frowned. "Not that I am aware of, why?"

She shrugged. "I have not spent much time with her. I wanted to be sure she's okay with everything." And find out if she did really disappear tonight with Puck!

"I'm sure she'd like that, after we finish the discussion about this quest of yours."

She looked at the ground as they walked in silence again, thinking over everything that had happened. It still confused her to know that none of the guys remembered her here in Camelot. Now that she was here, would they suddenly remember her being here in Camelot or would they truly forget all about her? A part of her wanted them to remember her. It bruised her ego to think that they would *all* honestly forget about her. She held back a sigh. Time travel was very, very confusing!

They entered their hall but she didn't realize it until Galahad stopped her in front of her door. "You seem lost in thought," he said with a smile in his voice.

She smiled sheepishly. "I've got a lot on my mind."

His face fell, like he was disappointed she didn't confide in him. "I will tell Sophvira you want to talk with her, when she wakes in the morning."

"Thank you." She turned from him, her hand hesitating on her door as she felt his stare on her back. She looked at him over her shoulder. "Good night."

He watched her until she shut her door, him on one side and her on the other.

22

Aliana looked around, confused by the warm air around her and contrasting cold stone at her back. *Where am I?*

She looked around the tall bookcase that she stood behind, the sound of two female voices drawing her like a fly to a halogen trap.

"Where did you find it?" another female voiced asked. This one was softer.

"It was right where he said it would be," the first voice said. Aliana peeked around the case as far as she dared. She recognized the pale blond hair and cold hazel eyes of Morgana, but the raven-haired beauty with caramel skin and gray eyes was a stranger to her.

"Let me look at it," the dark girl commanded. Obediently, Morgana took the box from the table and handed it to the woman, whose lavender-gray eyes roamed over the object. "It's perfect!"

"I know. He'll be so pleased. We're one step closer to finally conquering our enemies." Morgana laughed.

"Yes, my girl, but we must not make any hasty moves. We should wait awhile before revealing that we have the artifact. One very nice benefit of this box is it's the perfect vessel for holding things."

Aliana shot up in bed, the morning sun raining down on her. Her heart galloped, her breath coming in pants as she wiped the sweat from her brow.

"What's wrong?" Dagg was suddenly alert and on his feet next to her pillow.

"The woman I've been seeing around Camelot since the first feast…" Aliana took a second to slow her pounding adrenaline and get a deep breath. "I remember why she was so familiar! I saw her in my dream about Morgana and her bad-magic-room. It's Viviane!"

Dagg's expression changed to one of shock and concern. "If she is here in Camelot everyone is in great danger," he growled. "And Morgana may be close to turning on Arthur and our friends."

Aliana gulped down bile that threatened to rise. "If she's here then that has to mean Mordrid is close too." She shuddered. She had tried to think about the dark wizard as little as possible since arriving here. But the truth was, her brief time as his prisoner was never far from her mind. There would even be times when she could feel his lips on hers again.

"Now we really need to get to the Underworld and find that map and complete Titania's task to get home."

The Dragon nodded. "I know we are going to reveal more of who you are and our quest, but I think we must also be careful of what we reveal."

Aliana tossed the covers aside, her toes digging into the fur rug that was spread under her bed. "Because of her, Viviane?"

He nodded. "I do not know as much about this witch as I would like, but what I do know is that she is devious and stealthy and very, very deadly. We must suspect all that we have said may have reached her through Morgana."

"Do you think Merlin told her everything?"

Dagg shook his head. "I'm sure he's said some things, but he said earlier that he was doing this as a favor to the Fae Queen. From all we know of her, I'm sure there was some kind of warning given to him about sharing information. Even with his souls mate."

Aliana hoped he was right. It certainly fit Titania's MO.

Shaken by the dread and knowledge of Viviane's presence, Aliana ducked behind the changing screen, quickly grabbing her purple dress and slipping it on, using her magic to speed up the process.

Running fingers through her long chocolate hair she braided the mass, tying a heavy ribbon at the end to hold it. "We need to find Merlin and tell him we can't wait to go to the Underworld. We'll need to leave as soon as we finish last night's conversation." She paused, a cold feeling sliding down her spine like sludge.

"What's wrong?" Dagg asked, attuned to her feelings like he was.

"I don't know. I need to see Vira."

Dagg frowned but didn't question her as she slipped on her boots. He took her place on her wrist when she was ready. Aliana stepped out into the hall, turning toward Vira's door just meters from hers.

Galahad stepped out of his room as she got to the door. "Good morning." His voice was a little groggy. "Merlin and Morgana left at dawn this morning, but I made sure Percival had a vial of tonic for his head." He smiled gleefully.

But Aliana couldn't feel any humor. "Merlin and Morgana are gone?" she asked, hoping she didn't sound as panicked as she felt. What if Morgana was up to something?

"What is the matter?" Apparently she failed. "Why does their absence worry you? Merlin doesn't need to be present for the coming conversation, since he already knows so much."

Aliana forced herself to calm down. She didn't need to let on to Galahad right now about her suspicions. Not yet. "I was supposed to talk with him before." She shrugged for his benefit, trying to appear aloof. "I'll just have to speak to him when they get back."

The knight nodded, still looking unsure, but he didn't press her. "Is Vira up yet?"

He shook his head. "No I have not seen her all morning. It is unusual for her to sleep so late, but last night was a long one."

Aliana wished she felt as sure of that as he did. The cold sludge had returned to her spine. "I know I said I'd wait to talk to her until after we've all talked, but I'd like to talk to Vira now."

"Galahad?" Arthur's questioning voice drew their attention. They both turned as Arthur approached them.

The king smiled. "Good morning, Aliana, Galahad."

"Good morning," they both said back.

Arthur looked to the slightly taller knight. "Galahad, walk with me. There are a few things we need to discuss."

A look of understanding passed between them and Aliana could guess what it was about. Her.

Galahad nodded to his king. "I trust you and my sister will join us once you've talked."

Aliana smiled despite herself. "Of course."

The two men turned and headed down toward Arthur's rooms. Aliana knocked on Vira's door. She waited for a second but got no response. She knocked again. Still no response. She tried the door but it was locked. *"Something's not right here, Dagg."*

"I know. I feel it too."

Aliana used a small amount of her pink magic to unlock the door. The lock drew back and she pushed the door open and entered the room. "Vira? You in here?"

No answer.

She took another step in. The bed was unmade; the fire in the hearth was nothing more than dying kindling. Coldness spread like a frost around the room. A dead kind of coldness.

"Vira?" Aliana called a little louder, heading toward a connecting room that was off to one side. But she didn't get there.

As she rounded the small table in the center of the room she saw splayed out locks of brown hair stark against the stone floor.

Aliana gasped and knocked over a chair in her rush to get around the table. Her hand slapped over her mouth, her blood rushing to the pit of her stomach in horror.

"Vira!" she screamed, dropping to her knees beside the pale still girl. "Vira!" she screamed louder, cupping the girl's cold face.

Aliana slid an arm under the teen's shoulders lifting the girl's head. "Wake up, wake up!" she hissed, panicked tears building in her eyes. Aliana laid her shaking fingers on Vira's neck. She held her breath wishing with every ounce of hope in her that she would feel a pulse.

But there was nothing. Aliana ripped away the veil hiding her magic and Dagg leapt from her wrist, his glowing amethyst eyes running over the still body.

"She's dead," he growled quietly, anger and pain spilling from him.

"No, she can't be. Galahad will be devastated!" Aliana grabbed all the magic she could and pushed it into Vira, willing her magic to make her heart beat again, air to fill her lungs, her soul to return to her body.

Nothing happened.

She pushed her senses open further than she ever had, grabbed all the magic of the earth, air, energy and water elements surrounding them. With ruthless control, Aliana filtered it all into her own magic core, adding power from her ruby. Her chest felt like it was going to explode from the clashing magics warring in her muscles down to her marrow. But she ignored it and corralled it all into a single pool and pushed it with all her will into Vira's empty body.

Dagg wound around Aliana's shoulders. "Aliana, stop! You're going to hurt yourself."

She ignored his order. Yes, she could feel the weakness and draining effect of using so much magic. It was so much worse than the effects of waking Arthur, or all the other magic she had ever used. But she didn't care. Vira's life was more important.

"Stop right *now!*" His own amethyst magic ripped through her shields shredding her focus. Aliana's body jerked and convulsed at the sudden break. "We can't do anything for her now."

"No!" she screamed, hysterics starting to take over. "Guards, Galahad, Arthur, somebody help us!"

Before the last word left her mouth Arthur and Galahad came barreling though the door. They stopped dead, looking at Aliana cradling Vira's dead body in her arms. Lancelot, Guin and Delphina entered on their heels, stopping behind Vira's ashen-faced brother and the king.

"Sophvira?" Guin squeaked, her hand flying to her mouth as tears exploded.

"*No!*" Galahad sprang into movement, the shock that held him gone like shattered glass. He fell to his knees, took his sister from Aliana's grip, trying to shake her awake. "Little sister, wake up." His voice was hard and commanding, like he would use in a heated battle.

"Open your eyes, Sophvira!" he demanded, streaks of despair coloring the words. "Vira, come back to me!"

The gallant knight's shoulder's hunched as he hugged his sister's lifeless body close to his.

The dam of tears Aliana had been holding back broke and she started sobbing. Arthur knelt down next to her, wrapping his arm around her and pulling her to his side. His other hand went to Galahad's shoulder in silent support.

"How could this have happened?" Lancelot whispered, his own horror dulling his normally superior voice.

Aliana looked up to see all the members of the Round Table, except the absent Merlin and Morgana, in the room along with the queen. Everyone looked pained and devastated and frantic.

Igraine came to Galahad's side, got on her knees and wrapped a motherly arm around his shaking shoulders, kissing his hair lightly. He picked up Vira's lifeless hand, cupped it to his freshly shaven cheek. Aliana saw the small tear that leaked from his clenched eye.

Aliana was shaking all over, panic and guilt ratcheting higher by the second adding to the vast pain she was already suffering from magic drain. Desperate for answers, she focused again and opened her shields and connected with Dagg.

"Can your Dragon sight see something we can't?" He was silent. Aliana pushed the small amount of magic into him connecting her vision to his. The room's colors brightened, and everything in the room sharpened. But her eyes and magic immediately saw the evil that had killed the most beloved member of this family.

There was a thin gold bracelet with a small yellow diamond on her small, delicate wrist, hovering right below Galahad's own big hand, like a viper ready to strike another victim. Darkness leeched from the cold material, a black stream of death seeping into Vira's veins like a poisoned river.

Aliana grabbed at the bracelet; maybe if she could get rid of it Vira could be saved! Her hand closed around it and lava hot pain shot up her arm and through her body.

She heard her own howl of pain, felt fire shaking her body, trying to push her into unconsciousness. Her connection to Dagg and his magic snapped, her own magic falling to the way side in the rush of pain consuming her like a violent cloud.

Rays of sunlight broke through the clouds, air returned to her bruised lungs and the darkness faded into oblivion.

Aliana opened her eyes to see Arthur and Igraine both hovering, blocking out everything else in the room.

"Sophvira was murdered," she rasped out.

"That bracelet is poisoned with magic," Delphina's musical voice warned.

Aliana pushed out of Arthur's arms and reached for the bracelet again. Igraine's hand stopped her. "You cannot touch it, it nearly poisoned you too." She turned Aliana's hand over.

She gasped at the line of red angry blisters that ran across her palm and fingers.

Arthur shot to his feet, his anger and determination like a flare of red around him. "Lock down the city, no one enters or leaves until we've caught Sophvira's murderer."

The guys snapped into action. Percival, Leyon, and Lancelot shooting from the room.

"Gawain, Owaine, find Clara, the servant who attends Vira. She may know who has come and gone from this room."

They left immediately.

"Galahad," Arthur said, kneeling back down, placing his hands on his friend's shaking shoulder. "We will find who did this. They will pay dearly for Sophvira's murder."

Galahad didn't move from his smothering hold on his sister's dead body. Igraine continued to comfort the catatonic knight.

Delphina and Guinevere both sank to the floor next to Aliana, the three of them huddling together, muffling sobs of anguish and heartbreak.

How long had Vira been here like this? How could someone have gotten a magically poisoned bracelet into Vira's room?

"Morgana could have done it." Dagg seemed almost reluctant to blame the sorceress. And so did Aliana. Morgana clearly loved Vira, just like everyone else. It made no sense why she would have killed Vira.

Another face sprang to the front of Aliana's clenched and aching eyes. Viviane. Morgana's teacher. *"Dagg, take whatever power you need from me to remain hidden, but find her!"* She dropped the outer layers of her shields and fed it to him, ignoring her already aching body.

"I have enough without your magic. If you try to use any more you could kill yourself by depleting your own magic core!"

She sighed, finding a new reason to hate the way her magic functioned so differently from that of others. Even though Aliana couldn't see him, she felt his comforting presence go from the room. She hugged the girls tighter to try to stave off the panic and gut-stabbing guilt. Vira's room was right next to hers; she knew what fate planned for the girl. Why hadn't she taken more precautions, or watched over the sweet little sister better?

Arthur kept talking to Galahad in a low voice, signaling his mother to step back with a nod of his head. Slowly the big knight's death grip started to slacken, inch by agonizing inch. Aliana wanted to go to him, comfort him, but her shame held her rooted to the cement floor. That and the boneless feel of her whole body.

Gawain and Owaine pushed through the doorway, Clara's arms gripped in their big hands as they were coming very close to man-handling the servant.

She looked frightened and confused as they dragged her, stumbling in front of Arthur. "Sire, what is going on?"

Before Arthur could answer, Galahad got to his feet, his sister's lifeless head hung back, her arm dangling limply in the air. "My sister was murdered." His voice was as hollow and dead as his dulled blue eyes.

Clara gasped, and she looked unbelieving at Sophvira's body. Her eyes drifted to a small oval box lying on the ground by Galahad's feet, and then burst into tears. She would have fallen to her knees if the knights hadn't still been holding her.

Arthur stepped in front of Galahad before he could take a step toward Clara. "Do you know who did this?" His voice was even but stern. "She was poisoned by this bracelet!" He pointed to the gold band on Vira's dangling wrist. "Who gave it to her?"

"I don't know, sire!" she cried through hiccups and tears. "This is my fault! But she always got little presents…they have never…she's dead because of me!"

Galahad's face reddened, his eyes starting to return to violent life. Igraine stopped him before he could move, somehow holding the knight still.

"What are you babbling about, girl?" Gawain demanded, his voice hissing through his teeth. It was clear he was trying to restrain his own need to do violence on Vira's behalf.

Still on the floor, Aliana reached for the oval, wooden box. Gripping it she got to her feet, Guin and Delphina steadying her as she wavered. Faint traces of the dark magic clung to the box like a bad scent.

Arthur took it from her hands. "What do you mean she received gifts? How are you responsible for her death? Choose your words very carefully, Clara. They will determine your fate."

Aliana shivered at the cold warning.

"She's…Lady Sophvira has…has always g-gotten gifts like that one. She…she said they were from a-a secret fr-friend." Clara's body shook with her stuttered words. "They are…I always find them outside her door."

Guinevere went to Arthur's side, her face soft with understanding. "Have you ever seen who leaves them?"

Clara's shaking lessened as she focused on the less threatening Guin. "No, never."

Everyone in the room seemed to deflate a bit. Lancelot, Percival, and Leyon reentered the room, taking in all that was happening with silent focus.

"But…"

All eyes went back to Clara at the whispered word, attention fully on her. It was a wonder the girl didn't crumple on the spot.

"But what?" Arthur demanded. "Did you see who left this box?" He held it out closer.

She shook her head. "I didn't think about it at the time but…I saw someone, I've never seen him in this part of the castle before…"

"Who?" all the guys demanded together.

She flinched back, but the guys still kept hold of her. "The stable boy, Ra-Raven."

23

"What?" Delphina demanded, her musical voice hitting sharp notes. "It couldn't be him!" Aliana protested. "He's not the kind to hurt someone."

Arthur glanced at the two girls, his face filled with anguish but still determined. "Find him, now!" he ordered Lancelot, Percival and Leyon.

He looked to the shaking servant girl. "Is there anything else you remember? Something else you need to tell us?"

She shook her head once then stiffened. "I am so sorry for what has happened. I should have realized something was wrong."

Galahad seemed to fluctuate between mortified and ragingly vengeful.

Arthur's posture stiffened even more. "Gawain, Owaine, see Clara back to her room. You've been very helpful Clara, but I want you to stay in your room." He smiled at her, but it was purely for show, an attempt to soothe the terrified servant. "Place a guard at her door for her safety."

Gawain nodded. "Then we will join the hunt for our murderous traitor."

Owaine voiced his own agreement. "I will coordinate search parties with Percival." He looked to Galahad. "We will bring him to you in blood and chains."

With that they led a silent Clara from the room.

Aliana gripped Delphina's hand, trying to quell her nervous shaking. "Arthur, you don't know if Raven being in this wing is connected to that box!" But her gut told her that their assumptions might be right.

He shook his head. "This is not something we can take a chance on. We will find him and get the truth from him. One way or another." He glanced up as Lancelot returned, his face reddened with exertion. Guinevere went to her husband's side, taking his hand in hers for support.

"Lancelot, send out your most trusted scout. Find Merlin and Morgana. Get them back to the castle immediately."

He bowed to the king, kissed his souls mate's hand quickly and disappeared.

"Galahad, listen to me." Queen Igraine touched his flexed arm drawing the silent knight's attention. "You must give me Sophvira's body, we must prepare her for the funeral rites."

His grip tightened, his body shifting back from the queen. She waited calmly, her even, sunlight gaze wearing him down.

"Come." Igraine headed toward the door, Galahad took a step to follow then stopped and looked back to Aliana. For the first time she couldn't read what he was feeling.

Delphina went to him, her delicate face soft with sympathy. "You must see to your sister."

The knight looked to his king. Arthur nodded once, his face grave.

With Delphina, he followed the queen, Guinevere trotting after them as they disappeared from the room.

"We should not linger here." Arthur wrapped a steady arm around Aliana's waist. "You will wait for news in my chambers. They are the best guarded in the castle."

Her shocked state gave Arthur the distraction he needed to propel her from Vira's cold room, down the hall and into his own larger chambers. It was easily four times the size of her room, but then, that was to be expected. That and the rich drapings of red and gold and cream fabrics around his big bed, the massive hearth and long table that stretched away from it.

Arthur steered her toward one of the chairs furthest from the door, on the other side of the table.

"I will be joining the others in their search for Raven —" Heavy knocking pounded his now closed door. "Enter!"

"Sire, we have him." Owaine's grave frankness was helping to control the blood lust in his eyes. He, Percival, Galahad, Leyon, and Gawain entered the room.

"Lancelot and several of the guards are securing him in a cell in the dungeons." Gawain looked at Galahad, his hand resting on his brother's shoulder. "Do you want to be the one to get answers from him?"

Galahad was silent but nodded.

Aliana's blood pressure spiked. "You can't be serious!" They were not going to torture a boy, no matter his accused crime!

Sir Percival spoke for the group. "We will get the truth from this traitor in any way we must. If he somehow survives that, he will face the executioner." Quiet rage colored the words.

She shot up from her seat. "Arthur, Galahad, you can't! What if he didn't do it and he was seen by mistake?" Yet her twisting gut told her Raven could have something to do with what happened.

Leyon stepped forward. "We have no other option, lass. The longer we wait, the more chance something could happen to him to prevent us from getting our answers."

Aliana shifted back. "You think whoever poisoned Vira was working with someone else?"

Their silence was all the answer she needed. But they had no clue to search for Viviane. How could she tell them without revealing who she was to Morgana?

Aliana clenched her jaw. Dagg was searching for the evil woman. "I didn't think anything of it at first. There was a dark-haired woman I've been seeing around the castle since the games started. She was always sticking to the shadows, hiding her face."

"Why did you not say anything sooner?" Percival asked, taken back.

She shrugged, feeling helpless. "There were many visitors here for the celebrations. But I think she's the one we need to find."

"What does she look like?" Gawain asked.

Aliana described the witch in detail for them.

"That does not change the need to get answers from Raven." Arthur turned from Aliana to the knights. "Do what you must."

"No!" Aliana shouted. "Torturing someone doesn't get you the truth! They will say whatever you want to hear just to make the pain stop. That's not how you get your answers, or your justice for Sophvira. That's cold-blooded revenge. None of you are the type who would do such a horrible thing!"

"We have no other way." The finality in Arthur's rumbled rebuttal had ice crystals spreading through Aliana's veins.

Gawain and Owen nodded as Leyon spoke up, "We have already lost one person we love, Aliana. We'll not chance these murders taking another life."

Arthur agreed. "If Merlin was here, perhaps we could try another way, but he is not."

Desperation turned the ice into sludge. Aliana knew what she needed to do to keep her friends from losing sight of justice and the honor and chivalry that was a core part of their beings.

She went to Arthur, placed herself squarely in front of him boldly meeting his gaze head on. "What if I can give you a different way to get the truth? One that doesn't involve torture and will be certain that you get the honest facts?"

"How?"

"Give me an hour, I'll get you what you need to get real answers."

Arthur stared down at her. "How?" he asked again. "Unless you give us an answer, we do it our way."

She didn't have a choice now. She had to tell them about her magic. It was either that to let the men she cared about become monsters.

"I was going to tell you all this morning. I can do what Merlin can. I have magic too."

None of the guys seemed overly surprised.

"You finally confirm it then?" Lancelot asked, his voice hard.

"I'm sorry I didn't tell y'all sooner, but I had my reasons." She looked back to Arthur. "Give me one hour."

His gaze flickered down a fraction. "You have one hour."

"Sire!"

Arthur silenced the knight's protests with a hard glare. She turned and tried to look confident as she walked calmly past the guys and out into the hall.

She glanced over her shoulder, saw no one had made to follow her and took off running toward Merlin and Morgana's potion chamber.

"Dagg, have you found Viviane?"

She felt his frustrated growl through their link. *"No, she has hidden her tracks too well."*

"Keep looking then. We have *to find her."*

"I know what you are planning to do, be careful."

Aliana felt a ghost of a smile return to her face. *"Aren't I always?"*

"Only if always means never."

Flinging the door open to Merlin's potion room Aliana grabbed at one bottle then another and another. Merlin said he always kept potions and other magical things ready in case of emergencies. And this was an emergency. She couldn't let the knights, her friends, and her family do unspeakable things to a boy because they were blinded by a need for revenge. Even if he was guilty, the deed would still be cold blooded revenge.

Aliana slammed her hands on the wooden bench. "Damn it, Merlin! You have to have something here to help me figure out how to create a truth potion!"

The door opened again. Aliana's head snapped to see Igraine standing in the doorway, looking as calm and collected as always. All except for the faint stains of tear tracks still lingering on her cheeks.

Aliana's heartache threatened to return, but she held it back. She couldn't give into it right now. She didn't have the right to. "I need to find a way to make a truth potion."

Igraine stepped in and closed the door. "Magic strong enough to draw the truth from an unwilling mouth is not something that can be held at the ready. It must be created and used at once."

"I can't let Galahad and the knights throw away their honor to torture a boy because they're blinded by their grief for Vira," Aliana replied.

The queen's warm hand came to rest on her exposed shoulder. "Then you must create the truth potion they need."

Aliana shook her head. "I've never created a potion before. My magic has always been more physical and kind of spontaneous." She paused. "Apparently my magic is much different than everyone else's. Merl...I have no idea where to even start."

"What is the basis of all magic ability?"

Aliana looked up at the queen confused.

Then she remembered back to her first magic lesson with Merlin. *"We shape the power inside us to do our will."*

"Magic is shaped by our will."

Igraine smiled. "Exactly. You have to believe and command the magic to do what you want. You clearly have more than enough power to do this; you just have to want it enough."

She did want it enough. She took a fortifying breath and grabbed a small empty bottle with a glass stem that dipped inside the jar.

"Close your eyes and concentrate on what you want. Pull your magic and command it to do your will."

Aliana followed the queen's instructions, acutely aware that her hour was running out like sand through an hourglass. She held the glass between her palms drawing on her own core of magic, opening her senses and taking a large drop of the water element's power. She imagined it like a trickling fountain slowly filling the jar with an elixir that would get the truth they needed from Raven without the knights having to torture him.

Magic rushed through her to her hands like a warm spring through her blood and muscles before tapering off. Relaxing, Aliana opened her eyes and hands. The small jar in her hands was now filled with pale pink liquid glittering with dying sparks of magic.

"I did it!" Aliana wavered, her knees buckling before Igraine steadied her. She was dangerously close to a magic burnout.

"Yes, you did." The warmth and pride in her motherly voice reminded Aliana of her own mothers. Her adoptive mother's voice at least. "But you must use caution. Potions like this one can be very dangerous. If the person who consumes it has too much, it could cause them a horrible death before you can get the truth from their lips."

Dagg flew through an open window and wrapped himself around her shoulders. "I thought I told you to be careful." His reproach was softened by the flowing strength he returned to her.

Aliana closed her fist around the jar. "We have to get back to Arthur."

With the queen following her, and Dagg taking his hiding place on her wrist again, Aliana ran through the halls back to Arthur's rooms. Everyone was still there, the men pacing like caged animals ready to pounce. Delphina and Guinevere sat anxiously by the fire place, watching the men.

Aliana took a breath and went to Arthur, who had yet to leave the far side of the table across from his men. "I have it." She held the vial out to him. "It's a truth potion. Make Raven drink a little of it and you'll get real answers."

He took it, looking skeptical, and held it up to the light. "Are you sure this will work?"

Aliana nodded, letting him see how sure she was. "You have to be careful; you only need a few drops. Too much and you'll kill the person who drinks it."

Arthur handed the bottle back to her. "If there is another working with Raven we do not have the time to chance that this will not work."

"We have already wasted much time," Lancelot insisted.

Aliana ignored him, like she always did when she was in that mood. "It *will* work!" She held Arthur's gaze. "I promise you. Trust me, please."

He looked away from her to the others. They all seemed skeptical, but it was Galahad who finally nodded once when Arthur looked at him.

"Very well." He held the small bottle toward the knights, not taking his eyes from her. "You heard her. Only a few drops."

Aliana wanted to look away, to see the expressions on the knight's faces, but she didn't dare.

Feet shuffled, leather and weapons rustling as everyone left. The door shut with a click that seemed to reverberate through her very blood.

"Is your Dragon with us right now?" he asked after the door closed.

"Yes." The small silver Dragon appeared between them.

"Sire?"

"I am not sure what all it is you do, but leave us. I will see to Lady Aliana's protection."

Dagg appeared to hesitate, then cast a look at Aliana who gave him a ghost of a nod. "I will not be far." He flew out the small open window on the other side of Arthur's rooms.

They stood there for an endless moment. Aliana saw the hurt that lingered in his hypnotizing eyes. Hurt from Vira's murder and from the fact she was still keeping things from him.

"Thank you," she whispered, her throat too tight to speak louder. "For trusting me."

"I wish you would return that trust." His severe frown caused wrinkles around his mouth. He was stronger in so many ways than her.

She closed her eyes briefly. "I want to tell you, all of you, everything." She opened her eyes again, feeling tears pool there. "I don't hold back so much because I want to." *Not really a lie.*

"Then why?" he demanded.

"It's dangerous, for you, for the knights. I've been warned of the consequences of revealing too much." She took a steadying breath. "And I made a promise to someone I greatly respect that I wouldn't reveal…" She stopped herself. "Please believe I only want to help you, all of you…Vira." She felt the first tear fall. She shouldn't be focusing on her feelings for the king right now. She'd only just found her friend murdered!

Arthur sighed, his thumb and fingers stroking her face again, wiping away the tear before tangling in a lock of her loose hair. "I want to know everything about you. There are many things I would ask you, about so many different topics."

He closed the distance between them, his large hand resting on her shoulder. "But I understand better now why you hold back."

Aliana felt intimately aware of how close he was, the heat radiating from him, the smell of grass, morning dew and sweetness. He was the summer scent to Galahad's winter. Funny, summer had always been her favorite time of the year.

Golden threads weaved around them, pulling her attention to Arthur as other thoughts were pushed away.

"I'm not happy about the secrets, but I do trust you." He rested a hand on her hip. All he had to do was give a little tug, or for one of them to lean in a little and their bodies would be pressed together. His face inched closer, his golden eyes partially hidden by his lowered lashes, but it did nothing to dissipate the heart thundering emotions between them. He was just as intoxicating as he had been on the beach, during their moonlit dance, and again when he had taken their first kiss. She had cared for Arthur well before she had come to Camelot; even if she hadn't already been in love with him, she would certainly be now. Watching him these past weeks, seeing him as he was: confident, just, and beyond loyal to his kingdom and family—she had fallen even harder for him without realizing it.

She could see his own desire and feelings for her in his eyes. They held her ensnared, making her knees weak.

He took a cautious step back, almost like he didn't trust himself to be so close to her. Aliana felt her legs waver before she stumbled, catching herself on the table. What was she doing? This wasn't the time for her feelings to take over.

Heavy pounding sounded at the door. Arthur grabbed Excalibur from the table. How had she not noticed his sword there earlier?

"Who is it?"

"Sire, Lord Galahad sent me," a voice Aliana didn't recognize said from the other side of the closed door. "He says it is a matter of life or death."

24

Isis and Iris have been amazing teachers; they've shown me so much! I know more about Nymphs, my magic, and they even told me all I needed to know about the "time mirror" and what Lace and I will have to do for our plan to work. They are helping me stay in contact with Lacy and arrange everything, even keep the guys distracted while we do it. It feels good to have the guys in part of the loop, but neither Lacy nor I are stupid enough to tell them about the real risks of our plan. I find the anger and hurt I've been nursing, about what the guys did, about Wade, are fading. Maybe he and I will have a chance after all. If he doesn't kill me first, that is.

—Dawn

Aliana started to panic and moved to the door, but Arthur's hand on her waist stopped her. "Stay here," he ordered in his low, I'm-the-king-you'll-do-what-I-tell-you-to voice. "You are not safe to be out in the castle."

She wanted to argue, but her hazy mind wasn't coming up with a good enough argument.

Satisfied that she would obey, Arthur sheathed Excalibur at his waist and stormed over to the door. He opened it to the young soldier who stood ready to do his king's bidding. "I want four guards patrolling these halls and two more guarding my door." Arthur looked back at her. "No one but me goes in or out of my room. Understand?"

The man nodded solemnly.

Arthur closed the door behind him and Aliana sagged back in the chair.

She closed her eyes for a moment, calming her galloping heart. With Arthur gone and no longer taking all her attention, she realized what had just happened. Her bond with Arthur was forming and growing. Panic started to leak into her mind. She hadn't felt her bond to Arthur until now. She remembered feeling the sparkling silver bond between her and Galahad after he'd saved her life then nearly kissed the life out of her.

Had they both felt it?

She should kick herself. How could she have let this all happen? She wasn't from this time period! It wasn't right or fair to them for her to let them entertain feelings for her.

Aliana got to her feet, hoping to get to the window for some fresh air, to stave off her agonizing heartache, both from her untimely surge of feeling for Arthur and the tragic loss they all were suffering.

Dagg returned to the room through the window he had left. He was flying straight at her, his Dragon face scrunched and worried. "Are you all right?"

"No! Nothing about this is all right!" She didn't want to think about this anymore. It *hurt* too much. "Did you find anything about the map? Was Delphina right, is it in the Underworld?"

"Yes." His amethyst eyes lit up with his magic. The secret book appeared between them. Aliana caught it before it fell to the ground. Sitting back down, she laid out the small book. Dagg opened it to a page near the end. There was a drawing of an elaborate chalice surrounded by scrolling writing. Dagg's eyes glowed purple before the words shimmered and turned to English.

Aliana's eyes dashed across the page. It talked about the creation of the Grail, the story matching almost exactly what Delphina had told her. It spoke of the Grail's ability to restore what had been lost, even a person's life. But they already knew all this. She skimmed the page again looking for any mention of a map. She found it in a bottom corner.

"Here, Dagg!" She read the lines out loud, "'Should the Grail ever again be taken, only the map created of the Grail's magic will lead those who seek it to the prize.'"

She growled. "That was anti-climactic and a total waste of space! I need to know if the map is in the Underworld!"

"Then we have to trust that Delphina is right." Dagg closed the book, waving a claw over it before it disappeared.

"Finding it there is going to be a problem." She snorted. "That and figuring out how to convince the Underlord to give it up."

Dagg growled too. "There is something else I just thought of. Do you remember after we first arrived here? I left to try to find a magic that I felt around us, as you rode to Camelot?"

She wondered where he was going with this. He had said he thought that power was nothing.

"I've only realized now, that it was the power of the Well of Realms."

She shook her head. "Clear as mud, Dagg. I've got no clue what you're trying to say here."

"The Well of the Realms is a device that can allow us to communicate with another, no matter where they are in the realms, but it can also be used to watch someone without them knowing. I believe someone was watching us as we arrived here. I have felt the power to varying degrees since we've been in Camelot."

Aliana gasped. "Why didn't you say anything?"

He shook his angled, gray marbled head. "I thought it was the magic of Camelot. Now I know I was wrong. Someone has been watching almost everything we have done since arriving here."

"It has to be Titania!" Aliana said. "She's got to be the one!"

Dagg jumped into her lap. "Not necessarily. Every realm has its own Well. It could be anyone watching us, but I suspect it may be the Underlord."

Aliana sat back with a huff and stroked his scaly body and wings like she always did when she was trying to calm down or seek comfort. "Why?"

"I do not know, and that is a major thing to worry about. I find it hard to believe that throughout everything that had happened, that he is the only power in all the Realms that has not somehow inserted himself into the quest for the Grail or stopping Mordrid."

Aliana opened her mouth but snapped it shut when the door opened and Arthur came through with the somber looking knights. Igraine followed behind them and went to Aliana's side as the knights gathered around.

"What's going on?" Aliana asked.

Galahad's jaw tightened, his hand clenching his sword tightened.

"Your truth potion worked," Gawain said, his usually upbeat voice hard. "He *was* the one who placed that poisoned bracelet by the door."

Aliana's eyes widened. She had wished it wasn't true, that he hadn't killed Vira. "How? He doesn't even have magic."

Owaine shook his head. "Apparently he does, and so does the woman he's conspiring with."

"The dark-haired woman I told you about?"

They all looked at each other. Aliana's anxiety revved up. What on earth had Raven said to make them all so cold and distant?

"Yes," Lancelot said, his voice gravelly. "Her name is Viviane."

She should have realized who that woman was sooner. If she had, maybe Vira would still be alive! She looked at Galahad and Arthur, standing side by side. "What else did he tell you?"

Galahad's jaw unclenched for the first time since coming in the room. "That bracelet had not been meant for my little sister." His voice was so low, and spoken more to the others than her.

Aliana shot out of the seat. "What?" She looked from one knight to the other, her mind starting to realize the implication of Galahad's statement. "Who was it meant for?"

"You," Arthur said.

Aliana stared at him disbelieving, her entire body numb. "I don't think I heard you right."

"You did," Percival assured her quietly.

Guilt rammed into her like a one ton wrecking ball. Her legs collapsed as Igraine helped her sit back down. Tears of anger and disbelief prickled her eyes as she looked at Galahad. The white knight was staring at the stone floor, his knuckles white as he gripped the back of a chair.

It was all her fault. Vira was dead because of her. Galahad had suffered his most heartbreaking loss because of her! "Why?" she croaked. "I thought we were friends. Why did he do it? I don't even know this Viviane woman!"

"But they know you," Owaine spoke up, his grief and anger simmering. "The bracelet was supposed to place you in a deep sleep so they could spirit you away without anyone knowing."

"And magic works differently on everyone," Aliana breathed, looking at her clenched hands, her distress swamping her.

The queen's gentle hands settled on her shoulders. "When you touched it earlier it nearly did what it was supposed to. I was only able to save you because so much of its magic had already been used."

Aliana let the queen's words soak into her stunned and wrought brain. She raised her eyes to Galahad's, which were staring at her hard enough to go right through her. "I am so sorry, Galahad. If I had never come here, your sister would still be alive."

The white knight looked away from her.

"They also were responsible for the two men who tried to abduct you. They have been after you all this time, lass." Leyon's words and the sad, angry looks from the knights hit her like a rock.

Another possibility entered her mind. What if Guinevere is killed too because of another attempt against her? Her lungs constricted like a python was squeezing them. She had to leave now. She could go to the Underworld on her own and get the map. Maybe, once she had it, she could find a way to bargain with Titania to send her home.

Aliana got to her feet, her sadness and grief and guilt wanting to overwhelm her. But she didn't deserve to let herself give in, she had to leave now before anyone else was killed or hurt because of her. "I'll get my things together and leave immediately."

Arthur straightened, his face hardening. "You will not be going anywhere!" His order was that of a king.

Aliana shook her head, balling her hands into shaking fists.

Gawain spoke before she could. "The real question is why do they want you so much?"

Aliana bit her cheek. "Because I seek the Grail? And possibly my magic too."

"Why?" Arthur asked, still standing with his knights.

Her heart clenched, it almost felt like they were turning against her. Her hate of her magic resurfaced. "My magic is different than everyone else's."

"All who possess magic have different types," Gawain pointed out. "Merlin and Morgana have taught us that."

Aliana shook her head. "The way I use magic, the amount of power I can draw on is what makes me so different." She thought about showing them her ruby but shot the idea down as soon as it formed. She'd have to explain things she couldn't without breaking her promise to Igraine. "The best thing I can do is to leave, now, before anything else happens."

"No!" Arthur commanded.

"If I stay—"

"There is no *if* about it," Percival said, taking a step to his left. Owaine and Leyon moved to stand on both sides of him. A solid wall of undefeatable knights keeping her here.

Owaine crossed his arms. "You were sent here for a reason, and we all agree that we need to help you."

Aliana's eyes prickled. He looked so much like her cousin, it made her miss all her knights and sisters so much more.

Gawain agreed with Owaine. "We certainly have no intention of letting you go out on your own where you have no protection and no allies to help you."

"Vira is…*dead* because of me. I won't let someone else—"

"Sophvira is not dead because of you," Lancelot insisted, drawing her attention. "She is dead because of Raven and this Viviane. And we will not rest until we have captured this *woman* and put them both to death."

"You will not be leaving Camelot, Aliana," Arthur reiterated. "One of us will remain with you at all times. Extra guards, those whom we know are loyal to us, will patrol this hall and guard your door."

"But, Arthur…"

His shoulder's straightened. "No. My decision on this is final."

Distress flooded her again. She had to find a way to get away, no matter what these loyal knights and friends thought or said. This was her fault, and she would die before she let anyone else be hurt because they were after her.

"Aliana, do not do anything rash!" Dagg ordered.

Sunlight broke through the dark clouds that had descended on Aliana. She looked up at the queen who said, "We must prepare for Sophvira's funeral pyre."

Tears returned to Aliana's eyes. She looked at all the knights, but her eyes kept drawing back to the silent Galahad who had only spoken ten words to her in the few hours since his sister's death.

The sun had set by the time the funeral parade made its way down to the beach, lit by a wide path of blazing fire urns. The briny smell of the ocean had always been a great comfort to Aliana, having had so many wonderful memories on the beach by her house. But this time the familiar scent gave no comfort. It only added to the emptiness she felt in her chest and soul.

Leyon, Lancelot, Owaine and Gawain carried Vira's pale body on a decorative display overflowing with flowers, jewelry, and colored ribbons of silk. She was dressed in the green dress she had gotten for the opening celebration of Camelot's anniversary, her dark hair curled and sprawled around her head like a dark halo.

Aliana walked between Arthur and Merlin, behind Delphina and Guin who were on either side of a silent, stone faced Galahad. Merlin and Morgana had returned shortly after they got their truth from the traitorous Raven. Morgana had crumbled to the floor when she was told the news; her agonizing sobs still ringing in Aliana's ears, mingling with the more silent sounds of Delphina and Guinevere's. Even Merlin shed silent, angry tears for the lost little sister. Aliana had no doubt that Morgana was innocent in this murder.

More of Aliana's own tears slid silently down her cheeks, but she clenched her jaw even harder to keep from letting the sobs she didn't deserve to cry escape her mouth. She wouldn't deserve to grieve Vira's murder until she had found a way to make things right, until she'd found an impossible way to earn forgiveness for placing such a wonderfully sweet and totally innocent girl in the path of death.

As they neared the water, a small boat came into view. It was filled with branches of green leaves, a single bright torch strapped to the head of the boat illuminating the vessel that would take Vira's body and spirit to heaven. It was decorated with more of the same flowers and ribbons that covered her body. The four honor guard knights waded into the water, lifting Vira's body above the edge of the boat and settling her on the morbidly beautiful altar in the waiting vessel.

Galahad stepped forward, a bouquet of flowers tied together with silk in his hands. He made his way to the boat, while his brother knights and all the other members of the court watched quietly. He stepped up to the side of the boat and tucked the bundle of colored blooms in his sister's pale and still hands. He brushed her face with his fingers, bent over like he was whispering something in her ear, and kissed her forehead lovingly.

He stepped back and nodded to his four brothers. All of them gripped the boat. Together they launched it into the open ocean. They watched it float out with the gentle tide as they returned to the sand.

Arthur lifted his hand and a dozen archers stepped forward, arrows lit with tips of fire in their hands. They nocked the flaming arrows, raised their bows and took aim.

Galahad bowed to the king.

Arthur lowered his hand. The swish of the arrows flying from the bows was loud enough to drown out the sobs from the people around them. They sailed through the cloudy night sky like shooting stars before landing in Vira's funeral boat. The kindling caught fire, blazing to life like a moving torch as the clouds in the sky parted and the bright light of the full moon shone down on the lost member of their family, like the heavens themselves mourned the teen's loss.

After a long moment, Galahad turned back to the beach, his brothers by his side in a show of support.

Aliana's teary green eyes found his dull, pain-filled blue ones in the light of the fires raging on the beach. Their gazes held. She could read the despair that was churning in him, saw how he was trying to be strong for his sister, his family and himself.

Her lips trembled along with her hands. She wanted to go to him and hold him, to give him comfort. Aliana hated seeing him look so alone and lost. Her feet refused to move, her body locked with guilt. Why would he want comfort from the one who was the cause of his beloved sister's death?

Delphina went to him instead. She reached up, cupped his cheeks with her hands, and brushed away a tear with her thumb. Galahad's head bent and she pulled him gently toward her. That was when he broke and wrapped her in his arms, burying his face in her neck and apricot-colored hair.

Aliana's heart broke even more, sadness filling her. But the angry voice in her head screamed that she didn't deserve the knight. That Delphina was the one who should be comforting him.

The Fae held on to Galahad for what felt like an age before pulling him aside and back up toward the castle.

Arthur's hand touched Aliana's shoulder, drawing her mournful, wet gaze from Vira's floating pyre.

"You are shaking. We should get you back inside." He unhooked the thick cloak he wore and went to drape it around her shoulders.

She took a step back, shaking her head silently.

He frowned. Aliana saw Merlin nod once from her peripheral vision. His cloak draped over his arm, Arthur wrapped his arm around Aliana's waist and led her back to the castle. They passed the sobbing Guin and Lancelot, who had both treated Vira like their own child.

Aliana sniffled, trying to fight back more tears, knowing that more death was still coming. She made a silent vow to herself and the universe that, no matter what it took, she wouldn't let Guinevere suffer Sophvira's fate. She would find a way to be sure Lancelot got his Guinevere. That they would get to spend the rest of their lives together.

25

Aliana hadn't slept for a single second. Every time she had closed her eyes she saw the flaming arrows falling like stars on the ship that had carried Vira away into the night. She had seen the way Galahad slumped into Delphina's comforting arms, and how she saw him back to the castle. Even worse than that heart crushing image was the haunting sight of Vira's body, sprawled dead on the floor of her room, where Aliana had discovered her less than twenty four hours ago.

It didn't matter what the guys had said. It was her fault and she had to find a way to set it right. No matter what they all thought or insisted, she couldn't stay here. She had to find the map and then find a way home.

But Arthur had been true to his order. The clanking of the endless number of guards that patrolled the hall outside her room had added to the haunting, sleepless night. And before that, Arthur and one of the other knights had remained at her side while the last preparations had been made for Vira's funeral.

The sun was just starting to rise when she finally rolled out of bed. An equally tired and weary Dagg watched her go behind the screen to get dressed.

He had little to say, just like her, after telling her that he couldn't find any trace of Viviane, and that the room that would become Morgana's evil hideout was still undisturbed. "I know what you are thinking," he reminded her, his ageless voice soft and grumbly.

Aliana stepped from behind the screen and turned her back to Dagg so he could tighten the strings on her dress. Her shaking fingers couldn't grip it tight enough. "You know I'm right about this, Dagg."

His claws tied off the strings before coming to hover in front of her. "We knew she would die, Aliana. As much as it hurts, this was destined to happen."

Her anger flared. "Do not mention destiny right now! We have no idea *what* was or is meant to happen! We suspect and *hope* that my being here hasn't messed with history's timeline, but we have no way of knowing that for sure! And if I had never been reckless and impulsive and agreed to do Titania's stupid task, this might have never happened!"

Dagg's amethyst eyes flared with his own anger. "Aliana, stop this. You are doing nothing to help yourself *or Vira* or Galahad."

She crossed her arms and looked past him, out the window wondering if she could use her magic to help her escape out of the castle that way.

Dagg's hot, scaly claws gripped her face and turned her eyes away from the window. "We cannot run away from this. If you want to help our friends, you have to stay and finish what we've started. You owe it to them, to our family in the future and to Sophvira! Running away is the coward's way out."

She pulled his claws from her face, her cheeks heating. "I *am* a coward! Running is the only thing I can do right!"

"You are anything but a coward. You have proven that many times since you first stepped foot in Avalon and freed me and Galahad, and especially when you awoke Arthur! How many opportunities have you been given to turn your back from the prophecy of the Destined One, hmm?"

Aliana held his impassioned gaze for a heartbeat before looking away at the floor.

"You have not failed once since taking up this destiny. You cannot start now by abandoning King Arthur and his knights."

Aliana sank into her chair, her guardian and friend's words warring with her own guilt. She knew for certain now she didn't deserve Galahad or Arthur. But she still needed their help. She thought briefly of going to Merlin, trying to convince him that he alone was all the help she needed. But even he, last night after returning, had agreed that she couldn't do this without all of them.

"You are right. I have to do this for the guys if no one else." She ran her hands through her loose hair. "I just wish Lacy and Dawn were here with me. I really need their support right now!"

Aliana sat back and, after a second, took a deep breath, then got up. "We should go tell Arthur and get the others so I can finish my story from the other night. Tell them about my upcoming trip to the Underworld."

Dagg nodded, satisfaction relaxing his features as he returned to his bracelet form and she slid him into place on her wrist.

Aliana went to the door. The two guards she vaguely remembered meeting last night turned as she opened the heavy door.

"G'mornin', m'lady," they greeted her.

"Good morning. I need to go speak to Merlin; it is a matter of urgency."

"Yes, m'lady," the taller one said, then glanced at his counterpart. "But we must tell the king first. Our orders, you understand."

The other guard took off toward Arthur's room.

"Fine, you've done your duty." She turned to head toward the stairs and Merlin's chambers.

The guard's gloved hand gripped her arm. She turned to him, jerking her arm from his loose grip.

He looked sheepish, but stood his ground. "Our orders are that you are not to go anywhere without an escort, m'lady."

Aliana rolled her eyes, "Then let's go," she huffed, turning again. This time she avoided his grabby hand and made her way to the stairs.

"M'lady, wait. We are supposed to await the king's word," he called, his chainmail clanking as he hurried to catch up to her. By the time he did, they had already passed the great hall and rounded the corner that would lead to the wing of the castle Merlin resided in.

She saw Gawain just ahead, but didn't make a move to stop. If she did she might chicken out and not tell the guys the truth.

"Aliana?" Gawain questioned. "Where are you going in such a hurry? Why is Arthur or Galahad not with you?"

Aliana shrugged, taking a breath to steady herself. "I need to get Merlin, and…I…I need to speak to you and Arthur and all the other knights."

Gawain's face darkened. He watched her for a long moment like he was trying to see inside her head. "All right," he finally said, stepping back. "I'll gather the others at the round table." He looked past her to the guard following her. The man nodded to the knight.

Gawain touched her cheek briefly, a caress of support. He moved on before Aliana could turn her head away.

She watched him go, then made her way to Merlin's door. She knocked once, the door opening just as quickly.

"I thought you might be coming to see me," the Druid said, taking a step back to allow her in.

"What are you doing here?" Morgana spat, her face blotchy as she shot up from the ottoman she had been sitting on. Aliana flinched at the bitter venom in her voice.

"Morgana!" Merlin warned. He stepped between the two women. "Calm down. We are all upset and hurting."

Aliana looked at the Sorceress, her insides churning and twisting when she saw a glimpse of the vengeful, hateful Morgana she had always known. The air rushed from her lungs. No, this couldn't be the reason Morgana turned on the knights too!

"Aliana, what was it you wanted?" Merlin asked, his voice softer and kinder.

"We need to tell King Arthur and the others."

Those nine words were all she needed to say for the Druid to understand what she meant. His face set in resigned lines before he nodded.

"Gawain is already gathering everyone in the great hall."

Merlin turned back to Morgana and held his hand out to her.

The woman looked at Aliana with such hate and sadness, it was a wonder she wasn't ten feet under already. Morgana's face softened as she took Merlin's hand and rose to her feet. With her chin raised high, she glided past Aliana, Merlin following with an apologetic grimace.

They were in the throne room in minutes. Everyone but Delphina and the queen was already gathered around the large round table by the blazing fire pit.

Tremors started to race through her muscles, but she fought them as much as she could, even taking advantage of the reassurance that Dagg sent her through their bond.

Guinevere came to her and hugged her fiercely. "This is not your fault," she whispered. "Vira wouldn't want you to blame yourself like this."

Guinevere knew the teen girl better than any, and she wanted so much to believe what the redheaded woman said, but Aliana's guilt wouldn't allow the hope to settle. She pulled back and Guin returned to Lancelot's arms.

The guys all watched her, concern and curiosity mixing with their remaining sorrow. Morgana took a seat at the table, Merlin standing by her side. Aliana stood alone facing all the people who were and would become her family.

"We never got to finish our conversation from the other night."

She knew Merlin had told Morgana about her search for the Grail and her magic. Now, as much as she hated it, she had to be very careful about what she said. She couldn't risk Morgana tipping off Viviane.

Since they were alone in the throne room, Dagg took his true form. Aliana couldn't help but see the anger darkening the girl's hazel eyes.

The corner of Arthur's mouth turned up a little. Galahad just watched her silently.

"I am very sorry I've kept so much from all of y'all for so long."

"We know and we understand," Arthur said shifting to sit taller in his chair. "It does not change our resolve to help you, to protect you."

"I don't believe it!" Morgana hissed, rising from her seat. Merlin gripped her shoulder to stop her from storming over to her.

"Everything is going to be all right, my love," he assured her, then turned to Arthur. "Sire, I apologize for keeping this from you, as well, but I also believed it best to keep this knowledge a secret."

Aliana dropped her eyes as Dagg turned and wound himself around her shoulders. She stroked his wings again, trying to keep her courage together to tell them all the rest. "There is more to my quest y'all need to know."

"Like how you will find this map that you say leads to the Grail of Power?" Owaine tossed in.

"Or why you even need it," Percy added sending her a smile.

"Delphina has also told us what she told you about the Grail and its creation," Gawain assured her.

Leyon spoke up from his seat next to Galahad. "Do you know where it is? We need to plan the best strategy to retrieve it."

She looked at all of them. She saw no reproach in their faces, only friendly support, but she feared that wouldn't last for long. There was still more she had to tell.

Before she could continue the great hall doors swung open, a draft wafting through the room.

The queen and Delphina entered, three unidentified men trailing behind them.

Arthur came forward, stepping to Aliana's side, his hand hovering loosely near Excalibur. All the other knights got to their feet, watching the newcomers with great interest.

Aliana gazed past Delphina and the queen, her eyes widening when she saw the dark hair, pale yellow eyes and skin so white it was slightly tinted blue. They were Fae! Warrior Fae based on the weapons they carried.

"Your majesty," Delphina said formally, curtsying to Arthur. "Forgive our interruption, but these emissaries of my Queen Titania have arrived with disturbing news I thought you needed to hear immediately."

She stepped aside as the three Fae bowed their heads to Arthur. The one in the middle stood a little forward, and had an air of superiority to him. He was the leader of this company, most likely. "Great king, I am Falorn, a general in the queen's army." He motioned to his two companions with a sweep of his hand. "These are my seconds, D'varin and Echary." Both men bowed to the king.

Arthur nodded his head once, watching them all closely, assessing them. "You are welcome in Camelot, my friends. What news do you bring?"

Falorn, his melodic voice filling the hall. "Majesty, we…" The Fae choked on his words as he met Aliana's eyes.

Their mouths gaped open for a second before the three of them dropped to one knee, their heads bent low. "My lady, it is an honor to greet you," Falorn said when he finally looked up.

Everyone in the room closed in, forming a loose circle around them. Aliana's trembling returned, her face flushing with a fire that ran up her spine and neck.

"What is going on, Aliana?" Arthur asked.

Aliana opened her mouth to say something but no words came. This was NOT how she wanted to tell them about her ancestry.

"It is an unexpected honor to greet one of the queen's lineage, especially here in Camelot." D'varin spoke, awed, rising his head enough to meet her gaze briefly.

"We pledge our lives, weapons and service to you, princess. Whatever you need of us, you shall have." The strength of the devotion and admiration in Echary's promise confused Aliana. How could he feel those things so quickly? The other two echoed his words.

"Princess?" the knights all asked, staring at Aliana.

Aliana fought to keep from hyperventilating. "Please stand up," she ordered the three Fae breathlessly. "There's no reason for you to bow to me."

They did as commanded, like they couldn't obey her fast enough. She wrung her hands together.

"Explain yourself, Aliana," Arthur ordered her, turning his back to their visitors.

Echary took a step forward, his fine Fae features turning blade sharp. "Our princess does not answer to a *mortal king*."

The knights glared at him, their hands going to their swords. Arthur turned to the Fae and scowled. "And no foreigner gives orders to the King of Camelot."

"He meant no disrespect, Arthur," Delphina said, stepping between him and the Fae. "He does not understand things here." The Fae emissary glared at the young Fae when he tried to speak again. "He humbly begs your pardon."

"I'm only half Fae," Aliana interjected, not wanting any more trouble for her friends because of her. She met Arthur's eyes. "Titania is my grandmother."

Everyone was silent. Then Morgana spoke. "How have you kept all of this a secret for so long? What else are you hiding from us?"

Aliana fought the urge to run and hide. She hated all this attention.

"We will finish discussing this later," Arthur said to the Sorceress. He turned back to the three Fae warriors. "What is it you came to tell us?"

The three Fae looked to her as if needing permission. Aliana gulped but nodded once. Falorn's face became all business again. "There is a dark force in the forests around your kingdom. Five Druid encampments have been sacked, temples have been raided and four sacred treasures stolen. No one knows what this creature is, but it conceals itself with very dark magic."

"We have heard reports, and experienced our own problems with dark magic," Lancelot spoke, his voice even.

"What do these attacks in Camelot have to do with the Fae?" Gawain asked.

"The treasures stolen are objects of the Fae, given to the Druids, or hidden in sacred temples for protection. Several lifetimes ago, the Fae entrusted Camelot's ruler with one such treasure. We are here to see it is protected." Falorn looked to Queen Igraine who had come to her son's side. It was almost as if he wanted to remind the queen.

Leyon cleared his throat, drawing everyone's attention. "Why is this object we are supposed to have so important? How is it connected with your other stolen treasures?"

D'varin spoke up. "Those four missing pieces join with the fifth piece, here in Camelot, to form a weapon of unimaginable power."

"It's called the Spear of Hel," Echary added. "It is a weapon to create darkness itself. It can destroy any weapon or magic, no matter how indestructible."

Aliana snapped her finger, the name of the spear ringing a terrifying bell in her memory, something from one of her father's lessons in mythology. "Hel is the Norse goddess of death. She was said to be the daughter of the trickster god, Loki. In the underworld she sits in judgment of souls…" She trailed off, realizing what she had said.

Arthur raised a brow. "What do you want of us then?" he asked the Fae.

Falorn's shoulder's squared. "We want to return the final piece to our queen's kingdom for safe keeping, and we would ask your assistance hunting down this threat and reclaim these sacred treasures."

D'varin nodded. "Even separated, those pieces are very powerful and dangerous in the wrong hands."

Aliana steeled herself. "There was something else I need to tell all of you." She nearly crumpled under the weight of everyone's stares. "Thanks to Delphina's help, I now believe the map I need is in the Underworld."

"A map to what?" Falorn asked.

"A map to the Grail of Power," Merlin answered for her. "Aliana must travel to the Underworld and retrieve it."

Everyone was speechless, even the three Fae warriors.

"That is suicide!" Galahad raged. "You cannot go to the Underworld, no matter the reason."

Aliana sighed. "My friends need me to get that map; I can't go home without it."

The white knight looked ready to explode. Leyon and Gawain placed restraining hands on his shoulders.

Arthur's eyes narrowed before he looked back to the three visiting Fae. "You will have my decision in due time. Until that time you will leave us to discuss all of this information in private."

Falorn and the other two bristled at the command. They looked to Aliana, silently asking her if that was what she wanted.

She hesitated, uncomfortable, but nodded. They bowed low and let Delphina lead them from the throne room.

Everyone was silent until the heavy doors shut.

"Why have you not told any of us this before?" Galahad demanded, brushing off his friend's hands.

Arthur held up his hand, stopping the knight. "You need to tell us everything, now, so we understand all of this." Aliana heeded his order. "Everyone, take your seats."

The tension in the room was thicker than southern chili and just as heavy, as they all took their proper seats at the Round Table.

Arthur was the last to settle in his set. "Now tell us everything you can."

Dawn is up to something, her growing magic is proving very powerful. I'm worried she's keeping something dangerous from us. The two Nymphs, even Princess Varaness, seem to be aiding and abetting her as well. Wade agrees, and he's starting to panic. We've told Galahad our fears and he is of the same mind. Wade's popped off to find Dawn; we've not seen her in hours. My instincts are telling me there is more going on…Now I know I'm right. Wade's just returned, furious — an Elf told him Dawn and the Nymphs have gone to the Well! What the bloody hell does she think she's doing?

— Owen

Aliana explained that she needed the map to the Grail to save her friends and stop a great evil. Lancelot had been very upset when she admitted that Titania had sent her here on this quest. She told them about the book she had found in the market and gave them a general idea of the strength of her magic. But Aliana made sure to be very careful about the words she chose and how she described things. Morgana may not have turned on them yet, but she couldn't take a chance on tipping her hand about what little she knew of Viviane and Mordrid.

"Are you ready to tell them about being from the future?" Dagg's ageless voice filled her head while everyone sat, taking in all she had told them so far. No one had threatened anything or said she was crazy or demand she leave, but she still worried how they would all react when everything fully settled in.

"No, I don't think we should, not with Morgana here. And we promised the queen." Aliana wished she could still trust the girl who had become her friend, but the hate still swirling around the Sorceress warned her to keep her secret, for now.

She felt his hesitation, but he didn't protest.

"What's your next move then, Aliana?" Owaine asked, drawing her from the silent conversation.

She took a breath. "I need to go to the Underworld and get that map." She realized she still hadn't told them about Titania's other reason for sending her here. "And there is another reason, one I've yet to discover, for Titania sending me here. I have to have the map and complete this 'mystery task.'" Aliana wondered for a brief second if the mystery task had anything to do with the Spear of Hel.

Galahad sat back in his chair, his arms crossed, his face set in determined lines. He had been very quiet since his outburst. It seemed he wasn't talking to her again.

"How do you intend to find and get into the Underworld?" Gawain questioned, his tone filled with support and understanding.

"I can locate and open gates with my magic." She looked back to Arthur. "There is a portal near where you faced that Manticore."

He frowned.

Leyon cleared his throat, he and Owaine separating after sharing a quiet conversation. "Do we not think it odd that this weapon the Fae are worried about is connected to the Underworld, where Aliana needs to go?"

Aliana bit back a smile. *Still the smartest pair in the room.* "I thought the same when I was telling y'all about Hel. I don't think it is a coincidence."

"Needless to say, we cannot let such a powerful magical weapon fall into the wrong hands," Merlin said, his fingers stroking his chin.

Lancelot agreed. "I do not think we should return the last piece of this weapon."

Guin frowned at him. "Why not, my love?"

Lancelot took her hand in his, kissed it lovingly. "It must have been given to Camelot's protection for a reason. It has clearly remained safe for this long. That would not be true for no reason."

"Perhaps you all should help Falorn and his men while Dagg and I go to the Underworld," Aliana suggested, hoping they would see the importance of recovering the spear pieces.

"No."

"Absolutely not."

"You cannot undertake such a thing alone!" all the guys insisted together.

"I have to," she insisted. "This is my quest. If there is one thing I know about Titania, it's that she does not take kindly to outside interference. If any of you were to try to get involved…I'm scared to think what might happen."

"Then you do not complete this quest," Galahad said softly, his blazing blue eyes capturing hers. "You stay with us, in Camelot. You have a home here."

Her lungs frosted over, the intensity and sincerity in his words and gaze shooting straight through her. But why would he want her to stay after what had happened to his sister? She shook her head. "As much as I love Camelot, and all of you…" Aliana met each of their gazes, hoping they would see the truth in her words and understand. "This isn't my home. And my friends, my other family is counting on me to get this map and return to them. We have our own war to fight."

Galahad looked away from her, the broad muscles of his arms tightening.

Merlin rose from his seat drawing all attention. "Aliana is right. As much as we may not want to, we have to help her, or I do at least. The Fae queen is the one who sent me to her when she arrived in our kingdom."

Everyone was silent as he sat back down, all seemingly lost in his or her own thoughts.

Morgana's hands smacked on the table with a cracking snap. "I do not believe this!" She turned to Arthur. "She should not be here! She was sent to us with veiled motives, has kept dangerous and important secrets from all of us, she's deceived us, and worse Sophvira… Sophvira is dead because of her. She does not belong here and she is certainly not deserving of our aid."

"Enough Morgana!" Galahad shot up from his seat, his fist pounding into the table so hard it rattled.

Aliana's heart constricted then started to race in her tight chest, her pain and guilt still thudding inside her. "No she's right."

Every pair of eyes went to her. Galahad started to protest but Arthur's held up a hand to silence him. "For the last time, Aliana. None of us believe Sophvira's death was your fault. It was the fault of Raven and Viviane. And they will pay for their treachery with their lives."

Everyone voiced their agreement, even Galahad. Only Morgana remained silent, her face pinched so tight with frustration and anger Aliana half expected it to shatter like a pane of glass.

Arthur continued. "We will help you complete your quest, Aliana." He held his hand up when she started to protest again. "The Fae queen sent you to Merlin *and* Camelot, and that means you are in need of our help, one way or another."

Aliana looked around the table and saw the agreement and support of the others. All except Morgana, who had sunk back in her chair, her arms crossed as she stared out the window.

"We still need to decide what to do about the Fae and their magic spear," Gawain pointed out.

"I think Lancelot was right," Owaine said. "It has been safe here since it was entrusted to Camelot; it should remain that way."

"What is more important is defeating this dark force and discovering who has been stealing the other four pieces of the weapon," Leyon added.

"Sire," Gawain addressed the king. "What about the three Fae warriors here? We do not know how much we can trust them, but I believe we would be foolish to turn down their assistance. Fae are damn good warriors to have at our side."

"Agreed," Arthur said, sitting back.

"We have another advantage too," Percival added, pointing to Aliana. "She is royalty to them, so they will clearly do what she tells them."

Aliana realized what he was getting at, thought she didn't feel exactly comfortable with the thought. "I'll tell them to do whatever it is you want them too…"

"But?" Lancelot asked with a raised brow.

She swallowed the cotton in her throat. "I think it might be a better option if they accompanied me to the gate of the Underworld." She raised her hand when the guys started to protest. "Hear me out. You all are the strongest force in this entire realm, but only when you all are together. Separating would weaken your defense, and you'll need Merlin and Morgana's magic to help battle this dark force that's terrorizing your kingdom."

"Say you're right—" Arthur spoke up, silencing the other knights. "How do we know this isn't a trap? A way to separate you from us. We have no way to know with certainty that these three are not a part of the danger to Camelot. This is a Fae weapon they want, yet why was it hidden in our realm as opposed to their own?"

"Arthur's right," Owaine said. "We need to find out more."

"Then let me talk to them," Aliana offered. "But we don't have a lot of time. If this dark force only needs the piece of the spear that is hidden here in Camelot, it may already be on its way."

Dagg leapt from Aliana's shoulders and landed on the Round Table. "What if we attack two birds with one stone? We all ride out to face this dark force, with Falorn and his men, and face this threat head on. Then from there, Aliana, the Fae and Merlin can travel to the portal to the Underworld so she can complete part of her quest."

They all looked to Arthur, knowing the decision was his to make. Aliana held her breath, her fingers twisting together in her lap under the table. Even Queen Igraine watched her son with bated interest.

"You make a strong case, DragonLord. I agree with you."

Aliana let out a huffed breath at the king's words.

"But," Arthur said holding up his hand. "Galahad and I will also be going with Aliana after we defeat this dark force." He looked to his mother. "You will see to Camelot until we return."

The sunlight-colored woman smiled. "Of course, my son."

"Have Delphina bring the Fae back in," he ordered the guards standing by the door.

"Delphina?" Aliana reached out to the apricot-haired Fae mentally for the first time since arriving in Camelot.

"I beg your forgiveness for the way Falorn and his men exposed your secret. Honestly, it did not even cross my mind to warn you."

"No worries now, Delphina. Arthur is not sure we can trust Falorn and his men, what do you think?"

"I have known D'varin since I was a child, and I know Falorn by his reputation. They are good Fae. Strong, smart, loyal and deadlier than most. Echary is the only one I do not know, but D'varin has assured me he is trustworthy. And they will serve you faithfully, have no doubt."

Aliana took a deep breath, relaying all Delphina had said to Dagg. Her guardian nodded once as the doors opened and Arthur told Falorn his decision.

It was just after lunch by the time everyone had changed and prepared to ride out. Guinevere, Delphina and Igraine were the only three remaining behind in Camelot. Falorn and his two friends had not been happy when Arthur had said Camelot would not relinquish their protection of the fifth part of the spear, but they had no choice but to accept the decision after Aliana had explained the reason why.

The air was chilly with late fall wind and cloudy skies blocking out the warmth of the sun. Again Aliana feared how long she had been gone from her world, and what was happening to her friends.

Like when they rode out to face the Manticore, there was no fanfare, only the stone-faced knights and Fae warriors preparing for battle. Falorn and his men insisted on riding with Aliana, as their princess's honor guard, much to Galahad's apparent disapproval. Instead, the white knight rode next to Arthur who was just ahead of them.

Aliana glanced back at Merlin and Morgana, who would be riding just behind her and the Fae. Morgana had not even looked at her since her outburst, but the Sorceress had not stopped frowning since. Not even when her souls mate had kissed her passionately and tried to soothe her anger. The girl was currently tightening the buckle on one of her saddlebags. It was bulky, with a large bump protruding from it. Wisps of cool blue magic circled the bag for a brief second before disappearing.

Her heart broke for the blonde, and Aliana made another silent promise to try to repair the damage she had done, before the powerful Sorceress turned against her family. She had a lot of promises to follow up on, but she was determined to see them done!

They rode for hours, only sparse conversation starting here and there as they headed toward the last place the dark force had been seen.

Leyon and Owaine had mapped out the previous attacks, realizing that the threat was indeed headed straight toward Camelot. Aliana wondered if Viviane and Mordrid could be the ones controlling it, or even to have created it. Mordrid wanted total domination over the seven realms, and having a weapon as powerful as the Spear of Hel would certainly give him the strength he needed before and after the alignment.

"But what happened to it? We've never heard of it before now? Merlin would have mentioned it, wouldn't he?" She stroked her guardian's wings now that he didn't have to hide and rode wrapped around her shoulders.

"I would suspect so, yes. It could be that the spear is never fully recovered and still remains hidden, perhaps even still in the ruins of Camelot in the Isle. There is no way to know for sure as of yet."

Aliana sighed, drawing the attention of Falorn. "What is wrong, highness?"

She shook her head. "Nothing. And please, Falorn, call me Aliana. I am really not royalty, even if I do have the queen's blood in me. I'm just a girl."

"Your modesty does you credit, my Lady Aliana," he replied, his long hair shifting in the wind. "But you are royalty to our people. Trust us to protect you and share your burdens."

"Why is this spear so powerful?" she asked him instead.

"No one knows the truth of its creation, but each of the five pieces bears a jewel of great power. When the staff is whole, the gems reach their full potential, making it the destroyer of the un-destroyable."

Aliana needed to get her hands on that weapon. If Mordrid got it, or Raven or Viviane, they could destroy Excalibur and the only way to kill Mordrid once and for all!

A hopeful thought entered her mind, spurred on by Dagg's silent agreement. "Can this spear be destroyed?"

Falorn frowned. "I do not know. I suppose anything is possible, but it would take power greater than any I have ever seen to do so."

Aliana sat back in her saddle wondering if her magic would be strong enough.

They rode for a while longer before Arthur pulled his mount to a stop and held up his hand. They all searched the trees on either side of the path they were taking through the forest. Aliana opened her senses and connected her sight to Dagg's as he jumped from her shoulder and hovered a few feet in the air above her.

The sharpened colors and scenery was beautiful, but it was marred by a creeping darkness that felt terrifyingly familiar.

A grunting pig-like sound caught her ear as it traveled across the air around them. "Goblins!" Aliana cried out, recognizing the sound from her first few hours in Avalon so long ago.

Bolts flew from behind the trees aimed straight for their party. Aliana ducked forward as one whizzed past her head. "Seriously! Again with the damn bolts nearly hitting my head!" She huffed and sat back up as D'varin drew his long curved sword in a flash and deflected the next three arrows that came at her.

"Stay behind us, princess!" he ordered as the knights were all defending themselves with their shields.

"Maybe you all should stay behind me!" she muttered, raising her hand to grab the air element's magic. It came to her instantly, whipping out around their party like a hurricane. The deadly bolts were deflected and sent shooting back into the woods at the ones who sent them.

Grunting piggy cries were heard as she released the magic wind. Everyone stared at her in amazement, Merlin grinning like a mad man.

But the moment was short lived as grunts and angry battle cries rang around them.

"Dismount!" Arthur ordered as he drew Excalibur from its sheath. He gripped his shield and flung his leg over his saddle, quickly getting to the ground.

Everyone followed, the knights and Fae dismounting gracefully, arming themselves just as the hideously terrifying Goblins flooded out from the trees.

They were gruesome, pig-like creatures with blotchy brown-toffee-colored skin, pig noses, squinty black eyes and mouths full of blue, dripping sharp teeth. She hadn't seen these monsters in Avalon, a fact she was grateful for. They looked mean enough to scare even the bravest person with their bald heads and nasty snarls. If she'd seen them in Avalon…she would have turned tail and run. Just like she wished they could now.

Aliana shivered, but steeled herself and finally released the veil covering the true strength of her magic. Her ruby glove became visible again on the top of her right hand. She summoned her magic bow, ready to help fight. It felt good to have the magic weapon in her hand again.

The bulky Goblins charged them with squealing battle cries that hurt Aliana's ears. Dagg shot through the air, his purple Dragon fire incinerating the Goblin closest to them.

"My lady, stay with us!" Falorn ordered sharply as he, Echary and D'varin fought back the rushing beasts. She looked past them to the knights. Her gut lurched as Arthur and Galahad were fighting back to back with Gawain and Lancelot only feet from them. They were cutting down Goblin after Goblin, their swords slicing through bulky arms, legs and neck, all the while only taking a few hits themselves. Their scent was like bad body odor mixed with burning spice and mold.

A glint in the trees caught her eyes. She focused with her Dragon eyes and saw five Goblins aiming at Arthur and three of her knights. Anger and worry lanced her.

Instinct and training took over. Not thinking of anything but her friend's safety Aliana aimed her bow and drew her back, the sparkling pink arrow forming. She let it fly, twisting her ruby hand as the burst multiplied and sank into each grubby Goblin. They squealed as they fell from the trees, hitting the ground in dead heaps.

She didn't wait to see the knights' reaction, using her vision to see if there were any more hiding Goblins. She found them, aiming at the rest of the knights fighting on her other side. She nocked her magic arrows and killed them before they could hurt her friends. Dagg continued to circle her position, helping Falorn and his warriors destroy the Goblins around them.

The sounds of the battle were loud and brutal, but the knights and Fae warriors were making quick, blue splattered, bloody work of the attacking creatures. Her racing adrenaline kept her nerves steady and focus sharp. She searched around for Morgana but couldn't find the blond sorceress through all the dwindling fighting. Her gut twisted indignantly. The witch may have just betrayed them.

The darkness crept closer to them from the hidden recesses of the trees as the number of attacking Goblins was down to less than ten. Gray electricity crackled through the clouds of dark gray magic.

Oh no! Aliana froze, realizing what this meant for them.

The last of the Goblins fell dead in chopped off heaps at the knights' feet. They looked around the trees, their warrior senses probably telling them they were not out of danger yet. And they were right.

Shadowy figures lurked in the approaching darkness.

"Everyone, fall back!" Arthur ordered.

They all formed up around Aliana, their horses long having run off in the chaos of fighting. Aliana disconnected her vision from Dagg's, and opened her senses to feel the strength of the magic around them. It was not nearly as strong as she was used to, but there was a different element to it she had yet to feel from this dark magic.

Everyone shifted back and forth, ready to attack whatever came out of the darkness.

27

Aliana's heart galloped in her throat as she tried to brace herself. Evil laughter echoed around them.

Four shadows made their way forward in the gray mist, one on each side of the group, surrounding them. A taller Goblin, decked out with ragged pants and one piece of shoulder armor stepped into view near Leyon and the knights on her left side. He carried a blade that was curved like a slithering snake in one hand, and a large mace that dragged on the ground next to him in his other. It must have weighed a ton, but the monster hefted it on his shoulder like it was Styrofoam.

Viviane was the next to appear. She was decked out in rich black silk that draped across her body like a sexy Grecian dress accented with round gold pieces at the shoulder and under her ample breasts like a belt. Her raven hair stretched down to her waist, her hands hanging at her side crackling with a red magic so deep it was like burnt blood. She smirked at them arrogantly.

Morgana appeared next, behind them, her head held high as she stared down Merlin with a mix of contempt and sorrow.

"Morgana, what are you doing?" The Druid's usually confident voice full of pain, his strong face etched with devastating betrayal.

"I am joining the winning side, my love. You can too." Morgana didn't look as assured as she sounded, to Aliana.

"Never!" he spat out. "Why would you do this to us? To our king and our family?"

She snarled. "Because Arthur is not the rightful King of Camelot!" She turned her hate-filled eyes on Aliana. "And because this foreign interloper would see our kingdom ruled over by this weakling." The air crackled with her magic and fury. "Aliana is nothing more than that Fae Queen's puppet." She pointed a finger at Galahad and then Arthur. "You two would give her anything she wants. You drool over her like a pair of puppies instead of making Camelot the great power it should be!"

"Who is this *rightful ruler* you speak of, Morgana?" Arthur hissed, his molten gold eyes staring down the traitor.

"Why that would be me, Arthur." A familiar, high-pitched voice came from in front of them. Out of the dark magic stepped Raven, his clothes as regal as any Arthur would ever wear. He had a big sword strapped across his back as he looked down at all of them like a lord on high. He wasn't the shy, small boy Aliana had grown so used to seeing. He was taller now, his shoulder's squared with confidence and surety in his right to claim such power.

That sure as heck was not who I was expecting! "Raven? Why?" Aliana demanded, her clammy hands gripping her bow tighter. *How did he escape Camelot's dungeons?*

"You don't see it do you?" His cold calculating gaze studied her as the others tightened formation around her. "I would have thought you, with all your great magic, would have seen it before now."

Dagg growled fiercely as he circled above her, his eyes alight with magic.

"Seen what?" Leyon hissed, looking ready to pounce.

"That there is more to me than meets the eye." The air around him shimmered as his appearance changed. He appeared even taller, about Arthur's height, his body gaining a little more muscle as his night black hair grew to touch his shoulders. The change was over in less than a second and Aliana wanted to hit herself for being so blind.

"Mordrid!" she screamed, half terrified, half pissed off. *No wonder he escaped; it would have been child's play for him!*

The dark wizard's head tilted to the side a fraction as his black eyes bore into her. "And how do you know my true name, dear Aliana?" Her name rolled off his tongue like a caress.

She shivered, gripped her magic bow tighter, fighting to keep her hand and breathing steady. "Surprise, jackass," she growled. "I know a lot more about you than you think."

"And yet you failed to see through my clever disguise for so long," he taunted.

"Enough of this!" Arthur thundered, drawing the dark wizard's attention. "I am the rightful King of Camelot. You have no claim on my throne!"

Mordrid laughed his shrill, slightly-crazed laughter. "You are as ignorant as you are arrogant, *Arthur!* Camelot was never to be ruled by the likes of you."

"The hell you say!" the king spat, raising Excalibur higher.

Viviane laughed, making the hairs on the back of Aliana's neck stand on end. "Really, Arthur, you are so unenlightened about your own kingdom."

"Shut up!" Lancelot spat at the dark woman.

"You should have paid more attention to your mother's stories, cousin," Morgana sneered. "Maybe then you would have realized."

"Realized what?" Galahad seethed.

Morgana popped out her hip, her fist resting on it. "That the creation story of Camelot so many think a myth is true, and that blasted Golden Dragon stole Camelot from its rightful ruler, the great Onyx Dragon!"

Aliana's eyes widened as she made the connection. "You are crazy! That Onyx Dragon died ages ago! Why fight now?"

Mordrid's smirk widened. "His body may have long turned to bone and dust but his fathomless power remains and I am his only direct descendant. Camelot is mine to rule by right! Until Arthur's birth, his mother was the only living descendant of that pretender." His creepy gray black magic started to infest the clearing. "But her magic is not what it was, and her protection is failing!"

"I have always known the truth about Camelot's creation!" Arthur fired back. "And I know the Golden Dragon defeated the Onyx Dragon and banished him from Camelot!"

"Enough, Arthur!" Viviane commanded. "Hand over your crown with some dignity and we will grant you all quick deaths."

"Never!" they all cried, even Falorn and his men.

"Then die!" a forgotten Goblin grunted as he charged them, more of his army filing out from the trees.

Fear burst in her blood. There were too many monsters charging them! She had to do something. "Camelot will never be yours, Mordrid!" Aliana cried and pushed open her magical senses. She grabbed all the magic from the earth and energy elements and mixed it with her own ruby magic as she punched her hand into the ground.

Electric charged vines erupted out of the earth, shooting through the enemy before they could even reach her knights. They trapped and squeezed all the Goblins they could grab, leaving the rest to die at the hands of the Arthur and his men. The pig-like creatures squealed and thrashed but she pushed more of her ruby magic through the vines. The putrid scent of their rotting guts mixed with the smell of charring flesh made her want to throw up. She released the magic when the last of her captives stopped struggling.

Aliana gasped for breath as a chill ran down her spine. She snapped her head around to see a bolt of blue magic charging straight for her. Quicker than she could react, Dagg appeared in front of her, unleashing a stream of Dragon fire so strong the air sizzled around them and the icy magic shattered.

"Thanks!" she said to Dagg, getting back to her feet, looking around at the battle raging on all sides of her. Mordrid and Viviane watched from their perches as Arthur, Galahad, and Gawain slaughtered the minion Goblins around them. Merlin tried to fight his way past the small army to get to Morgana. Leyon, Percival, Owaine and Lancelot were thrusting and slashing their swords, facing off against the nasty Goblin leader. All her knights were bleeding from cuts and gashes, but they fought like they didn't feel the pain, and she hoped they didn't. Falorn and his men struggled against the few Goblins that tried to break the fighting circle all the warriors had formed around her.

Grim determination filled her mind. She needed to stop this, before someone got killed. She leveled her bow at the two in front of her. She drew back, released her magic arrows, and fired them. She whipped around and finished off the last two just as one was about to stab Echary with its rusted sword.

The young Fae looked over his shoulder, sending a quick smile in thanks. She returned it before he stepped to the side to avoid the barreling club of the Goblin before him. Another cold chill went through her, her eyes darting past Echary toward Morgana just as she threw another spear of blue icy magic straight at her. Aliana raised her bow to counter it, sweat dripping down her temple. The blast was flying through the air so fast she wasn't sure she'd deflect it in time. Echary severed the head of the Goblin he had been fighting as Aliana summoned her bubble shield and aimed. She released her pink magic just in time, the two energies exploding in the air as they collided violently.

Another darker power surged from her side. She looked too late as Viviane sent her own burnt-blood-colored blast at her. Echary stepped in front of Aliana just before the blast reached her. It pierced his heart with a bang that rang in Aliana's ears like a gun shot.

"Echary!" Aliana cried out, catching the pale Fae as he fell backward. His skin turned a deeper shade of blue, his lips darkening to a deep purple. "Echary, stay with us!" she ordered frantically as she sank to the earth under his weight. Her entire body trembled in outraged anger and despair.

Dagg returned to her shoulder, his watchful eyes and presence helping to protect her.

The others glanced at them, the worry and fear doubling on their faces. But so did their rage. Falorn and D'varin roared in denial and charged the remaining few Goblins to try to get at the woman who had hurt their friends.

"Pri-Princess—are…are y-you hurt?" Echary asked, his eyes unfocused as he tried to move around.

"I'm fine, you idiot!" she whispered, trying to fight back her tears. "Why did you do that? I would have been all right!"

"You're m-my pri-princess. It's my…my…duty." His eyes rolled into the back of his sockets as his last breath left him and his body went slack.

"No!" Aliana screamed. Her powers rushed inside her, her magic senses opening wide and absorbing all the energies around them. She felt Morgana and Viviane gather more power to attack, fueling her fury. "You won't get away with this!" Aliana seized all the magic she could as Dagg wrapped himself tighter around her shoulders.

All the magic she corralled exploding outward like a rippling pink waves. The Goblin leader shrieked and squealed with his remaining army in the valley before he too fell dead on the ground. Her magic slammed into their enemies obliterating the cloud of gray magic and blasted Morgana, Viviane and Mordrid back through several trees.

Everything was statue-still for a long second as Aliana's shoulders heaved from the magic backlash. The knights all stared at her in amazement. Then the world moved again and she pitched forward. Galahad got there first, wrapping his arm around her shoulders as he knelt beside her. Falorn and D'varin took their dead friend from her slackened grip.

"What the hell was that?" Galahad demanded gruffly.

She shook her head, leaning against him as Dagg pushed healing energy into her. Aliana felt a few silver sparks fire up through her weakened bond with Galahad helping to heal her.

"You have more magic than I ever suspected!" Mordrid hissed through his heaving breath with delight as he steadied himself against a tree.

Aliana pulled out of Galahad's arms, her body screaming in pain. Through squinted eyes she saw Morgana and Viviane both get back on their feet, though all three had torn, burned clothes, were bleeding in several places on their faces and body and couldn't stand on their own feet without support.

"I must have you even more!" Mordrid raised one hand, palm toward her as Morgana and Viviane did the same.

The knights raised their shields but everything in her knew that wouldn't be enough. She took the last of her ruby magic and her own bubbling pink magic and created a shield around all her friends just as the three attacked. The combative magics slammed into her shield, but Aliana felt the power like it was ramming against her own flesh.

Aliana barely held back her agonizing cry as her shield imploded under the weight of their power. Everyone was knocked back, good and bad as the very earth vibrated with the force of the collision.

When Aliana raised her head she saw all the knights out cold, Falorn and D'varin lying next to their dead warrior. Her heart kicked and her stomach twisted as her eyes frantically looked over all of them.

"They're alive," Merlin groaned, pushing himself up, his hair disheveled with clumps of dirt in his hair and on his face and clothes. "Unfortunately, so are they." He motioned to their enemies, who were getting back to their feet.

"Why would you betray your souls mate, Morgana?" Aliana demanded in a pain-choked voice as both girls got back to their feet.

"I am not!" Morgana looked at Merlin. "He will come to our side now that he knows the truth, now that he knows we will prevail!"

"Never, Morgana!" Merlin stared at her, his devastated and desperate face pleading with the witch. "What has happened to you? You are not this hateful, evil person. You are good and beautiful and loyal and strong. We are your family!"

Dagg wrapped himself around Aliana again, both helping each other recover again. What was she missing here?

Morgana held Merlin's gaze, the anger in her face lessening for a second as indecision warred in her eyes.

"Please, my love, do not do this! You have not done anything Arthur and our family would not forgive! These two are confusing you."

"Viviane raised me, taught me about my magic, taught me how to use it! My mother was of her blood. That was why Uther sent me away, especially after he married Igraine." But Morgana didn't sound too convinced.

"Then why come to Camelot?" Merlin demanded. "Why fall in love with me?"

"Because I told her to," Mordrid snapped in frustration. "I sent her there to gain the trust of the fabled Knights of the Round Table and infiltrate your *family*. You fools made it all too easy."

Merlin growled. "Stay out of this, you murdering whelp!" He looked back at Morgana. "He killed Sophvira, our little Sophvira! He and Viviane murdered her!"

"No," she denied, shaking her head. "That bracelet was for Aliana! That stupid servant messed everything up! Her and *Aliana!*"

"That's not true, we talked about this!" Merlin pleaded.

She shrieked. "Why do you keep defending her? Maybe you are in love with her too, like those fools Galahad and Arthur!"

"You know that is not true! I *love you!* You're my souls mate, don't do this to us!" he begged.

Aliana's heart broke. Morgana was doing all this because she thought Merlin loved her? Her resolve tightened, she needed to help Morgana see.

"Morgana, there was *never* anything—"

"Shut up!" Morgana lashed out with another spear of icy magic.

Merlin appeared in front of Aliana, his own shield deflecting the blast as he defended Aliana.

"Why? You still protect her!" The blonde's eyes filled with tears.

"You see it for yourself, my dear," Viviane crooned as she came to stand next to Morgana, Mordrid appearing behind them both. "He protects her from even you, he turns his back on you. He loves her. She is already stealing your souls mate bond from you. She wants him and the others all wrapped around her finger to do her bidding."

Mordrid stepped up to Morgana's other ear. "If they truly loved you, cousin, they would be standing by you right now, your lover would not be protecting her. He would be helping us."

"Don't listen to them Morgana! They're manipulating you!"

"You know what you need to do, my dear." Viviane held out a solid black onyx dagger in her hand. "Pierce his heart with it and he will be yours!"

Merlin's face turned ashen as he stared at the dagger. Whatever it was, it scared the normally unshakeable Druid.

"Don't do it, Morgana!" Aliana cried out. "Don't you see they're lying to you?"

"You would know!" Morgana gripped the dagger in her trembling hand. "All you've done is lie to all of us. Everyone but *my souls mate.*"

"That dagger won't make me yours, Morgana. You know what it will do, it will destroy me in every way!" Merlin took an unsteady step forward. "My mind will be gone. I will be nothing but a puppet. My magic will be nothing but darkness."

"You are letting them fill your head with lies and half-truths, Morgana." Arthur groaned, getting back to his feet. Aliana sagged for a second in relief. Everyone else was still out cold, but at least Arthur was back on his feet, with Excalibur in his hand. "We are also cousins, Morgana. Uther's blood flows in you just as much as in me. You *are* a member of our family, *we* care for you."

Morgana wavered, her eyes going between the onyx weapon and Arthur and Merlin as they stood side by side. Aliana kept her mouth shut, realizing that she would only make the situation worse.

"Don't be taken in by their weasel words, my dear," Viviane whispered. "They are trying to fool you. We are the ones who truly care for you. *We* are your true family, you are a descendant of the onyx clan. Remember everything you've been through. Mordrid and I were there for you, not them."

"Enough of this," Mordrid ground out, another onyx dagger appearing in his hand. "I will do it for you, cousin."

Aliana screamed as he threw the dagger straight toward Merlin faster than anyone could move. Everyone but Morgana. She magically appeared in front of Merlin at the last possible second.

Merlin cried out in denial as she was struck and engulfed with rays of pure blackness. Aliana rushed forward only to have Arthur hold her back. Merlin was already at his souls mate's side, but even as he poured his orange rays of magic toward Morgana, they couldn't penetrate the unbreakable darkness surrounding the blond sorceress.

Tears leaked down Aliana's cheeks as Merlin watched helplessly as the evil magic filled the woman he loved more than life. He tried again to penetrate the magic, but it was no use. Aliana's own magic was so depleted, she would be of no help.

Morgana and the sphere disappeared from sight. "No!" the Druid cried into the sky.

Mordrid and Viviane laughed in shrill delight.

"I will kill you!" Merlin raised his hand in the air and summoned down the strongest bolt of lightning she had ever seen him use. Every strand of air crackled with the mighty power, the charges popping against her skin.

It raced toward the evil duo only to be stopped by a dome of unbreakable ice that formed above them. The ice vanished with the lightning. Morgana, transparent like a ghost, stood between Viviane and Mordrid once again.

"My love?" Merlin's voice cracked.

The witch's body slowly took on corporeal form, like she was being reborn.

Aliana gasped, seeing the so familiar hate and malice she had known from Morgana for so long.

"You will never stop us," the blonde said arrogantly. "We will destroy all of the Knights of the Round Table and claim Camelot for its rightful ruler." Her cold eyes landed on Aliana.

Arthur's arms tightened around her as he shifted her closer.

Morgana sneered. "And I will not stop until I have ripped your new pet from your grasp."

"I am not a pet!" Aliana seethed under her breath. But her anger was more at herself than Morgana. Morgana's evil magic came because she had sacrificed herself to save Merlin from taking that blade!

Groans sounded all around Aliana. The knights and Fae warriors all started to shake off the residual disorientation they must have felt from the blast. They got to their feet, weapons back in their hands, and stared at Morgana in disbelief.

"I have one more piece of information you should know, *my king*," Morgana snarled, taunting Arthur. She held out her hand a long spearhead with a bright emerald on its base appearing in her hand. "We are the ones who have been claiming the pieces of the Spear of Hel, and thanks to those foolish Fae, I finally realized where the final piece was hidden in the castle. I took it right under all of your noses."

"Traitor!" Percival hissed.

"You can't give it to them!" Owaine insisted, panic on his handsome face.

Morgana laughed and handed the piece over to Viviane. "You can't stop me. And once the spear is assembled, not even Excalibur will be able to save your pathetic life, Arthur!"

Galahad burst into motion, Falorn, D'varin, Gawain, Lancelot and Leyon all moving with him as they charged the trio. Their evil laughter filled the forest as they vanished before the warriors could attack.

28

Aliana believes that her task from the Fae queen was to help Delphina and Arthur come together. I have never agreed with this thought. Now that we know of this Spear of Hel, I believe that may truly be our quest for the queen. I never once heard a tale of this weapon in the centuries I traveled the realms before the Sidhe imprisoned me. I wonder now if that is not because of something Aliana or even Mordrid may do. And now we've walked right into his trap, and Morgana's betrayal has finally come to light. My instincts are telling me the worst is still to come.

— Daggerhorne

Merlin fell to his knees, staring blankly at the spot where Morgana had stood side by side with their greatest enemy. Falorn and D'varin knelt down next to their fallen comrade murmuring soft, sad words Aliana realized were in Faetine, the language of the Fae.

"Percival, Leyon." Arthur's voice was low and solemn. Everyone looked to him for his next orders. "Search the area, be sure we are alone." The two moved toward the trees, their injuries making their movements slower and rougher. "Lancelot, you are our best tracker, find the horses. Get them back here, we return to Camelot immediately. Take Owaine with you."

The two nodded, faces grim and bloody, and hobbled off, following the hoof prints in the ground.

Aliana knelt next to Merlin. The Druid didn't even seem to notice her. She touched his shoulder with her shaking hand, the sharp pain and burning in her muscles still punishing her from her overuse of magic. Dagg's wings moved against her shoulder.

"We have to fix this, Dagg."

Dagg's rumbled hum rolled through her body. *"Our only chance to save Morgana, to rid her of that evil, is the Grail of Power. Only elixir from its enchanted metal will destroy that darkness. It has the power to restore and return anyone to what they were. Or it can grant unimaginable power, if the person who possesses it knows what they are doing."*

Shivers ran through her again. Merlin had the Grail of Power when he made the bargain with Titania, after Mordrid nearly killed Arthur. Aliana looked down at the ruby glinting on the back of her hand. The Fae queen had used the Grail to create this magic ruby, the prophecy stone. She knew what she needed to do next.

"Merlin," she called him again, hoping to draw his attention. But it didn't work. She sighed heavily, her heart breaking for the lost Druid. Aliana glanced over her shoulder at Arthur, Gawain and Galahad who were talking quietly with Falorn and D'varin. Merlin needed to get the Grail of Power, and maybe knowing what it could do would help give him hope.

Aliana scooted around to face the ashen Druid. "Merlin, you need to listen to me!" She cupped his clammy cold face with her hands, the touch of skin on his flesh finally drawing him from whatever haunted world he had been trapped in. "I know how we can save Morgana."

His brow furrowed.

"The Grail of Power!"

His sky blue eyes widened, the first sign of hope and life returning like little sparks.

Aliana let a little of her own hope show in her small smile. "Think about it, the Grail can destroy the darkness that took her. If we can rid her of that, she will be your souls mate again!"

Then the Druid's face fell. "I have no way of getting to it. I would need the map *you* need to return home."

She shook her head. "No, you don't." She smiled again. "Delphina can show you the way. Her people know where it hides in Avalon, remember?" She knew, from the fact Morgana was still evil in her time, that Merlin wouldn't be able to save her now. But giving him the hope would be enough to ensure he got the Grail. He'd need it if their future were to happen.

Hope returned to his face and he started nodding.

"Avalon is the realm of your father, you can draw so much power from that magic land. If you and Delphina go there, I *know* you can find the Grail!" She hoped that the smart man would read between the lines of what she was saying. "So much rests on that fact."

Merlin's sky blue eyes studied hers for a long moment. They widened as he realized what she was hinting at. "I suppose you *are* from the future," he whispered. "All right."

Together they both got back to their feet. He hugged her fiercely. Aliana was shocked for a half second then she wrapped her arms around him and returned the hug. "You will get her back, Merlin! I'll make sure of it."

He nodded against her shoulder then pulled back. He led Aliana to where Arthur, Galahad and the others were watching them both.

"As soon as the others return, we will ride back to Camelot." Arthur's face was set in hard lines. "We have a war to prepare for."

Aliana's restored hope dimmed. She couldn't go back with them. She knew she was about to start a heck of a fight, but it was one that needed to be settled. "I need to continue on with my quest, Arthur."

"No." Galahad denied her before the king could. "Our enemies now have the one weapon that can defeat even Excalibur, they will not wait to strike again."

"Sickening as it is, we know that Raven…" Arthur shook his head. "Mordrid wants you. We cannot make it easy for him by letting you go jaunting off to another realm."

Aliana steeled herself, setting aside her heartache for now. "This isn't something you have a choice about," she said softly, trying not to rattle this beehive too much at once.

"He seemed surprised you knew his name," Falorn stated. "How did you know who he truly was?"

Aliana gulped. She still had to tell them about being from the future, why she knows him.

"Because she has faced him before," Merlin said beside her.

She took a breath. "I told you that I was sent here to find the map, because I need it to fight an evil that is threatening *my* family, *my* world…" She cleared her throat, about to break her promise to the queen, but if felt like the right thing to do. "In *my* time."

Galahad shook his head. "What are you saying, Aliana?"

Falorn took a step closer, his eyes lit with awe all over again. "She's saying she is from the future."

She nodded, looking from him to Galahad and Arthur, terrified how they would react.

"That's impossible," Arthur denied.

"And yet…" Aliana shrugged her shoulder. "Now do you understand why I have been so careful about revealing my secrets?"

"Did you know all of this, any of this, was going to happen?" Gawain asked, his voice very quiet.

Aliana shook her head. "No, just because I am from the future does not mean I have any answers." She looked to Galahad. "Please tell me you understand why I have to go to the Underworld."

His stubborn mouth remained shut, the silence cutting through her heart.

D'varin stepped between them, his severe face softening with sympathy for her. "You knew who Mordrid was, does that mean you face him in your time? He is the enemy you must prevail against?"

She looked past him to Arthur. The king watched her with heavy golden brown eyes. His king mask was in place, but she could guess he was dreading her answer. "Yes."

Arthur turned his back to her, Galahad and Gawain's face lighting with a realization. Aliana could only imagine that meant they were starting to realize what that meant for their future.

"Princess," Falorn said, drawing everyone's attention. "You should not reveal too much to us of the future." The older Fae looked at Galahad and the other four knights who were returning with the horses. "Even if the future is determined, no man should know what his fate is to be."

Aliana nodded as Gawain caught the others up. Arthur and Galahad stood side by side as Aliana went to them. "Please say you understand that I *have* to go. I have no idea how my being here has affected my own timeline. The sooner I complete these tasks for Titania, the sooner…" She let her words trail. They knew what she was saying.

"Then we will all go with you," Galahad insisted. "Morgana knows where you are going and why. They will no doubt be laying a trap for you."

Aliana's gut twisted, the voice in her head questioning that suspicion. Assembling a weapon as powerful as the Spear of Hel would take time and power. The three of them had to be weakened after this battle and the magic used. If *she* had that weapon, her first focus would be on getting it together.

"Maybe," Aliana told the white knight, trusting her instincts. "But we don't know that for sure, and this isn't something I can avoid any longer. Maybe if I had done more sooner, learned of the map sooner, none of this would be happening."

The two were silent as everyone gathered around waiting for the king's decision.

"We cannot let you go on this quest alone." He held up his hand to silence her as she started to protest. "We know, you think none can travel through the portal with you, but *you* don't know that for certain."

Aliana bit back her argument. Fighting would do her no good right now.

Arthur looked over her shoulder to Merlin, who had come to stand behind her. "You said you were sent to Aliana when she arrived."

The Druid nodded.

Arthur's golden eyes came back to her. "Then you will go with her. Protect her and travel to the Underworld with her. You and Sir Gawain."

"Sire," Galahad started.

The king shook his head. "You and I are needed in Camelot."

"Falorn and I will also accompany our princess," D'varin added.

Aliana tore her eyes from Arthur, her sadness at their loss returning through all the other swirling emotions flying around them. "What about Echary?"

Falorn smiled solemnly. "We will send him home to the Isle where his sister Freya can bury him with honor."

Aliana jolted at the name. He couldn't possibly mean Leo's Freya, could he?

It had taken Arthur finally ordering Galahad to return to Camelot with the rest for the white knight to finally accept Aliana leaving with Gawain, Merlin and the Fae warriors. She hated that he was so upset, still so raw over losing Sophvira. But then being separated for this part of her quest was for the best.

"Do you believe having any of the guys go to the Underworld with us is a good idea, Dagg?"

"Sadly, no."

"I'm gonna need Merlin's help to keep them from trying to follow." Dagg's reluctance was like a wet blanket but he also knew she was right.

"Aliana?" Gawain's gruff annoyed voice broke her from her private conversation.

"What were you asking, *Sir* Gawain?"

"I was *saying* that we should stop and water the horses and try to find out how much further to this portal of yours."

She followed as he veered to the left. They came to a small running stream not far off the trail they had been using. Aliana dismounted, her thigh muscles protesting the long hours they had rode and the lingering weakness of her magic drain.

She led her horse to the water, pulled free her own water sack as her mount drank her fill. She looked to Merlin, a few feet down from her. He was silent and brooding and she couldn't blame him. Gawain and the Fae were in the middle of a quiet conversation so she made her way to the Druid.

"Merlin?" She rested her hand on his shoulder. "We need to talk about the Grail of Power."

"What of it?" His voice was low and hollow.

"After I enter the Underworld, you need to send word to Delphina and go to Avalon."

The Druid sighed, running his hand through his wind tussled hair. "Arthur will not like it."

She squeezed his shoulder reassuringly. "If anyone would understand, it's Arthur." She smiled dreamily. "He understands love and is compassionate."

Merlin frowned. "And is very serious about us protecting you."

Aliana pursed her lips. "Don't be so thick headed, Merlin. This is your chance to save Morgana. You *have* to take it. Besides, none of you can go with me to the Underworld. You will be sitting around until I come back. Might as well make good use of that time."

The Druid nodded once. "You are asking me to distract them, keep the others from following you through the gate, yes?"

She shrugged sheepishly. "You know the Fae Queen, do you really think she would want, much less *let* anyone else interfere with my quest?"

Merlin shook his head and turned to pat his horse on the neck as it drank.

Understanding the dismissal, Aliana turned back to her own horse, where Dagg was perched on her saddle. "Let's see just how close this gate is." She called on a small bubble of ruby magic and summoned the holograph-like globe with all the portal points like Merlin had taught her in their first magic lesson.

"Amazing," D'varin said, coming to stand by her side. The others followed, each taking in the map.

Merlin's mental voice stole into her mind. "*Where did you learn this?*"

She looked at him through the map and shrugged, not wanting to have to lie.

"*I see.*" The Druid's mind pulled from hers.

"How close are we, Aliana?" Gawain asked, rubbing his hand over his stubbly jaw. Aliana couldn't help thinking all the guys needed a good shave right now.

"Not far." She pointed to a bright pink star only inches from a flashing brownish green one. "We are maybe another hour or so away. We need to keep heading northeast."

A few minutes later, they were all back in their saddles and riding toward the portal. It was early night, judging by how low the sun had gotten when they arrived. She opened her senses, felt around for… something she had never felt before. She had never had any exposure to the Underworld, so she didn't know what to expect.

A rolling earthly power drew her attention leading her toward an open stretch of grass left bare by the surrounding trees.

"We are very close to where we faced that Manticore," Gawain mused. "There is no doubt now that it had to come from the Underworld."

Merlin nodded. "But we still do not know who or why it was sent."

"It had to be Raven and Viviane, right?" Aliana asked, dismounting. Dagg settled around her shoulders as she looked around the small clearing. "Raven…Mordrid was there, he could have easily been controlling it."

Falorn circled the area studying the trees like he could see through them to find any hidden enemies. And maybe he could. The Fae were a very gifted race. "If that is indeed true, then you could be in even graver danger, Princess."

D'varin agreed. "If they had control of the Manticore, then they may have allies in the Underworld. All the more reason for us to escort you, Princess."

Aliana held back a groan. She was grateful for everything they were willing to do for her, but she didn't like how they thought she couldn't do this on her own. She needed to be back in control again. Nothing had gone right since she first arrived here. Now was her chance to change that.

"That's lovely, but I need to figure out how to open this portal first." Aliana crouched down, following her instinct to touch her fingers to the ground. A different kind of earth energy came to her. Stronger, but somehow more silent and charged. She followed it with her magic senses to the center of the open area. "Well that seems a little obvious," she muttered.

The power called to her, whispering in her ear how to open this gate. Much like the attack she favored to destroy and free the conscripted black knights, Aliana felt the power take root and push up through the soil. Sprouts grew up into a twining, thick trunk before splitting apart and twisting through the air, forming a long oval. When the roots met again, it was like a mirror had grown from the earth, complete with three steps that ascended to the vine portal.

"That was not exactly what I was expecting," Aliana said, getting to her feet. "I was expecting more doom and gloom, maybe some creepy split in the earth or something equally terrifying."

Merlin came to her side. "Many do. But they are wrong. The Underworld is the land of death, yes, but it is also a land of great power and life." Merlin's gray blue eyes met hers. He nodded ever so slightly, telling her he was ready to keep the others back.

Aliana connected with the magic of the Underworld again, asking it to open the gate so she may cross over. Electric green flashes of power shot across the open space between the vines. "I guess that means enter."

Dagg circled tightly around her shoulders and she stepped up on the first step. She paused, waiting to see if the magic of the gate would reject her or bring forth a crazy creature like the Banshees that had attacked them when they tried to enter the Isle.

But nothing happened.

She looked back at Gawain and the others and smiled. She waved once, then climbed the last few steps. In the magic's reflection she saw Gawain and Falorn rush forward. Before Merlin could stop them, jade green magic shot past her creating a barrier that kept them all from following.

Be careful. Merlin's last mental words rang through her mind as she crossed over into the realm of the Underlord and his son, Death.

Aliana pushed herself up from the cold jade floor she had fallen on. "That's gonna hurt in the morning," she mumbled, rubbing her shoulder and neck. "Dagg, are we in the Underworld?" She looked around but found no sign of her marble scaled guardian. Her anxiety spiked. "Dagg? If this is a joke, this so isn't the time!"

She looked around, but the almost total darkness made it impossible to find her Dragon, if he was even there. But why wouldn't he be? Taking a big breath Aliana sought into herself to check the strength of her returning magic. She was shocked to find that she was back to full strength. "I never recover this quickly!" Then again, who knew how long she had been here already. She opened her link to Dagg, hoping to find some hint of where he was, but she felt nothing but a vast emptiness.

She shook her head, trying to dispel her loneliness, and summoned her bubbly pink ball of magic to illuminate her current predicament. The light from her glowing orb lit up the dark space around her, revealing a dark winding labyrinth below the cliff she had landed on. Looking at her feet she realized she wasn't on a cliff, but at the top of a staircase. Behind her was a wide, arched Gothic style doorway made of dark green jade.

Vines crawled up the archway with black blossoms clinging to the stone. "Unreal," she said, looking back to the labyrinth. The labyrinth that was supposed to surround the Underlord's castle: Galkamish.

29

Lacy has snuck off again and Percy is rightfully angry. My instincts are telling me there's more to it this time than just seeing Puck. I have only allowed this to continue for so long because Delphina assured me it was necessary. Leo has told me of his doubts about her words, but Delphina is helping, I am sure of it. She is part of our family, and from what I have seen since she returned to us, she knows far more about everything that happened than she has let on. She may even have the answer I need.

— Arthur

A glowing orb of purple and silver light appeared in the distance. It pulsed in sync with her pink ball of magic. "Well if that's not a sign to go that way, I don't know what is."

Walking to the edge, Aliana saw a dark and roughhewn set of stairs leading to the labyrinth entrance several stories down. Her vision tunneled for a second before she calmed herself. She couldn't turn back now. There was too much at stake. "Dagg, I hope like heck you're at the center of this death trap maze."

She descended the stairs as quickly as she could. The closer she came the more she realized this wasn't an ordinary labyrinth. Most mazes had towering walls that made it impossible to see where to go. But the walls of this maze were shorter than her! She thought to question it but decided to thank the stars for the fact she could keep the purple orb in sight.

It turned out the short walls didn't help her like she had hoped they would. Fifteen minutes into her search Aliana realized she couldn't see enough of the path to figure out which turn to take. "I'm not about to give up. Time to get creative!"

Using her magic, Aliana boosted herself up onto the wide flat top of the wall. From this angle she could see a direct path to her prize. She walked along the edge, feeling like she was traversing a wide balance beam, jumping to a new wall ledge when the one she was on ended. "I should make it to Dagg in no time!"

Yet every time she thought she was getting closer, the purple light seemed to move further away. "This is ridiculous!" Maybe this was the labyrinth's way of paying her back for cheating.

Aliana was starting to get desperate. Who knew how time was passing here and in her world. She hadn't tried shifting since she was in the Isle and she and Lacy had shifted everyone to the ruins of Camelot, but it seemed like the only way she was going to get to that glowing purple and silver ball. Closing her eyes, she opened her senses to the charged earthlike magic all around her. Aliana imagined herself next to that purple light and willed her magic to take her to it.

Power rushed around her; her body felt tingly and like liquid as she felt herself being pulled way. Her eyes fluttered open, pink sparks popping before her for a long second, before she saw the tree enclosed Zen garden she had ended up in.

"That is still one heck of a rush!"

A low growl caught her attention.

She snapped around to see her guardian trapped in a circle dome that could have been made out of diamond. It hung from a branch of a low wisteria tree, covered in black blooms, like a hanging lantern. Bands of purple magic swirled around the globe cage like a barrier to be sure she couldn't free her friend.

"Dagg!" She tried to open their connection again, but still felt nothing. It was a profound loss that left her feeling hollow and totally alone.

"What's going on? Who's doing this?" Aliana shouted into the empty garden.

A ringing high voice pierced the empty space. "There is no need to shout, Destined One."

Aliana swung around, but saw no one. "Who's there? Why have you trapped my friend?"

"So many questions," that voice teased.

Aliana turned, her green eyes coming in contact with a pair of pure white eyes just in front of her. "What the…"

She jumped back as a woman's head appeared to go with the eyes. Her body soon followed, like the Cheshire Cat from Alice in Wonderland. She turned into a beautiful Sphinx with long tapered paws and a muscular but feminine body. She wore jade green chest armor to match the dark Greek style helmet on her head.

"You're beautiful," Aliana let slip before she could stop herself.

The legendary creature grinned. "Flattery will not return your friend to you, Destined One." Her mirth didn't seem friendly. It felt more like she was sizing Aliana up, like a great predator looking for a weakness to exploit.

Aliana crossed her arms. "How do you know who I am?"

Her lion/human shoulders shrugged in a fluid, unreal like motion, the first move she had made since appearing. There was a smug tilt to her mouth and wide white eyes. "I know much. My master has talked often of you."

"Your master?" Aliana shifted to place herself between Dagg and the creature. If she noticed, she made no mention of it. The Sphinx just shifted her head in that same eerie, fluid motion.

Shivers ran down Aliana's spine like a snake slithering down her back. "I want my friend back, now." Aliana hoped the Sphinx thought her as strong as she sounded, because she was really starting to get creeped out.

The Sphinx woman remained unmoving like a still lake. "But you did not come for your Guardian. You came for the Grail map."

"Yes, but my friend came with me. You had no right to take him."

Her lips pulled back in a wicked smile revealing pearly white canine teeth. "I did not take him from you. You are in the Underworld, realm of the great Underlord. Everything and everyone here bows to his will."

"I still want Dagg back, and the map. I need to get home and I can't do that without either of them."

Her head shook from side to side, like rippling water and earth. "It is only within my power to grant you one or the other. Choose wisely, Destined One."

Aliana stared at the female Sphinx dumbfounded. She couldn't choose between Dagg and the map! *There's gotta be a way around this. Think, Lia, think!* She scolded herself. Her papa had told her the different tales of the Sphinxes of old. The female creatures were of Greek mythology, while the more recognizable male versions were Egyptian myth. But one thing they both shared in common was a pension for challenges.

Aliana met the white gaze defiantly. "If there's one thing I've learned it's that there's always another way."

Those white eyes narrowed slightly, a smirk appearing on one corner of the Sphinx's fang-tipped mouth. "Indeed, but many have found that the other way does not always grant satisfaction."

"Let's say I'm gonna go on faith that this one will work out." Now she just hoped fate didn't prove her wrong.

The beautiful woman lion creature flowed back. "Very well. Answer my riddle and you will get both your Dragon and the map you seek."

Aliana took a step forward, hoping she looked more confident than she felt. "And if I lose?"

"You get nothing and will remain here for the rest of eternity," the Sphinx finished.

Her palms were sweaty, and a bead of sweat formed on Aliana's brow. The last deal she'd made had quite literally blown up on her and trapped her in the past. The stakes seemed almost too high. But what other choice did she have?

Aliana made the only decision she could. "You have a deal. Ask away."

The Sphinx got up to her paws, her body rippling with muscles and magic. She prowled around Aliana, moving more like she was gracefully floating rather than stalking her prey. Aliana held still as the creature studied her.

After two circuits around her, the lion woman sat back on her haunches, her fathomless, eerie white eyes fixed on Aliana like they could see straight into her heart and mind. "What is the one thing no one can change, outrun, or defy? It knows no bounds and is one of the two creations of this universe that is truly uncontrollable."

Aliana rolled the words over in her mind. What was the one thing no one could change? She looked around the blackness of the

Underworld thinking about the possibilities. *Death?* she wondered. This was the Underworld after all.

Where the Underlord and his son Death reigned. And that fearsome general did control death. *Damn.*

"We do not have all eternity, Destined One," the woman lion mocked.

Aliana scowled. "Give me a minute, all right? Geesh."

The Sphinx chuckled.

Stop calling me Destined One, she wanted to hiss at the creature, but held her tongue. The Sphinx was right, this was a part of her destiny, and she should know this. Aliana looked back to Dagg. He watched her silently from his diamond cage. Even without their mental bond, she knew her friends well and she could see his belief in her.

"Something no one can outrun or change or defy…" she muttered twisting her fingers together.

"I grow weary of this game. You have one minute to give me your answer or you forfeit the wager."

"That's not fair!" Aliana snapped.

"Life is not fair, Destined One. I should think the answer is quite obvious. Only fifteen seconds left."

A mental light bulb went off. *That's it!* "Destiny!"

The Sphinx snarled. "Took you long enough." She shook her head in her fluid movement. "And the Underlord thought you so clever."

Aliana's annoyance sparked her temper. "Hey, I solved it, didn't I? Shut the commentary down, free my friend, and give me my map." She cocked a hip, her balled fists resting on her hips.

The Sphinx smiled, one that actually looked somewhat friendly. Then she slashed out her big paw with long talon-like claws. The blow struck and shattered Dagg's cage. The small Dragon shot out of the shards of diamond, straight for Aliana.

"Dagg!" Aliana cried out, grabbing her guardian in a tight hug as he flew into her arms, his wings flaring to wrap around her shoulders. The hole in her heart filled again, quashing the lonely pain their separation had caused. *"I am so glad you are all right!"*

"I am too. You did wonderfully to bet the Sphinx the way you did. They are cunning and very dangerous."

Aliana smiled. *"Thanks, Dragon boy! Now let's get our map and get out of here. I'm ready to go home."*

Dagg's wings folded in as he crawled around her shoulders like a stole. With her guardian and friend back where he belonged, Aliana faced down the Sphinx. "I won. Now I'd like that map so we can go home."

"Of course, my lady." The creature bowed to her. "But I am not the one you must retrieve it from."

"Oh come on!" Aliana shouted, stalking up to the giant mythological creature. "You lost! Are you going back on our deal?"

That beautiful and fierce face swooped down to Aliana's level before she could blink. The growl that rumbled from her vibrated through Aliana's muscles. "Watch your words, Destined One. I have cut others down for far less of an insult. If I were not under orders to see no harm comes to you, I would have already cut your destiny short."

Aliana took a step back, her brow pulling together. "Orders from who?"

The Sphinx straightened, silent. She inclined her head one more time before vanishing.

"Wait! Orders from who?" Aliana cried out, looking around the starless surrounding.

"Those would be my orders."

A man only inches taller than her appeared. He was dressed in exquisite, Asian style jade and amber silk robes. He had sharp features that reminded Aliana of a bird of prey, like a raptor or a falcon, especially with his black eyes. They weren't terrifying like Mordrid's black eyes, but rather wiser and kinder. Power rolled off him from the way he stood. Like a military man, shoulders squared and perfect posture.

"Are…are you the Underlord?"

He nodded.

He held out one hand, palm up. For a second nothing happened then green lightning crackled in his palm, a yellowed roll of parchment appearing. "I believe you won this."

Aliana hesitantly took the map from him. "Thank you."

He chuckled. "You did well to defeat the Sphinx."

Not sure what to say or do she nodded. "Um, so can I go now? I really want to get back to my time."

He cocked a brow. "And which time is that? Your past in Camelot or your present in the mortal realm?"

Aliana tilted her head a fraction and used her bubbly magic to hide the map in her ruby. "Present time, obviously. We need this map to stop Mordrid. And honestly I am terrified that I may have inadvertently done something to mess up my time, being back here."

"You have spent much time worrying over this fact. What would you say if I were to tell you that you being in Camelot did happen in King Arthur's past?"

"What?" Aliana's face scrunched as she looked to Dagg. "I'm totally confused. I couldn't have been here. The guys would have had memories of me in Camelot, before I even awoke Arthur and freed Galahad form the Sidhe."

The Underlord waved a dismissive hand. "So you think. As I told another, there was and still is much you have to do in Camelot to ensure your future unfolds the way it did and still must. There is nothing I cannot divine with my Well of Realms. Past or future. Though neither makes a matter in my realm."

Aliana rubbed her temples. All this confusing talk of time travel and affecting the past was really starting to give her a headache. "Why is that?"

"Because my realm exists outside of the laws of time. And no other living or dead being knows the uses of the Wells as I do."

Chills ran through her. "Can you see my future?"

His head tilted a fraction, his eyes glowing with green light. "I see a future for you, several in fact."

Aliana reeled back. "What?"

His eyes returned to normal. "It would seem your fate has not yet been determined. Your destiny is still being written, with many possible outcomes. I have only ever seen this one other time."

"Well, aren't you special?" she muttered, exhaustion suddenly settling in. "Please, I need to get home."

He chuckled. "And here I would have thought you would have so much more to ask me, Destined One."

She crossed her arms. "My name is Aliana, not Destined One. And I need to get back to my friends."

"Very well." He held his hand out, a mirror appearing similar to the one she created in the field. "Your passage home lies before you."

Aliana stepped past him.

"I would have thought you would demand to see your parents. Know the truth of your heritage."

Aliana stopped dead, glanced back at the Underlord. "What do you mean? What could you know of my parents?" She caught herself. He could see her past…he could see who her birth father was, what really happened to her Mama and Papa! She wheeled around. "Tell me what you mean! Do you know who my real father is because of your tricks?"

He turned to her. "I do not need my *tricks* to know who your birth father is. He is here, in the Underworld, along with your mother and adoptive parents."

Aliana felt the blood drain from her face and her legs start to shake. "They're here? My father and mother, Selene…my mama and papa too?" She felt Dagg shift restlessly on her shoulders.

He nodded. "Would you like to meet your birth parents?"

"Careful, Aliana," Dagg warned. *"I do not trust his motives."*

"At what price?" A tremble penetrated her voice. She cleared her throat. "Nothing comes without a heavy cost."

A sharp smile broke out on his eagle face. "You have learned much, have grown into a wise and strong young woman, indeed. But this I offer free of any strings or cost; as I am offering it for the sake of others as much as my own."

"Now you've totally lost me."

"It's quite simple really. Do you wish to meet your birth parents, and know it is them this time?" When Aliana hesitated he added, "It's a yes or no question, my dear."

Her anger sparked. "What do you mean *know it's them?* Of course I want to meet them! I've wanted little else since I learned I was adopted…but—"

The Underlord clapped his hands together, the sound echoing like thunder. "Then it's settled." He waved his hand, a mist mirror forming between them. Aliana saw herself standing on the pier watching as the boat carrying her Mama and Papa exploded. Tears misted her vision as the man and his wife caught her before she could jump into the water, unknowingly into Morgana's trap.

"Why show me this? Do you think I needed a reminder?"

"You still are not seeing the truth that is right in front of your eyes."

Aliana angrily dashed away the moisture in her eyes. What was she missing? The man whispered to her, the woman stroking her arms as she sagged back against the strange man who was protecting her.

"But how…?"

The image vanished, a new voice behind her making her spine go stiff. "We have protected you since you were born."

That rough voice was gentle, with just a hint of hesitation. Aliana screamed at her body to move, but she stood frozen where she was.

"You can do this." Dagg jumped from her shoulder.

She blinked rapidly, tears clogging her eyes and nose. Everything seemed to slow down as she managed to get her legs to work. She turned toward the male voice behind her, shaking like a leaf with so many emotions she couldn't sort them all out.

Her emerald eyes landed on a tall man with jet-black hair, hot red eyes, and strong, sharp facial features like they were carved of marble. He wore dark pants and black boots, and an Asian-like wraparound tunic with intricate stitching revealing a prowling tiger that seemed to be watching her with similar red eyes. For as hard as his face was, there was an impression of hesitation she would have never expected to see.

"Who are you?" she choked out.

His foot moved like he wanted to take a step forward but caught himself. "I am General Alaki."

Aliana's eyes widened. "Death?"

He nodded, his eyes darkening. "Yes, others know me as Death, and many other names. But *I* am Alaki, son of the Underlord…and your father."

30

Aliana stumbled, blood rushing through her so fast it was like hot lava.

General Alaki was there, his hands on her arms steadying her. Aliana looked up at him, her tears finally falling. She had no idea what to do or think or say.

He reached up and brushed away the tears. Something inside her shattered and she threw herself in his arms, burying her face in his shoulder as sobs wrecked her.

"Shh," he whispered, his arms coming around her, one hand cupping the back of her head, the other rubbing up and down her back. "I've got you now. Your mother and I have waited for this day for so long."

Another cool presence appeared and touched her shoulder. Aliana looked up from the general's shoulder. She met emerald eyes, exactly the same as hers. The woman standing next to them was a face Aliana had memorized from the only photo she had ever seen of her birth mother.

Delicate flowers were draped in the short, dark brown hair that curled at her shoulders. She had a heart shaped face with the same "half lips" Aliana had, and rounded cheekbones. She wore a long, flowing dark purple silk gown, stitched with beautiful colored flowers and a golden phoenix, with a square neck line that came up to tie behind her neck. A thick matching purple and jade green sash was wrapped under her chest, accenting another piece of jade green silk that appeared from under the dress forming long, wide bell sleeves. She was beautiful, and enchanting, and so much more in person than Aliana had ever imagined she could be.

The general's arms relaxed as Aliana pulled away and turned into her mother's open arms. Aliana squeezed her eyes shut as more tears escaped and she clung to her birth mother. Strong arms encircled both women. Aliana turned her head to see the general watching her with bright happiness in his hot red eyes.

"I don't understand," Aliana said when she finally pulled back. "I don't get any of this!"

Her mother laughed softly, running a hand through Aliana's hair. "I understand. You've had a lot of shocks lately."

"It is a very long story, my Aliana," the general started. "The simple version is this…your mother, Selene, is my souls mate. After she fell pregnant with you we discovered Titania's plans, the prophecy she had built upon."

"We also knew you would be in great danger, from Mordrid, Morgana…" her mother hesitated "…and possibly from Oberon or even my mother."

Aliana frowned, but listened to their story with rapt attention.

Her father continued. "We realized the only way to protect you, to give you the chance of a normal, happy childhood was to give you up." He choked on his words a little. "It was the hardest decision we ever made."

Her mother nodded. "Carrie and Allen were very dear friends to us. I had known Carrie since we were kids. She knew the truth of who I was." Selene looked at her souls mate. "And she knew the truth of who Alaki was. Carrie was unable to have children of her own, so when I came to them, after you were born, they agreed to take you in, and raise you as their own."

Aliana wiped away the last of her tear streaks. "But why couldn't I stay with you?" She looked at her father. "You're Death, couldn't I have been raised here?"

They looked at each other and shook their heads, sadness radiating from them. "I," Alaki started, "am bound to the Underworld. I can be away from the realm, yes, but never for very long. And your mother is my souls mate. As soon as we accepted that bond she became as I am. Bound to the same restrictions. Raising you here would have changed destiny and would have been even more dangerous."

Aliana looked to the Underlord, who had watched all of this silently. "You're the Underlord! Why couldn't you change this? Make it possible for my mother and father to stay with me?" The injustice of it all burned her. He was one of the greatest powers in all the realms!

"Even I have my restrictions, and time stands still here; those who reside in this realm do not age. You would have remained a babe, dear granddaughter."

Her eyes widened, he *was* her grandfather! She rubbed her forehead, trying to stave off the headache that was forming.

Her mother's hands took over, rubbing her temples. Cool gentle power flowed through her, easing the building pain. "Even though we could not raise you, we have protected and watched over you every moment of your life." She smiled warmly, cupping Aliana's face. "We are so proud of you and all you have accomplished."

Aliana took her mother's hands, pulled them from her face and held them as she looked to her father. "If you couldn't be in the mortal world for so long, how were you able to be there to save me after...on the dock after..." She let her words hang.

"We can be in the other realms for any amount of time, but the mortal realm is the opposite of the Underworld, so it drains us if we remain in human form for too long." He looked at Selene, stroked her cheek. "The year I spent with your mother, before you were born, was the longest I had ever attempted in human form. I can spend unlimited time, when I am there as Death, we both can, but then you would not have been able to see us. My immortal army helps me gather the souls of the departed from all the realms."

Aliana let all this new knowledge sink in. She didn't want to touch the whole army-of-the-dead thing with a ten-foot pole right now. "You said you had been protecting me all my life, what did you mean?"

"Titania had already seen to one level of protection for you," her father said. "But we added to those shields."

A light went off in her brain. "The extra power in the shields around my house and flat."

The three Underworld beings nodded. "Yes," her mother said. "And other ways as well."

Before Aliana could ask, the general answered, "Do you remember when you were in the mountains of China a few years ago?"

Boy did she! It was the first trip abroad she had taken after her parents died, well before she discovered that she was adopted. "I was there for one of Wade's tournaments, and I went to visit a monastery in the Wudang Mountains."

"Yes, and you decided to go wandering off just before sunset, on your own, with no map or guide," her mother said with a disapproving frown. "You nearly scared the life out of me when you fell down that hill, and hurt your leg like you did."

Aliana flinched, both from the reprimand and the phantom pain of the long gash that had been torn in her calf. "Yeah. I admit it wasn't my smartest move."

Her father sighed. "Do you remember what happened next?"

Aliana shivered. She wouldn't soon forget. "That king cobra came along. I was so scared."

"I know." Her father stroked her hair again.

"But a tiger saved me. It came along and somehow scared away the snake." She looked at the tiger on her father's silk tunic. "That was you!" After scaring away the cobra the tiger had circled her, Aliana had been sure she was going to be tiger kibble, but the beast instead started to lick her wound. She had been so freaked she didn't dare move, but then something strange had happened: her leg started to feel better. At least enough that she was able to put weight on it again.

"I guided you back to the monastery after that." Her father's strong mouth turned up in a smile.

"Then Wade seriously laid into me for going off on my own like that." Not that she hadn't deserved it for being so stupid and impulsive, but she hadn't been in a really good place then, so soon after her Mama and Papa's deaths. "I learned to start making my own maps after that, and being more careful when I went exploring."

"Thankfully," the Underlord tossed in. "And though I do regret this, you cannot remain here much longer, granddaughter."

Her chest tightened. "But I've only just met my parents!"

Selene wrapped one slender arm around her. "It is hard on all of us, but you need to get home to your friends. They need you far more than you realize."

Her father wrapped his arm around her shoulders from the other side. "This will not be the last you see of us. Now that you know, and have tapped into the full powers of both your heritages, it will be much easier for you to come see us, here. And us to come to you."

"Before you go," the Underlord interrupted, "There is one more thing I have for you."

"Seeing my Mama and Papa?" she asked hopefully. She felt a slight tension enter her parents. "Sorry," she whispered, not meaning to upset them.

"Do not worry," her father told her. "We owe Allen and Carrie much and do not begrudge them your affection."

"I am truly sorry, Aliana," the Underlord cut in again. "They are here in this realm, yes, but now is not the time for you to see them again." His sharp features softened a fraction. "But that time *will* come."

Aliana swallowed the heavy lump in her throat and nodded to the Underlord. She held her hands out to Dagg, who had been watching all of this silently. She bit her cheek as he came to her arms. She stroked him seeking comfort from his presence as he resettled around her shoulders. "What was the one last thing?" she asked her grandfather.

"I offer each of my descendants one boon in their lifetime. Your father used his to find his souls mate, I am now offering you yours. You can ask anything of me as there is very little outside of my powers to grant."

Aliana sucked in a breath. She could ask him to let her mother and father be with her in the mortal realm! Or ask him to give Vira her life back; or give her Mama and Papa their lives back! She remembered Titania's final challenge before she had awakened Arthur in Avalon. She remembered her answer to Titania's similar offer. Her parents wouldn't want her forsaking the safety of everyone for her own selfish happiness. Neither would Vira. She couldn't let everyone down like that. What she needed was to get Arthur allies to help in the fight against Mordrid. And her father did mention he had an army.

"Then I would ask that you grant us General Alaki." She looked up at him. "My father," she corrected herself, "and his army to fight with us, King Arthur and the Knights of the Round Table, when we need them to finally defeat Mordrid and Viviane and Morgana."

The Underlord cracked a wide and pleased smile. "I was hoping you would ask for that. Your wish is granted. Death and his army will be at your disposal whenever you need them."

Aliana looked at both her parents, their pride shining in their eyes. She hugged them both fiercely.

"Before she must depart, my lord," Selene said, her arms tightening around Aliana. "I would ask one last moment alone with my daughter."

The Underlord allowed it. With a kiss dropped on her forehead, the general went to his father. Dagg left her shoulders and followed the two men.

"Come," her mother said, leading her a short distance from the two men. She waved a hand creating a beautiful Chinese garden, with a long stone bench covered with colored cushions.

"I'm surprised everything here had such an Asian feel to it. I would have expected a more…"

"Doom and gloom, hellfire and brimstone atmosphere?" her mother finished for her.

Aliana giggled. "Something like that, yeah." They sat down on the bench. Aliana glanced at the Underlord who had his back to them and met her father's red eyes over her grandfather's shoulders. He smiled affectionately.

"I am so very proud of you. You have endured far more than anyone your age should have too. But you have done so with grace and great strength and honor."

"I don't feel like I have. I just feel so lost all the time," Aliana said. "I'm so confused by all the different stories and magics and destinies! I mean, my best friends are half Fae and half wood Nymph! I'm terrified I'm going to mess something up in Camelot and screw with my friends futures, and everyone expects so much from me. What if I'm not strong enough or smart enough? What if I make a wrong decision or trust the wrong person or do something wrong and I let everyone down! I mean, Merlin has beat it in my head from the day I met him that my *destiny* is to help save the realms, for god's sake!" Her hands fell to her lap.

"And then there's the fact I'm in love with two guys at the same time. I feel these strange, wonderful and sometimes terrifying bonds with both of them. But Galahad broke my heart, my trust, and Arthur…even after all he's done and said and…I can't help worrying that Titania may want him with Delphina, that he may truly love her. That doesn't even take into account that fact that Galahad's little sister is *dead* because of me."

"Oh my sweet girl," her mother lamented, brushing a strand of hair behind Aliana's ear.

"And if the Underlord is right, that I was here originally…or… oh whatever! Why don't they remember me?"

"Hush now," her mother said gently. "No one can truly understand how time works. There may yet be some explanation as to why the memories of you were taken from the knights."

Aliana sighed and leaned against her mother. She felt Selene's lips brush her head as she wrapped a comforting arm around her shoulder. "What do I do? Before Mordrid kidnapped me, after I first kissed Arthur and he and Galahad fought…" She stuttered over her words, not sure how to explain what she had felt. "After I helped Galahad, and he kissed me, it felt like those two bonds started warring against each other. It *hurt* so much." Tears started to well in her eyes. "I just want to know what the heck is going on in me! This can't be normal, at all!"

"Aliana…"

"I know," Aliana said bitterly, pulling away from her mother. "I'm the Destined One, nothing about me is normal, and I'm just a freak creation of Titania's magic prophecy."

"Stop that right now," her mother ordered in a stern, motherly voice. "You are not a freak! Everyone is created as they are meant to be, unique and special."

Aliana sighed. "I just don't *get* all of this. I just want to feel like I have some control of my life again. I've been moved around like a pawn on Titania's chessboard, and Mordrid's ridiculous bid for ultimate power." She got up and paced wringing her shaking hands together. "What Galahad and I had made me feel like I had something solid to hold on to, to help find some kind of stability but…I have been pushing this horrible worry aside for a while now, because I don't want to even think about it. But what if what I feel for both Arthur and Galahad isn't real? The instant attraction I felt for Galahad doesn't just happen outside a teen romance series! What if this *love* is just a side effect of this prophecy or even worse, some kind of manipulation?"

Her mother stood. "The riddle the Sphinx asked you…she said, 'One of the two creations of this universe that are uncontrollable.'"

Aliana frowned, what did that have to do with anything?

"Think. What is the one thing besides destiny that is stronger than any other magic or force in all the universe?"

Aliana dropped her gaze, huffing out a breath. "I don't know." She truly didn't.

Her mother's cool fingers touched her chin, guiding her emerald gaze to hers. "Love." She smiled softly, casting a glance at her husband. "There is no force in all of creation stronger than true love. It transcends even death. Magic cannot create love; it can only enhance or manipulate the true feelings that already exist. That is why you did not feel the full force of the bonds you share with both Galahad and Arthur right away. You had to grow into them."

"But I love both of them," she whispered.

"Perhaps, but a person cannot truly be *in love* with more than one person at one moment. If the bonds you are feeling are truly not real then you have to seek that out, inside yourself, and discover the truth of your true heart. You have told Arthur several times to listen to his; it is time you do the same. You are strong enough to figure out the truth. Your father is my souls mate. Morgana is Merlin's as Lancelot is Guinevere's. You have felt the strength of those bonds, use that as your guide if you must."

Aliana looked at her mother silently, letting her words settle in. Could it really be that simple? Could her fear, the fear she hadn't let herself truly consider until now, be true and the bonds she felt with both Arthur and Galahad were fake? A creation of Titania's prophecy? But Morgana hadn't fully turned her back on her bond with Merlin. She'd hesitated, but she hadn't really forsaken it, not in the end. The blond sorceress had saved Merlin. She had sacrificed herself for him.

"I just wish I could get some kind of clarity."

Selene hugged Aliana fiercely. She whispered, "You are my daughter, the daughter of Death himself, and granddaughter of the Fae Queen and the Underlord. You have the blood of heroes and cunning scoundrels running through you — that comes from your father's side, I assure you. If anyone can find this truth, it is you."

They pulled back as General Alaki and Dagg came to them. "I am truly sorry my love, my daughter, but you have to return to Camelot now."

Aliana nodded as Dagg coiled around her shoulders and her parents guided her from both sides. She felt warm and safe and loved. Her mother's words gave her a little confidence that she could yet figure out the mystery of her heart.

"Okay, I'm ready, I think." She turned and hugged her parents tightly one last time.

Her father kissed her head and whispered, "I am always with you, call for me whenever you have the need. No one will dare harm those who Death loves and protects."

Her mother kissed her cheek, cool, flowery magic flowing through her. It circled her heart and her mind and eased some of Aliana's remaining fears and pain. She felt the cool blossoming strength of her mother and father's love for her.

Aliana pulled back, went to the Underlord, where he stood by the mirror portal. On impulse she reached out and hugged him too. The fierce man hesitated, and then rubbed her back briefly. "You are certainly full of surprises, granddaughter," he said when she pulled back, a wicked smile on his face that told Aliana that the news pleased him.

"I will see you all soon…right?"

"Indeed, my daughter," Alaki and Selene both assured her.

Aliana called on the rolling, earth-charged energy she was now assuming was the power of the Underworld and ran her finger down the middle of the mirror. The surface rippled like water then crackled with jade green magic.

She looked back at her parents one more time and waved before following Dagg through the portal.

The magic flowed and rippled through her giving her another kind of clarity she had not realized until now. Her earth magic, the energy magic she connected to so strongly was because of her father, because he was of the Underworld and by default so was she. Her magic so easily killed the black knights because, like Excalibur, she had the power to kill even what was already dead. Maybe that was why, after the first time she used that magic, back in their battle in London, she had felt that spirit thank her for freeing it after defeating the black knight army.

The power ebbed and vanished after that moment, and she felt the chilled air of Camelot as she stepped out of the mirror and down the stairs of the portal she had created.

31

Inner conflict is the very devil to deal with. It's not that I don't trust Delphina, she's family, but she is not telling us everything. I worry why that is. At least we know now where Lacy is heading. Thanks to Freya. Lacy is heading to the Well. She's told us of her and Dawn's plans, but it worries me that she has just gone off without us. I fear there may be severe consequences to their plan, and she's kept it from us. Freya wants to come with us, but it's too dangerous to get her any more involved in this quest than she already is, not that she agrees with my opinion, the stubborn lass.

—Leo

"My lady, you've finally returned!"

Aliana met Falorn's excited pale eyes. She blinked away the remains of the magic, turned from the Fae and raised her hand. Her ruby glowed as she closed the portal and let the earth return to what it once was.

"It's good to be back," she said to the Fae as Gawain snatched her up in bear hug. "Put me down Gawain!" She laughed.

He did and hugged her again. "We have been going insane with worry! You've been gone almost a month!"

Aliana pulled back, her eyes wide and shocked. "Son of a monkey!" She looked around and saw the fallen leaves, and the winter dark evening setting in around them.

Gawain stepped back as D'varin came over and bowed to her. "'Tis true, Princess. You have been gone a long time, and much has happened."

"We need to get back to Camelot, immediately," Gawain insisted.

Aliana looked around. "Where's Merlin?" She hoped the answer was the one she wanted.

Gawain's face pinched as Lancelot stepped out from the woods. "He went with Delphina to the realm of Avalon." Lancelot's voice held a frustrated, long angry edge about it. "He is attempting to claim the Grail of Power."

Well, he certainly doesn't approve, she thought. But she was glad Merlin did it. He understood how important this was.

"Are you able to ride, Princess?" Falorn asked.

She nodded. "All recharged and ready."

Gawain crossed his arms. "You got what you needed then?"

Aliana held up her ruby glove. "I did indeed. And a lot more." She smiled at Dagg. She missed her parents already, so much so it was an ache in her heart, but she was also glad she finally knew the truth and got to be in their arms.

"What has happened since I've been gone? Have Mordrid and Viviane put the Spear of Hel together or attacked Camelot?"

Lancelot shook his head. "Neither, that we know of. Queen Igraine discovered that in order for the Spear to be connected, revived, it must be done on the first winter harvest moon."

Aliana shivered as a particularly cold gust of wind blew through the small valley. Falorn grabbed a velvety looking cloth from his saddle and held it out for her. It was a Fae cloak that would protect against even the bitterest chill. "When is that?" she asked, securing the soft material. It was light and very warm.

Gawain's face darkened even more. "Tomorrow night." He ran a hand through his hair then grabbed his horse's reins. "We are still searching for the site they will use, but without Merlin…that task is far harder."

Aliana took her mounts reins from him. "Maybe I can help, now that I'm back."

Lancelot agreed and said that they needed to ride all night to get back to Camelot, so that they would have enough time to find the location.

Her guardian settled around her shoulders after she mounted. They set out for Camelot riding at a fast pace, Aliana thanking the stars that her time in the Underworld had refueled her energy. She didn't think she would have the stamina for an all-night ride otherwise.

After a few hours Aliana started to recognize small landmarks she had seen the last time she had ridden this path. They were maybe halfway back to Camelot already. When the horses started to lag, Lancelot led them to the river where they would rest for a while.

Everyone was feeling the cold of the night and the wind that had been thrashing them on their long ride. She opened her magic senses and pulled on her ruby power to create a warm pocket of air around them all.

"Are you doing that, Aliana?" Gawain asked, grinning.

She nodded. "I thought it would be nice for everyone since we don't have time to build a fire."

"We are grateful, Princess. Thank you." Falorn bowed his head to her.

"Please call me Aliana, Falorn." She looked to D'varin. "You too."

Lancelot opened his mouth to say something but a flash of fire soared through the air, hitting the valiant knight in his left shoulder.

The guys scrambled. Aliana ran to Lancelot, panic flowing through her as she looked at the burning arrow that had pierced him. He was moaning through clenched teeth, his face a mask of contorted pain and sweat. More arrows started to fly. Aliana opened her magic and summoned her bubble-like shield to cover her and Lancelot. With her other hand she held it toward the river, calling on the dripping, rippling power of the water element. She doused the burning arrow.

She leaned over him as Falorn, D'varin and Gawain wielded their shields, forming a barrier between their injured knight and the attacking arrows.

"I can heal you, Lancelot! But I have to remove the arrow first!" She looked around and expanded her shield to their other side, just in case the enemy tried to attack from the other side of the stream. She looked to Dagg. "Go invisible!" she ordered. "Find who's attacking us and from where!"

Her guardian nodded. She felt the slight pull of him taking a bit of her magic. She turned back to Lancelot. "This is going to hurt."

"Do it," he bit out.

Gritting her own teeth, she grabbed the arrow and yanked before she lost her nerve. More arrows flew at them as Lancelot's howl of pain was muffled in his mouth. Aliana gripped more of her bubbly sparking magic and sent it into his body, healing the torn muscle and flesh.

"You'll still be weak for a few minutes," she said, panting. "But you will be well!"

"Thank y—" Lancelot shoved her to the left as he rolled right.

A burnt-blood-colored crack of magic smashed against Aliana's shield. She looked at Gawain and the Fae, relieved when she saw they had dived to the side as well to avoid the blast.

"Viviane!" Aliana's anger flared, her temper igniting. That stupid witch was the cause of all this.

The evil woman's leering voice floated from a nearby cluster of trees. "We have been searching for you for quite some time, Aliana." Viviane and ten other men on horseback filed out of the woods just as the first light of dawn broke over the horizon.

"Sorry, I had more important things to do," she snapped back, getting to her feet and calling on her magic bow.

"Ah yes, your magic toy. I'm afraid it will do you no good this time." She pushed back her long black hair over her shoulder.

"That's what you think!" Aliana sighted down the witch and quickly released the strongest blast of arrow magic she had yet summoned.

Viviane threw back her cloak and raised her hand just as the blast was about to strike. The dark pink magic shattered into falling sparks and a flash of light.

Aliana's eyes widened when she saw what the evil Sorceress held in her hand. The spearhead of the Spear of Hel. A fine tremor ran through her. How could one fraction of that spear stop her magic?

Lancelot got back to his feet, his chest heaving, looking a little unsteady as he grabbed his shield and drew his sword. "You will take her over our dead bodies!"

"That can be arranged, and incidentally my pleasure," she assured him with a shrill laugh. She signaled the men to attack.

The men swarmed them. Gawain blocked a swinging axe with his shield while thrusting his sword up into the horse bearing the rider that attacked him. The horse whinnied in pain and fell, taking the man with it, crushing his leg under its weight.

Falorn batted away the slashing swords easily as he jumped toward the nearest tree. His feet touched the trunk briefly before he launched himself into three of the riders, knocking them from their mounts. He looked calm, but Aliana could almost feel his anger.

D'varin had already taken down two of their attackers with daggers lodged in their throats. He grabbed an arrow from his quiver, nocked it in a flash and sent it spiraling into the eye of another rider. A grim smirk appeared on the Fae's face.

She looked at the remaining four attackers that surrounded them, her own panic spiraling.

Viviane raised the spearhead again, its magic pulsing out. Whips of fire shot down toward them. Aliana panicked, sweat pouring down her as she watched the fire race toward her. For a brief second she was back on that pier, watching her parents die, with Morgana's magic fire trying to reach out and consume her too. The prize it had been denied, by her father and mother's protection.

The thought of her parents snapped her out of her fear. At the last second she summoned her bubble shield, pushing it out to dome around them. The fire struck it full force, not dying out but circling around it like a terrifying pattern of wires and fiery lines.

The heat of the magic pushed against her shield. It was like she could feel the fire burning her skin. Aliana cried out, falling back on her arms, but her shield held.

"Aliana?" Gawain asked, kneeling next to her.

She looked at him with frantic eyes. "The fire, I can't…the fire, it wants me…I can't…I'm too scared." The fire raged brighter, searing her skin.

She cried out again, red angry burn slashes forming on her arms. She started to panic and scramble back.

Gawain wrapped her in her arms, trying to calm her as Falorn helped D'varin.

"Control your fear, Aliana! You know what you must do. Open yourself to the fire element. Make this magic yours. As long as you do not keep control of your fear, the fire's power will only grow." She knew Dagg

was right, but she was so scared. She felt the cool presence of her mother's magic blossoming in her heart.

"I'll try," she whispered to him. She shut down their mental link and took a breath. Lancelot met her eyes and for the first time she saw something from him she never thought she would. Trust. He trusted her to save them.

Aliana focused on her shield and expanded her senses. The fire snapped and crackled, her fears surged but she fought them back. *I am not afraid anymore! Morgana ruled that fire, but I'm strong enough now to fight back!*

Sparks ignited inside her. Bright pink sparks of magic fire similar to Dagg's purple magic fire. She concentrated, felt the warmth and comfort from the flames easing her fear and the searing hot pain that attacked her. She opened her eyes, her vision a haze of pink, like looking through colored lenses. The attacking fire wavered and snapped again before it burst into bright pink flares.

She did it! She had connected with the fire element! She turned her pink tinted gaze to Viviane.

She raised the spearhead again.

Aliana expanded her senses and gathered magic from all five elements. Earth, air, energy, water and fire.

A flash of fear appeared in Viviane's eyes as she realized the depth of the power Aliana was calling. "You won't succeed! Evil never wins!"

The ground vibrated with the thundering of horse hooves and a shrill warning of more danger. They needed to get out of here. With her newfound magic, Aliana visualized the six of them back in Camelot, in the throne room.

Power ripped through her like a dizzying white light. It was agonizing for a second before everything stopped.

The forest had vanished, replaced with the warmth of the main hall of Camelot. Opening her eyes she saw the questioning gazes of Arthur, the queen, the knights and Guinevere. They descended all at once.

Aliana sagged back into Gawain. There went all her recovered strength.

Everyone started asking questions at the same time, but it was Galahad's voice she heard over all the rest.

"What happened?"

Aliana sat up from Gawain's hold. "Good news, I got the map. Bad news, Viviane attacked us on the way back and Lancelot got hurt."

Everyone looked at the olive-skinned knight standing with his wife's arms around him.

"She healed me," he said, his pale green eyes filled with gratitude. "Then brought us all home before their reinforcements could get to us."

Falorn and D'varin helped Aliana to her feet. "They have also learned to use the magic of the spear pieces." The Fae commander shook his head. "We need to find them before tonight's harvest moon."

Dagg wrapped himself around her shoulders, his power filling her, helping to fight off the magic backlash having a go at Aliana's body. "Where's Merlin? Is he back yet?"

"In the library with Delphina." Aliana met Arthur's pale gold brown gaze. So many emotions were there, clear for her to see even through the mask he wore like a shield. She looked away. She couldn't do this right now.

With the Fae warrior's help Aliana sank into a chair at the round table covered with maps and other random pieces of research.

Owaine sat next to her. "You said you got the map, what about the task you didn't know of?"

She leaned back against the hard wood back of the chair. "I don't know. But I've started to wonder if it doesn't have something to do with the Spear of Hel."

Her stomach growled loudly. Heat flared on her neck and cheek as the guys cracked small smiles. They probably hadn't had much occasion to smile since she'd been gone. "I don't suppose anyone has anything to eat?"

"I'll get you something." Guin left the hall quickly.

"Any luck finding where Mordrid, Morgana and Viviane are going to be tonight?" She looked to Galahad, who was standing next to Arthur.

"We've narrowed it down." He pointed to six small stones all placed on the largest area of the map.

"Merlin is trying to find more on the spear, maybe find another indicator that could help us find where they are keeping it." Arthur leaned his hands on the table.

"If we don't find the location soon it'll be too late for Camelot." Galahad straightened.

Aliana swallowed the dryness in her throat and looked out the dark window. "It's barely dawn, why are you all awake?"

"None of us will sleep until we know where our enemy is hiding," Percival said.

"And we *are* closing in on their location," Leyon added, laying a supportive hand on the giant knight's shoulder.

Lancelot took a seat across from Aliana. "After you returned from the Underworld you said you thought you might be able to help find them. What did you mean?"

All the others followed suit, taking their places around the table.

"If there's one thing I've learned about magic, it's that it's strongest at a grid point. It's one of the first things Me—I was taught about magic." Aliana scolded herself for the near slip.

D'varin spoke up, "The map you created when we were traveling to the Underworld portal, that showed all the magical grid points, did it not, my lady?"

"Yeah." She looked at the Fae. "Go get Merlin. Let's see if he agrees and can help narrow the location."

The Fae bowed to her, Gawain rising to accompany him. Guin returned as they left, carrying a plate filled with fruits, cooked vegetables and a decent sized piece of bread in her hands. Several servants followed her carrying more plates.

"All of us are going to need nourishment if our plans work and we find the location where they are held up," Guin said, taking her seat. Aliana and Dagg dug into the delicious food immediately.

The guys continued to talk strategy as they ate. Aliana listened but took the time to really study them all. Gawain said she'd been gone a month; judging by the ragged, tired looks on all of the guys, it hadn't been a good one.

"What's happened while I was gone?" she asked Guin quietly so as not to interrupt the guy's planning.

The dark eyed woman dropped her gaze. "Several villages have been sacked, crops burned. Mordrid and Morgana have spread terror throughout Camelot and even into the other kingdoms of Albion."

Aliana's heart fell. "I'm sorry."

"It's not your fault, none of what has happened is."

"I know, but I can't help feeling guilty. How have you been? The others?" Guin seemed to realize right away she was talking about Sophvira.

"As well as can be expected given the circumstances." She sighed, looking at her husband. "Galahad has had the hardest time, but he won't admit it."

Aliana looked at the white knight, really looked. She could see and even feel his exhaustion but she also saw his ruthless determination and his fears. Her heart broke for him all over again. "I wish I could make his pain go away."

Guin's soft hand covered Aliana's. "You need to stop blaming yourself for everything. I've seen Arthur wearing the same looks. All the knights have at one point or another. I'll tell you what I always tell them. No matter the circumstances, no one is responsible for the actions of another. Only for their own actions."

Part of Aliana knew she was right but that didn't make it any easier.

Merlin burst into the chamber with D'varin and Gawain hot on his heels. "I've found it!" he declared, placing an opened book in front of Arthur.

She recognized it right away. It was the artifact book they had found in the secret library room! "They need the power of a grid point, right?" She was right! Excitement poured through her muscles.

The Druid grinned, a cunning glint in his sky blue eyes. "And I know how to find one."

32

— Galahad

Aliana tugged at the boot strings again before tying them off. Queen Igraine had insisted that she take time to wash up and change. She was wearing a pair of thick leggings tucked into fabric wrapped around her ankles. She stood up, securing her belt to hold the fur-lined collar of her vest closed over the layers of wool shirts she had on underneath.

Merlin was sure that with them working together, they could narrow down the search for Morgana and Merlin's hideout. The knights and Camelot's army would then ride out to face the evil triad before they could get their hands on real power with the reformed spear.

There was one thing still bothering her. When they faced Mordrid, when Morgana had betrayed them, she had known instantly that Mordrid wasn't as strong now as he was in her time. *"Why?"*

"We can worry about that later," Dagg whispered into her mind. *"The king just summoned everyone to the Round Table again. He and Merlin want to go over the final plan of attack."*

"I'll be down in a few minutes."

The growing strength of her bond with Dagg was as amazing as it was helpful. He had gone with Merlin while she cleaned up, yet they had been able to stay in perfect contact with each other the whole time.

She looked down at her ruby glove. It felt good not to hide her magic anymore. There was a rightness to having her power free. She could tell the others had been itching to know more about it. Leyon and Lancelot had even asked her about it, but Queen Igraine had shut them down faster than a cop manning a roadblock.

Igraine had declared after her return that for Aliana to reveal any more would put everyone in grave danger. So despite all wanting to know, none had asked again.

Aliana opened her door, looking around the room. She had a feeling this would be the last time she'd set foot in here. Closing the door, she went to Sophvira's door.

How had she not felt the poison magic of that bracelet? No, that wasn't right, she had felt a wrongness, a sludge-like feeling, but brushed it off. If she hadn't been distracted by Galahad and Arthur…

Her hand reached out and touched the cool wood. Even the door felt dead.

You're being overdramatic, Lia! Lacy and Dawn would have told her the same thing if they were here. She missed them, everyone, so much.

"Aliana?"

She jumped, spinning around so quick she knocked her shoulder against the stone door frame. "Galahad?"

The knight's amazing blue eyes were filled with sadness and worry.

Letting out a breath, Aliana ran her hand through her hair. "You've got to stop using those sneaky ninja skills of yours on me."

His brow pinched. "I don't understand."

Oh my stars, help me. "Never mind, is everything okay?"

He shrugged silently.

Heated tingles flashed up her spine to her cheeks. He was looking at her like…like she was someone special. Still backed against the wall Galahad took another step closer. It was torture waiting for him to say something. They hadn't been alone since before Vira died.

Aliana's guilt came crashing back like a tsunami wave. How could he even stand to be around her?

"I haven't been able to ask," he said, his voice pitched low. "How have you been? You…we all have been through a lot these last few weeks."

"I feel like I should be the one asking you that." She knew the pain of his loss. She could all but taste it.

His eyes shifted away from her. "I am a little better now that you've returned." His eyes found their way back to hers. They were so open, so searing. "You may not want to hear or believe this, but I feel calmer, more in control of…what I'm feeling, when you are near me."

Aliana swallowed the dry lump in her throat, her heart thundering in her ears. What was she supposed to say to that? She couldn't do this, to either of them.

She changed the subject instead. "I thought you'd be down with the others."

He shifted back a fraction. "I was, but I needed a break."

"When did Merlin get back?"

"Just days before you." Galahad rubbed the back of his neck roughly. "I don't think he's slept since his return. He's taken to keeping to himself far more than he has ever done. Morgana's betrayal has changed him greatly."

"He lost his souls mate." Aliana could imagine what that felt like, after what her Galahad had done. "She sacrificed herself for him. Merlin would be a monster if that didn't affect him."

Her words clicked home the secret she had been trying to figure out since she first met the Druid.

Merlin had never been able to catch up to Morgana in all the centuries he wandered the realms. Just like Titania's refusal to let Lancelot die and escape the haunting memories of Guinevere, the Fae had kept Merlin separate from his fallen souls mate. She not only robbed him of his greatest magical source of power, his blood link to Avalon, but also to his love. But that still didn't explain the small vial she had seen him drinking from, and why, in her time, Merlin seemed so much stronger at times than others.

She deserved to be smacked, she should have realized this right away, when she arrived in Camelot!

"Aliana?" Galahad's cautious call drew her from her realization.

"What?"

"I asked if you were ready to return to the Round Table. Merlin should have some answers by now."

She hesitated, looked to Sophvira's dead door. "I'll be down in just a minute." She needed to at least say good bye to the girl.

Like he understood her desire, Galahad left the hall, leaving her totally alone.

Pulling herself from the wall she touched the door gingerly, resting her forehead against the rough surface.

A giggle, so much like Vira's, echoed in her ear. A small sad smile formed. It was so unfair that she had been stolen form them all, from Galahad.

The giggling became louder. The ruffle of a heavy wool skirt mixed with the innocent sound. Out of the corner of her eyes a girl in a green dress, exactly like the dress Vira always favored, appeared.

Aliana straightened, her eyes going to the ghostly figure. Sophvira stood there, a bright smile lighting her brilliant blue eyes.

Aliana rubbed her hands over her deceiving eyes. The ghost remained, giggling again.

It couldn't be Sophvira! *Maybe it's her spirit.* If it was her spirit, maybe the teen was trying to tell her something.

Aliana boots thudded against the stone floor as she rushed to catch the ghost that had turned the corner.

"Come on!" Vira's ghost called, waving her hand for Aliana to follow as she rounded another corner.

Vira's ghost led her down one hall then another. If she had to guess she was in one of the halls along the backside of the castle, overlooking the ocean and cliff below.

Aliana skidded to a stop in a dead end hall. "Why?" she asked the deserted hall, searching for a reason Vira's ghost would lead her here.

"Here!"

Aliana looked left, toward Vira's call. Her eyes landed on a dark green scrap of cloth on the floor. She went over, picked it up, bracing her hand on the unusually cold stone. The barest hint of a breeze touched her flattened palm.

Aliana straightened, jerking her hand back and staring at the wall. She touched it again, the tips of her fingers dancing over the stone. Expanding her magical senses she touched the air element's power, saw the flowing current of air through a nearly microscopic crack that ran from the bottom of the wall and stopped two-thirds of the way up.

She ran both hands along the wall as adrenaline trickled into her blood. "Please be a secret door!" she muttered. A small piece of stone shifted under the pressure of her fingers. She pushed it harder.

The crack widened, the stone door pushed in several inches.

"Yes!" Aliana pushed harder, revealing a steep winding stone staircase.

But it was pitch dark, so dark you could barely see past the first two steps. Aliana summoned a dozen of her glowing sphere lights and sent them to light the hidden passage. The stairs lit with a rosy gleam. There were patches of moss and splinters of wood mingled with the heavy stones. Camelot, it seemed, was full of surprises. Carefully she stepped onto the first stair, testing its strength.

The stone gave no sign of trouble. She moved to the next stair then the next, each time taking a second to be sure nothing started to crumble or collapse. Briny air hit her nose as she made her way down the descending passage.

Aliana's heartbeat kicked up again. Maybe this passage led to the beach. But why would Vira show her this? Maybe she was trying to warn Aliana of a possible danger. If Morgana knew of this, it would give her and Mordrid and Viviane a way into the castle without any trouble.

Aliana hurried down the flight, determined to see if there was anything hiding that could cause Arthur and his men problems.

Bright rays of sunlight mixed with her pink orbs of light. Calling them back, Aliana stared at a large rock formation that seemed to grow out of the side of the wall but ended abruptly. It reminded her of the labyrinth she'd gone through in the Underworld. Another rock formation, from the other side was the same. It was exactly like a labyrinth!

"Dagg! You're not gonna believe this."

Her guardian's worry hit her immediately. *"Where are you? I can't feel you inside the castle. The knights are getting anxious for you to join us. Merlin thinks he knows where to find Mordrid."*

"There's a secret passage that leads from the halls by Galahad's rooms down to the beach! Sophvira's ghost led me to it!"

"No, Aliana!" her Dragon snapped, his panic flooding her. *"You mustn't leave the castle without us. Without me."*

"Too late for that, Dragon boy, I'm almost out on the beach." No sooner than she finished the thought she stepped past the last rock and onto the shifting sand.

She was on a different part of the beach from where Sophvira's funeral rites had been performed.

"Don't go any further, we're coming to you." The order sounded harsh and frantic, but Aliana couldn't understand why. Vira had shown her this, surely there was something to be learned here, maybe even found that could help her or the others.

She looked around, staying close to the cleverly concealed entrance. Maybe that would satisfy Dagg when he got here. She looked back at the hidden passage. If she hadn't known it was there she'd have never found it.

An energy flared behind her. She turned as a dark shadow descended from above.

Rushing forward, she managed to avoid the attacking thing. She pivoted and looked right at Mordrid, who stood between her and her passage back to the castle.

"My trap worked then," Mordrid hissed, an arrogant, triumphant grin on his long face.

Aliana fought back the shiver of dread that slithered down her body like a snake. Glaring at him, hoping to look annoyed rather than terrified, she demanded, "What are you doing here?"

"That's not the question you should be asking. The question you should be asking is what are *you* doing here?" He advanced on her.

She took a step back, desperate to keep distance between them. She needed to stall until the knights got here with Dagg.

He tsked like a disapproving teacher. "Naughty Aliana, running from the knights and that buffoon Arthur, right into my trap."

Aliana glanced around quickly for signs of anyone else, good or bad. "Vira led me here."

"You still don't see. I created an illusion of that girl to lure you here."

Angry embarrassment colored her cheeks. She should have realized something was strange, but she had wanted so badly to see the teen again. She threw a ball of pink sparkling magic at the dark wizard.

He jumped out of the way but Aliana was ready and threw another. Not waiting to see if it hit, she dashed toward the hidden entrance.

Mordrid appeared just in front of her and grabbed her arms. She jerked to the side, shifting her weight and bringing her hands up to break his hold.

His gray electric magic sizzled through her muscles as he pushed her to the side.

She smacked into the unforgiving rock wall, her moan of pain mixing with the sound of crashing waves.

"I should have come after you myself, instead of sending those two fools to abduct you." Mordrid sneered as he trapped her against the rocks. His face was inches from hers.

Aliana wanted to move, but she had nowhere to go. "*Dagg, it's Mordrid! He's here!*"

"*We're coming, hang on! Stay calm and use your magic.*"

Aliana steeled herself. She refused to be a victim to another psycho guy. With all the strength she had, she shoved his chest, adding her magic to the attack.

The wizard fell back, a look of surprise on his face.

Aliana kicked out her leg, connecting with the dark wizard's kneecap. He cried out in pain as she turned and fled again. His hand caught the back of her fur collar as he tried to pull her back, but she ducked to the side, striking her palm against his shoulder as he went past her, sending him stumbling to the sand.

She shot past him, her lungs ready to burst.

"Enough!" she heard Mordrid yell behind her, but she didn't stop.

Not until whips of black gray magic smoke circled her arms.

Her wrists were yanked behind her back, bound by the gray-charged smoke that expanded to wrap around her arms and chest. The magic was like bruising coarse ropes around her. He gripped the back of her head, pulling her back against his chest. His other arm wrapped around her waist, his hand splaying on her stomach. She wanted to vomit at his touch and the shivers that went through her.

She sucked in breath, trying to keep her fear and emotions in check. She needed to be in control of herself and her magic if she wanted to escape this madman. "I will never be yours!"

"I need you to be mine, *want* you to be mine. And I know exactly how to make that happen."

The superior, know-it-all confidence in his voice chilled her very marrow. Whatever he had planned was bad.

"I have learned many things over the years, chief among them how to control others, bend them to my will."

"Like that onyx dagger you wanted Morgana to use against Merlin."

She felt him nod before his hand moved her tussled hair aside and his lips touched her neck. Aliana jerked forward, trying to escape the chilling touch. The magic binds around her tightened until she cried out.

"Struggling will only make the suffering worse. You don't want that, now do you?"

Aliana refused to answer him, clenching her jaw to keep any more cries of pain from escaping.

His hand released her hair, his fingers touching her neck where his lips had been, right over her racing pulse. "What I have in mind for you will leave your mind and spirit as they are, but your magic will be a slave to mine."

"What are you going to do?" She tried to keep her fear from showing, but she knew she failed by the quiver in her voice.

"Aliana!" Dagg roared in her mind. *"I'm here, hold on!"*

But it was too late.

Gray smoke started to surround her. It smelled acidic, burning her eyes and nose. She coughed and coughed, trying not to breathe in the poisoned magic. But she could already taste the bitterness of it. Small puffs filled her lungs and she couldn't stop it.

"Aliana!"

The roar of Arthur, Galahad and the other knights was enough to help her fogged mind clear.

They burst from the rocks like avenging warriors, her wonderful silver Dragon leading the way.

"He's trying to kidnap me!" she told Dagg. She struggled against him again but the dark bonds tightened as she cried out in pain.

"Let her go, Mordrid!" Arthur ordered, Excalibur gleaming deadly and bright in the sunlight.

The stolen spearhead appeared, held in Mordrid's hand. "Too late, *Arthur.* She's mine, just like Camelot soon will be. We have a ritual to complete," Mordrid said to her as he touched his piece of the spear to her temple. Then darkness took over.

33

Lancelot watched Merlin throw the scrying bowl against the wall, and shook his head, his already low spirits falling even more. They had been in Olympus for over a month. Thanks to Merlin's tracking marks, they knew the others were still in the other realms, and Aliana had still not returned to them, that she was still stuck in the past.

Despite what the Destined One probably thought, he did not hate her, never had, even after Sophvira. It was a realization, after she was taken, that he was jealous of her. Jealous that she had found love, while he was haunted every hour of every day by his Guinevere. He held a groan of pain in his chest, not wanting to alert his Druid friend.

The pain of not having his Guin was getting worse and worse by the day, the madness of her loss driving him into lunacy. How many times had he thought he'd seen her out of the corner of his eye? Thought he'd heard the soft notes of her laugh or voice? He had even tracked her ghost several times through the magic lands of Olympus, coming up empty every time.

"Curse all the gods!" Merlin grabbed and threw the glass bowl, again, down into the flowing pool of mystical water. "I can find no hint or trace of this Atlantian that could lead us to the Grail!"

Merlin got to his feet, straightened the orange and brown robes he had taken to wearing since arriving in Olympus. "I must continue our search for this Atlantian. Until Aliana returns to our time, with that map, he is our only hope." Merlin turned and left the garden room.

The knight knew his own sanity was slipping, the side effect of Queen Titania's punishment. Now it seemed Merlin's was sliding toward the same dark oblivion. He punched his fist into the stone bench he had been on, splitting the solid piece of earth into two neat halves. Arthur had told him once, after his fight with Aliana in her mother's piano room, he believed he could prove himself again. Somehow earn release from the Fae's punishment. But how could he accomplish such a task? His loyalty to Arthur had become rock solid since he left Avalon. He had never wavered in his devotion. He had fought by the king, supported him and his brothers since their return. What more need he do?

"Wouldn't you like to know?"

Lancelot spun around toward the high-pitched, sarcastic voice. His pale eyes landed on a short Imp looking boy with orange tinted skin and molten silver eyes. He recognized the intruder almost immediately. The others had told him several times about the mysterious halfling.

"You're Puck."

"Ten points to the knight!"

Lancelot growled. "I do not have time for this." He stalked past the short troublemaker.

"Even if it means freedom from the Fae queen's punishment and the chance to hold your Guinevere again?"

Lancelot looked back at him, meeting those silver eyes over his shoulder. "Explain yourself!"

Puck raised one hand, his fingers rubbing over his pointed chin. "Do you realize how much you sound like that tight wad, Arthur?"

Lancelot's hand gripped his sword hilt. "Do not insult my king!"

Puck waved him off with a dismissive hand. His body lifting from the ground, his legs curling up like a Dijin's from an Arabian tale. "I wonder if you even know the true reason for your punishment."

"I will not tell you again, explain yourself."

Puck shrugged like he was humoring a child. "You've had eight centuries in the mortal realm to contemplate your decision after leaving Avalon." Puck floated closer to Lancelot. "Tell me what you've discovered of yourself and that decision since."

Lancelot's teeth ground together as words locked in his throat.

"Come, come now. You want your sanity back right?"

"I left because of my own selfish desire to escape losing my souls mate." The self-loathing he felt seemed endless. It ate away at his soul as much as the Fae's punishment.

A cunning grin appeared on the Halfling's fine face. "Very good, let's see what else you can glean from that pearl of wisdom as we go." Puck shot past Lancelot so fast, his raven hair rustled in the forced breeze. "Follow me if you want your freedom."

Lancelot didn't hesitate. He was already going mad. If this trickster could be of even the smallest help, it was worth the risk.

They made their way through a labyrinth garden near one of the large Greek temple like buildings of Olympus. The realm, for being so immersed in Greek and Roman myth, was a surprising mix of architecture from all over the realms. There were no influences that were not represented. Forests and landscapes to rival the Isle of the Blessed and Avalon, cities carved into mountain and earth to match the homes of the Atlantian tribes, enchanted creatures and Dragon nests like you would find in Tir Na Nog. Even the Underworld had its own corner of dark Gothic buildings and mountain passes. Those didn't even take into count the influences of the mortal realm's different cultures.

They exited the maze, stopping outside a small temple like one would see in ancient Greece. He had ended up in front of this very building several times when tracking his Guinevere's ghost. "Why are we here?"

Puck scoffed and rolled his eyes. "You are not that dumb, Sir Lancelot. You should have at least guessed by now."

The knight felt the blood drain from his face.

"Ah," Puck said gleefully. "So you're not a total hopeless cause after all."

"Is my Guinevere really in there?"

The half-breed pushed open the iron gate blocking the entrance to the temple. "See for yourself."

Lancelot raised his chin at the challenge and strode past the insufferable Imp. He bound up the few steps and walked into the darkened cathedral like space inside. He reminded himself that nothing was as it seemed here in Olympus. This small temple was towering on the inside as candles and torches exploded to life along the walls.

The knight's hands fell to his side, useless, as the red hue of the firelight illuminated two lifeless bodies hovering at the center of the room. They looked like they were floating in non-existent water, the skirts of their dresses flowing and waving around their feet. The dark brown hair of the smaller girl floated in the air like a dark halo, her head tilted back like she was staring at the stars. The other's red hair floated around her head and shoulders.

"What is the meaning of this?" he demanded, running toward them, unbelieving of his own sight. "Why are both Guinevere *and* Sophvira trapped here?"

The knight had seen Sophvira's dead body himself. How could she be here, looking exactly as she had in Galahad's arms?

Puck appeared between the two females who meant the world to Lancelot. "It would seem you have a decision to make."

Lancelot's temper snapped. "For once, explain yourself, and be damn sure you are crystal clear in your detail!"

Puck vanished, reappearing in front of the enraged knight. Lancelot saw the move coming and drew his sword, the blade touching the halfling's throat just as he became corporeal.

"Really? I am here to bring gifts, and all you knights seem to want to do is put your swords to my throat."

"If you want my blade gone, *explain this now.*"

"Very well." Puck threw up his hands. "Your punishment came as a result of your abandoning Arthur and your vow to the Fae Queen Titania. Your own selfish actions brought this curse on your sanity. You wanted so badly to die to escape the tearing pain of losing the other half of your soul. In doing so, you lost the right to your own soul and the chance of ever truly being at peace again."

Lancelot pulled his sword back. The full implication of his crimes hit him. It was nothing he had not realized on his own, but no one, not even Arthur, had dared criticize him on all of it. Aliana had been half there; if she had known everything she no doubt would have "called him on it."

Lancelot's pain leaked onto his face. His desperation to be free of this curse and regain his honor was a frantic cry inside him. "I know my crimes. But how can I make them right? How can I prove myself again to my king and the Fae queen?"

"You have already done much to prove your loyalty to the king. You *have* stood by him, and your brother knights, even before the Destined One reawakened and reunited you all."

Lancelot swallowed the ball of grit in his throat, his attention flickering between Guin, Sophvira, and Puck.

"But there is one final test to prove your ways have changed. That you are once again the noble, honorable knight you once were."

He could feel his freedom rising inside him, the burden he had born for so long lightening. "What? I'll do anything!"

Puck evaporated, appearing again between the two girls. "Pick one."

The knight reared back. "*What?*"

Puck smacked his hand to the side of his head. "Are you deaf now too?"

"Do not toy with me, you bloody Imp!" Lancelot roared.

Puck stared him down with a sinister smile. "Then do not act like the court fool!"

Lancelot growled, reflexively sliding into an attack position, his fury focused on Puck. Then his gaze shifted to his beautiful Guin and he eased up, sheathing his sword.

Puck threw his arms in the air. "Finally, a wise decision."

"Why do I have to pick?"

"*Because*, like I said, you have already proven much in your quest to redeem your soul. It is believed you deserved the right to have one loved one back. Now choose."

"You also said this was a test."

Puck wiggled his eyebrows but remained silent for once.

His heart went first to the girl who was like a little sister to all of the knights in Camelot. She was innocent and wrongfully taken before her time. Her death had nearly destroyed Galahad and cost them a loved member of their family, Morgana. All would be thrilled to have her back.

But the return of his Guinevere would do much the same. She had grown up in Camelot, with all the knights. She was the light of his existence. She made everything he did worthwhile. Arthur had his loyalty, but Guin was his reason for getting up in the morning. His cursed memories surfaced, recalling the day Arthur had wed them. The vows he had made to her. To love her, honor and protect her. To serve and cherish her. He had promised to love her until the sun no longer rose, to be faithful and to treat her not only as a wife, but also as an equal. To listen to her council and value her thoughts and wishes as he would his own and his king's.

His heart ached at the beauty of the memory and her vows, so similar to his. She was his heart; they deserved to have the life they were robbed of. No one would fault him for choosing her.

But she would, his conscience whispered. *You vowed to listen to her council, value her wishes. Would she wish you to save her over the girl she thought of more as a daughter?*

Lancelot had his answer. No, she wouldn't.

He stared at both women, torn by the pain of knowing what his only choice was. Every time he looked to Puck to answer, the words died in his dry throat. He would never have this chance again, to hold his Guinevere, to kiss her, to share a bed with her…to hear her laughter and soft voice. To feel her fingers on his skin or know the softness of hers.

He reached up, touched Guinevere's peaceful face. Her skin was cool to the touch, like Chinese silk. He cupped her cheek, memorizing her face again even though the visage had never once left him or faded in detail. Lancelot's heart swelled and thudded like an eviscerated limb. It was literally killing him to make this decision. Once he did, he knew his heart would be gone, but at least he would be one step closer to regaining his honorable soul. Though it would be so lonely without its mate.

He dropped his hand and stepped back. He bowed on one knee to Guinevere, saying a silent prayer that she would find peace and happiness and hopefully be granted a new happy life.

He rose up, met Puck's calculating stare that had not left him since they entered this temple. "I choose who my Guinevere would have chosen." He cleared his throat as his voice cracked. "Sophvira."

The room shattered, light splintering the red hued room like a mirror. Lancelot threw up his hands to shield his eyes from the blinding release. When he opened them again, he was standing alone in an empty field of gravel. He fell to his knees as energy rushed from his body, taking with it all the insanity that had plagued him. His countless lifetimes of memories dimmed, though remained. The pain that had plagued him for over eight hundred years, the centuries he had suffered since leaving Avalon, the searing loss he was so used to feeling eased like a boulder being lifted from his chest. He still felt the heartbreaking loss of his souls mate, but he felt whole in a way he had not since before he left Avalon.

Sucking in air, he got to his feet and looked around for Sophvira, but found nothing but the rubble of the former temple.

"Puck!" he roared. His anger at this betrayal rose like a monster from the darkest pits of the Underworld.

"No need to shout!" Puck's high, sarcastic voice came from behind him.

Lancelot wheeled around, his breath rushing from him as he saw a rosy cheeked Sophvira being cradled so carefully in the trickster's arms. Puck held her, her head resting on his shoulder, his face turned so slightly to hers in protection. She was cradled with the most exquisite of care.

Lancelot was the best at tracking magical signatures, could see magic in a way few others could. The silver gold magic of Puck was wrapped like a cocoon around the young girl. If the knight didn't know better he would have entertained the thought that the halfling cared for Sophvira.

But he shook that thought away. "Give her to me," he ordered.

The Imp hesitated for a half second then took one step then another toward the knight. Lancelot placed his arms outside Puck's and lifted the precious treasure from his arms.

A soft sigh came from Sophvira as her body shifted. His world felt even more right. He may not have his Guinevere, but he could at least give the girl they both loved the life she was robbed of. And he could give his brother knight, Galahad, his sister back.

"She will sleep for several days while her body fully recovers. Once she is well, you may leave Olympus and return with her to the mortal realm." Puck vanished before Lancelot could say anything.

Wasting no time, Lancelot took off in a run, being careful not to jostle the healing girl too much. He spotted the brightly colored onion dome-topped tower that Rothik used as his teaching and healing quarters. People, students and those who lived in this realm stared openly at him as he rushed past, but he paid them no heed.

"Rothik!" he called out in the long hallways after entering.

The large, bull-like man stepped out of one of the rooms, Merlin right behind him. The Druid looked like a good wind would have knocked him over when he saw Sophvira in his arms.

Rothik stepped back and ushered a panting Lancelot into the room they had left out of. "Place her on the bed," he ordered, his deep voice vibrating in the room.

"What in the name of Camelot is going on, Lancelot?"

The knight told them both everything that had happened. The only detail he kept were his own shattered feelings, but Merlin knew him well enough that he would understand what he was not saying.

"This Puck was right," Rothik said afterward. "Your Sophvira will sleep for days. Her body is returning to what it once was, so she will be strong enough to live again."

Merlin apparently detected a hesitation in the Chimera Lancelot missed. "What aren't you telling us?" the Druid asked somberly.

"Did she ever have magic before?"

Both men shook their heads.

"She does now, and whatever created it in her is very strong."

Sweat built on the back of Lancelot's neck. "What does that mean?"

Worry creased Rothik's broad forehead. "It means she may have her life back, but she is not wholly who she was in Camelot."

They were silent for a long moment. Until another girl, about fourteen, burst through the open door. "Lord Rothik…" She paused, taking in the heavy atmosphere of the room.

"What is it, Niss?" the Chimera asked, his demeanor calm and easy.

"You were asking around about an Atlantian that used to reside here in Olympus. Lady Nimuah told us about him, what he looked like, because she had known him."

Rothik nodded. "What are you saying, Niss?"

"I saw him."

"Where?" Merlin demanded.

Lancelot jumped to his feet. "When?"

The girl flinched at the raised voices of the two knights.

Rothik held out a soothing hand. "Do not fear, Niss. Just tell us."

"He was just here, I was walking through the gardens when I saw him standing at a statue…he looked…sad." Sympathy washed over her oval face. "I didn't recognize him, so I went to talk to him. When he turned around I recognized him." She glanced at Lancelot and Merlin again, her arms wrapping around her middle. "White blond hair, silver eyes and orange skin and pointy ears. Lady Nimuah said his name was—"

"Puck!" Lancelot hissed out in surprise and outrage.

34

Aliana woke, her head pounding much like she imagined a hangover would feel, if she'd ever had one. The events of the day came rushing back as her moan of pain died in her throat. She peeked open her eyes and saw Viviane just feet away from her holding a small scroll of paper. Aliana recognized it instantly. It was the piece of paper she had hidden in the iron-box-of-death that said the daughter of Avalon would have to sacrifice her life to stop Mordrid!

The dark-haired witch set down the scroll, still unopened. Why hadn't she read it yet? Aliana could tell she hadn't, because there was a different seal around it that hadn't been there when she retrieved it from the iron-box-of-death. Viviane turned toward her. Aliana held perfectly still, slowing and evening out her breath.

The witch seemed satisfied that she was still out cold and left the small cave-like room Aliana was trapped in, tucking the small scroll up her sleeve.

The door closed, but Aliana waited what felt like an eternity before she dared move. When she was sure she was alone, she got up and found she was not bound, much to her surprise. She was lying on a small bed with fur blankets. Shaking away the last of the magic that had knocked her out, she headed straight toward the door. She peeked through the circular opening near the top, but it was hard to see into the dim cave hall.

She felt for her own magic, but it was different, like there was a thick cloud surrounding it, only letting the vast power trickle through. The bitter taste of Mordrid's poison filled her mouth as she fought back the instinct to retch. She turned to the power of her ruby, felt its swirling depths, but not nearly as strongly as she should. Something was very seriously wrong. *I'll have to deal with that later. First order of business is getting the heck out of here!*

Aliana expanded her strained senses and searched for any traces of magic or life. She found it, recognized the feel of Viviane, Morgana and Mordrid's powers all near the one side of the area, by the exit she assumed, along with the burn of something else. Almost a dozen something else's.

She huffed. This was not going to work very well. Caves usually only had one way out. Kneeling down, Aliana sent a small amount of her bubbly magic into the lock of the door, turning the tumblers, letting the door glide open on silent hinges.

"Dagg?" She took the chance of calling out when she left the room. *"I am close."*

Aliana sagged against the cave wall. She hadn't realized how tense and worried she had been until she heard his voice. *"Please tell me the guys are about to come storming in like the knights in shining armor they are!"*

She felt his brief amusement. *"We are close. I am using our bond to find you. I am also leaving a trail for Arthur and the others to follow."*

"I guess you're faster on your own. Are you and the guys all right?"

"We are, and are also very, very angry with you. What were you thinking going down a secret stairway without reaching out to me first?

Why didn't you tell me the moment you decided to not come down to the Round Table?"

"I saw Vira!" Aliana flushed again. *"But I realize now it was just an illusion created by Mordrid to lure me. I played right into his hands."* Taking a silent, deep breath Aliana moved closer to the entrance of the cave. *"I'm sorry. I didn't even think to tell you until I was already down there."*

"It's too late to do anything about it now, but in the future you must always tell me these things."

She nodded, then realized he couldn't see her. *"Okay."*

"I am waiting for an opening to slip into the cave undetected."

"Are Mordrid and the others out by the entrance then?"

"Viviane and Morgana, yes. But I do not see Mordrid."

"What?" Panic resurfaced. She was sure she had pinged his magic with the others. *"I need to go."*

"Be safe." Aliana cut him off, quickly looking around the hall she had been creeping in. She could go back to the room she had been locked in; Mordrid would never know that she had been out of the room. *Keep breathing, Lia, and move!* she told herself.

It was slow, trying to be as quiet as she could and listen for signs of her kidnapper. She kept close to the wall, partially for support, as she made her way toward what she hoped would be the entrance. Sounds like gusting winds and roaring fire grew louder. That had to mean she was getting close, right? But what on earth was making that noise?

"And where do you think you're going?" Mordrid hissed in her ear.

She froze stiff. *Oh my stars, could he use any more cliché of a line?* "You know…" She shrugged trying to go for calm candor. "I just thought I'd stretch my legs for a minute before you get on with your plan to take over the world and all."

He scowled for a quick moment before a rueful, evil grin spread over his face. "I must admit, I do not quite understand all you say, but the magic coming from you and that stone are too great to not possess."

Aliana went pale. The Mordrid in her time knew that taking her ruby from her would kill her. He had made it clear that was not something he wanted, but what about this Mordrid? Not knowing what to expect from him terrified her.

She moved to run but his foot tripped her sluggish legs, sending her face planting in the dirt.

"Really?" she muttered, hoping like hell Dagg had found his way into the cave by now. She pushed herself up and got to her feet, facing the lunatic that wanted to rule the seven realms and unleash Armageddon. Her panic and pumping adrenaline helped push away the lingering fogginess that felt like a wet blanket. It felt like her magic was being drained away.

"You do not know how special you are, do you?"

Aliana rolled her eyes. "I am really sick of people saying that."

"I will have you and your vast magic. But I can already sense the deep connection you have with that jewel. It would kill both of us if I tried to take it by force."

Aliana's eyes widened. That was something she hadn't known. "Then what are you planning? I will *never* help you. You're evil, you want to destroy thousands of lives for your own selfish desires."

He stalked closer to her. Aliana stepped back, her back hitting the cave wall. Her heart kicked, the cheetah returned, racing through her blood. This was too similar to Josh's attack; he was trapping her, trying to control her. She took heavy breaths to keep herself calm and not give in to her impulse to freeze up. She wasn't that same scared, helpless girl.

"You are right and you are wrong. I want what is mine by birthright. Camelot."

"You can't seriously think you're a descendant of that Onyx Dragon!"

He growled, his eyes darkening even further. "Your Arthur is a descendant of that blasted Gold Dragon. Why is it so hard to believe I am a descendant of the other creator?"

Aliana hesitated. She needed to stall for time, for Dagg and Arthur and the knights to find her. Her magic wasn't strong enough yet to fight her way out. Not against the evil trio.

"What do I have to do with any of this?"

His smile turned even wickeder. Something she didn't think was possible. "Like any magic, no matter how powerful, it is limited by the strength of the one who bears it. I've seen your magic, felt its strength, and I know you have not yet even reached your potential. When I make you mine, take you over, your abilities will be tied to *my will*, and your endless strength will guarantee that I will conquer all the realms and rule them for all eternity. Not even Death or time will stop my eternal rule. And I'll need a queen of worth by my side."

He stepped closer and Aliana darted to the side, freeing herself from the trap of being cornered.

Aliana raised her chin, her eyes trapped on his. "You can't be that deluded. Nothing you could do would ever make me your queen, much less let you use my magic to further your psychotic plans."

He tracked her, ignoring her words. "I watched you, since the first moment you arrived in Camelot and smiled at me. Stood up for me in front of those bullies of knights. There was a feel about you, but I never thought it was magic, not until we were on that field with the Manticore and I saw your Dragon and your amazing magic. I knew then you were beyond priceless."

"You did set the Manticore on us. On Camelot."

He tilted his head to the side. "I did."

"Why?"

"To test the strength of Camelot and, by default, you." He raised a hand to touch her. She flinched to the side, narrowly avoiding being cornered again. "You may not have revealed all of your magic then, but it was enough." His hand shot out, grabbing her right hand. He raised it between them, his thumb running over the magic stone.

She felt that caress all the way to her bones. Her magic was tied too deeply to the stone. "That still doesn't tell me why you think I would ever be your queen." God why did her voice have to sound so shaky?

"I will make you mine, have no doubt. In fact I've already started."

Aliana tried to jerk her hand free, but the sluggishness in her muscles made her too weak. And her connection to her magic was terrifyingly weaker.

"You are already feeling the effects." He pulled her roughly forward, her body crashing into his. "You took in my magic, and it will in turn consume you. Sadly, for the magic to have full effect it must first bring you to the point of death. After your heart misses three beats, my magic will bring you back to life, your memories gone and then, you will be my jewel, my queen."

Burning cold terror singed her down to the marrow. If Mordrid succeeded…there would be nothing to stop her magic, bent to his will. All her friends and family and countless innocents would suffer.

She felt Mordrid's hot breath by her ear. "You will be mine."

She heard Dagg's enraged roar before she saw him appear. He slammed into Mordrid, knocking both of them back. The wizard's grip fell away as they hit the floor. Aliana touched the power of her ruby, felt its connection even weaker than it had been, but used what she could to attack Mordrid. Dagg zipped to the side as Mordrid deflected the attack. Her heart gripped, its beat becoming weaker.

"There's nothing you can do now. It's too late, my magic is already doing its work."

Sweaty, furious and scared beyond belief, Aliana let her temper fly as she threw a ball of pink sparking energy at Mordrid. He deflected it, again with a flick of his hand, sending it colliding directly into Dagg.

Her guardian fell to her feet in pain. Aliana felt it like her own, on top of the fading power of her pulse and muscles, and it became harder to breathe.

"The more you use your magic, the quicker my poison works, and the closer you get to being mine." Mordrid held out his hand toward Dagg, the smoke that had poisoned her earlier wrapping around him like a cage.

"No!" she screamed, getting back on her feet.

"I know you two have a special bond. I suspect he is able to help you heal, but it will not work this time." The cage trapping her guardian rose. "However, no need to take chances."

With Dagg trapped, her magic leashed, and her strength fleeing her, Aliana was truly at his mercy. Terror shook her.

"Come, there's something you need to see." He gripped her around the waist and led her, like a caring boyfriend, out of the cave and into the valley where her lungs frosted over.

Aliana watched Viviane use blue magic chains to strap a beautiful creature with red, orange, brown and gold feathered wings onto an altar.

"What are you doing? Stop this now!" she demanded.

"It's far too late for that. This is the last of the eighteen Firebirds we captured."

Tears sprang to her eyes as Morgana drove her curved blade into the creature's neck. Aliana's scream came as the bird exploded into a tower of magic fire that rushed into Morgana's magic bloated body. Even with her weakened senses, she could see the abundance of power gathering inside the sorceress.

How could she have forgotten this part of the story? Titania herself told her of Morgana's sacrifice of Firebirds to create the army of black knights that fought with Mordrid in the final battle in Camelot.

"No," she moaned, sagging. She knew what happened next, or at least she thought she did.

"Mordrid!"

Aliana's head snapped to the trees ahead of her as Arthur rushed from the forest, Excalibur raised, his shield at the ready. "Release Aliana now, return the pieces of the Spear of Hel and I will let you live!"

Viviane and Morgana appeared in front of her and Mordrid. The evil wizard laughed shrilly. "You will let *us* live? I think you have that backward."

Mordrid shoved Aliana back so hard she tumbled to the ground. Even from across the field she could see the anger in Arthur's hard face.

Arthur lowered into an attacking stance, his eyes fixed on Mordrid. He charged them; Viviane and Morgana raised their hands summoning spears of magic. Aliana's heart hopscotched more beats. Where were the others?

Her question was answered when orange lightning poured down, colliding with and exploding the evil magic. Galahad, the knights, Falorn and D'varin flooded the field from all sides. Viviane threw spear after spear of burnt blood red magic at the four who rushed her. They deflected the attacks with their shields, Aliana's weakened senses feeling the magic Merlin must have infused them with to make them resistant to attack.

The evil trio spread out, dividing to take on the attacking Fae and knights.

"Morgana, stop this," Merlin pleaded as they exchanged blows, the other guys striking when they could. "I have the magic needed to free you of the evil darkness!"

She sneered. "But I don't want to be freed!" She lashed out with her whip. "I *like* this power. You'll soon see. You'll join us, I know it."

Merlin fell back a step, the others swarming the witch.

Gentle hands grabbed Aliana. *"My lady, I am here, cloaked to remain hidden. I will get you away."*

"Delphina? I can't," Aliana said as the invisible Fae pulled her back. She didn't dare try to use her mental voice for fear it would weaken her even faster. "He's poisoned me. He wants control of my magic and is going to bring me to the point of death to get it."

She felt the Fae's horror and surprise. *"I know this magic; it is the darkest kind used only by the evilest of Dragons!"*

Aliana's hope dimmed even further. She watched Mordrid fight Arthur with a gray magic sword he conjured. Arthur again proved to be the better swordsman, his shield deflecting strikes as he moved like water and cut gushing wounds into Mordrid.

She looked to Viviane, who was faring just as badly against Percival and Owaine and their team. The Sorceress was being cut and injured faster than she could heal the wounds or fight back. "End this, Morgana!" she screeched.

The blond witch glanced briefly at her counterparts before a wave of icy fire magic blasted out of her like a rippling wave. All the guys were knocked back, their bodies crashing to the ground, against rocks or into trees. Delphina's hands were ripped from Aliana. She heard the startled cry before a loud smack of a body hitting the mountainside. The apricot-haired Fae became visible as she slid into unconsciousness.

Mordrid looked back toward them and sneered. Aliana immediately shifted to place herself between the evil man and her Fae friend.

"She is of no threat to me," he said, dismissing the fallen girl.

He turned back to the battlefield as the knights struggled to get back to their feet. "Do it, Morgana! Let these pathetic wasters see what true power is."

Viviane, Morgana and Mordrid vanished only to reappear surrounding the altar that Morgana had used to sacrifice the beautiful Firebirds. Both witches pulled out four of the five pieces of the Spear of Hel, Mordrid summoning the fifth piece he had used to knock her out earlier. The pieces jumped from their hands, lining themselves up in the air like they had a mind and will of their own.

Knowing the story behind the spear, it was quite possible it did. Fear churned alongside the black magic slowly poisoning her as she studied the fearsome weapon.

Seeing all five pieces together, Aliana's suspicion was confirmed. The five jewels that decorated each piece of the Spear were in fact the same jewels that had decorated the sword the Fire Elves had made for Arthur until he reclaimed Excalibur, the same weapon they had given Titania!

That was when the panic truly set in. She struggled to push it away, tried to touch her fading magic, anything to find the strength to stop what was about to happen.

Magic stronger than any Aliana had ever felt flared, coming from the five pieces of the spear.

Aliana's desperation won out when neither of the men she loved moved. "*Help! Someone! Father, Titania, anyone!*"

"Ask and you shall receive."

"What do you think we are, chopped liver?"

Aliana's head snapped up, her eyes wide as she stared at the ghostly figures of her best friends, Lacy and Dawn.

3⁵

"What…how are you guys here?" She looked around but no one seemed to notice them. *"Dagg can you see them?"* She risked weakening her magic even faster to keep anyone from realizing what was happening.

"Yes. "

Her hope returned.

"How?" she asked, mentally ignoring the irregular beats of her heart.

"The Well of Realms. Duh, Lia," Dawn chastised with fake annoyance.

"Why can't anyone else see you two? How are you even using a Well? Where are you guys?"

"The magic of the Wells." Lacy grinned. "We've learned some very helpful tricks in the other realms. I'm in the Isle with Arthur and Percy and Leo. Merlin and Lancelot are in Olympus."

Dawn added, "I'm in Avalon with Owen, Wade and Galahad. Your Elf friend, J'alel is hot too, Lia."

Tears burned Aliana's eyes. "*I've missed you two so much! And I can feel how much your magic has grown, both of you.*"

"Yeah, we're just as hot stuff as you now, Lia." Lacy's face turned serious as she looked at the evil trio. "What are those things floating around like bad Halloween decorations?"

"And who is that truly old woman in need of a serious fashion police intervention?" Dawn added.

Aliana grinned. "*Says the girl who wears KEEP CALM shirts.*" But it was time to set her happiness aside and get down to business. "*That's Viviane.* Readers Digest *version, she trained Morgana and Mordrid in magic, is a corrupting force who killed Galahad's little sister with a poisoned bracelet that was meant for me. Morgana only turned against Merlin and the knights because she took this crazy I-will-control-you dagger that was meant for Merlin, saving his life.*"

She ignored the girl's gasps of outrage and rubbed her hand over Dagg's leathery wings for comfort and strength.

"*The three of them gathered together those five spear pieces that form this Excalibur type of indestructible-crazy-deadly-power-mythical weapon called the Spear of Hel. And Mordrid is far more psycho then I ever thought he was and he's infected me with a poison that will all but kill me, then bring me back to life and enslave my magic to him.*"

The two stared at her as she struggled to her feet before looking out and taking in all that was happening around them. But she lost her footing as sheer magic rained down from above, like a powerful G-force weighing them all down to the ground. Dagg fell from her shoulders, also pinned.

"Lia?" both girls cried out, unaffected.

"*We have to stop them!*" She tried to push her body up. It would have been difficult with her normal strength, but now with this life-sucking poison, it seemed impossible.

Cool magic, like liquid moonlight, gripped one of her arms; leafy pale purple magic gripped the other.

"We've got you, Lia!" Lacy smiled at her as Aliana managed to lift herself up.

Dawn nodded. "We're sisters, in every way that counts, and that means we support each other."

Aliana's tears fell. "*I've* missed *you both so much!*"

Lacy wrapped one arm around Aliana as she managed to straighten. "You already said that, silly," her sweet and loyal friend joked.

She met the surprised eyes of the guys and the Fae who were all still bogged down.

Dawn wrapped her arm around Aliana's other side. "But you can keep telling us how bad ass we are."

The trio giggled then sobered. "How do we do this, Lia?"

"Best I can figure we blast it with everything we've got." She studied the gems again, all five glowing like her ruby would when she used its magic. *"I have a sneaking suspicion the real power is those jewels."*

"Like your prophecy ruby?" Lacy asked.

"That makes total sense," Dawn cut in. "The wood Nymphs have been teaching me a lot about the magic of the earth and have said some of its strongest conduits are jewels of the earth." Dawn hesitated.

"What is it?"

"Iris said that magic gems are almost impossible to destroy."

Lacy spoke up, her idea a stroke of genius. "Then we destroy the spear pieces. Is there a way to dampen the power of those jewels?"

"There might be." Aliana thought back to the veil that hid her own prophecy stone for so long here in Camelot. *"Leave that part to me."*

Dagg clawed his way up Aliana's body and wrapped around her shoulders.

"Glad you could join the party," Dawn said with teasing affection.

"Me too, but to do what you want you will need what's left of my strength as well."

"That's the first time you've spoken to us in our heads!" Lacy sounded amazed.

"Time to do this, girls."

The others watched her while they struggled to get to their own feet.

She lifter her ruby gloved hand, her palm facing the evil trio that were so immersed in the magic to bind the spear they were ignorant to what was around them — the first stroke of luck Aliana had had since returning to Camelot. Pushing aside the pounding fear that she might be speeding up the magic killing her, Aliana opened her senses wide, calling on all five elements and the strength of her own magic.

Her ruby glowed, much like the jewels of Hel. Moonlight magic flared next to her, as bright as the largest full moon on a crystal clear night. Pulsing pale purple magic brightened like the most beautiful of leaves in the summer sun.

Aliana looked at Dawn, meeting her loving and strong, determined gaze. Her sister raised her right hand, palm forward, skin to skin with Aliana's. "*Thank you.*"

She turned to Lacy who brought up her left hand, mirroring her and Dawn, loyalty, hope and determination glowing around them. "You don't even need to say it."

Together the three focused on the spear of Hel and the ones who wanted to control the realms with it. Dagg's silver purple magic swirled around their hands. "Fire at will," Aliana commanded.

The magic tore through her, for one blinding second ripping open the poison cloud to blast free. The girls watched amazed as their magics swirled and twisted together like winding beams of pure light, soaring through the air. They split apart and wrapped around the spear like constricting ribbons of magic.

Mordrid's head snapped back to Aliana. What he saw, she didn't know, or care. She poured even more of her remaining magic, heedless of the cost, into the attack.

"No!" Morgana and Viviane shrieked as cracks started to form on the five pieces. The girls' magic took advantage and sank into the weapon until it imploded like a bomb.

Five bright flares pulled at Aliana, almost like they were responding to the magic of her prophecy stone.

On instinct, Aliana summoned five individual magical veils, wrapping each of the gleaming gems up skintight before tying it off so tight not even air could get in or escape. The world stopped around the three girls.

All were weak, Aliana fighting off the pull of the poison. "I love you both, you know that right?" Since she had landed here in Camelot she had wished for little else besides having her best friends back by her side. A feeling of almost nostalgic desperation filled her.

"Of course you do!" Dawn sniffled, her weary eyes telling her she sensed Aliana's fading life force. "You will come home to us, yourself. I'll kick your butt if you don't!"

Aliana blinked back her tears. She needed, for just a moment, to feel like her old self again.

"You're going to make me cry." Lacy wiped her eyes. "D's right." She squared her shoulders. "You're our sister, nothing else is acceptable."

Aliana felt them fading, along with her own strength. "I couldn't have done this without you guys. I couldn't have asked for better sisters or friends!"

"We'll see you soon!" Lacy promised, blowing her a kiss.

"Girl power rules!" Dawn grinned and waved once.

Their banter may not have seemed appropriate to others, but right now it was the only thing that gave Aliana a little hope to hold on to. "See you soon." *I hope,* she added silently as the girls faded completely and she crumpled to the ground.

The weight holding the guys prisoner vanished. They sprung to their feet, rushing the evil trio. Mordrid flung himself to the side as Excalibur cut into him, blood flinging and seeping as he scrambled away from Arthur's furious pursuit.

Viviane blasted herself free of Owaine, Leyon and Lancelot, trying to make her way to Morgana, who was facing down Merlin. But Galahad stepped into her path, his sword spearing toward the vile woman. She vanished, reappearing on the other side of the field.

"This night is done for us!" she yelled to Mordrid and Morgana. "We must go now!"

Mordrid disappeared as Excalibur almost skewered him, reappearing at Viviane's side. "She's right Morgana." He looked at Aliana, lying helpless by the cave entrance. "But I *will see you soon.*"

"No!" Morgana's shriek shook the earth.

The guys fell back. With vengeance in her eyes, she took a step toward Aliana. "We don't leave until I've had my revenge!"

She raised her hand toward Aliana, who struggled to move but was too close to death. Blue flames flared, Morgana's hateful gaze fixed only on her.

Merlin moved behind her.

Those evil cool hazel eyes widened in shock, her mouth falling open as a soundless gasp escaped her. She looked down at the blood-covered blade that had speared through her abdomen.

Aliana gasped, tears escaping as Merlin pulled his sword from his souls mate, his face tortured worse than she could ever imagine. It was too horrible to describe, as Morgana fell to the ground, dead.

It was hard to remember everything that happened after that. Mordrid's poison was having too great an effect as Aliana's heart struggled to keep beating. Her lungs felt like piles of wet blankets were weighing them down.

Fury pulsed over the entire field. Viviane screamed shrilly, like that dead firebird, her wild eyes fixed on Merlin, who was huddled on the ground next to Morgana's lifeless body. Burnt-blood-colored magic speared into the Druid, throwing him from his dead souls mate's side. His already tortured eyes widened as the blond witch's body vanished.

Mordrid's last words before he evaporated with Viviane rang through her mind. *"Soon you will be mine, and there is nothing that can be done to save you."*

Arms wrapped around Aliana, lifting her prone body from the hard ground. She looked up into Arthur's stone-hued face. She tried to tell him she would be okay, a lie, but she couldn't get the words out.

"Don't try to speak," Arthur commanded, brushing her hair from her sweat and dirt-coated face. "We will save you from this!"

Galahad appeared over them, a weak Dagg in his arms. She moaned and tried to reach out to her guardian but pain seared her veins and muscles. The white knight knelt immediately, placing Dagg in her arms, the weight of her dear friend a burden she'd happily bear. Silver purple magic sparked, trying to help her, but she knew it was too late.

"Dagg, what are we going to do? I don't want to be Mordrid's slave!"

"I...I don't know."

She could feel his guilt and devastation, the pain of knowing he had failed to protect her.

"Not...your fault...Dragon boy." She closed her heavy eyes.

"Aliana, stay with us!" Galahad's rumbling voice was too hard to ignore.

She lifted her lids, tried to smile, but couldn't feel her face to know if she had succeeded. The white knight's hand cupped her cheek as Arthur's arms tightened around her.

"Merlin!" the king roared. Aliana managed to turn her gaze and saw Leyon and Gawain supporting their friend who looked almost comatose. "Snap out of it! We need you here."

Everyone gathered around them, Falorn and D'varin supporting Delphina between them. All the knights looked on anxious and worried, each one covered in injuries she wish she were strong enough to heal. Tears gathered and leaked from her eyes. She had tried so hard to fight back her terror of being a slave to Mordrid that she had failed in her quest to help Arthur save the seven realms.

She felt a rising magic growing in her like a vine. It could only be Mordrid's magic trying to take over.

Orange light flared, but it was far away, unable to penetrate the gray stealing her away. "I can't heal her!" She vaguely recognized the Druid's voice, but couldn't see him through the dark clouds.

A strange accented voice roared. Leyon, their whip smart Scot. "You have the Grail of Power! That can save her!"

The voices of the guys swamped her pounding head until one feminine voice silenced the bunch. "It will not work." The musical lilt to Delphina's voice soothed her abused ears. "That stone she bears, it was created with the Grail's magic. I can feel it now."

"Then that should help even more!" Gawain tried to reason.

Falorn's low voice came next. "No. She already has the Grail's power inside her…if it hasn't helped her yet…it never will."

The last of Aliana's hope burst like a popped balloon. Everything drifted away slowly; the frustrated bursts of denial and sorrow from the knights fading like the last notes of a song.

The scent of flowers and the warmth of sunlight touched her, drawing her away from the realm of pain. She lifted her eyes, the world around her was black and white, like she was trapped in an old silent movie. She could see the guys clearly, all huddled around her. Galahad gripped her hands, his blazing blue eyes staring down at her. Arthur's hands brushed her face, her hair. He was saying something, shouting it maybe, judging by the way his face pinched.

Delphina was crying silent tears as she knelt on the ground, bowing her head as her shoulders shook. D'varin and Falorn mimicked her, their shame radiating like a fire's heat. Gawain was punching the earth, Owaine and Leyon looked sick. Percival stood by Lancelot's side, both men silent and stiff as statues in their grief. Merlin stood apart from the group, his face turned from Aliana, but she could feel the pulse of his own devastation.

"We shouldn't be here."

Aliana turned and saw Dagg hovering next to her. She wrapped her arms around him instantly.

"Are we dead?" She shook her head. "No, my…father would be here if we were." Her fear returned. "Is Mordrid's magic about to take us over?" She whispered the question, looking back to her knights and Fae friends.

The scent of flowers returned, growing so strong it was like being in a garden. Rays of sunlight broke through the black and white world, warming her body which she hadn't even realized was so cold.

"Mordrid's magic will not take you this day, my sweet girl."

Aliana snapped around and saw her birth mother standing next to Queen Igraine. "Mother? I don't understand. Mordrid said…"

Camelot's queen smiled reassuringly. "The magic the dark wizard used was *nearly* undefeatable."

She studied both women with cautious hope. "Was?"

The Dragon Queen's smile was a warm comfort as she looked to her son. "The world is a balance of light and dark, good and bad, pain and pleasure, life and death. Everything is created with an opposite equal in strength. Gold Dragons are the opposite of Onyx Dragons. It took the power of my lineage to save your life and free you from becoming Mordrid's slave."

"Then why am I here? Am I—" She looked at Dagg. "Are we dead?"

General Alaki, her father, appeared beside his wife. "I told you, no one can take what Death protects."

Aliana nodded once, her heart thudding with the happiness of seeing her parents again so soon. She followed Queen Igraine's gaze back to the knights. "Then why am I here?"

A light started to grow from the still chest of her body, cradled in Arthur's arms. Aliana looked down as that same light heated her chest under her shirt. She pulled out the pendant Arthur had given her. It glowed with the same light that pulsed on her body.

She turned to Igraine, who held out a matching necklace. Aliana's strength started to return, her aches easing as color started to seep into the world. Realization hit her like a brick. Her eyes grew wide as she looked from the queen to her mother's resigned face to her father's reassuring one.

Tears burned her eyes as she looked back to the queen. "You're trading your life for mine."

Igraine smiled and spoke before Aliana could demand she stop it. "I have known for a long time that this was how my life would end. I have lived so many long centuries without the comfort of my father or brother, but I knew I had to give birth to a child to carry on my family's line. As Arthur was born, I was gifted with a glimpse of his future. I saw your arrival and everything that would come of it. I knew I could not leave my son until his future was secure. You have seen to that now."

Aliana gave into her anger, panic and guilt. "But he'll never forgive me! Vira already…I can't let someone else die because of me!"

Her father took her shaking hand. "But this is not really about you, is it? Queen Igraine's decision was just as much for her son and for Camelot. The kingdom *her* father built."

Her anger whooshed out of her. Her father's words rang with a truth she hadn't seen earlier. She looked back to the king holding her body. "What about Arthur? He'll be crushed."

"He knows."

Aliana's eyes snapped to the queen. "What?"

"Before you were pulled into this plane, he called out to me, begged me to save you. I shared with him what I have with you. He agreed."

Aliana stood there at a total loss of what to think or feel.

Igraine's warmth started to bleed into her again. "He knew my time was coming, I had told him so before your arrival."

Aliana felt her strength returning little by little. She placed the pendant back under her shirt.

"There is something else you need to know." Igraine stepped closer, holding out a small scroll of parchment with a mercury-colored seal.

Aliana stared at it, blinking again and again. It couldn't be… "Is that?"

"It is the first prophecy of the Destined One."

It was the scroll she had stolen from the iron-box-of-death back in Charleston. "But Viviane, she just…I saw her. She just had it." Her face fell. "And I already know what it says." She looked sadly at her father. Dagg rumbled softly against her skin as he crawled around her hunched shoulders.

Igraine shook her head. "I was on my way back to Camelot, just as you arrived in this time. I came upon a halfling who told me about this Fae elder who lived in the forests of Camelot. He was gifted with the magic of prophetic sight. I went to him and he gave me this. It tells about a time when one girl, a lost daughter of Avalon, would rise. It was then he told me not only was another coming for the scroll, but he had also told the Fae Queen of this prophecy. It was too late to keep Titania from knowing, but I created a forgery, changed the prophecy and got the elder to agree to keep the true words a secret."

"But, Titania created the Prophecy of the Destined One, didn't she?"

Selene shook her head. "No, Aliana, she built upon the words contained in this scroll. Not even my mother possesses enough magic to create Prophecy."

Igraine took Aliana's hand, still hanging at her side and placed the small piece of life altering paper in it. "You need to know the truth. This is your secret."

It felt like Aliana was in a dream, separated from her conscious body as her trembling fingers broke the seal and she read the words.

"With the full force of alignment magic and a pure heart, the lost Daughter of Avalon will have the power to change the realms for the good of all or raze them to the ground."

Aliana looked up at the queen and her parents. "But I thought…" She read the words again. "I thought I was supposed to die to stop Mordrid…"

General Alaki shook his head. "It is like my father told you. Your fate is still being written. And like it or not, that promise you made to Merlin saved your future."

Heat rolled through her as she looked to her father with shocked disbelief. "What do you mean?"

Her mother sighed. "Had you gone that night, to that exchange with Mordrid and Morgana for Dawn's mother and Joe…"

"You would have been killed," the general said heavily. "It was one of the visions the Underlord saw in the Well. Queen Igraine, through the actions of Merlin, saved your life before she even met you."

Numbness desensitized Aliana for an endless moment. "But how…how could you even foresee something like that?"

The Dragon queen shook her head. "I told you, fate has a mysterious way of working out the way it's supposed to."

"I don't know what to do, what to say to any of this."

Her parents surrounded her on both sides. Her mother kissed her cheek. "You must return to your body now. You cannot stay much longer."

The general stroked her hair. "We are with you, always. It may not always seem like it, but when you need us most, we will be here for you." He looked to the knights. "For all of you."

Dagg's claws tightened on her skin as invisible hands started to tug at her. Her eyes turned back to Igraine. Her words choked in her throat, but she forced them out. "Thank you, for everything. I don't know how I can repay you."

"Help my son save his kingdom, help him be happy. My son and the knights know you are from the future now. No matter what, you cannot tell them what your future is like, what fate is to befall them and Camelot. That is all I would ask of you."

Aliana nodded. She had failed to keep the knights from finding out before. She would absolutely do this for Igraine. No matter what. She owed the queen no less.

"Your body and magic will still be weak when you return; you must take care of yourself." The queen bowed her head to Aliana.

36

Her parents and Igraine started to fade as the world brightened. She closed her eyes against the blinding light, as the hands pulling her away grew stronger.

When the light and phantom hands faded, she blinked her eyes open, sucking a heavy breath into her starved lungs.

"Aliana!" Happy cries and cheers rang around the field.

"You're alive!" Galahad's hoarse voice croaked as he kissed her hands. Silver sparks trickled into her.

She tried to move, to sit up. Arthur's arms tightened around her. She turned her sad gaze to him, her heart breaking for the loss he had suffered. She owed him and his family so much. He nodded to her, his face set in harsh lines of grief, but the way his arms tightened ever so slightly and his taut shoulders relaxed told her he was relieved she was safe.

Her emotions overwhelmed her. So much had happened just in this day alone. Her heart swelled with passion for both men who still held her, everything twisting together like a giant ball of tangled emotional strings. She couldn't deal with it all right now so she shoved it in her already overstuffed mental box until she could.

Aliana turned from Arthur as he helped her sit up, Dagg climbing to wrap around her shoulders. She looked around at the friends who had gathered around. "Hi everyone."

"You have more surprises in you than one would ever suspect." Gawain's relief softened his gruff voice.

Delphina touched her leg. "What happened? How were you freed of Mordrid's poison?"

Aliana met Arthur's gaze. "It takes a Dragon to fight a Dragon, I guess." She looked back to Delphina. "And being the daughter of Death seems to have unexpected benefits."

"I think there is much you need to tell us," Lancelot insisted.

She nodded. It was time to fill everyone in on everything; everything except what the future held.

With the supporting hands of Arthur and Galahad she got to her feet, looked around the ruined area, her eyes lingering on the altar where Morgana had slain all those Firebirds.

Her eyes sought out Merlin who had been silent. Hoping she wouldn't trip on her own feet, she went to him. Cognizant of everyone watching her she whispered, "She was sacrificing Firebirds." The Druid's face filled with even more grief. They must have seen it before they attacked from the woods. "Think about what that means. What powers that granted her." She'd read from the Fae book that Firebirds had the power to regenerate themselves, almost like a rebirth. Viviane had taken Morgana's body. The power of new life that Morgana stole was the greatest of the Firebird's magic abilities.

"There is always hope, Merlin."

The Druid's shoulders sagged like a heavy weight had fallen from them. Gawain and Owaine came to his side. Letting the knights support their friend, Aliana went to Falorn and D'varin and thanked them for everything they had done. Delphina hugged her tightly with tears in her pale green eyes.

Percival cleared his throat. "Not to seem insensitive, but we still need an explanation of all this."

Aliana couldn't help but smile.

The sound of horse hooves came from their right drawing everyone's attention. Suddenly on guard, the guys drew their weapons, ready to face the intruder. They relaxed, as Guinevere appeared from the trees.

Lancelot all but ran to her side. "My love, what are you doing here?"

Guin dismounted. "The queen sent me." Her face fell as she looked to Arthur.

"I know." His heavy words caused a deafening silence to fall over the field.

"Know what?" Owaine's hesitation seemed to age his pale features.

Arthur met the eyes of each of his men. "The queen is dead."

A small platoon of guards appeared just after Guinevere had, ordered by the queen to accompany Lancelot's wife before her death. The news had been hard for all the knights to take.

Aliana told them everything, what had happened in her trip to the Underworld, the truth of her parents, and everything Mordrid had said before they came charging in. They searched the cave thoroughly, at Leyon and Owaine's insistence. Maybe they would find something to help them against Mordrid and Viviane.

Aliana used the opportunity to pull Delphina and her Fae warriors toward the altar while she told Dagg to stay and keep the guys distracted. She gathered the five fallen stones from the Spear of Hel, hidden in the tall grass like Easter eggs. Their colors were muted, their power almost nothing compared to what she had felt from them earlier. Her veils had worked. These jewels were needed to create the sword the Lady of the Lake gave to Arthur after she'd awoken him in Avalon. Titania now possessed the sword, which must have been the mystery task the Fae had wanted Aliana to accomplish. If she wanted to go home, she needed to see it done.

"Delphina, you know Avalon and its people, right?"

The apricot-haired girl nodded. Falorn and D'varin frowned as Aliana held out the five stones. "Take these to the fire Elves, tell them to forge them into a sword for Arthur, one they must give to the Lady of the Lake."

Delphina's eyes widened. "I don't understand?"

Aliana gave her a tight smile. "You don't need to."

It had to be done if she wanted to ensure the future. She met the eyes of all three of the Fae. "I have one more thing to ask of all you."

D'varin bowed his head to her. "We are yours to command."

She took a breath. "You can't tell the others what I've asked you to do. The truth of these jewels needs to stay hidden from all but us four. No one must know that the jewels were not destroyed with the Spear of Hel."

The three were reluctant, but in the end agreed to her wishes.

The Fae secured the gems in an empty pouch she tied to her belt. "I will leave immediately, my lady." Delphina bowed to Aliana.

"Thank you." She looked to D'varin and Falorn. "She can't travel alone. You two need to see her safely to the fire Elves."

They bowed and went to ready their horses, Delphina making a beeline to Arthur to say good bye.

"Where are they going?" Galahad asked, coming up behind her. Dagg wrapped himself around her shoulders.

She turned to him. He and Arthur had remained out in the field with her and the Fae while the others searched the cave. Both men had given her space but it seemed she couldn't avoid them any longer.

Aliana watched Arthur walk Delphina to her horse. Her chest tightened but she let it go. "They need to go to Avalon, and then return to the Isle."

"Why?" the white knight asked, his body moving closer to hers so she could feel the warmth rolling off of him and smell his winter spice scent all around her. A scent she had been addicted to in her time.

Arthur came and joined them as she answered the knight. "There is a war coming." She looked at Arthur. "You'll need all the allies you can get to fight Mordrid and the army he's going to amass. The armies of Oberon, and maybe even Titania, are your best hope."

Realization dawned on both men's faces. "We will see to it."

Aliana wanted to feel relief, but she knew what was going to happen. Not yet, but soon. Galahad had told her once that Mordrid's final attack had happened a month or so after Guinevere's death. Icy shivers wrecked her. A death that was fast coming.

"Arthur!" Merlin came pouring out of the cave with all the others hot on his heels. All looked equally excited and worried at the same time.

Arthur went to him. "What is it?"

"They left this in their haste." Merlin held out a crumpled piece of parchment. Merlin spread it out, and Aliana recognized it immediately.

"We found it in a large chamber toward the back of the cave," Percival explained.

Aliana's eyes roamed over the familiar symbols she had seen in the ruins in the Isle, when they were searching for Excalibur. The same symbols that told everything about the alignment Mordrid needed to conquer the realms.

Merlin explained the story, pointed out the iron-box-of-death, but the words that followed were like being gob smacked. "I know this box, and where it is kept. If we get this, we can stop him."

Arthur agreed after a silent moment. "We must find this first; no doubt he and Viviane are already on their way to it."

"They may be weakened by all that has happened," Owaine voiced.

Leyon took over the sentence. "We will have no better chance to get ahead of them."

Gawain gripped the Scot's shoulder. "And we can get some justice for all the wrongs they have done."

Galahad echoed Gawain's words. "We can take our justice for what they have done to our family."

Aliana recognized the swirling emotions in all of them. "You need to be sure you get *justice*," she insisted, "not revenge."

Everyone was silent.

Arthur finally relented. "We leave immediately."

Aliana sighed, relieved. She trusted Arthur's judgment, trusted that he would keep his men from breaking their code of honor. "You and Guinevere will return to Camelot with the guards."

The order surprised her. "No, Arthur…"

"He's right, Aliana." Dagg's eyes illuminated with his returning power.

Aliana looked down to hide the despair that was overcoming her. So many people had already given their lives, sacrificed so much. She vowed to herself, on her destiny, that she wouldn't let Guinevere die too.

They were almost halfway back to Camelot and Aliana was beyond exhausted. Igraine had been right; she was still recovering from the effects of Mordrid's poison, physically and magically. It was hard for her to open her senses long enough to connect with the elemental powers that could help speed up the process.

And riding a horse didn't help the matter. She had tried to hide how much pain she was still in, but Guin had guessed it after the first hour of riding and ordered the guards to move at a slower pace.

"I saw Igraine," she told Guin, realizing she hadn't heard the explanation she had given the guys about everything that had happened. "She came to me…" Tears started to prickle but Aliana cleared her throat, shaking them away. "She was with my birth parents."

"Death and his wife, I know. Lancelot told me everything already, while we were searching the cave."

Aliana nodded silently. At least she would be spared the pain of having to tell the story again. "Did she…was Igraine…"

Guinevere reached over from her horse and gripped Aliana's hand. "She didn't suffer."

She took a breath, reminding herself that this was Igraine's choice. Being selfish would dishonor what the queen had sacrificed for Camelot. She focused instead on something she could control, the attack that would steal Guin's life. She remembered Galahad's story, that Lancelot's wife had died just after Morgana's death, while being escorted by a patrol of Camelot guards. She opened her magical senses, pushing aside the taxing pain it caused to protect her friend.

"Let me do that!" Dagg insisted. *"You need to conserve your strength."* Of course the Dragon had figured out what she was planning. He knew her too well.

"Okay."

The attack came less than two hours later. A few dozen black knights, even more zombie-raccoon-eyed monsters and Goblins surrounded them. Dagg took to the air ready to fight.

The black knights could only mean that Morgana had managed to save her life with the power of the Firebirds. It was the only thing that explained why, after Merlin killed her, she had managed to survive, or how she was able to create the black knights.

Guinevere veered her horse close to Aliana's as the guards circled them, furiously fighting back the evil army. She drew a sword from her saddle as Aliana summoned her magic bow. Guin's jaw dropped; she hadn't seen this part yet.

"I'll take care of the black knights, your sword won't kill them." Aliana watched for the first enemy to get through the line. "The black eyed freaks can be killed with their own weapons—"

"And I can kill a Goblin with my sword." Guin sent her a confident smile. "Don't worry."

Aliana didn't get to respond as the first black knight charged through the guards, who were being efficiently cut down by the enemy. She drew back her arrow and released it. The knight's rusted dark armor wriggled before falling to pieces with oozing, foul smelling rot. She nocked more arrows, releasing one after the other at the evil knights and zombie creatures.

But her magic was already growing weaker. She couldn't keep this up for much longer. Dagg rained down his magic fire, frying several Goblins in the process, and wearing himself down.

Guin fought as hard as any of the guys, slashing and stabbing the Goblins that came at her, grabbing one of the zombie creature's spiked sticks and killing three of them with it. She was a fierce warrior, but Aliana stayed close to her side.

She ached as more guards died at the blades and clubs of the black knights and Goblins. "This is going really badly," Aliana muttered, her senses guiding her to look just past Guin.

An arrow was already whistling toward her friend. Acting on instinct Aliana swung her leg over her saddle and knocked herself into Guin, both women falling from their horses to the ground in a jarring crash of body parts.

Aliana groaned as she pushed herself up. "Are you okay?"

Guin nodded, but hissed in pain when she tried to use her right arm. "I think it's broken." The girl gritted her teeth.

Panting heavily, Aliana looked around the battle. Only five guards remained, the others scattered along with the rotting pieces of armor and dead Goblins. Dagg dive bombed a zombie, a broken piece of a barbed stick between his teeth. It ripped through the monster like a hot knife. The little Dragon zoomed through the army, taking out one zombie after another.

"Aliana, look out!" Guin cried.

She ducked to the side just in time to avoid the spiked stick that almost impaled her head. Rolling to the side, Aliana kicked the zombie's leg from under him, grabbed his stick as it fell from the gnarled hand, and thrust it up into the vile monster.

It glowed and shriveled into itself before disappearing.

The last few guards rushed to Aliana to aid her. She didn't stop to think, just moved to the flow of the battle. She had to be sure Guin survived!

Gripping her bow, she nocked three magic arrows at once and fired them, dropping three of the charging pig-like creatures. But others rushed past, leaping over the corpses, their clubs raised.

Aliana danced to the side of one that came down on her, summoning a spear of pink power and jabbing it down into the Goblin's shoulder. She let out all her fear and anger that had been bubbling over, fueling her determination to stop these monsters before they could take another friend. She ducked another club from her left and summoned a ball of her sparking magic, launching it into his gut. Both creatures fell to the ground as smoking corpses. The last two guards fell, impaled on rusted swords. Dagg came rushing toward her.

"Aliana!"

She turned just in time to see Guin run a Goblin through that had snuck up on her. The redhead wielded her sword in her other shaking hand, her broken arm cradled to her chest. The girls put their backs together, watching their enemies.

"What are we going to do now?" Guin asked through heaving, painful gulps of air. The last six Goblins circled them like a pack of rabid hyenas.

Dagg swooped down like a demon, toasted one with his Dragon fire. Aliana shot two with her arrow but was too slow to avoid a club that came hurtling toward her from the side. It smacked into her shoulder, barreling her to the ground. The adrenaline that helped fuel her was ebbing and the price of using so much magic started to take over.

From the ground she watched Guin stab one through the heart then whirl around, her dirty, tattered skirt flaring out, and slice through the nasty gut of another. The girl was amazing to watch. How had she never guessed Lancelot's love would be such an amazing warrior?

"Look out!" Aliana threw out her right hand, her ruby giving her one last blast of magic to fry the remaining Goblin.

Guin nodded in thanks but Aliana couldn't respond as her body seized from the pain of using her magic. Dagg's magic invaded her, assuaging the pain enough that she could think clearly again, but neither was strong enough to stop it completely.

Guin dropped to her knees. "You're suffering from the use of your magic! You were still too weak!"

Aliana looked at her with cloudy eyes. "Worth it…you're not dead."

"What?" Guin shrieked.

Aliana had the insane desire to giggle; it had to be the pain getting to her addled brain. Something moved from the corner of her eye. She looked over as the Goblin Guin had cut across the gut rose up and hurtled a short sword directly at them. It happened so fast Aliana didn't have time to react before the blade sank into Guin's side and the Goblin breathed his last breath.

Aliana screamed as she turned a gasping Guinevere over to lie on the ground. She ripped a long part of the redhead's tattered skirt off, pulled the blade from her side and jammed the cloth to her side tightly.

"Aliana…" A small stream of blood trickled from the corner of her mouth.

"No, Guin! I won't let you die!" What little of her magic sparked and flared, but it was only enough to slow the bleeding. Aliana crumpled, her shaking hands all that kept her from falling on the girl. "Dagg…"

A dark shadow passed over them so big it blocked out the last of the dying sunlight.

The ground rumbled as a large silver Dragon landed beside them.

Aliana's eyes widened in shock.

"I am too late," the gravelly voice rumbled mournfully. "I am sorry, young ones."

"Silzik?"

37

*I am never letting Lacy out of my sight again. The second the
Well's magic releases her I grab her up and kiss the life out of
both of us. "I knew you'd come," she says. "I felt you here
and it gave me courage." I still don't know what to say to her,
so I've taken her away, back to our camp, with Arthur and
Leo in tow. As we're packing, Queen Titania arrives. That
crazy queen is more dangerous than a rattlesnake and a control
freak to boot. I'm glad Delphina and Freya have already left.*

— Percy

The Dragon's head tilted to the side as he regarded her with his
endless silver eyes. "Hmm…The queen *did* say you were from
the future." He said it more to himself than to her.

"The queen?" Aliana's brows pulled together as she tightened her
grip on Guin's wound. "You mean Queen Igraine?"

He wuffed, smoke pouring from his scaly nose. "Of course, dear
girl, whom else would I be referring too?"

The insane desire to giggle returned. She kept it in as Dagg went
to his longtime friend. The two Dragons regarded each other, their
eyes glowing.

"I see…it will be a pleasure to watch your destinies unfold." Silzik bowed his large head and Dagg bowed back.

Aliana snapped. "Sorry to interrupt this bonding moment, but Guin is dying and I don't have the magic to heal her!"

Silzik ambled over to them, his semi-truck huge body and massive wings hovering above them. His long neck swooped down and he sniffed Guin's wound. He made a sneezing sound and pulled back quickly. "Poison," he spat out. "The blade that struck her was coated in a poison I have never come across."

"Oh for the love of the stars, is there one damn weapon or magic in this place that isn't poisoned?" She threw her hands up. "Does no one have any imagination?"

"I think you are asking a might too much there…" Guin laughed at her own words, then started coughing and groaning.

"Aliana," Dagg growled in warning, winding himself around her shoulders. His calm influence swept into her.

She returned her hands to Guin's side. "I'm sorry." She looked back to the big Dragon. "I *need* to get home, to my time. Maybe Merlin can save her?"

As soon as the words fell from her mouth Aliana understood what had truly happened. They had never found Guin's body, because *she had* been here in the past and brought Guin back to the future to save her life!

Her eyes went back to Silzik's frantically. "Please tell me that Igraine sent you because you can help us get home!"

The big Dragon grinned, his angular head bobbing up and down. "Indeed, Destined One," he added with a whisper. "As I said, the queen told me much."

She ignored him, another thought plaguing her. If she had truly been here, as she realized now Igraine had been hinting at all along, why didn't the guys remember her?

She regarded him with wide anxious eyes. "What else did the queen tell you to do?"

The Dragon cleared his long throat. "No person, no matter how great, should know what their future holds. Life is, after all, about the journey and not the destination."

"Then the queen asked you to…take everyone's memories of me too."

He nodded. "All whom you have touched, that are still in this realm, will have their memories of you hidden away, only to return when they are needed."

Guin coughed again, more blood dribbling from her lips.

"Oh my god, Guin." She looked back to Silzik. "I'm not sure if you will be able to send me home. I don't know how Titania even did it."

Silzik started to shimmer with magic. "I may not be the Fae Queen, but my magic is nearly as powerful."

"Then, please, send us home to my time and my realm. I need help to save Guin!"

The giant Dragon nodded. "Traversing time is no easy thing, and I cannot guarantee your friend will survive it." His eyes turned to liquid silver.

The cloth in Aliana's hands started to heat. "What the?" She pulled it away and saw Guin's wound glowing the color of Silzik's eyes.

"I cannot save your friend's life, but my magic may just be enough to help her survive this journey." He reared back, rising to his hind legs, his wings flaring wide like an eagle. He threw his head back as his entire body glowed with his breathtaking magic. The very stars seemed to brighten in the early night sky as wind swirled and sizzled around them.

Ever so carefully, Aliana shifted Guin so she was half lying against her as she hugged the redhead tightly. "Dagg!"

Her guardian wrapped himself around her shoulders, his claws and wings clinging to her. If this was going to be anything like when Titania sent her back to Camelot, this trip could end up hurting… a lot.

"Are you prepared?" Silzik's voice was like booming thunder in the night.

"Yes…Silzik you need to know—"

"No." His glowing eerie eyes turned down to her. "I appreciate what you wish to do, but you have to understand that someone knowing their future, what is to happen to them, can be a dangerous burden to bear. Igraine knew her future, and fortunately had the wisdom to understand what it meant and what she had to do. I fear I do not have that same resolve."

Aliana nodded, understanding. She didn't know hers either, not anymore. She had thought she did when she read that fake paper saying she had to die to stop Mordrid, but now she knew the truth, that the queen had the true paper…and that the Underlord was right when he said her destiny was still being written, that her future was not set yet.

"Safe journey," the Dragon said as his power exploded out and surrounded them in an unbreakable cocoon. The magic fizzled before searing pain gripped her, ripping the three of them from Camelot, away from the family Guinevere had grown up with and back to the family Aliana had been building for herself since this strange quest started.

Weight returned and all pain vanished as she came back to herself. Aliana looked around, found herself on her front lawn still clutching a moaning Guin, whose wound was bleeding worse than ever.

"Help! Anyone, please!" she cried out, hoping the others had returned from their own journeys. She could still feel her own weakness and never hated the cost of using magic more than she did in that moment.

The front door flung open so fast and hard it smashed into the side of the house. Aliana looked up and saw Galahad frozen on the porch. He vanished, and then his arms closed around her, his solid muscular chest pressed tight to her back. Dagg rushed from her shoulders, landing on the ground to inspect their friend's condition.

"You are home." He looked from her to Guin. "We should have known."

Before she could ask, Dawn came charging out of the house with Lacy and the other knights and Pixies. The guys froze, just as Galahad had as the two girls fell to their knees beside Guin and Aliana. Flora was hot on their heels, zooming through the yard toward them.

A smile broke over her face, a real smile for the first time in ages. "I am so happy to be home, but I need you two to heal her. She's been poisoned with something we don't know and I have no magic to save her with."

"Then let's see if we can help," Lacy said, placing her hand on the bleeding wound.

Dawn placed her hands over Lacy's. "Thank god Merlin taught me some of his healing magic!"

"I can help too!" Flora pulled a small vial from around her neck. "Pixie dust," she explained to the wide-eyed girls. "It's able to heal any poison."

Lacy took the bottle with one bloody hand, thumbed off the stopper and poured the glittering powder onto the wound.

The knights all circled around. Everyone but Lancelot and Merlin.

Dawn's leafy, pulsing purple magic flared, along with Lacy's liquid moonlight magic, both swirling together under their hands and around Guin.

Their dying friend started coughing so hard her body shook. Aliana tightened her hold; Galahad's own arms gripped Guin's shoulders helping to hold her still until the fit passed. The blood that had been spilling, staining Guin and the girl's hands, faded into nothing.

The magic ebbed and disappeared. Both Lacy and Dawn fell back on their butts, gasping for air and wiping the sweat from their brows. Percy swooped in immediately, cradling Lacy against him. Both Owen and Wade supported Dawn.

"Guinevere?" Arthur asked, kneeling, inspecting the now healed wound. "Guin?"

Aliana held her breath as Galahad released his grip, his hands briefly touching her hips before he pulled back a fraction.

Guin moved in her arms and groaned, stealing Aliana's focus from Galahad and his bond to her.

Her rich brown eyes fluttered open. Everyone breathed sighs of relief, some hooting with joy. Aliana couldn't hold back her giggle as Flora danced around in the air like a pop star.

"Guinevere!" Arthur cupped his dear friend's cheeks, his own eyes misty as he looked up to Aliana. "You've brought her back to us."

She laughed, her aching body filled with relief and joy. She had finally managed to save one of her friends' lives.

Guin sat up gingerly. She hugged Arthur before the king helped her get to her feet. Aliana remained where she was, even though her muscles were aching to be stretched. Galahad offered his hand to her. She looked at it, then to him, felt her eyes widen with so many emotions she didn't know what she was feeling.

Bracing her hands on the ground, she got herself to her feet. Dagg hovered at her side, his reassuring magic brushing against her sensitive skin.

Guin cleared her throat. "Someone is going to need to explain to me what is happening here and where in Camelot we are." She looked around. "Where are Lancelot and Merlin?"

"They've not yet returned," Galahad said, his voice controlled and calm. "And the explanation is going to be hard to understand at first."

Arthur went to Aliana. "Welcome home." His voice was low and gruff and she could see the pent up passion sparking in him. She hugged him, his morning dew smell calming her taut nerves.

She pulled back, only to have Dawn and Lacy steal her away into a group hug. This time a few of Aliana's tears did leak out as she gripped her best friends and sisters tightly. "Thank you!" she whispered to both of them.

"No need," Lacy insisted.

Dawn squeezed a little harder. "We always have each other's backs."

Aliana giggled and pulled back, swiping away her tears.

Dawn winked at her. "And now I don't have to kick your butt for falling to that rat ass Mordrid's poison."

They broke out in roaring laughter. Wade came to them, pulling Aliana from the girls and swung her around in big hug. "It's good to have you home, Lia."

He set her down only to have Owen sweep her into his arms next. "You scared the bloody piss out of me, cousin. Don't go off like that again, yeah?"

She nodded against his shoulder and pulled back to exchange hugs with all the other knights and Pixies. She whispered her thanks again to Flora.

Everyone turned, making their way to the house. Aliana shivered as a cool wind blew past them. Fear returned. "How long have I been gone?" How long did they have until the eclipse?

"Christmas is in a week," Wade told her, walking between her and Dawn.

Aliana stopped dead. "WHAT?"

"That's what we said," Lacy told her with a grin. "We only just got back from the Isle a few days ago."

Owen piped up. "We've been back for almost a month, from Avalon."

"You all remember everything now?"

Leo nodded, a content smile on the Scot's face. "Yes, lass, whatever blocked our memories of you in Camelot have been fully lifted."

"That was Silzik." She glanced up at Arthur. "Your mother sent him to us to return me home and help save Guin's life."

Exhaustion started to set in again as they climbed the stairs to the front door. Aliana stumbled into Arthur, the king steadying her as she closed her eyes and leaned into him. "I'm so freaking tired I could sleep for a year or two."

Everyone chuckled, and it was a wonderful sound to hear after so much pain and death. Her world tilted as Arthur scooped her up in his arms. "I'll take you to your room. You need to rest."

In that moment she felt her emotional anxiety float away. Maybe it was because of his strong, warm arms; or maybe it was because she was deliriously tired and it felt like the world was finally giving her a moment of peace. Aliana nestled her heavy head against his shoulder as he addressed the others. "Lacy, Dawn, please see that Guinevere gets settled. I'll be back down shortly so we can plan our next move. Hopefully Merlin and Lancelot will return soon from Olympus with the good news we need." He smiled fondly at Guin. "I know we have good news for them."

Aliana let her mind drift as the girls followed Arthur up the stairs, pulling Guinevere into their room after opening the door to Aliana's room for the king.

He kicked the door closed, laying Aliana down on her bed, his warm hand brushing her hair aside. She felt a real smile creep onto her lips as she turned her sleepy eyes to him. It felt so good to not worry about her feelings for a few minutes; she decided to enjoy it while she could.

"Thank you, Arthur." She sighed, snuggling into her pillow as the bed dipped.

Arthur leaned over her, his face hovering inches above hers. Aliana sucked in his scent and let her eyes roam over his delicious upper body. Her heart fluttered as his face descended closer, his left arm braced by her head, the other stroking through her hair. She felt ghost-like strings weaving around and through them. The same golden threads she had felt when she had kissed him awake, and when they had kissed on the beach by her house. She was drowning in the bond that was only theirs.

His fingers touched her neck lightly before hooking around the leather cord that held the Pendragon pendant. He ran his thumb over the pendant, then took her hand from him and placed it in her palm. "I didn't tell you the whole story behind this pendant."

"What do you mean?"

"This has been in my family for generations. My mother said the Golden Dragon forged three of them. One for him, one for his son and one for his daughter. They are meant to give the wearer a link to the one who gifted it to them. My mother gave this to me when I was five and started to train as a knight."

"Then you should have it back." Aliana went to remove it, but Arthur stopped her. He held her hands between his, brought them to his lips, brushing feather light kisses on her curled fingers, his eyes never once leaving hers.

"I gave it to you as more than a token for you to wear during the games. My mother always told me, the person I gave this to should be the person who holds my heart. You're the only person I have ever considered giving this to. My heart tells me you're meant to have this. I have faith that things will work out for us." He closed her fingers around the pendant that was now hers.

Aliana looked at the beautiful thing in her hand. How many times had she told him to listen to his heart and to have faith? Now he had it, and he was certain about his feelings for her. The golden strands she had felt for so long with Arthur weaved a tighter net around her heart, drawing every bit of her closer to his own soul. She had only realized she loved him before she was taken by Mordrid and then thrown back into Camelot. Seeing Arthur as he was, as a king confident and sure, she had only fallen even more in love with him.

Then she remembered. "Do you remember Delphina clearly now?"

Surprised by the sudden change of subject Arthur's head jerked up. "What?"

Aliana sighed, hoping her heart wasn't about to break into shards again. "You remember her now, right? Your ghost girl you always said you thought you loved but couldn't remember. At least you couldn't remember her besides her green eyes."

He shook his head, a confounded half smile on the corner of his mouth. "I have never forgotten Delphina. Not for a moment."

Aliana frowned up at him. "But…you never mentioned her… you said the woman you couldn't remember had green eyes." She huffed in confused frustration. "I know you care for her, have had an intimate relationship with her."

He shook his head, twisted a finger around a lock of her hair. "A relationship I clearly remember telling you was over long before you came to Camelot."

She looked away from him. "But your green eyed ghost girl…"

He cupped her chin between his thumb and forefinger, turned her face back to his. "Is you."

Her entire being went stock still at his husky confession. She felt like a stalked animal again, and this kingly Dragon was about to swoop in to claim his stunned prize. "What?" She wasn't sure if he heard her whispered gasp when he remained just as still, watching her like he was afraid she would bolt. Too bad she couldn't do much more than suck in breath.

"When you awoke me in that cave, do you remember what I said?"

She remembered all right. She remembered him touching her cheek gently and her lips. The way she had leaned into his touch, not understanding why she felt so connected and safe with a virtual stranger.

"It is you," he had whispered.

Slowly, the realization hit her, but she was scarcely able to believe it.

"From the first memory of you in Camelot, I knew for certain you were the girl I was dreaming of for so long. Despite my memories of you being taken, my heart would never forget you. Nor would my soul."

Her tired heart stuttered. "I'm not really sure what to say." She touched his cheek lightly. "I care for you. Very much so."

Arthur leaned his cheek into her touch. "I didn't tell you this to force a decision from you. I simply needed to tell you. As for what to do, you listen to your heart," he said boldly. "You taught me that." He took her hand, kissed the palm, his eyes still holding hers.

Aliana's eyes fluttered again, as she tried to stay awake. She liked having Arthur this close; she wanted him to kiss her again, like he had in Camelot.

He laughed huskily. "You do realize you said that out loud?" he whispered, bringing his lips close enough to brush teasingly on hers. Their inflamed eyes locked fiercely as he rested his forehead against hers, both breathing heavily. She could read every emotion he was feeling. He made no move to hide his passion, his love for her. His desire. The golden strings of their bond tickled against her skin. He pulled back, his lips sweeping her cheek like a butterfly's wings. The sweetness of the moment remained even as he sat up, moving slowly.

"I need to go, before I lose all sense and self-control." He traced his fingers down her cheek.

Her hand tightened around the pendant still between them. Aliana felt so relaxed, so safe and warm she fought to keep her eyes just barely open.

"Do not regret what my mother sacrificed to save you. I don't, and I know she didn't either."

Those were the last words she heard from him as she finally fell into a deep sleep.

3⁸

Something was buzzing in her ear.

Aliana took a short breath, lifted her heavy eyelids, her tongue touching her dry lips. The buzzing, deep and even, grew louder. With a small moan she turned her head to see Dagg curled up on her other pillow, his wings settled against his body, his tail curled around him like a cat. His ears twitched as he took another snoring breath.

A smile broke out on her face. She rubbed her hand over her sleep-fogged eyes and looked around her moonlit room. Why wasn't she in her room at the castle? Reality came back to her. She was finally home, back in Charleston, in her own time.

A glass of water sat on her nightstand. She grabbed it and drank it down greedily. Her cottony mouth now less annoying, she slid from the bed, careful not to wake her sleeping guardian. She was still dressed in her stained, ripped clothes from Camelot. She shuddered and grabbed a pair of jeans, fresh undergarments and a graphic T-shirt before dipping into her bathroom. The running water from her shower felt amazing as she scrubbed herself clean two times.

As great and wonderful as Camelot was, Aliana didn't think she'd ever willingly give up modern plumbing again. Not that she'd had much of a choice this time. Testing the strength of her magic, Aliana opened her senses and felt the flowing magic of the water element. It trickled through her, trailing little rivulets over her body as the water slid over her magic ruby.

When she finally stepped out of her steamed filled bathroom, Dagg was still asleep. Shaking her head she went back in and peeked into Dawn and Lacy's room through the connecting door. Percy was wrapped around Lacy, almost possessively, in a bed that was too small for the giant knight. Dawn's bed was empty, un-slept in judging by the unwrinkled covers. Where was she? Maybe she had made up with Wade while she was in Avalon.

Aliana closed the door quietly, not wanting to disturb the sleeping couple.

It felt so good to be home, back in her own house, with her own bed and clothes. She glanced at her bedside clock. It was five a.m. Sunrise would be soon. She grinned and grabbed a light wrap sweater and headed down the stairs. She had a thought to wake Dagg, but he needed as much rest as she did.

Her stomach grumbled. She made a beeline to the kitchen to grab a morning snack. Estrelle was humming as she zipped around the kitchen, preparing what looked to be fresh cinnamon rolls and coffee cakes. The rarely seen redheaded Pixie smiled at her when she saw her standing in the doorway.

Her dragonfly-like wings shimmered as she fiddled with the hem of her brown dress. "Welcome back."

"Thank you, Estrelle." Aliana inhaled the smell of baking sweets. Her stomach rumbled again, loudly. Both girls broke out laughing. "You wouldn't happen to have anything I can munch on until breakfast is ready do you?"

She nodded excitedly. "I have just the thing." She held up one finger as she disappeared into the pantry. She emerged holding a very large red and green apple Aliana immediately recognized as an apple from Avalon.

Galahad had given her one after they had escaped the Sidhe's keep. Her mood turned heavy as Estrelle put the fruit in her hand. Aliana could still recall that moment perfectly, including all the wild emotions she had felt after realizing she was crazy attracted to him. Her conversation with her mother about the magical bonds between her and Galahad, and between her and Arthur, came back to her.

Estrelle was watching her cautiously. "Is everything all right, Aliana?"

Aliana put on a smile. "How did these apples get here?"

"Sir Galahad brought them back when he returned from Avalon. He insisted that we store them so you would be able to have one when you returned." The Pixie's cheeks pinkened. "He said you were fond of them."

Aliana bit her cheek; she did like them, a lot. Her throat was tight when she said, "Thanks," and walked out of the kitchen, straight toward the back door.

She stepped out into the chilled early morning air, wrapped her sweater tighter around her and stared at the ought-to-be-forbidden fruit. Why had Galahad done this?

She decided to not read into the thought. She took a big bite, the familiar sweet and tangy flavor bursting in her mouth like a small party. She demolished the apple, its magic filling her very empty stomach. She thought over her romantic situation as she walked the path she'd memorized years ago. By the time she reached the sand, she was even more confused and tangled up inside. She tossed the core into the tall grass and slipped off the ballet flats she had put on before leaving the house. The sand shifted under her weight, its normal warmth dulled by the slight chill of the season.

The last time she stood here she had kissed Arthur for the first time, watched him and Galahad fight a grudge match and then been torn apart by the conflicting power of her unnaturally strong bonds to both of them.

A cold breeze drifted from the water, playing with her hair as she wrapped her arms around herself and stared at the setting moon and fading stars from her spot at the edge of the surf.

"Aliana?"

She saw Galahad making his way to her from the left side of the beach. Her eyes went to the dagger she had enchanted for him, which was strapped at his waist. She opened her mouth to ask him why he was outside but couldn't find her voice through her tangle of emotions.

"How are you feeling? You slept for quite some time," he asked when she remained silent.

"Fine. Much better, thanks." She frowned. "How long was I asleep? And why are you up?"

"You've been asleep for two days. And I was unable to sleep and decided to go for a walk."

His eyes darkened, telling her it was more than that.

The tension surrounding them held her, the heat and intensity spearing through her, straight to the mending part of her heart. She saw his regret, longing, determination, control and love.

"I..." Aliana choked on her words. There was so much unsaid between them. Even leaving aside the new feelings that had taken root in her heart for him, they still hadn't talked about all that happened when he gave in to his impulses to protect her.

Seeing him in Camelot, how he had been, as a knight, with his sister, the others...it complicated her once-simple emotions of regret and a shattered heart. If she was ever going to figure out this bond they shared, she needed to talk to him about it. She just couldn't make her treacherous vocal cords work.

Or control her racing heart at his nearness.

Galahad reached out and captured her hands in his. Silver sparks ignited, but they seemed muted compared to what she had been so used to. It was like when they first met, and it was more of an awareness than anything real and solid.

"I've been needing to speak to you of what happened," he started. "Before you were taken."

She waited for him to go on.

"No apology I could give you would make up for the enormity of the mistake I made, trapping you in your house like I did. I have no excuse for it, not even that evil Mordrid infected me with. I regret my actions more than anything I ever have in my long life."

Aliana swallowed, opened her mouth to say something…but she still had no words to give him. She didn't know what to say.

"I know I cannot expect your forgiveness, but I will never stop proving to you how much I have changed. Because of you. I will do whatever I must to earn back your trust and friendship."

The bubbles burst in her stomach. "Galahad, you have never lost my friendship! Being back in Camelot, learning about your parents, Vira…" She cleared her throat, blinking away tears. "I will always be your friend, we will always be family. A part of me will always love you, but…"

Cautious hope swirled in his watchful eyes that studied her so intently.

"But, I do not know if I can ever trust you enough to open my heart to you again." His face fell the merest fraction and it broke something in her. She reached up and touched his cheek lightly. "I don't want to hurt you, Galahad. I care for you too much for that. But…I have feelings for Arthur too. I think I have for a while, I just didn't realize it. Not until after…" She let her words hang. He knew what she meant.

He swallowed again, his jaw tight, but he nodded.

"I am so confused right now, about everything. You, Arthur, my feelings, Vira, this quest and how the heck I am supposed to help stop Mordrid…I hate the thought that I am hurting you—"

"Don't."

His word confused her.

"Don't worry about hurting me. It is nothing less than I deserve for what I did. All I want for you is to be happy. Even if that means you and Arthur…" He cleared his throat. "If he is the one you truly love, then you should be with him. As long as you are happy, I will be content with that. You deserve to be happy in your life, Aliana."

Tears burned and prickled her nose. His selflessness and sincerity made the healing part of her heart swell, the silver sparks of their bond becoming stronger.

He reached behind and pulled something from his back pocket. Holding out his palm, he revealed a small piece of jewelry, just smaller than his palm.

Aliana gasped, the tears she had been fighting returning full force. In his palm was a very small replica of the oval music box, with a heart shaped lid, which her father had given her mother for one of their anniversaries. She had told Galahad about it back in London, before the party where they found Merlin and Wade, after he saw a picture of it. She hadn't been able to find the original after their death.

Aliana's hand hovered around his, almost afraid to touch the small, beautiful locket. "Where did you…how…" She looked back up to him.

"When we were on our date, we passed a store that made custom jewelry."

Aliana remembered. They had looked around briefly, but she didn't remember Galahad talking to the store clerk.

The white knight turned over her hand, placing the delicate piece in her upturned palm.

"Before Percy and Lacy left us to continue their date, I told Percy I wanted to have a replica made for you." His finger brushed away a tear she didn't realize had fallen. "He and Lacy helped a lot. She told me the song it played and gave the artist a picture of it. I know how much it hurts you to not have their music box, because your parents loved it so much. I hoped that this locket would make that hurt a little less for you."

Aliana was well and truly speechless. And her surprise didn't stop there. He reached out and opened the heart lid. The soft, old world melody of her parents' wedding song filled the world around them with its delicate beauty and notes.

"Galahad…" Aliana was beyond elated that he remembered such a tiny detail from so long ago. "I can't believe you did this." More tears fell as she took it from him. "Thank you." She touched it gingerly, the warm metal a comforting weight alongside the playing melody she'd watched her parents dance to too many times to count.

Her fractured heart healed a little more. His smile was as loving as his fingers that brushed away her tears.

She brought the locket to her mouth and kissed it lightly before gripping it tight. "I can never thank you enough for this."

He took her other hand, their sparks flying, and kissed it. "I do not need thanks, I just need you to be happy."

Pulled by her blooming feelings she reached up and hugged Galahad tightly. "I think I forgave you when I realized Mordrid's magic had poisoned you. I was just so hurt, so confused."

He gripped her tighter for a second before pulling back enough to look at her. "I should have had more control. I've worked tirelessly, since that night, to be a better master of my deeds and emotions."

She sighed heavily and laid her cheek against his chest, the rapid drumming of his heart like a soothing rhythm. She inhaled his wintery spice scent which she had grown to adore. "Like I said, you've never lost my friendship. Part of me loves you even still. But…" She raised her head, needing to look him in his eyes when she finally said it. "Trust is not something that comes easily to me. Especially after learning my parents had adopted me but never told me. After Josh and what he tried to do to me."

Galahad's arms tightened around her. She almost felt his anger for her ex-boyfriend.

"My horrible track record with guys…not to mention trusting Raven." She shook her head again. "I could have stopped him from killing Sophvira."

Galahad's fingers touched her trembling lips. "I have never once believed that her death was your fault. Indeed, now that I have my memories back I remember it even more, and I *know* it was not your fault." He let her see the truth of his words. "Mordrid, Morgana, and Viviane are to blame."

She felt another familiar presence brush against her senses. Jerking from Galahad's arms she looked to the path that led to her house. There was Arthur, his left hand gripping Excalibur's hilt strapped around his waist. Did neither of them go anywhere unarmed?

Aliana shifted on her feet, looking out at the ocean, hoping this very emotionally awkward and confusing moment wasn't happening. But she couldn't run from this. Not now. She couldn't run if she ever wanted to find out the truth of her heart.

"What are you doing up, Arthur?"

Arthur cleared his throat. "I saw you leave the house. You've been asleep for two days. I wanted to be sure you were all right."

Her emotions started to rattle like a pinball. Her worry that the feelings between her and these two brave, noble men may not be real stabbed vengefully. Her mother had said that *if* these bonds were indeed manipulated ones, then she would have to discover that for herself, by listening to her true heart. Heck of a lot easier said than done. Especially when the pull she felt for both men was only growing stronger and she wasn't really sure *who* she was anymore. She had been changed after her adoptive parents' deaths, and was still changing every day of this crazy quest. She hardly recognized herself anymore.

She looked out at the vast ocean, her mind racing as she made a decision that would probably hurt all three of them. "Maybe it's good we're all here."

The knights shared a confused look.

"I want to talk to both of you, and this seems like the only time we'll get the privacy we need."

Galahad shifted uncomfortably. "I think we know what this is about."

"I don't think you do." Aliana took a big breath. "You know I care for both of you very much…that I love both of you, very much."

"But?" Arthur asked quietly, watching her like a silent predator.

It was time to take her mother's advice. "There's so much…we've all been through so much…" She sighed and ran her hands through her hair. She couldn't figure out how to say what her gut told her she needed to. They both waited for her to find the words.

"I don't want to hurt either of you. So much has changed…" she watched both men trying to gauge their reaction to her decision "… since I have been in Camelot and even before that."

The white knight's face darkened, his mouth thinning, but he said nothing.

"Between my *destiny*, Mordrid, my weird magic, and my fear that my feelings are all part of some crazy chess game Titania is controlling…" She held up her hand when Arthur tried to speak. "Please let me say this. I don't know if I'll be able to again."

The king inclined his dark head, his face impassive behind his king mask she saw through so easily. She was hurting him, hurting both of them, and that broke her heart.

"I am so confused, and hurt, and it kills me that I'm hurting you both with my feelings for the other, or that I may eventually cause a rift between you both."

"Aliana…"

She shook her head, cutting Galahad off. "I know you both think that won't happen, but I can't take that chance. And honestly,

I'm not sure I really understand what love is, at least not true love. There's too much we don't know, too much *I* don't know about who I really am and what I'm really meant to do."

"What does that mean?" Arthur asked, his arms folding across his tensed chest. Even Galahad was standing rigidly, like he was exerting an unrelenting amount of control over himself.

"I can't be with either of you —" she took another breath "— until I figure out the answers to those questions. Figure out who I am."

They stood there in silence for endless moments, the only sound the breaking of the waves against the surf and the whistle of the breeze.

Galahad was the first to speak. "I think I can safely say that all either of us wants is for you to be happy." He and Arthur's eyes locked, both nodding silently. "But I also believe neither of us is willing to give up on the hope of being with you."

Arthur dropped his arms to his side. "You worry you will come between us, but you have to *trust us* when we say that won't happen."

Aliana's fingers clenched her sweater even tighter. That was the crux of it all, trust. "I can't promise either of you anything." If what she feared was right, that what she felt wasn't real, just a sick game... she shuddered.

Galahad took a step closer. "We should go back inside, you're shaking."

Not from the cold. She let them think he was right nonetheless. She needed time to think, to adjust.

She led the way, both her gallant knights like shadows at her back. The hair on the back of her neck stood up as the magic of an opening portal sizzled on her skin.

Aliana looked back at the beach, her senses tracing the power trail back to the beach. Her feet were moving to get there before she had the conscious thought to. This was a magic she hadn't felt yet. It was breezy, thin like the wind.

"What's that?" Arthur asked, both men trailing her, their weapons drawn.

Aliana searched, the first light of day illuminating the world. Until she saw the rippling of a gate, feet from the water, like hot air in the desert. "Someone's opening a gate."

The very air split open as Merlin stepped through the portal. Aliana let out a relieved breath.

"You're back!" She looked past the Druid. "Where's Lancelot?" She finally had a chance to do something good for the suffering knight. His Guinevere was finally going to be his again!

Merlin turned as Lancelot came through, his hand holding another smaller one as they both stepped onto the beach.

Galahad's dagger dropped from his hands landing with a thud in the sand. His blazing blue eyes were fixed on the short, dark-haired teenager beside his brother knight. "Sophvira?"

The girl's blue eyes lit up with her bright smile. "Big brother!"

39

Sophvira ran straight for her shell-shocked brother, flung herself in his arms and hugged him fiercely, burying her face in his chest as a big sob escaped her.

Almost like he was afraid she would disappear, Galahad wrapped one arm around his dear little sister and stroked her dark hair with the other. "Is it really you, Sophvira? How is this possible?"

Aliana covered her mouth, muffling her own gasp as tears brimmed in her eyes. She looked to Merlin and Lancelot, silently asking for the answer to the question her clamped throat wouldn't let pass her lips.

"It's a very long story," Lancelot said, a somberness in his eyes mixing with the relief and contentment he clearly felt at reuniting brother and sister.

Arthur stepped to her side as Galahad picked Vira up, swinging her around in big circles, both laughing loudly. A few tears escaped down Aliana's cheeks. Vira was still wearing the same dress she had when the poison had taken her from them.

She had thought the sweet teen was lost to them forever. She should have been. Mordrid and Viviane's poison had killed her! Her guilt over the tragedy surfaced, but was muddled with her happiness of seeing the girl was alive and well. But how?

Worry invaded her; what if this was a trick? She opened her magical senses, felt the air around Sophvira and recognized the kind, loving spirit she had always felt from the girl. But there was an underlying current, barely there. Magic! Her emerald eyes widened, shooting to Merlin.

He nodded, silently reading her worry. "*We will explain all, once we've gathered the others.*"

The others! Guinevere! Excitement poured through her. She looked to Arthur, the good news ready to fall from her tongue. Arthur shook his head ever so slightly.

She frowned, her brow knitting together, silently asking why not.

"He'll need to see her to believe it." His words were a quiet whisper. He was probably right. Arthur knew Lancelot best.

Galahad finally set Vira down, kissing her forehead lovingly. The teen's bright smile made Aliana'a heart soar. Vira stood on her tiptoes, kissed Galahad's cheek, then dashed toward Aliana.

Vira barreled into her, both girls almost falling to the ground as they hugged like long lost sisters. "I am so glad you are alive!" Aliana whispered before pulling back.

"I know, I've got a lot to explain," the teen said with a shy smile. "Merlin and Lancelot told me everything that's happened since—" she shrugged "—you know."

Aliana let the girl go as Arthur pulled her into a tight hug. "We've missed our favorite little sister more that I can say, Sophvira!"

A flush broke out over her cheeks before she kissed the king's cheeks. "I've missed all of you!"

They broke apart. Aliana looked to Galahad, who had been watching his sister and king, his blazing emotions searing her straight to the bone. Her heart galloped again. A large part of her hesitation of being with Galahad was because she had blamed herself for what had happened to his sister; what did this mean for them now? *Nothing,* she reminded herself. *I need to figure out who I am first, and if what is between him and me and Arthur is even real.*

Lancelot broke through her reverie. "We should head up to the house, wake the others, and explain everything." The knight went to Arthur. "We found more than Sophvira in Olympus. We know who the Atlantian is."

Arthur's eyes hardened. "Who?"

"We can explain all at the house, sire." Merlin clapped his hand on Arthur's shoulder. "For now, we should not linger in the open."

Galahad wrapped his arm around his sister and steered her toward the house.

Sophvira looked back at Aliana. "Merlin said we are at your house?"

Aliana nodded. "Yeah. I'm so glad you're here."

They made it to the house, Flora and Dagg awaiting them, hovering by the back door. Both pairs of magical purple eyes widened when they saw Vira. "Who is this?"

"Flora, meet my little sister, Sophvira."

The Pixie's eyes widened even more. Aliana hid a giggle behind her hand imagining Flora's eyes bugging out like a cartoon characters.

The Pixie zoomed up to Vira. "I've never met a Pixie before! I'm Vira." Her blue eyes swung to Dagg. "It's a pleasure to see you again, DragonLord."

The small silver creature grinned broadly. "My lady, it is I who am pleased to see you again. I regret not getting to know you better in Camelot."

Straightening her shoulders, Vira curtsied. "A pleasure," she said, giggling.

Flora's face lit up, her wings fluttering faster. "I can tell we're going to get along great! And wait until you meet Dawn and Lacy!"

"Don't get carried away, Flora," Merlin cautioned. "Go wake everyone, we have a lot to discuss."

The Pixie zoomed through the house, leaving a trail of yellow magic in her wake.

Aliana touched Vira's shoulder, drawing the girl's blue eyes from the fading trail of magic. "Are you hungry? Estrelle was making breakfast when I came out earlier."

Vira nodded ecstatically. Galahad led her inside, his gaze lingering on Aliana for a long second. Ignoring the fluttering of butterflies in her chest she turned to Lancelot, Dagg settling himself on her shoulders.

Both he and Merlin stopped when she held out her hand. "You two have your memories back now, right?"

Merlin nodded. Lancelot's face turned stone hard but he nodded too. She thought back to the night she had heard him playing the piano, a sad ballad he had written for his lost Guinevere. The night she learned why he really left Avalon and Arthur.

"You're not the only one with a surprise visitor." She watched his eyes scrunch together as he tried to figure out what she meant. She barely contained her smile when she felt the presence of the others coming toward the back door. "I was riding with Guin, remember?"

The knight and Merlin went completely rigid.

"Then you know what happened to her?" Lancelot's words were little more than a choked plea.

The back door opened and everyone came pouring out. Lacy and Dawn were still dressed in their pajamas, Percy and Wade holding them. The guys all broke out in wide smiles. Even Lacy and Dawn looked relieved to see the two knights home safely. Then the crowd parted as Galahad and Vira came back out.

Lancelot's jaw fell open, his eyes zeroing in on the redhead that was dressed in a pair of Dawn's jeans and a black T-shirt. "Guinevere?" He looked like he was seeing a ghost, one that tortured him as much as it thrilled him.

Guin's brown eyes misted over, a small sniffle escaping her. "Yes, my love. I'm here."

They both ran forward at the same time, meeting each other halfway as everyone watched the happy reunion. He cupped Guin's face in his hands and kissed her like a starving man at a banquet. The redhead buried her hands in his raven hair and pressed herself flush against him and kissed him back with everything she had.

Even without opening her magic senses Aliana could see the bright flares of pale blue and white glowing light that burst from them. Their souls mate bond, she realized, wiping a happy tear from her cheek.

The two broke apart, both panting, Lancelot resting his forehead against Guin's as their eyes locked on each other. Her fingers brushed the sharp planes of Lancelot's face before trailing down his chest. His own were wrapped tightly around her, holding her to him like he would never let her go again. They stood there looking at each other like nothing else existed in the world.

Aliana finally looked away, as she remembered feeling like that with both Arthur and Galahad. She looked to Lacy and Percy, the blonde hugging her southern knight, tucked in his arms. Happiness warred with her own longing as she watched Dawn place a loving kiss on Wade's cheek, as the playful knight held Dawn against his chest.

She dropped her eyes again before they could wander to Galahad or Arthur. She had made her decision, now she had to live with it.

Merlin cleared his throat. "Not to spoil the lovers' moment, but we have much to discuss."

Lancelot shot him a nasty glare as Guinevere giggled, resting her head against her souls mate's chest.

Arthur grinned, patted Lancelot's free shoulder. "He is right. You two can continue your reunion *privately*. Later."

The guys chuckled. Wade whistled a cat call. Dawn and Lacy shared a knowing look with Aliana when she finally looked up. Aliana wiggled her eyebrows, setting aside her own jumbled feelings.

Everyone started making their way inside, Lacy and Dawn leaving their knights' arms to come to her side, Vira trailing behind them.

Aliana closed the patio door after everyone entered, the girls all hanging back a second, with Galahad as his sister's shadow.

Aliana grinned realizing Galahad was probably going to be hovering around his little sister a lot. Not that she could really blame him. "Vira, meet my best friends, Lacy and Dawn."

The teen nodded, a bright smile on her face. "Merlin and Lancelot told me about you two."

Lacy raised a brow. "Well *that* couldn't have been good!"

Vira broke out in laughter. "Maybe a little. Lancelot seemed a little worried I would get into trouble with all of you!"

Dawn's cat-ate-the-canary grin had Aliana's spirits lifting. "Stick with us kid, we'll make sure you go down the right path of trouble making!"

"Dawn," Galahad said sternly.

The girls laughed at his solemn face and crossed arms. Shaking her head, Aliana led them all into the kitchen where Sabine had magically enlarged the kitchen to fit the two extra diners.

Lancelot sat next to Guin, his arm draped around her shoulders. Lacy and Dawn took the open seats between Percy and Wade. The rest of the guys were seated in their usual spots.

Aliana gulped, realizing she was going to be in her normal seat between Galahad and Arthur, Vira on her brother's other side. Not wanting to let on anything was wrong she sat quickly and grabbed a steaming cinnamon roll from the plate in front of her. Sabine and Estrelle had outdone themselves, making enough food to feed an army, but with the way the knights packed away the food, it seemed like they were feeding an actual army.

Dawn's voice broke into her mind. *"Lia, what's going on?"*

"Yeah, you look like you're waiting for a firing squad or something," Lacy added.

"I'll explain later, guys." She shut down the conversation as Dagg used his magic to fill his own plate next to hers.

"So where are we going to start with all this?" Dawn asked, swallowing a bite of eggs.

Wade frowned eying his girlfriend and sister. "Why don't we start with a full explanation of the stunt you two pulled with the Well of Realms."

Vira perked up. Aliana bit back a smile. The teen was so going to be corrupted by the three of them. But she had a sneaking suspicion the teen was more mischievous than she had ever let on in Camelot. Especially if she was already friends with the trickster. She remembered seeing Vira with a person she thought was Puck.

Aliana cleared her throat. "They were helping me destroy the Spear of Hel."

"It's not that we doubted you would find the Well," Lacy said. "But we didn't know that the Well's waters were the same as the time mirrors. And we thought this was a way to bring her home."

"Even before we all set out on our journeys, Lace and I had been having weird dreams about needing to find Lia in Camelot."

"And once we found the Wells…we just knew we had to do it." Lacy offered Arthur an apologetic smile. "We were afraid you guys would stop us if we told you our plans."

"You weren't wrong," Owen said.

"But if you had explained everything, we would have helped you," Wade said. "I think we've all learned our lesson from the last time we tried to control your actions." Several of the guys, including Galahad, agreed.

Aliana stopped mid-chew, her eyebrows nearly shooting off her face. Did they all really just admit that? *"Well I'll be damned."*

"You act like you didn't already know they all regretted their actions."

Aliana pursed her lips at Dagg. "I wouldn't have been able to use my magic without them."

Merlin nodded but he looked like he was haunted by the memory. And why wouldn't he be? He had lost Morgana in that battle. "It was fortunate they were there to help. I only wish I had realized what was happening at the time."

"The guys already know." She looked to Lacy and Dawn. "But you two don't know yet. I found my birth parents. I know who my father is."

Dawn's hazel eyes grew big, Lacy's mouth fell open. "Who?" they demanded together.

"General Alaki, son of the Underlord, and Death himself."

Dawn and Lacy looked at each other, then her, then back at each other. Aliana couldn't remember a time when both of her friends had been so speechless. It wouldn't last long.

"I'll fill you in on all the details later. But the Underlord—" she shook her head "—my grandfather…gave me one boon."

"That's a hell of a thing to not mention," Merlin mumbled.

An embarrassed flush crawled up her neck. "It wouldn't have made sense if I told you back in Camelot."

Arthur placed his hand on her shoulder in a show of support. "Let's move on."

Grateful, she continued, "I used it to ask that General Alaki, my father, and his army of death fight with us when we finally face Mordrid, Viviane, and Morgana in battle."

The silence around the table was thicker than pumpkin soup.

Aliana looked around the table feeling more out of place than ever. "Someone please say something!"

Lacy clapped her hands together, her stunned stupor disappearing. "Dude, you're a double princess!"

Dawn's lips twitched with glee. "Does that mean you now have a three-headed dog for a pet too?" Dawn winked at Dagg.

Happiness bloomed in her; leave it to the smart mouthed girls to break the heritage ice.

With a rueful smile on his face, Arthur spoke up. "I also had a private audience with the Fae queen. She came to me before we left. She has also pledged her Fae army to our cause, when the final battle comes."

Reassured relief was on all the guys' faces.

Galahad spoke up too. "Princess Varaness has also said she will speak to King Oberon about his Elf army once again fighting with us. She also commands a smaller army that she has promised would stand with us even if her brother's army won't." Galahad touched Aliana's arm ever so lightly. "J'alel among them. He insisted I tell you that."

Aliana's grin widened.

"You really are the key we need to defeat Mordrid, cousin," Owen said.

Leo nodded. "Not only did you find the map but you secured us the aid of the strongest army in all the realms, lass."

"All lives eventually answer to Death," Merlin added. "With him on our side, many others will rally to us. Even those who may have been tempted or even already promised to side with Mordrid in the final battle."

The relief pouring through Aliana was like a weight off her shoulder. She looked around the table, grateful for all the support of her friends. Her family.

"This is all very good." Leo rubbed his chin. "We are gathering the support we are going to need, but all of this will be for naught if we do not have the Grail of Power."

"I have the map." Aliana held out the ruby set atop her right hand. It glowed as she imagined the map in her other hand.

"Amazing!" Vira gasped.

Aliana handed it to Arthur. "I have no idea how to use it. I haven't really even had a chance to look at it."

Arthur unfolded the wide parchment with time-ravaged edges. Everyone leaned in to see what secrets the magic document contained.

"It's blank!" Owen stated when no one else did.

Leo took it from the king's hands, held it up before turning it different angles and up to different lights. "Strange," he murmured before passing it to Merlin.

The Druid ran his hand over it, everyone watching with rapt attention. "Very strange indeed." He looked up, met Arthur's questioning frown. "This will take some time, the magic used here is not one I have ever felt before. I will need some time to study it."

Aliana's brows shot up. A magic Merlin knew nothing about? Was that even possible? Then again, she existed. No one could explain her magic, or had ever seen anything like it.

"That does not frame our next piece of information in a favorable light." Lancelot pulled Guinevere closer to his side, her fingers tangled with the hand he had wrapped around her shoulder. "We found the identity of the Atlantian we believe may know the location of the Grail."

"Who?" Lacy asked, perking up in her chair.

"He was seen in Olympus by Lancelot and another student. Thanks to Lady Nimuah, we knew who to look for. Puck." Merlin and Lancelot both looked at Sophvira.

Galahad straightened from the relaxed position he had been in, his eyes alert and on the defense. "Why are you looking at my sister like that?"

Aliana wanted to know too, but she already had a kernel of a suspicion. If they had seen Puck in Olympus, and she had seen him in Camelot with Vira…The servant girl, Clara, had said Vira would receive gifts from an unknown person, trinkets and jewelry. And Vira had known more about the Manticore attack than she should have, lied right to her when she said she had gotten it out of Galahad.

Aliana could put two and two together. She looked at Vira who had seemed to take an interest in her cold eggs, a light flush on her face.

Guin placed her free hand on Vira's arm. "Sophvira?"

"When I was in Olympus, it was Puck who led me to the temple where Sophvira—" he kissed Guin's cheek "—and Guinevere's bodies were. It was he who put me through what I believe was a test to prove that I had changed, proven myself a loyal and true knight again. When I chose Sophvira, I felt the strain, the magic that had been my punishment for leaving you in Avalon, lift. I can even recall all the entrances to Avalon now. I hadn't been able to before. It's strange that the Fae queen would have used that test, and had Puck be the one to administer it."

Aliana sat back in her chair stunned. There was more to the story, but for now, she was content to know that he had found his release. It couldn't be a coincidence that it happened just as she saved Guinevere though, could it? She rubbed her temples. This was all getting very. Very. Very. Confusing.

"That's wonderful, fantastic news, mate!" Owen raised his juice glass to Lancelot.

The guys all followed, the girls grabbing their own glasses in salute.

Vira pushed her plate away. "I know Puck, I've known him for over three years…well, three years for me, I think." She looked at her brother from under her lashes. "I'm sorry I never told you."

Galahad frowned, his dark brows pinching together. Aliana watched the surprise, hurt, even anger and worry on his face. He finally took a deep breath. "There is nothing we can do about it now."

Aliana blinked rapidly. What was going on today? It was one miracle after another! From the covert looks Lacy and Dawn shared with her, they thought the same.

Vira smiled at him. "When I first met Puck, he was trapped. He never told me how, but he got caught up in some kind of magical trap. Because I wasn't magical, I was able to free him." She looked at Aliana with a hopeful expression. "He said he owed me a life debt, I told him I just wanted a friend."

Galahad sucked in a barely audible breath. Guin looked to Lancelot with a sad glint in her brown eyes.

"Clara said you would receive gifts from an unknown person. It was him, wasn't it?" Aliana wanted her suspicion confirmed.

She confirmed it. "He told me all about his home, in Atlantis, the Isle of the Blessed and Avalon. We became good friends."

"So I wasn't imagining it when I thought I saw you leaving with him from the Champion feast?"

She sighed, a dreamy expression on her face. "I hadn't seen him since the Manticore attack."

Dawn pushed her plate away. "Okay, this is lovely, but I'm confused."

"Yeah," Lacy added. "What does any of this have to do with…all of this?" The blond girl frowned. "None of this is making any real sense."

"Actually I think it is, lass." Leo looked to Sophvira. "He owed you a life debt, so he saved you from the poison bracelet."

"My soul, at least. Or that's how he explained it, anyway." Her young face fell. "After it happened he said I had a choice. I could move on to a new life, or he could protect my soul until he found a way to give me my life back."

"You chose to wait," Lacy said, sounding awed, looking at Vira like she was seeing her in a whole new light. Dawn was too. Aliana looked at Guin, their eyes meeting. They both knew how strong a spirit the teen had.

"How he managed everything, I don't know. The last thing I remember is him putting me to sleep, then waking up in Rothik's chamber with Merlin and Lancelot hovering over me like a pair of nanny goats."

The girls cracked up, and even Guin hid her giggle behind her hand.

Arthur decided to call everyone's attention back to the original conversation. "All right, settle down. We need to focus on our next move."

Dawn apparently decided to take that as her cue to speak up. "If Sophvira is friends with Puck, can't she just ask him to come and tell us where the Grail is?"

Vira looked down sadly. "Before I woke up, he said he wouldn't be able to see me for a while, and he always found me."

Aliana frowned, not sure that was the whole truth. But she would get the answer from her later, privately.

"Then we're back to square one," Percy moaned.

Merlin held up the blank piece of magic paper. "No. We have the map. I will study it."

"We have time on our side," Dagg said, speaking up for the first time. "Viviane and Morgana cannot know the location of the Grail either. They would not hesitate to use that kind of power, especially if they are still busy trying to free Mordrid from whatever dark hole Queen Titania put him in when she sent us to Camelot."

Aliana nodded. "Dagg's right. I would think, with all of us scattered, they would have tried something if they could have. You all were at your most vulnerable being divided."

"Then let's hope that is indeed the case." Leo motioned to Owen and Lancelot. "Sire," he turned to address Arthur. "Owen, Lancelot, and myself can help Merlin study this map. Four minds are better than one."

Arthur agreed. "While you do that, the rest of us will put together a strategy for traveling through Atlantis, learning all we can about its peoples and terrain."

Aliana sat back in her chair taking in all the chatter of the knights in full planning mode. This was where she belonged, even as hard as it had been, and as hard as it was all guaranteed to become. She may have always been meant to be the Destined One, but until Mordrid had nearly killed her, she hadn't ever really accepted the title.

Despite what Vira said about Puck, Aliana had a feeling she needed to find the trickster sooner rather than later. With Vira's new life, their family, their Round Table was truly whole again. Now she just had to make sure it stayed that way. She was the Destined One after all.

EPILOGUE

King Oberon sat back in his imperial throne as he watched his Lady wife, Queen Titania, carry on a reserved conversation with one of the Elf princes. The winter celebrations were already in full swing, but all the king could think of was what his scheming wife had planned next.

Despite their nearly eight hundred year separation, he had never stopped *caring* for the only woman who had ever captured his affections. There was no other to match her, none other he would ever want by his side. But he also knew that her grand plans stretched far beyond all the power and realms she already controlled, starting with one of her bloodline on the throne of Camelot. Even before his lady queen had conjured the Dragon's ruined city into her realm, she had made a bid for such power. A bid that failed when her niece had not wed the golden king after years at his side.

Titania wanted ultimate power.

He couldn't let her get it.

Not without needing him to help her acquire and maintain it.

He needed the Grail of Power, had to have it before his wife got her elegant hands on it. With the Grail, she could unlock all the hidden power of the Hel gems her Destined One had so cleverly sealed away. He recalled the first whispers of the Jewels, when a stray Fae had come to his loyal fire Elves and demanded they be set in a sword for the Golden King of Camelot.

He had never been able to glean the information he wanted from that charming Fae, who was his queen's niece, after he had his assassins bring her to him. To this day, it incited a rage in the Elf king that he did not know *how* or *who* had helped her escape questioning. He had his suspicions, but Puck had proven impossible to blame for the daring rescue. Perhaps Titania herself had aided in the escape. It was rare, but his vixen queen had shown many times she did care for the fate of her blood kin.

The silver wine goblet in his hand bent and cracked, red liquid running down his palm and wrist like blood. He cast the ruined cup away, the tarnished metal vanishing before it hit the floor, the wine spilling down his arm fading with it.

It was time King Oberon took matters into his own hands. If he had the Grail, then Titania would need him to help her unseal and restore the great powers of the Hel jewels. He could bargain with her to remain by his side. Such unstoppable magic would only serve to make both of their ruling realms that much more powerful.

Oberon understood Titania in a way he was sure even she didn't realize or understand, but one thing eluded him. Would she seek to revive the sword, take the power of the eclipse herself, or wait until after the dark Wizard faced the Golden King and the Destined One in the final war?

His sister had just finished requesting that he once again send his armies to aid the king in that very war. Varaness made a passionate case, but her own feelings for one of the human knights, Sir Galahad, had always clouded her judgment. He had assured her he would think on it, but he would not once again give his warriors over so easily.

His lips turned up in a smirk as Titania bowed her head ever so slightly to him, her ringlets of copper red brushing her sharp cheeks. He bowed his head to her in respect. Her emerald eyes gleamed as she held his gaze, a move no other living being would have ever dared do.

Except the Destined One, Aliana. His queen's granddaughter and the granddaughter of the Underlord. He himself had realized her true heritage when he held her captive in the Isle, for that short time. The Fae king had learned much from that one invasion into her mind. But she would be of no real use to him, or his queen, until she rid herself of the magics battling inside her. Foreign magics she didn't even realize his lady wife and another had cast upon her even before her birth. Forces that were hampering the true strength of her magic.

A flash of black behind a marble pillar caught the king's attention as Titania moved to where Varaness stood with the other four members of her council.

One of his most trusted assassins inclined his head, his deadly silver eyes alert and pleased.

"We have him, my king. The trickster awaits you in the pits."

Oberon rose from his throne. Titania came immediately to his side.

"My Lord, do you mean to leave these celebrations?"

He took her free hand, brought it to his lips. His kiss was quick, but he felt the minute change in her pulse, the awareness of the effect his touch still had over her.

"I must see to a matter of Avalon, my lady. I shall return with all haste."

She nodded, stepping back as he made his way through the throngs of Elves and other magical creatures. They all bowed low as he passed.

He had truths to get from Puck, one way or another. The Atlantian trickster was finally going to be made to tell his king all he knew of the Grail and where it was hidden in the underwater realm.

He was King Oberon, his will would not be denied.

Acknowledgments

I want to thank everyone who helped put this book, and my series together and bring it to life. First up are my editors Bev and Sean, whose honesty and support helped bring everything together. My publicist, and friend, Jenn for being the amazing person she is and putting up with my craziness. The entire Omnific family for their continued support. And of course, all my readers. Without you, no author would get to share their stories.

About the Author

LH Nicole is a seasoned pastry chef in our nation's capitol and a lifelong fairy tale (Disney and Grimm) lover. She believes in love at first sight, is addicted to eighties and nineties cartoons, and anything that can capture her ADD-way-too-overactive imagination. Joan Lowery Nixon and L.J. Smith were the first authors she became addicted to, and they inspired her to steal away whenever she could to read and write. You can keep up with LH and all her news and adventures on:

Facebook: www.facebook.com/LHNicoleAuthor

Tumblr: LHNicoleLegendary.tumblr.com

Blogger: LHNicoleAuthor.blogspot.com

Legendary Saga website: LHNicoleauthor.com

www.ingramcontent.com/pod-product-compliance
Lightning Source LLC
Chambersburg PA
CBHW020248120726